A CURSE IN KYOTO

A HUNTER & HIGASHI MYSTERY
BOOK 1

S.J. Cullen

HADEDA PRESS

GET YOUR FREE EXCLUSIVE MYSTERY NOVELLA!

She's a tourist in Japan.
It's her first time on the bullet train.
What could possibly go wrong?

To instantly receive the exclusive free novella, ***Death on the Bullet Train***, join the S.J. Cullen Readers' Club at **www.SJCullen.com**

CHAPTER I

From the viewing platform of Kiyomizu-dera Temple, a lone figure was staring out over the city of Kyoto.

Anyone seeing them would have presumed they were simply admiring the view like anyone else. But this person was not admiring anything. They were searching. Not for the many temples or historical landmarks, but for the buildings that made up the British School of Kyoto, somewhere between the Palace and the Botanical Gardens in the north of the city.

This is where it would all be happening, and today it would begin.

Only minutes earlier, the figure had drunk from the wish-granting waters of the Otowa Waterfall beneath the temple's main hall and asked for success in what lay ahead. Now they cast their eye over the deep reds and yellows of the autumn foliage, which was already setting in across the landscape. Catching sight of the school's distant collection of blocks, a smile formed across their lips.

They took in a deep breath, checked their watch, and before a clutch of early-bird tourists standing nearby had even noticed them, they were gone.

CHAPTER 2

One hour later, in the auditorium of the British School of Kyoto, one particular girl was making a point of being utterly uninterested in what was happening in front of her.

At the centre of the stage, behind a lectern, stood the headmaster, Mr Murphy, a tall and chubby man with permanently red cheeks, a haircut designed to hide a growing bald patch, and a shirt and belt struggling to contain his overhanging belly. Behind him, a giant screen displayed the school's crest – a golden lion standing in front of a large red circle, depicting the combination of British and Japanese cultures. Beneath that, in bold type, were emblazoned the words: *BSK in partnership with the Kyoto National Museum.*

To the headmaster's right stood what looked like a large Chinese harp, the kind which lay horizontally on top of a stand, not upright like the Western version. To the headmaster's left,

3

two women waited by the curtain, one of them at least twenty years older than the other. They appeared slightly nervous and awkward as they listened to his speech but hid it behind polite smiles.

"It's an honour to be partnering with the museum in this unique and unprecedented scheme," came the headmaster's loud voice, which the girl found highly irritating like so many other things in the school. She scowled as he droned on about how the museum was loaning BSK one of its exhibits as part of a new scheme that was to do with the museum becoming more interactive, or something like that. It was also to mark the Jidai Matsuri, a historical festival that would be taking place at the Imperial Palace in a little over two weeks' time.

In this case, the exhibit was the harp, but the girl couldn't quite see what all the fuss was about. She'd only been in Japan for a little over two months, but this was not her first international school, nor her first experience of living in Asia. She and her parents had been based in India and then China for two years respectively. She was used to seeing Asian cultural artefacts, and this harp looked like any number of similar Chinese versions she'd seen being played back when Beijing had been her home.

After the headmaster had waffled on for a few more minutes with a speech that seemed to place himself as the hero and architect of this whole scenario, he introduced the older woman and stood aside as she took his place at the lectern. Her name was Miss Nakamura, and she was a senior curator from the museum. She was around forty-five years of age, perhaps older, with a serious yet not unfriendly demeanour that was made more formal by her glasses and the black suit and white shirt she wore. Speaking in slightly broken English, she explained she would be speaking in Japanese while her assistant translated.

With a flick of her hand, she referenced her assistant, Miss Yoshida, who bowed her head as she came forward and stood beside the lectern with a microphone in hand.

Miss Nakamura told them about the history of the instrument, which had been built at the request of a nobleman, especially for a talented musician sometime during the late Edo period of the 1800s. The koto would be on display, she said, in the school's main foyer from today until the festival, when the school would be holding its own special performance evening to celebrate Kyoto's history.

The girl, whose name was Jessica Hunter, was preparing to switch off when a figure emerged onto the stage, bowing to the auditorium before taking a seat in front of the koto so that she was still facing the audience.

The person was a maiko, a novice geisha. She couldn't have been much older than twenty, though with the heavy white face-paint masking her features, she looked more like a human doll. She wore a stunning kimono of red and pinks and greens – a floral pattern stretching over her small form like an artwork itself. And her hair, arranged into the most immaculate bun, and adorned with flowers, looked almost too perfect to be real as it shone in the beams from the stage lights.

As the maiko began to play the koto, the light murmur which had erupted amongst the pupils at the sight of this strange apparition began to fade. As both of her hands glided and plucked artfully at the strings, the whole room, with its six hundred or so pupils and teachers, remained in silent awe.

Miss Nakamura and her assistant watched on proudly from the sides. Close by, the headmaster beamed, no doubt already planning his next speech.

When the maiko was finished, she stood and bowed her head demurely. The auditorium erupted into applause, and the young woman scuttled off the stage in her peculiar little sandals as Miss Nakamura returned to the lectern. "Did everyone enjoy that?" she said into the microphone.

"Yes!" came a unified reply, mostly from the younger pupils at the front.

"You're very lucky," continued Miss Nakamura. "Not many people have the opportunity to see a novice geisha play an instrument. Now, if anyone has any questions, please feel free to ask."

Several hands went up around the hall. Miss Nakamura smiled with delight and picked out the first pupil.

"How much does it cost?" said a Year 7 boy.

Miss Yoshida moved closer and translated quietly into Miss Nakamura's ear.

"Ah," said Miss Nakamura, giggling. "It is definitely quite valuable, but that is why we chose your school for this great project, because of its excellent facilities and security. We will also have our own museum staff monitoring the koto while it is here. The museum is delighted to be loaning artefacts to schools, but we must also treat them with respect, just as we would in the museum."

Though delivered with convincing calm, Jessica saw the veiled warning in Miss Nakamura's words: *Keep your hands off my koto!*

Miss Nakamura pointed to the next raised hand, which belonged to a girl in Jessica's year.

"Is this the koto that has a curse on it?" said the girl. "I remember reading about it."

At the mention of a curse, Jessica's and half the auditorium's ears perked up. Jessica watched closely for Miss Yoshida's translation, after which Miss Nakamura's professional smile slipped momentarily, only for her to regain it before answering.

"Of course, there are such tales around many historical artefacts, but they are just stories for our entertainment, nothing more."

Miss Nakamura was already shifting her attention to another hand, but the girl called out again. "I read that the previous owners of this koto all had bad things happen to them."

All eyes went from the girl to Miss Nakamura. The shy assistant seemed to hesitate before translating, but Jessica could see from the stiffening of Miss Nakamura's expression and posture that she'd probably understood.

"Well, I think we should all give Miss Nakamura a huge round of applause," said Mr Murphy, stepping forward before Miss Nakamura herself could speak.

Perhaps irked at not having the question answered, pupils reluctantly applauded again as Miss Nakamura and the assistant bowed and waved.

"As Miss Nakamura said, the koto will be on display in the school foyer as of today. Now, before we all go to our lessons, could you also wish our Scholar's Cup team some luck. They will be competing in the regional finals tomorrow in Osaka, and we're really hoping they'll be Kansai's winners for the second year in a row. Let's have a big round of applause for the team and the captain, Yudai Matsumoto of 12H."

Mr Murphy broke into a final round of clapping, and the rest of the room followed suit.

Jessica recognised Yudai in the row in front, the Scholar's Cup team's key member. He was in her tutor group and was clearly one of the school's genius kids. Every school she'd been to in Asia had at least a couple of them. She watched as he lowered his gaze and stared into his lap as numerous eyes turned towards him. A pang of pity, or was it relief, came to Jessica. She didn't imagine it was always much fun having that pressure and expectation put on you. She was the type who preferred to remain under the radar, and that was the way she intended to keep it.

Once the headmaster was finished and some final announcement had been made, the pupils began to file out of the auditorium a class at a time.

As Jessica made her way out, she strained for one last sighting of the young maiko on the left side of the stage. Just before she passed through the doors she was rewarded, as a parting in the giant velvet curtains allowed her a brief glimpse into the backstage area – where she saw a flash of patterned fabric and a ghost-white face watching as the pupils went out.

CHAPTER 3

Kenta Higashi, a fellow Year 12 pupil, though not from the same tutor group as Jessica, was glad that the Thursday morning assembly was over and the important football match he was due to play was about to start.

History wasn't exactly Kenta's thing, but it didn't turn him off either. He liked having a real historical artefact before his eyes rather than simply reading about it in a textbook, which was why he'd never minded the school's many museum trips. But football was one of his passions, especially as he was the main striker in today's game. His stomach was a mash of nerves, and he half wondered if he might be sick. *That* would be the real curse.

In the end the game, against a rival international school, went well. They won 3–2, with Kenta scoring the winning goal ten minutes before the final whistle. It was his fifth goal so far after just three games, which made him the team's top scorer. He'd been made the captain too after proving a reliable player and leader during the previous school year.

After the game, he stayed behind to practise taking penalty shots, and so by the time he was showered and dressed, he was the only person left in the changing rooms.

On his way to the foyer the only other people he came across were the two cleaners who normally worked the lower corridors in A-block. One was an older, heavyset lady in her forties who'd been working at the school as long as Kenta had been there. The other was new. She was probably in her mid-twenties and came across as extremely shy.

They were both mopping the corridor floor, though they barely noticed as Kenta passed by. He offered a quick apology as he trampled over the freshly mopped surface, but the young cleaner wouldn't even acknowledge him except with a little nod as she drained the mophead in a bucket.

His legs were tired and sore, but he was pleased with himself and his performance as he approached the row of doors at the entrance. He saw the reception area was empty. The security guard's chair near the koto was empty too, and Kenta presumed he was off on a break somewhere.

Glancing to his right for a peek at the koto exhibit itself, Kenta saw there was already someone standing in front of it. It took a second look for him to see that it was Yudai Matsumoto.

He was staring at the koto, which earlier in the day had been placed inside a large display box to great fanfare. Normally,

Kenta might have thought nothing of it, but there was something in the intensity with which Yudai was staring at the instrument that made him slow his steps and stop.

Yudai's nose was virtually touching the glass of the display box. His face was illuminated by the display lights inside. It was as if he were in a trance. Kenta would've expected him to already be at home studying furiously in his room in preparation for the final the next day. Not only that, but Kenta couldn't remember Yudai ever showing any real interest in history. He'd always been far too concerned with Maths and IT.

When Kenta spoke, Yudai didn't hear him at first. He was still seemingly too spellbound by the koto with its golden patterning and smooth mahogany body.

"Good luck tomorrow," Kenta repeated, this time louder.

Yudai snapped out of his reverie and turned his head to face Kenta. For a moment, his eyes showed no signs of recognition, as though he'd never seen Kenta before in his life. Then slowly he seemed to regain his senses.

"Oh… thanks," he muttered. He looked about him, almost like he was only just realising where he was, then lowering his gaze he swung his bag over his left shoulder and marched suddenly for the doors as a bemused Kenta watched on.

He was about to continue on to the doors himself when he saw another person had entered the foyer. Under closer scrutiny he saw it was the new girl from his English class. She was British, he remembered. Jessica something. She flashed Kenta an inquisitive, almost questioning look, and he guessed she'd just witnessed the odd exchange between him and Yudai.

He went to speak or at least nod, but perhaps it was the awkwardness he was feeling, as though he'd been caught in the act of doing something wrong, or maybe it was the brazenness of the girl's piercing stare, but he could only remain where he was, standing in the heart of the foyer as yet another person scurried away from him and out into the night.

He could hear the guard returning along the corridor in A-block and began making his own way out. It was only as he was walking to the doors that he caught sight of the display case from the front and saw what had been done to it.

CHAPTER 4

Waking just as the first slivers of the dawn's light were reaching around the distant mountains, Yudai Matsumoto got out of bed without a moment's hesitation.

He took one look out of his bedroom window, across the roofs of the neighbouring houses and apartment buildings. His eyes, though sleepy, took it all in with the same sharpness with which he saw everything.

After showering and putting on his school uniform he went downstairs to the kitchen, where his mother had already laid out his breakfast on the table – okayu rice porridge with a side dish of vegetables.

They exchanged only a brief "Good morning," as Yudai took his seat and began eating while his mother prepared him a small omelette. There was a slight tension in the air. Yudai could sense it and knew his mother did too, though she was behaving as though nothing were amiss. His father managed a chain of local restaurants and had already left the house. Before going to bed the night before, he'd knocked on Yudai's bedroom door to wish him good luck with a solemn nod, which Yudai had responded to with a nod of his own.

Once his breakfast was finished, Yudai stood and picked up his schoolbag. He was aware of his mother watching him closely with a nervous twinkle in her eye.

"Good luck, son," she said quietly, and Yudai hid his annoyance at hearing those words yet again, as she came towards him and hesitated before pecking him on the cheek. Looking into his mother's face, Yudai thought he saw even a glimmer of fear there in her pupils and in the tautness of the muscles around the lips.

He thanked her, nodded, then headed to the door.

The bus ride to BSK normally took him twenty minutes. The number 57 bus was already close to full, occupied by young men and women in business suits seated alongside various pupils, most of them from local Japanese middle and high schools.

Normally, Yudai would get off the bus less than a five-minute walk from the school, but for the first time in three years of school mornings at BSK, he didn't leave when he was supposed to and remained on the bus for a further four stops, only alighting at Takaragaike in the northernmost suburbs of the city.

Later, the bus driver would say he only noticed Yudai as he'd stood to get off. He recognised the uniform and wanted to tell

Yudai he was in the wrong place, but Yudai jumped off before he could. The bus driver would also remark on Yudai's general behaviour, how in the rear-view mirror he could see the pupil's expressionless face as he moved quickly along the aisle.

Once he was off the bus, Yudai moved ahead with purpose. It was a pleasant autumn morning, with only a few wispy clouds in the blue sky, and all around the flaming reds and yellows of the season, but Yudai didn't care for any of it. Several witnesses in the area would later claim to have seen him walking fast in the direction of Takaragaike Park.

When he was sure no one was looking, he removed his phone from his blazer pocket, then took out the SIM card before breaking it and dumping them both in the next rubbish bin he came across.

When he was satisfied no one had seen him, and that he wasn't being followed, Yudai moved swiftly onwards towards the park.

Beyond this point, there were no witness accounts of his movements, nor any trace of him on camera. He was simply gone.

CHAPTER 5

For the remainder of the previous evening, Jessica had found herself thinking of two things. The first one was the koto. She wasn't entirely sure why this particular item had captured her imagination, except that she didn't like knowing only half a story, and Miss Nakamura's limited presentation had left several blanks in this one. Moreover, it was a distraction from the frustrations and boredom of school.

The second thing on her mind was what she'd witnessed in the foyer when she was leaving the school. She pictured Yudai again standing in front of the display box. When the other boy had spoken to him, it was as if he were being pulled from a deep sleep. And that was when Jessica saw the black marker pen in his right hand.

He dropped it into a pocket so the other boy wouldn't see, then made a hasty exit. Then she turned her attention to the display cabinet itself and saw the two large black circles he'd drawn on the front panel side by side.

She wasn't sure if the other guy from Year 12 had seen Yudai drawing the circles or even noticed them at all. They exchanged confused, questioning glances, neither one of them quite sure how to respond. Then before it got any stranger, Jessica took the easier option of simply leaving, looking back only once at the koto and its display case daubed with strange new markings.

She made the decision there and then to find out what it was about. Figuring out people and their behaviour was something she'd always enjoyed. It was only the fact that BSK offered psychology as a subject that had lessened the blow of having to move country and schools yet again. It wasn't that she liked people either. She often wasn't too keen on them, and they didn't exactly warm to her either. Nevertheless, she enjoyed studying others – their tics, habits, motivations, neuroses. In any given lesson, she would spend as much time surreptitiously analysing her classmates and sometimes the teachers, as she would actually focusing on the subject at hand. As a result, she knew which classmates had the most pronounced phone addictions, which ones were the most serious gamers, who got on with their parents and who didn't, and who was depressed as opposed to simply a bored adolescent.

It was with these keen observational powers of hers that Jessica had noticed the deeper meaning behind Yudai Matsumoto's posture and behaviour during the assembly.

On hearing his name called out by the headmaster, he hadn't bowed his head or cast his hands together out of self-consciousness or humility. No – a closer look would have revealed the whiteness of his knuckles where his hands were throttling one another, along with the incessant twitching of his jaw muscles. And then there was the troubling glare in his eye. This wasn't a shy boy, it was a seriously determined one, a determination fuelled by anger. As Jessica saw it, this was a classic case of the awkward geek seeking to vanquish his foes by crushing all with his superior abilities.

This troubling glare had been there too when she'd caught him defacing the display case in the school foyer. But when Jessica entered the school the next morning, the black circles had been removed. The headmaster was there too, arranging a group of pupils from varying year groups around the koto. A couple of photographers were standing close by waiting, no doubt for another promo opportunity. And then Jessica saw precisely the person she wanted to speak with.

Without invitation, she walked over to the group and joined the line of older, taller pupils. The headmaster went to say something, but she quickly appeased him with a bright smile, and he returned to ordering them about.

Jessica glanced at the girl to her right. It was the one from the assembly who'd asked the question about the curse. Her name was Rina Mitsustuka. She was in Jessica's year and sat in front of her in English class. She was quiet and normally didn't say a lot during lessons, which was why Jessica had been surprised to hear her piping up in the assembly. However, she knew her to be a smart student who routinely received top marks.

After a sufficient pause, Jessica said, "Nice job."

Rina jerked her head. "Sorry?"

"Your question yesterday morning," said Jessica. She grinned as the photographers began taking photos. "About the curse... I wish the headmaster had let her answer you."

"Oh, thanks," said Rina, visibly relaxing. "Do you know about it too then?"

"I've heard a little," Jessica lied. "But not much. Where did you find out about it?"

"I saw this koto before on a tour at the museum. The tour guide made a joke about the curse and something about it being haunted by the geisha who'd owned it, but when I asked them more questions, they didn't seem to know anything."

Continuing the pretence of posing for the cameras, Jessica said, "You mean the talented musician Miss Nakamura mentioned?"

"Yes, that's the one," said Rina. "Apparently, the court noble who had it made asked for the finest koto that had ever been built, kind of like a Stradivarius."

"So where does the curse come in?"

"The story is, the geisha was caught stealing something from a senior geisha, and as a punishment she was thrown out on the street. The worst part was she was forbidden to play the koto ever again."

To Jessica's annoyance, she found the conversation suddenly interrupted as the pupils were repositioned for more photos. Keeping herself close to Rina, she forced a smile for the cameras as a barrage of flashes came at them. Through the corner of her mouth, she uttered her next question. "What happened after that?"

Rina revealed her perfectly white teeth for the photographers and angled her head slightly towards Jessica. "They say she cursed the koto before she left, so that anyone who owned it from then on would meet terrible misfortune."

Though her powers of reason told her this was all rubbish, Jessica couldn't help but flick a brief look over her shoulder at the koto itself, seemingly so harmless and untouchable behind the glass casing. "And did they?" she said under her breath.

"Did they what?"

"Did the people who owned it meet any misfortune or untimely ends, anything like that?"

Rina waited while the group was ordered to smile more. "According to a few websites I found, two of the families did have some messed-up stuff happen to them."

"Like what?"

"No talking please, face the cameras!" barked the headmaster.

Both girls waited until the photographers were done and they were told they could go. Rina made her way towards the main corridor and Jessica made sure to follow.

"What happened to the families?" asked Jessica, catching her up.

"I can't remember all the details." Rina checked her watch. "You know, weird deaths, unexplained accidents, that kind of thing."

They passed through the main corridor, which connected the school's two main wings. It was form time, and pupils were filing towards their form rooms.

Jessica wanted to press Rina on the details concerning the families, but seeing her window of opportunity was closing, she opted for one last question.

"What was that you said about the koto being haunted?"

Rina checked her watch a second time and shrugged. "That was just something the tour guide said, to make it more entertaining. I guess it was just some joke about the koto playing by itself at night, or a ghost of a geisha walking about? I can't remember. Sorry, I have to go to my locker," she added, already speeding ahead.

"Oh, okay. Thanks!"

"No worries," called Rina over a shoulder, before she was lost amongst a sea of uniforms flowing into the corridor.

CHAPTER 6

It was clear from the moment Kenta entered his form room for registration that something was wrong.

"Kenta, have you seen Yudai?" asked Miss Bennett, his form tutor, who was unable to hide the mild alarm in her voice.

A bamboozled Kenta shook his head. *We're not really friends any more*, he wanted to say. Instead, he simply said, "No, sorry. Why?"

"He hasn't arrived yet. He was supposed to be here half an hour ago – the Scholar's Cup team are leaving for Osaka in five minutes."

It was then Kenta noticed the other four members of the senior Scholar's Cup team standing around her desk. One of them, a tall Year 13 Japanese boy with broad shoulders and spiky hair, was pacing the room with his phone to his ear. Kenta guessed that like Miss Bennett he was trying to contact Yudai.

"Where the hell is he?" he growled after the call rang out yet again.

Kenta took his seat near the back left corner of the classroom and watched on helplessly as the drama continued to unfold. Soon the headmaster had arrived, along with the teachers leading the Scholar's Cup team. The usual registration had been abandoned entirely, and Kenta's classmates seemed to be enjoying the spectacle.

At one point, Kenta himself felt it okay to break school rules by consulting his own phone under the desk, before realising to his dismay that he no longer had Yudai's number.

"His mother says he got on the bus at the usual time," said Miss Bennett to the headmaster, loudly enough for Kenta to hear. By this stage, the team were already twenty minutes late. Mr Murphy's complexion was turning ever deepening shades of red with each passing minute.

On hearing this news, he ordered the rest of the team to follow him, leaving an anxious Miss Bennett to pretend everything was fine.

For the rest of the morning, Yudai's failure to turn up on time was on all the pupils' lips. From those around him, Kenta learned that Yudai had never arrived, and Mr Murphy had been forced to choose another pupil to go in his place at the last minute.

By lunchtime, the currents of gossip were rife with graver speculations, which were only encouraged by a sighting of police officers going into Mr Murphy's office at lunchtime.

Kenta himself had seen both Yudai's parents leaving the headmaster's office in the early afternoon. He'd been passing the foyer on his way to the science labs when he saw them. He knew them fairly well from the days when he'd occasionally visited Yudai at his home. Yudai's mother had always been a pleasant and kind woman, though often a little nervous.

She looked pale and frightened as she walked alongside Yudai's father, a taciturn man who was looking more stony-faced than ever.

***

When the weekend went by and still there was no sign of Yudai, it officially became a missing persons case, and an emergency assembly was called at the school on Monday morning.

Kenta had been up half the previous couple of nights thinking about his old friend. Mostly he continued to see an image of Yudai staring at the koto, the haunted look he'd given Kenta on turning to see who'd spoken to him. And then there was the strange graffiti, namely the two large O's drawn on the front of the display case. He hadn't seen Yudai do it, but Kenta was certain it had been him. What it meant or why he'd done it, however, were beyond Kenta. Like everything else that had happened, it was totally out of character for Yudai. But the most confounding thing of all was that he'd chosen that day of all days to disappear. Not only was he the school's star pupil, but no one was more competitive than him when it came to the Scholar's

Cup, and no one could have wanted to succeed again more than he did.

At school that morning, Kenta had tried to block out the more sinister comments from those around him. The rumours were that Yudai must have buckled under the pressure. The fact he'd last been seen heading for Takaragaike Park also didn't bode well. Kenta had heard the word "suicide' more than once, and as hard as he tried to ignore it all, he couldn't help also pondering the same unbelievable possibility. It wasn't an uncommon event in Japan, especially these days when many pupils were often under so much pressure, but Kenta hadn't known of anyone from BSK doing that, and he was still struggling to comprehend how Yudai might have gone that way.

During the special assembly, the headmaster told the school what they already knew concerning Yudai's disappearance. Standing with him was a Japanese man in his early fifties, smartly dressed in a dark brown suit and with neatly combed hair that was greying slightly at the temples. He was introduced as Detective Yamada from the local police force.

With Miss Chisaka, Kenta's Japanese teacher, translating for him, the detective spoke to the pupils, asking for anyone to come forward with any information they might have concerning where Yudai was or why he'd gone missing. He relayed the information concerning Yudai's movements the previous Friday morning, including the fact he'd got off the bus near the park and dropped his phone in a bin along the way.

The detective spoke slowly and carefully, lowering his head while he waited for Miss Chisaka's English translation. His tone was deep and sombre, as though delivering a eulogy at a funeral.

They all think he's already dead, thought Kenta as he listened, feeling sick at the end of it even as he was irked that people immediately thought the worst in these situations. But why? He was burning to know. *Why, Yudai? And where were you going?*

Detective Yamada finished by saying anyone who'd spoken to Yudai the day before his disappearance, no matter how trivial, should come to the conference room where a police officer would be on hand to speak with them.

It was then, with a dropping sensation in the pit of his stomach, that Kenta realised he might have been the last pupil to see and speak with Yudai that day.

As the pupils filed silently out of the auditorium, Kenta knew what he had to do. He felt he might vomit as he headed in the direction of the conference room, but steadied himself with several deep breaths before knocking on the door and being beckoned in.

Sitting at the giant mahogany meeting table were a young female police officer and Miss Eguchi, one of the Japanese teachers.

"Come in please, Kenta," said Miss Eguchi with a weak smile. The police officer followed suit with a nod and smile of her own, gesturing for Kenta to take a seat opposite her. She was surprisingly young, thought Kenta, barely older than his sister who was halfway through university.

She confirmed Kenta's name, age and tutor group, then asked if he wanted to tell them anything. He proceeded to relay the events from the foyer the night before the Scholar's Cup. The officer wrote down everything he said while a small digital recorder in the middle of the table captured the conversation.

She asked about every little detail – time, location, his reasons for being there, whether there was anything off or unusual about Yudai's behaviour that evening, to which Kenta said he seemed a little spaced out maybe, distracted, but that he'd put it down to the competition. He didn't say anything about his suspicions regarding Yudai and the two big O's on the display case. He figured there was enough heat on his friend as it was.

When Miss Eguchi mentioned that Kenta and Yudai had once been good friends, the police officer stopped writing for a moment and considered Kenta more closely, before releasing a barrage of further questioning to which he kept on saying the same thing – they hadn't been friends for a long time now.

It was true they'd once been close. For all of their first two years at BSK they'd been virtually inseparable, and for much of their third year too. They'd bonded in the after-school computer club. Yudai was incredibly talented when it came to coding and most other computer-related endeavours. He had a dream of going to MIT in Boston one day and inventing his own world-beating software. Kenta was also reasonably proficient when it came to coding, but he was mostly doing it because he found it interesting and guessed it might be useful one day.

It was obvious to Kenta and Yudai that they were quite different in many respects. In contrast to Kenta's fun, relaxed and popular persona, Yudai was a very serious person who didn't make friends easily. But in Kenta he saw a natural intelligence and a lack of judgement that made their friendship flourish.

They spent much of their free time discussing programming. At one point, they'd even worked together on an app Yudai was developing to make researching easier for pupils, but Kenta soon reached the limits of his interest and capabilities and dropped out.

It was around midway through Year 9 when Kenta noticed a natural distance beginning to open up. Yudai was committing himself to more and more projects on top of several after-school classes. His parents were as invested in Yudai's future as he was, and certainly seemed a lot pushier than Kenta's mum and dad. But from Kenta's point of view, most of the pressure seemed to come from Yudai himself. He was driven by some unknown force, almost as if he were being chased by something only he could see. Kenta began to notice a change in Yudai's behaviour too. The serious glint in his eye became even more fixed, and he began to walk at a near-manic pace wherever he went, often with his head down.

The cooling of their friendship began harmlessly enough when Yudai started telling Kenta he was too busy to hang out after school and at weekends. Kenta didn't take this personally, but then Yudai began avoiding him at school as well, often electing to sit by himself at the back of the classroom rather than beside Kenta as had often been the case since Year 7. It got to the point where Kenta had to stop Yudai in the corridor one day and ask him if he was okay, to which Yudai had replied that he was "Perfectly fine," in a dry and expressionless tone. When Kenta had pushed further and asked why Yudai wasn't hanging out with him at school any more, Yudai had sighed rather impatiently, as though he had far better things to do, then told Kenta it was nothing personal, it was just that he wasn't a serious enough person. He said this matter-of-factly before walking away, leaving a rather stunned Kenta standing in the corridor, watching him go.

Kenta wouldn't have denied he was hurt and confused by this whole episode, for a time at least. He'd wondered afterwards if it all stemmed from his dropping out of the joint app-building venture – but whatever the reason, that was the last time they spoke, and Kenta soon gravitated towards other friendship groups while Yudai became more and more of a loner. From Kenta's side at least, there were no hard feelings, and on the occasions when he passed Yudai in the corridors, or saw him in class, he would remember their time as friends with fondness, and even found himself feeling sorry for his old friend who was becoming more and more obsessive as the school year went on.

The split had also coincided with Yudai's first success in the Scholar's Cup. As the captain of the under-16s team, Yudai had taken them to the regional Kansai final where they beat Osaka's top Japanese school. Now he had a platform with which to demonstrate his prowess and raise himself above the crowd on his way to future tech glory, which was why Kenta couldn't understand why he'd chosen to disappear now of all times. It didn't make any sense.

Before letting him go, the police officer said, "Aside from the security guard, was anyone else there at that time?"

Kenta thought about it for a moment. He was about to say no when he remembered the girl. "Yes," he said. "There was a girl from my grade. I think her name's Jessica. She's in 12G."

The police officer's pen continued its quickfire movements over the page.

"Jessica Hunter?" asked Miss Eguchi.

"Yes, that's her. She was also walking through the foyer at that moment."

The officer looked up from her notes. "Did she say anything?"

Kenta shook his head. "No, she just looked at me then left."

The officer's hand scribbled several more notes before she stopped quite abruptly. She smiled at Kenta. "Thank you, that's all for now. We'll contact you if we have any further questions."

"Thank you, Kenta," said Miss Eguchi. "You can go to class now."

Kenta bowed his head and thanked them before heading for the door. He wasn't sure now what help his information could possibly be, and there was a definite underlying guilt, a niggling and unreasonable sense that he was somehow partly to blame for Yudai's disappearance. He could have said something, maybe asked Yudai if he was okay. And what about the previous year? If there was something up with his old friend, Kenta might have picked up on it had he shown more interest.

His thoughts returned to Yudai and what the hell could've happened to him. He was distracted enough that it wasn't until Kenta went back out into the corridor, closing the conference room door behind him, that he saw Jessica standing there waiting to come in. She considered him with those large inquisitive eyes of hers. He was sure he registered a hint of surprise in them at the sight of him, but otherwise she gave little else away.

Just like the other evening, Kenta found himself pausing uncertainly in the beams of her attention. There was something about her that unsettled him. It was as if she was analysing him, taking him apart, measuring and comparing like he was some random subject she was studying.

He thought he should really say something this time, but her odd scrutiny and strange silence suddenly annoyed him.

He walked away without so much as a nod. Over his shoulder he heard her knuckles rap firmly on the door, but he refused to look back.

CHAPTER 7

They were parked across the street from the school when Jessica arrived on the following Tuesday morning.

There was one TV van with aerials and small satellite dishes piled up on its roof. Jessica recognised the name of the news network – it was a local TV news station she'd come across when flipping through the Japanese TV channels at home, most of which she found utterly perplexing.

She counted at least three men with large cameras waiting around alongside various technicians, and one smartly dressed man and woman who must have been the reporters. The young woman in a red suit was in the middle of recording a segment as Jessica was crossing the road to the school gates. Overhead, the sky was a solemn, ashen grey, and a cool breeze shivered the yellowing foliage of the trees lining the street. It was the first day since she'd arrived that it had felt properly autumnal, and it brought back memories of the south-west London neighbourhood she'd grown up in, where she'd always loved walking, kicking up the fallen leaves littering the pavement.

As she was going through the school gates, the teacher on duty and three volunteer Year 8 pupils greeted her with a "Good morning' and a bow, and Jessica turned away awkwardly, looking back across the road as a second TV news van pulled up.

Well, if Mr Murphy wanted publicity, he'd certainly got it, she thought, picturing him silently fuming in his office while the school became famous for its missing star pupil rather than his fancy museum stunt.

Yudai had been missing for four days now and there was still no sign of him. The police had already combed Takaragaike Park and found nothing. One witness sighting had him possibly somewhere further north in the Kita ward, not far from the Kyoto Sangyo University, meaning it was possible he'd headed into the deep forests and hills west of Mount Kurama and the Hira mountain range, which also tended to be a bad sign – Jessica had heard the stories in Japan of people wandering off into forests and never coming back. From the various local websites she'd been reading and translating the night before at home, she'd gathered the police had little in the way of leads, and the undertone did not seem altogether positive.

To make matters worse for BSK, the Scholar's Cup team had been humiliated in the regional final in Osaka. They hadn't even made it to the last round, being soundly beaten by a school they'd easily quashed the year before. It hardly seemed to matter now with all that was going on, but it didn't do anything to lift the ominous mood amongst the pupils and teachers.

Jessica was sure she could sense it the moment she entered the school foyer. Even the security guards by the doors seemed graver, as though on high alert in readiness for some imminent attack. The two young women at the reception desk were more subdued, failing to address all passers-by with their normally pleasant smiles and greetings, and the other pupils behind and in front of Jessica were eerily quiet.

Passing close to the koto, which sat proudly in its display box, Jessica couldn't help recalling what Rina had said about the curse. Of course it was ridiculous, but there was no doubt in her mind that the koto had at least something to do with Yudai's disappearance, however indirectly. There was no logical explanation for why this would be the case, but she'd seen the look on his face as he'd stood in front of the display box with an almost disturbing fixity, as though he were seeing in the koto the portent of some terrible thing. The strange markings he'd drawn there had been wiped off by the next morning, and there'd been no mention of it at the school. But surely it had to mean something.

She knew the other boy had seen it too, or had at least noticed something was off. Jessica had mentioned this to the police officer in the conference room the day before, and knew from the officer's questions that the boy must have mentioned her too. She'd learned his name was Kenta Higashi, and had casually asked Miss Eguchi if he and Yudai were friends. "They were a while ago," was all she'd said.

Jessica hadn't mentioned anything to the officer about her theory concerning Yudai and the koto, knowing it would probably have sounded absurd, and that she had no evidence other than a hunch. She hadn't mentioned the circle markings either.

Today there was a security guard posted much closer to the koto, and also a representative from the museum, a young woman clutching a handful of pamphlets, her nervous eyes glancing over the people streaming by her. Needless to say, she probably wouldn't have quite so many people enquiring about the exhibit now. The plan had been to allow members of the public in as well, but that had been put on hold while the investigation into Yudai's disappearance was ongoing.

The strange spell that had been cast extended also into the classrooms, where teachers who were normally more relaxed had become uncharacteristically stern, and the ones who were already sticklers became outright tyrants. As with the tense security guards at the school entrance, there was a visceral feeling in the air, an aura escaping from each and every person, which said something was amiss. Like villagers of old anticipating an attack, pupils were suddenly cagey now that the initial buzz and speculation surrounding Yudai's status as a missing person was no longer new. Now no one wanted to mention his name lest they jinx themselves and become further infected by the fear and dread that had found its way into their normally safe and predictable lives.

Jessica hadn't experienced anything this exciting in any school she'd been to. In one fell swoop, her days of drudgery and resentment had been infused with new purpose. She wasn't entirely unsympathetic towards Yudai and what might have befallen him, but she hadn't known him either. He was a stranger to her, which meant she could analyse his case with the necessary detachment.

Later that day, while her brain was still fizzing with new possibilities, Jessica found herself presented with a golden opportunity.

In English class, Miss Sissons surprised them with an interesting assignment. She tasked the pupils with carrying out a research project on a topic of their choice. They would have almost two weeks to complete it, after which they needed to submit an essay of at least 1500 words and a ten-minute PPT presentation to be given to the class. The essay would need to include a rationale for why they'd chosen their topic, and they had to consult her about it first, but otherwise they were free to have fun with it.

While Jessica listened to her classmates discussing in pairs which topic they would choose – half the boys seemed to want to do theirs on either a video game or a manga book – she knew instantly what hers would be on.

Later in the lesson, when Miss Sissons called Jessica over to her desk for a quick chat about her project, Jessica told her immediately that she wanted to do it on the koto in the foyer – its history, and also that of the famed geisha musician that Miss Nakamura had mentioned during the special assembly.

"Oh?" Miss Sissons said, peering questioningly at Jessica over the top of her bright orange glasses. "I didn't know you were interested in history?"

I'm not really, Jessica wanted to say. "Well, I suppose it's an opportunity to familiarise myself with the local culture," she replied, pleased with herself.

An impressed Miss Sissons nodded. "Well, I like your attitude, Jessica. This is also a great cross-curricular opportunity. I'm sure your history teacher could help you with it."

"Absolutely," Jessica replied with her most eager smile, knowing she had zero intention of consulting Mr Wilkins on any topic.

With her project given the green light, Jessica relished the opportunities that lay ahead. What she hadn't told Miss Sissons was that the whole thing would also be a potential cover for her interest in the fate of Yudai Matsumoto. It was, she told herself, as much a psychology project as an English or history one. She needed to understand, to know what had happened to him and why.

And so she went away from the English classroom formulating her next moves. Regarding the koto, there would be much online research to do at home, but in the meantime there were more pressing tasks at hand.

One in particular had been bugging her since the previous day. It was after she'd finished her quick interview with the police officer, consequently finding a queue of pupils waiting outside, no doubt eager to report any tiny interaction they might have had with the mysterious missing boy. Returning to her locker, which was with all the other Year 12 lockers along a first-floor corridor in A-block, Jessica came across two police officers removing things from one of them. She knew it must have been Yudai's, and purposely slowed down her own movements so that she could surreptitiously watch them.

The two male officers were wearing latex gloves. One was kneeling and pulling things out while the other dropped the items into a transparent bag. Mr Takagi, the head caretaker, was standing close by and watching on with a key in his hand. Jessica knew this was the master key, which she'd seen him use several times before when pupils had forgot their locker codes, which seemed to happen all the time.

Mr Takagi was a short man of slight build. He had on the blue overalls he always wore, as though he were always in the middle of a job that might make him dirty. Jessica estimated he was close to sixty years old. He had a full head of neatly cut grey hair, and a lightness in his eyes that she interpreted as a kind inquisitiveness. Seeing him smiling at people as he passed them in the corridors, including pupils, which wasn't the case with most adults in the building, Jessica had gathered the impression he was not only a gentle and friendly man, but a wise one too. He had a stoic quality about him as he went about his daily tasks, and a quickness in his movements that one would expect from a far younger man.

As she loitered by her locker, Jessica saw them remove several textbooks and school exercise books, along with a pair of trainers and a few miscellaneous objects. There were loose pieces of paper scattered about on the locker's bottom shelf. The officer removing the contents looked through them briefly, then clearly deciding they weren't significant, tossed them back in and closed the locker door.

The officers left with their stash of evidence while a troubled-looking Mr Takagi closed the locker. Noticing Jessica watching him, he smiled at her and said, "Hello' in English before going on to whatever other tasks were calling.

Jessica finished packing her bag with the necessary books, but her eyes remained on Yudai's locker a while longer as she considered what secrets might still lie inside.

Coming out of the science lab at the end of the final period, Jessica had made up her mind to start scratching this proverbial itch. It was no use simply speculating on things; action was required.

And so, as she had the previous day while watching the police officers collecting Yudai's books, Jessica remained stationed in front of her open locker, pretending to be reading through some notes while her fellow Year 12s buzzed around her, chatting about all manner of inane topics as they loaded rucksacks and canvas bags with the books required for that night's homework. Not one of them looked at her or talked to her, which was how she wanted it.

After a further couple of minutes, all the remaining pupils had already dispersed on their way to school buses and taxis and walks home. There was the odd teacher or pupil passing by along the busier adjoining corridor, but it was still early enough that her presence wouldn't draw any attention, and the security guards would be busy at the front gate for a while yet.

Jessica remained crouched by her locker for several more seconds, glancing furtively about. She knew there was a security camera at the furthest end of the corridor near the English classrooms, but it wasn't angled in a way that would capture her movements.

With a final check over her shoulder for measure, Jessica closed her own locker, stood up, turned around, and crossed the floor to Yudai's.

There was no time to waste. She quickly removed a coin from her purse and immediately set to jamming it in behind where the PIN lock was set into the locker door. This was a trick she'd picked up at her school in Beijing. It was something the pupils did whenever their friends had intentionally changed their PIN as a prank. It was only possible with these PIN code lockers, which BSK had in abundance.

It only took Jessica a few seconds to get the small coin in behind the lock, and then several more for her to pop it out with a slight thud.

She checked the corridor on both sides, finding it empty. Then she carefully pulled the lock out, leaving a small rectangular hole in the door. A small thrill shivered through her as the door opened and she peered inside.

Scattered there on the locker floor were the several loose A4 papers she'd seen the officer disregard. Reaching in, Jessica gathered them up in her hand and began sorting through them all. The first few were simply worksheets from a couple of weeks earlier. There was an essay too, written in Japanese characters which were still utterly alien to her. At the bottom, the teacher had written comments in purple ink and given him an A*.

Rifling through them impatiently, Jessica cursed under her breath when she realised they were nothing at all. There were no salacious diary entries, no receipts offering an insight into habits and movements.

To her left, a blur of movement registered in the corner of her eye.

It was Miss Hart, one of the English teachers, marching at speed along the other corridor with her coat on and bag over her shoulder, clearly eager to end her working day. She didn't so much as glance in Jessica's direction, and even if she had, all she would have seen was a pupil looking into a locker.

Jessica let out the breath she'd been holding onto and returned her attention to Yudai's near-empty locker. With a sigh of dejection, she went to throw the papers back inside as the officer had, then noticed something she'd missed on the first look.

It was on the rear side of one of the worksheets – the letters OO had been scrawled all over it like many pairs of eyes, just like the ones on the display cabinet. In places they'd been penned haphazardly in varying sizes – some miniature, others cartoonishly large, while in one section they'd been written in a neat row of lines. There were hundreds of them on just this one side of paper.

Sifting through the other papers a second time, Jessica chastised herself for not having looked more closely. On two of the worksheets, the O's in the words "lock' and "box' had been underlined in red pen, and the same pair of blank circles had been written in the margins and corners of two further worksheets.

Still crouching in front of the locker with the PIN lock lying uselessly on the floor by her feet, Jessica puzzled over what it meant. She tried to recall if she'd heard of any pupil or teacher with the initials OO. It was possible this near-demented scrawling was a symptom of an obsessive crush, or there was the less likely chance that it had to do with some vendetta, as though the mad scribbles were an incantation against an enemy.

"What are you doing?"

The voice startled Jessica enough that she dropped the papers on the floor. She looked up at the source of the rude interruption and immediately recognised the voice's owner.

Kenta Higashi was standing over her, bag slung over a shoulder, his eyebrows furrowed angrily.

"Excuse me?" Jessica replied, recovering quickly as she gathered the papers up from the floor.

"That's Yudai's locker."

"Oh, is it?" She stood up with the paper still in her hand. "I just found it open and wondered whose locker it was."

"Bullshit," snapped Kenta, his fierce gaze unrelenting.

Feeling her fake innocence being quickly replaced by indignation, Jessica dropped the act and returned fire with a glare of her own. "What's it to you?"

"He was my friend. You've no right to look in there."

"Yes, I heard about that. Emphasis on the word *was*. You were thick as thieves back in the day, then you don't speak for years. What's that about?"

Jessica saw Kenta's outrage falter briefly at the sudden accusation.

"Who the hell are you anyway?" he snapped, the anger flaring again, reddening his cheeks. "You've only been at the school five minutes. You didn't know Yudai, so why d'you give a shit what's in his locker?"

There was a momentary pause in which the two of them simply stared at one another, each waiting to see who would buckle first. Jessica realised she could have simply turned and walked away, and her right foot shifted slightly in readiness, but that might look like an admittance of defeat, an acknowledgement that she'd been ruffled. No, she wasn't going anywhere just yet. Plus, something told her she could use the situation to her advantage if she held firm.

"I was intrigued," said Jessica finally, shrugging. "I want to know what happened to him."

Kenta screwed up his face. "Why?"

"Why not? Don't you want to know where he is too?"

"Of course I do, but I actually know him. We were good friends."

"So you keep saying," said Jessica. "So what are you doing about it?"

It was as if she could see the new calculations working furiously behind his eyes.

She held out the bunch of papers towards him, pointing at the back of the scribble-covered worksheet. "I know you know it was him who drew the circles on the display cabinet."

Kenta started. "I didn't see anything."

"I saw the marker pen in his hand. It was him all right. And now I find all this in his locker. Do you know what it means? Is there anyone with these initials in the school that you know of? A teacher or a pupil?"

Kenta's eyes narrowed as he looked the paper over. He shook his head. "I don't think so."

"What about a book, a film, a singer, a game even? Anything like that?"

Again, Kenta shook his head.

"Well, whatever it is, it's probably significant. If you check the date on the worksheet, he did this a little over a week ago, and people don't obsess over words and symbols unless it means something to them."

Kenta looked up at Jessica then back at the papers, clearly undecided on how he should deal with this odd girl standing in front of him.

"I guess it has something to do with that koto," Jessica added.

"What?"

"We both saw it, in the foyer. That wasn't an innocent fixation. He was looking at that thing like it meant life and death, and I don't know about you, but I intend to find out what it was about."

With that, Jessica pushed the papers into Kenta's hands and picked up her bag, sending one last questioning glance his way.

"What's in it for you?" he said.

"Something actually interesting happening at school," replied Jessica before turning and walking away, leaving a bemused Kenta standing beside Yudai's open locker, the papers bunched uselessly in his hand.

CHAPTER 8

It took longer than usual to get home as the public bus stopped and started its way through the downtown rush-hour traffic.

The anger was still there following his unsettling encounter with Jessica Hunter. It was lodged in his chest and throat, a hot stone pulsating as the frustrations surrounding Yudai's disappearance melded with Jessica's infuriating brazenness. Who the hell did she think she was anyway? The arrogance of some of the foreign pupils could get to him sometimes, particularly the privileged ones – the way they acted like they owned the place when they'd only been off the plane five minutes. They often believed they had Japan and Japanese people pegged from the get-go. It was all temples and neon lights and manga comics.

He scoffed at nothing and no one as he glanced through the bus window at the passing scenery. Mostly, though, it had been one question that had really pissed him off. *Don't you want to know where he is?*

He heard the words coming again from her lips and imagined all the things he could and should have said back to her, a tirade of witty remarks that would have wiped that self-satisfied look from her face. But instead, he'd been left questioning himself. What *was* he doing about it?

Stepping off the bus near his home, Kenta shivered against a cold, sweeping breeze. He and his parents lived in Minami ward, south of the city centre, on the fifth floor of a six-floor apartment building close to the Katsura River. From his bedroom he had a decent enough view of the river itself, though the kitchen on the other side of the apartment looked out onto a loud and busy intersection close to the Katsura River Bridge. There was none of Kitayama's glamour or neatness in this part of Minami. It was mostly industrial buildings interspersed with cheap motels, collections of small homes and apartment blocks, and large vegetable patches, so that overall it was like some industrial park mixed with farmland.

Kenta had been living there for more than five years now and was used to it, even though he wasn't unaware of the significant differences between the kinds of areas the majority of his fellow pupils came from and the one he was in. It was for this reason Kenta largely avoided having friends over to his place at weekends and holidays, instead engineering meet-ups so that they would always be in a neutral spot or occasionally at his friends' homes.

Growing up, his family had lived closer to the downtown area, not far from Kiyomizu-dera Temple. Back then, they had had a small but comfortable traditional home, but they'd sold it for reasons Kenta hadn't understood at the time. Since then, he'd gleaned that the family had hit hard times and had no choice but to downsize.

Kenta's older sister, Mizuki, was now in her second year at Tokyo University and hadn't been living at home for a while now. She still came back during longer holidays, but for the most part it was just Kenta and his parents.

It was rare that Kenta found himself resenting the lifestyle gap between himself and the others at school, but what he did find troubling was his own part in it. It was when his father had insisted he go to an international school that the family's money belt really began to tighten, and in Kenta's mind there was no denying that he was technically the cause.

At first, he'd resisted going to the BSK primary school when he was nine years old. Kenta had wanted to be in a Japanese school like everyone else, but his father had insisted on him going to a British school, despite how expensive the fees were compared with his parents' modest pay cheques.

His father worked for a medical supply company, selling products to hospitals, clinics and health centres. His mother was a kindergarten teacher. They weren't flashy people at all. They didn't go on expensive holidays and rarely travelled abroad, but for as long as Kenta could remember, his father had openly dreamed about his son one day being an international businessman.

"English, son. You must learn it!" his father had often said to him. "The kids in the local schools aren't good enough. You must learn alongside foreigners. That is the way to truly immerse yourself in a language. Only then will you be able to study at the London School of Economics, and then the world will be yours!"

That was another of the more specific details within Mr Higashi's dreams for his son. Namely, he'd always talked about Kenta going to LSE to study business. Kenta was aware of how famous and reputable this university was, but he was never sure why his father had settled on this particular institute.

"Because it's the best," his father had once said when he'd asked this question. "Why would we want anything less?"

Over time, Kenta had developed a two-pronged suspicion – firstly, that when Mr Higashi was a young man in Hiroshima, where he was from, LSE had indeed been the world's best in the field of business studies, and he'd never relinquished this impression. Secondly, it wasn't exactly a secret that his father also had unrealised business ambitions of his own. He often lamented his decision to go into medical supplies rather than taking a job in car manufacturing.

Perhaps it was because of this that Kenta had never really rebelled against the plan that had been laid out for him. Now that he spoke English fluently and was doing well at BSK – and had recently taken business as a new option for his final exams – his father was particularly happy, and if Kenta's father was happy and Kenta appeared happy, then his mother was happy too. He wasn't exactly against the idea of going into some business either, since he figured it might be interesting and involve travel.

Still, it didn't sit well with Kenta whenever he got off the bus in front of their apartment building and considered that they could be somewhere better if it weren't for him. He could hear his sister's nickname for him – the golden child – something she'd started calling him during her teenage years on account of their father's blatant favouritism towards his son. She liked to tease him by sometimes calling him a 'half-gaijin' and joking that he would soon forget how to speak Japanese if he wasn't careful.

When he came in through the front door of their apartment, the hallway was already filled with food smells wafting from the kitchen.

His mother was at the counter chopping vegetables, and there were two large pots boiling on the stove as she turned to see him. "My, that was a long practice."

"The bus got stuck in traffic," replied Kenta, taking out a carton of fresh orange juice from the fridge and pouring himself a glass.

He sat down at the kitchen table and waited for his mother to ask about his day, a routine they kept up most school days. They started chatting in Korean, which they usually did when Kenta's father wasn't home. His mother was from Seoul. She had met Kenta's father at university in Kyoto when she came over to study as a young woman.

For the most part, Kenta considered himself a fully fledged Japanese, but he didn't ignore his Korean heritage either and had visited Seoul and his Korean grandparents several times. He was aware now of the past troubles and difficulties between Japan and Korea, and eventually he'd learned of the problems his Korean grandparents had had with their daughter's marriage to a Japanese man. Kenta knew his sister had actively hidden her half-Korean status from her friends and schoolmates when she was younger, though he hadn't felt the need to do the same. If anything, the pupils at BSK were used to mingling with people from all over the globe, and more than a few had parents from differing countries and ethnicities. In reality, the few Japanese people who knew Kenta's mother was Korean thought it was cool, just like K-pop and pretty much everything else that came out of Korea these days.

Sitting in the kitchen, Kenta relayed his ordinary school day to his mother, missing out the part about his run-in with Jessica. After that, he asked her about her day.

"Fine," she said with a shrug and a mild sigh. "Nothing unusual."

Kenta knew his mother worked hard teaching three- and four-year-olds in a local kindergarten. There were several Korean parents with children there, and Kenta's mother was well known in the local Korean community in Minami.

Kenta had visited her at work a couple of times when he was younger, and couldn't believe how difficult it was controlling small children. That explained why she was often tired after work, but she clearly enjoyed it too.

When they'd finished chatting, Kenta stood up. "I'd better start my homework. Got a lot to do."

"Okay, dinner will be ready shortly," said his mother. "Your father will be home late," she added, which was a familiar sentence in their home.

Just as Kenta was going out of the door, his mother spoke again. "Any news on Yudai?" she said tentatively, knowing it was a delicate subject.

Kenta shook his head. "No, nothing."

His mother nodded sadly then return to the chopping.

Kenta set to his homework – an English essay, a maths assignment and a geography project. These days he struggled, like everyone else in his year, to keep on top of it all, and judging by his friends at Japanese schools, it was even worse there.

It took him more than two hours to finish all his work, pausing only to wolf down his dinner with his mother in the kitchen. By the time Kenta was done, it was already 9.30pm and he could feel the languid fingers of exhaustion working themselves into his limbs and eyes. But instead of getting ready for bed, he took out a blue notebook from his desk drawer and began writing.

This was what he did most evenings. It was still a secret activity, and if his mother or father happened to see him bent over his blue notebook, he would tell them he was writing a draft of a story for English class. Writing by hand instead of on a laptop also made it easier to hide.

His parents knew he enjoyed writing stories and that he was good at it too, judging by his English teacher's enthusiasm for his creative writing, but what they didn't know was that Kenta was writing a novel.

He'd had the idea for a long time but had finally started it during the summer holidays prior to Year 12. It was a sci-fi story based loosely on ancient Japanese and Chinese history, and while it was still early days, it was slowly taking shape.

Tonight, however, he was struggling to concentrate. Normally, he could get down a few pages in no time, even when he was bleary-eyed with tiredness, but the words just weren't coming. Since the summer holidays, Kenta's spare moments at school had been taken up with thoughts about the novel and what he would write that evening, but since Yudai's disappearance, his creative ideas had been crowded out by thoughts about his friend.

The front door clicked open out in the hallway, and Kenta instinctively placed a hand over the notebook. He listened to his father's footsteps, then muffled voices as his parents spoke in the living room.

Kenta knew that his father would say hello soon, and so he hid his notebook underneath a geography textbook. He had no real idea how his father would react if he knew his son was spending his spare time writing a novel. Perhaps he wouldn't mind as long as it didn't interfere with his schoolwork, but then Kenta didn't want to take any chances. More than that, there was some small pleasure to be derived from keeping it to himself, even from his mother and closest friends.

Just as he'd expected, a few minutes later his father's footsteps sounded in the hallway again and a knock came at the door.

"Hi, come in," Kenta called over a shoulder. He swivelled round to face his father in the doorway.

"Hello, son. How was school today?"

Kenta repeated the edited version given to his mother earlier while his father listened carefully, nodding throughout. He looked even more tired than usual. He'd been coming home from work close to 10pm most days for a while now. Standing in the doorway, he looked suddenly quite small. Kenta was already several inches taller than him. The height came from his mother's side apparently, but he had his father's thick hair and shy nature.

"How about you?" said Kenta.

His father smiled thinly. "Oh fine, you know."

With that he wished Kenta goodnight and went to have his dinner alone in the kitchen.

After Kenta had readied himself for bed, rather than reading or falling straight to sleep as usual, he reached for his rucksack and pulled out a folded piece of paper from the front pocket.

He looked again at Yudai's scrawled double O's over the back of the worksheet and experienced yet again the flowering of anger he'd felt as Jessica had pushed it into his hand. He puzzled over what it could mean, racking his brains for any person or anything at all bearing these initials. Kenta could feel his eyelids trying to close, but he forced them open and reached for his laptop.

He typed two letter O's into the search box and pressed enter. Whatever it was, if it could offer any sort of clue about what had happened to Yudai, then he wouldn't rest until he'd figured it out.

CHAPTER 9

Jessica wandered home along Kitayama Dori, the main road running east to west through the Kitayama area. Her home was only a fifteen-minute walk from the school and barely five minutes from Kitayama Station and the Botanical Gardens.

She knew this was a popular area, though she was just glad she had easy access to the subway and didn't have far to go to school. In that respect, her parents had at least put her first. It was her mother who'd insisted they move to an area close to Jessica's school, unlike in Beijing where she'd had to travel an hour to get to the British international school there. It was also her mother who'd insisted they move to Kyoto instead of Osaka. When it became clear they'd be leaving China for Japan, her mother had put her foot down on where they would live. Initially, Osaka had been touted as the best city for them, but her mother had refused to live in another busy metropolis. She hadn't enjoyed the pollution and overcrowding in Beijing and wouldn't budge on this. So, in the end, they'd decided on Kyoto, which was close to Osaka but also much smaller and more liveable, with easy access to nature.

After Mumbai and then Beijing, Kyoto felt more like a town to Jessica. The fact that she could see hills and mountains in every direction was both refreshing and odd. She remembered the English countryside well from her childhood, but she'd been born in London and was a city girl through and through.

Needless to say, she hadn't fully settled into Kyoto yet. It wasn't just her anger at being uprooted yet again; the slower pace and relative quiet, not to mention the totally different culture, were things she needed time to adjust to. And there was always the lurking suspicion that they'd have to move again soon anyway, even though her father had promised they'd be there for at least a few years this time. But that was the downside of being the granddaughter of Massimo Morelli, the owner of Morelli Olive Oil, a major Italian company based in Milan where the family was from.

When Jessica's mother, Eleonora Morelli, Massimo's only child and heir, had married Jessica's father, Peter Hunter, a lawyer from London, Jessica's life was forever tied to olive oil. Her father had been quickly recruited into the Morelli family business, whereas ironically, Jessica's mother had never wanted to work with or for her father. She had her own online jewellery business which took up most of her time.

Massimo Morelli had always harboured a desire to conquer the Asian market, and since Jessica's father was proving himself a very capable businessman and had travelled extensively in Asia as a young man, he was assigned this most important of tasks. And so, the family found themselves first in India, and then when the Massimo name had been firmly established there, it was on to the mighty Chinese market.

Jessica's father would still be travelling regularly to China, but as Japan was Asia's largest olive oil market, her grandfather wanted a strong foothold in both countries. And what Massimo Morelli wanted, he tended to get.

As Jessica made her way along the main road, passing cafés, restaurants and boutiques, she felt her phone vibrate in the pocket of her rucksack.

When she took it out, she saw it was a voice message from her mother in Italian – they often spoke together in her mother's native tongue. This was Eleonora's way of keeping in touch with her own language and culture while also instilling it in her daughter, but Jessica also knew her grandfather wanted her to keep their Italian sharp. He'd sometimes joked that he didn't want her becoming too English, but Jessica knew her grandfather was also quite serious about this.

The message confirmed what Jessica had already guessed – her mother wouldn't be home from the jewellers exhibition in Shanghai until tomorrow. Their cook and cleaner would be making Jessica's dinner, as she had the last few nights since Mr Hunter would be back late from Osaka.

Not bothering to reply, Jessica dropped the phone back into her bag and turned into the small residential side road where their new home sat.

Another new aspect of being in Kyoto was having an actual house to live in. Jessica had lived in a house when she was a small girl in London. In Mumbai and Beijing, they'd been in apartments and private compounds. Now they even had a small garden with a little pond and perfectly crafted bushes and trees which a gardener tended to twice a week.

The house itself was a modest size, but Jessica knew they were living in a good area and were lucky to have it – her parents had first used this fact to sell the Japanese move to her, then when she said she didn't care, they'd changed tack and told her she should be grateful.

When she got home, Yuko, their cleaner, was busy hoovering the living room. At the sight of Jessica coming in, she waved enthusiastically and stopped the hoover. Jessica waved back, flashing a quick smile.

Yuko was a kindly lady in her mid-fifties. She was originally from Nagoya but had lived in Kyoto for half her life, as her husband was from there and her two daughters had been born in Kyoto too. Jessica's parents had hired her almost as soon as they'd arrived. Most days she was there to keep the place clean and tidy since Mr and Mrs Hunter had little time for housework, but also it was to keep an eye on Jessica when her parents weren't at home, which was most of the time.

As Yuko barely spoke any English, she spoke to Jessica in Japanese, often encouraging Jessica to practise with her, and though most of the time Jessica really didn't want to, she did her best to humour Yuko with a little conversation. When this failed, she simply resorted to using the translation app on her phone, which Yuko still saw as a small wonder.

"*Konnichiwa, Yuko-san*," Jessica said, remembering to bow a little and add the "san' to Yuko's name as a mark of respect.

Yuko broke into a wider grin on hearing Jessica speak Japanese, and came towards her. "*Gakko wa do datta?*" she said, which they'd practised before. Jessica knew she was asking how school was.

"*Yoi*," said Jessica, which meant "good'.

Again, Yuko grinned, clapping her hands together. She was an easy audience.

Next, she directed Jessica to the kitchen, saying a few things that Jessica didn't understand, although she knew they were about food.

On the kitchen table there were several dishes laid out and covered over with cellophane. There was noodles and dried seaweed, a soup and a few small bowls containing salad and a variety of vegetables. Jessica wasn't hungry, nor was she much of an eater anyway, though she'd learned that it was much easier to pretend she had an appetite than to resist, as had often been the case in her younger teenage years.

Dropping her bag to the floor, Jessica decided to get it over with and sat at the kitchen table. She picked up her chopsticks, which she could use well now after living in China, and proceeded to pick at the food while Yuko watched on with interest. This was another aspect of their routine together. Yuko would prepare food for Jessica, then would watch her eat to judge her reaction and to make sure she had at least a little something in her belly.

Making sure to smile and nod as she ate, Jessica made herself eat enough noodles and vegetables and salad to keep Yuko happy, then told her she had to get to her homework and would eat the rest later. This seemed to be good enough for Yuko, who nodded and ushered her away with a pleased smile.

Once she was alone in the bedroom, Jessica didn't change out of her school uniform or put on any music or watch any YouTube clips. Nor did she do her homework, which she had a lot of, and which she knew she should be starting right away. As with food, she'd learned that to do just enough when it came to homework was the easier way. She was more than capable of getting top marks in most subjects, though she knew this normally involved long hours of homework and diligence, which wasn't high on her priority list. But her previous tactic of simply not doing the work, or doing it in a horrid and slapdash manner, had only resulted in earache from teachers and then eventually from her parents after so many emails and phone calls from the school. To just do enough to get a half-decent mark was all it took to keep the teachers off her back, and therefore her parents also.

But the homework could wait. Instead, she opened up her laptop on her desk and set to the real task at hand. She knew she would have to start researching the koto and the story of the young geisha, which she was at least interested in on some level. But right now, all of this paled in comparison to finding out the meaning of the two letters "OO', which she found herself typing into Google the second the screen came on, the letters almost on her lips as she pressed "enter'.

Chapter 10

The corridors of BSK stood silent and empty, with most of them cast into darkness where security had already switched off the lights.

In the foyer, the koto stood in its case. Nearby was a young security guard, the same one who had got into trouble when Jessica and Kenta reported that he wasn't at his post when they'd last seen Yudai Matsumoto. He'd been told not to use his phone on duty and to remain more vigilant from now on, especially during the after-school hours.

Walking the main corridor of A-block, Mr Goto, the most senior of the security team, was halfway through the hourly patrol. This was one of his favourite elements of the job, as he appreciated the quiet and the exercise.

Moving close to the Year 12 locker area, his torch beam cutting left and right through the darkness, he paused for a moment. Ear cocked, he shone his torch along the smaller adjoining corridor, sending a powerful beam of light all the way to the end. Caught in the beam was the expected row of lockers and classroom doors. He was aware there was still a handful of senior pupils in the IT room upstairs, but they shouldn't be messing around in this area, in the dark.

"Hello?" he called out, his voice reverberating ever so slightly in the tunnel-like space.

No reply came, but he was sure he could still hear it. Perhaps it was a phone. Those disrespectful youngsters were always playing noisy videos on their phones. One could even have left it on in their locker by mistake.

But then it got louder, so that the sound was unmistakable. It was music. And not just any music. It was without a doubt the soft, plucked notes of a koto, made all the more haunting in the blacked-out space.

Squinting his eyes, yet still not seeing the source of the music, Mr Goto kept the torch trained on the end of the corridor while he reached for the walkie-talkie in his belt. "Tomo?" he called into the mouthpiece. "Tomo!"

A moment later, the young guard's dozy voice clicked into life through the speaker. "Yes, sir."

"What's going on in the foyer? You hear any music?"

"Er... no, sir. Nothing here."

"Well, keep your eyes open. I think there's some stray ones messing about in A-block, playing on their damn phones."

"Yes, sir," said Tomo before the walkie-talkie went silent again and Mr Goto placed it back on his belt.

"Damn it," he whispered quietly to himself as he took a few steps forward. Whoever was playing the music, they were coming around the corner at the far end, and he would catch them at it.

He waited a moment longer, eager to bark at the first youth he saw for wasting his time. He'd take their names and have them standing in front of the headmaster first thing in the morning.

Standing alone there in the dark, however, with the koto's sad, echoing notes drifting through the air, he had to shake off a mild sense of unease. He couldn't be nervous, or worse, scared. He was the one who did the scaring. He'd been doing it for eight years at BSK and was good at it too, not to mention the fact he'd never been afraid of the dark in his life.

There! Movement at the far end.

He shone the torch beam on them at once, his lips poised to shout a warning. But as the figure appeared, moving slowly yet purposefully around the corner, almost gliding, Mr Goto saw what it was.

His eyes widened. A strange clicking sound came from his throat in place of the words he'd intended to scream.

And then the only sound was the torch clattering to the floor, and the koto's continued sad melody.

***

Only a couple of floors above, Trudy Chen was finishing up in the IT room. As a Year 13 pupil studying for her finals, she had permission to be there after hours until 10pm. A number of pupils often opted to study there rather than at home, where there could sometimes be distractions and nagging parents. Here, pupils could also help one another with homework and enjoy the camaraderie of being together through the dreadful slog of the last year of high school.

As the last person out, she was sure to switch off the lights and close the door.

The third-floor corridor lights were still on, but she knew the ones downstairs would be off. She was used to it and switched on her phone torch to guide her down the stairwell to the ground floor. They were only permitted to use this particular stairwell, as the rest of the school building was off limits after hours.

Trudy let out a yawn as she reached the ground floor. Her eyes were sore and tired from staring at a computer screen for hours, and she was already looking forward to the hot food and warm bed waiting for her at home.

Turning right into the corridor nearest the main way out, she thought she heard something.

Slowing her steps, Trudy directed her phone torch ahead of where the music was coming from. She recognised the music too, and at once recalled the assembly from the other day when the maiko had entertained them with her amazing musicianship. There was no doubting it had been miles better than the normally dull affairs that passed for assemblies.

Just at the end of the phone light's reach, she could see a figure standing, a person dressed entirely in white.

Peering further into the murky corridor, and still moving tentatively forward, Trudy thought she could make out something lying on the floor beside the white figure – a dark shape, and there was another pinpoint of light shining there too.

It was only when she was around forty metres away that Trudy knew what it was.

The shape on the floor was another person, dressed in dark clothing. It might even have been a security guard, and the light was coming from the torch lying uselessly on the floor beside him.

But it was the other figure who made Trudy stop walking.

At first, she didn't believe it, or thought it was a prank, but as the figure turned to look at her, she saw the ghostly white-painted face, the elaborate hair, the haunting eyes.

And Trudy's piercing scream resounded along the corridors, bouncing and echoing so that it could be heard throughout the four corners of A-block.

CHAPTER II

Kenta had a distinct sense of déjà vu as he approached his form room for registration. There was a flurry of activity in the corridor outside – excited conversations and pupils rushing in and out of classrooms. At first, he thought it was about Yudai – he'd been found perhaps, or at least Kenta hoped that's what it was.

He went up to Milo, the Italian boy from his form who he was friendly and who was one of the school's best footballers. "What's going on?"

"We've got a ghost! It gave one of the guards a heart attack. It's freaking unbelievable."

"What? What ghost?"

"A geisha. Like, a proper one. It's freaky shit, man. It's that koto curse, I'm telling you."

"What about the security guard, is he okay?"

Milo shrugged and turned to chat with a Spanish girl in their year.

A perplexed Kenta saw Shun nearby, another football friend he was sure he'd get more sense out of.

"Hey, Kenta. You hear about the ghost?" was the first thing Shun said.

Kenta sighed inwardly. "Yeah, Milo told me. Sounds like a load of crap."

"Nah, a Year 13 girl saw it too. It put her and a security guy in the hospital."

Kenta raised a dubious eyebrow.

"Seriously," Shun went on. "That curse is no joke."

Kenta was looking to extricate himself from all ghost-related talk when he heard two teachers behind him. It was Miss Bennett, no doubt on her way to clear the ruckus in the corridor. She was crossing paths with Mr Tanaka, the IT teacher who was emerging from the direction of the auditorium. All Kenta heard at first was Miss Bennett saying, "Two giant circles? Oh my god." After which Mr Tanaka went on his way and she clapped her hands to get all the pupils' attention.

Kenta, however, was already heading for the auditorium. When he got there, he found Mr Takagi and his assistant staring up at the stage. He couldn't see whatever it was from the doorway and wandered further in, at which point his mouth simply fell open as his eyes took in the scene before him.

There was no person or object on the stage itself. What he and the two caretakers were staring at was the giant screen at the back, onto which all videos and PPTs were projected during assemblies and performances. It was about ten metres wide and four metres tall, and a fairly new addition to the auditorium, which had been given a high-tech upgrade the year before. There was no image or projection on the screen now, however. Instead, someone had painted two giant O's in black paint across almost the entire surface. The paint had dripped in several places, giving each huge circle a hurried and scrawny appearance.

The sight of them hit Kenta with a force that almost floored him. In the backpack hanging from his right shoulder, he still had Yudai's worksheets with their frenzy of identical double zeros. He clutched instinctively at the bag strap as if to protect its secret contents from any prying eyes. He wondered if anyone else knew the significance of what he was looking at – but then of course there was one person who did, and she was there too, standing off to the right in the opposite aisle.

Kenta and Jessica locked eyes from across the space. Neither one of them needed to say a thing. Something was happening, something big, and they were probably the only ones who had some idea of who it pointed to.

CHAPTER 12

Jessica was already waiting close by Kenta's locker when he appeared during the morning breaktime.

Watching him approach, she noted his mild surprise at seeing her there as his steps faltered slightly, before he proceeded to blank her and open his locker to swap his geography books for his maths ones.

Jessica waited, then as soon as he was done, followed him outside. She caught up with him as he crossed the badminton courts beside the main playing field. "Well?"

At first, Kenta said nothing, only walked straight ahead, hands buried in his pockets, gaze locked on the ground a few steps ahead of him. Jessica wasn't sure if he was thinking furiously or simply ignoring her. Either way, she didn't have time for hesitation.

"What do you have to say?" she added, louder this time.

"I don't know," muttered Kenta, still avoiding her gaze.

"What do you mean, you don't know? You saw it, same as I did. A great big bloody sign!"

"I said I don't know," repeated Kenta with a hint of irritation. "Did you even find out what it means? I couldn't find a thing."

"Well, I... I did find a manga character called Ougi Oshino when I searched it online. It's the name of some female character from a series called Bakemonogatari. It's about vampires apparently. Is there any chance Yudai was a fan?"

Kenta shook his head. "No, definitely not."

"You sure?"

"Yes, I'm sure."

"Well, we still have to figure all that out. What matters is that that thing in the auditorium is linked to your friend, or at least something that involves him too."

"We don't know that for sure."

Jessica rolled her eyes and let out an impatient sigh. She was already wondering if she was wasting her time with him. "Next you're going to tell me it's just a coincidence."

Perhaps seeing he wasn't going to get rid of her any time soon, Kenta looked over his shoulder then made a beeline for the edge of the school grounds, close to C-block, a smaller building in the far-right corner. There was a long section of wooden decking there with benches and a row of trees. He stopped beside one of the larger trees. The wooden decking was littered with fallen leaves, mostly brown or yellow. Normally, pupils liked to sit there in groups, or loners chose the spot to read their books, but now it was empty.

Kenta kicked at the nearest leaf then looked Jessica in the eye for the first time. "Look, what exactly do you want me to do?"

"Help me find out what this all means – I thought that was obvious. It's not just the letters in the auditorium, there's all this ghost business too."

"Yeah, I heard some people talking about it in form time. Something crazy about a geisha."

"Except," said Jessica, "it was seen not just by a senior pupil, but by the head of security."

"How do you know?"

Jessica smiled to herself. "You can learn just about anything that goes on in this school by listening to large groups of girls chatting by the lockers. The Year 13 girl who saw it isn't in school. Too traumatised apparently. One of the girls I was eavesdropping on is friends with her, so I'm guessing this is first-hand information, albeit with possible embellishments here and there. The Year 13 girl – I think her name is Trudy – saw the geisha standing over the guard on the floor. She claims she heard music too, a koto. After she screamed, she said the geisha disappeared."

"They're saying the guard had a heart attack," added Kenta.

"There's one of those embellishments. I already checked with the receptionist. He didn't have a heart attack, only fainted. He does have a heart condition though, hence why he's off work resting. But it also confirmed the girl's story regarding the geisha."

Kenta raised a dubious eyebrow. "Really?"

"When I asked the receptionists about the so-called ghost, they got all cagey and said they didn't know anything about that. If it wasn't true, they simply would've dismissed it."

"So, there's some lunatic dressed as a ghost walking around. What does it have to do with anything?"

Jessica raised a questioning eyebrow of her own. "I suppose you're going to say this is just a coincidence as well? A few days after a koto shows up with a geisha backstory, a geisha just happens to appear the night the auditorium's vandalised with a symbol we both know has something to do with Yudai?"

Avoiding Jessica's mocking stare, Kenta looked off into the distance. "I have to get ready for maths."

"What you need to do is wake up. This is just like yesterday. One minute you're all about finding out what happened to your friend, the next you're acting like this is all a massive inconvenience for you."

This time he glared at her, just as he had when he'd found her rooting through Yudai's locker.

"I'll ask you one last time," said Jessica. "Do you want to help Yudai or not?"

A brief stand-off commenced, in which Jessica, hands on hips, glared back with equal ferocity.

"Obviously I want to help, but what can we do? Just because Yudai scribbled a few zeros or O's on a page... that's not evidence of anything."

"No, but evidence is exactly what we're going after."

"How?"

"By first finding out what this whole geisha thing is about. It was clearly a distraction so that whoever it was could paint up the auditorium, that and a smear campaign of some sort."

"A smear campaign?"

"Isn't it obvious what the main motivation is behind all of this?"

When Kenta failed to reply, Jessica shook her head. "It's to make the school look bad, that much is obvious – first the star pupil goes missing before a crucial competition, then the publicity for the whole museum thing goes down the toilet, and now we've got ghosts and vandalism on an industrial scale."

"But why?" said Kenta.

"Exactly! That's the real question. And that's what we're going to find out tonight."

"Tonight?" Kenta bellowed the word louder than he'd intended. He scanned the area again to ensure there was no one within hearing distance.

"Yes," Jessica went on. "I know it's an inside job. Whoever's behind it, they must have had help from someone who knows the building."

Kenta's eyes flitted about nervously. "Let me get this right... you want to go into the school... *tonight*?"

"Precisely," said Jessica, grinning widely. "Well, we won't be going out of school, so technically we'll simply be staying in the school until tonight."

"How? We'd get caught."

"Ye of little faith! I've already got that covered. I know exactly where a person can remain undetected until the building's empty."

"It's crazy," said Kenta in a harsh whisper. "Especially after what happened last night."

"That's exactly why we need to do it now. Strike while the iron's hot. Either way, I'm doing this with or without you, I just figured two is better than one. You can keep a lookout, plus you actually know the building."

"No way," said Kenta, taking a step back. "I can't. It's insane." He started walking away.

"I'll see you by the lockers at 4.00pm," called Jessica after him.

"No, you won't," he fired back before speeding up in the direction of B-block.

What he wouldn't have been able to see was that as Jessica watched him go, a wide and knowing smile was stretching its way across her face.

CHAPTER 13

The time was 4.00pm, and Kenta was heading to the main doors in the foyer like every other pupil in A-block. He was going to walk out and get on the bus home just as he always did. There was no shame in it, none at all. It was unthinkable to entertain the idea even for a second.

He'd made sure he had everything he needed before last period so that he wouldn't have to go to the lockers. On top of that, he'd avoided Jessica for the rest of the day, including in English class, their one lesson together, when he'd made damn sure to avoid her eye and get out of the classroom before she could accost him again.

So why, as he entered the foyer and briefly caught sight of the koto on his left, did Kenta find himself slowing down?

"Out of the way!" grunted a Year 13 boy, finding Kenta momentarily blocking his path.

Standing off to the side as the usual mass exodus of pupils streamed past him, he found his agitation growing. Twice he went again towards the main doors and twice he held back. It was as if the koto itself held some strange power over him, and he did his best not to look at it again – until with an inner groan of frustration Kenta found his legs taking him back into the corridor and all the way to the Year 12 lockers as he muttered angry, disbelieving jibes against his own self.

Jessica was waiting by the lockers as she'd said, leaning against the wall with arms folded. The other Year 12s had already been and gone, so it was just the two of them.

He expected her to greet him with a self-satisfied smirk, or something similar, which might just have given him the push he needed to turn back while he still could. But she only glanced at her watch and said, "I was a minute away from giving up on you."

Careful as always, Kenta made sure there was no one nearby before he spoke. "I'm here because I want to find out what happened to Yudai, no other reason."

"Fair enough."

"I can stay a couple of hours, maybe three, but no longer, all right?"

Jessica shrugged. "If you say so."

"So, what the hell are we supposed to do now?"

She jerked her head in the direction of the corridor behind them. "Follow me. It's best if you keep a good few metres behind so it doesn't look like we're together. There aren't any cameras on this route as far as I'm aware, but you can't be too careful."

"Where exactly are we going?"

"The gym," replied Jessica.

"The gym?"

"Yes, it's the best place to keep a low profile for a while. You'll just have to trust me on this one. And if you see any teachers, you just tell them you're looking for something, your football kit or whatever."

With that, Jessica calmly turned and began walking away, leaving Kenta to stand there, near frozen to the spot as he'd been in the foyer. This was her funeral, he thought. He didn't have to get involved, but whether it was some sense of a challenge, or a deeper compulsion, he once again found his legs carrying him forward.

He followed a good distance behind Jessica, as she'd instructed. She walked swiftly yet evenly, face forward, moving like she had every right to be there, which was the exact opposite of how Kenta was feeling at that moment. His rational mind told him he was simply walking in the school just as he always did, albeit a few minutes past the time when pupils should be on their way home. But it was the very fact they'd soon be breaking the rules in a big way that flooded his system with an unpleasant jangle of nerves. This wasn't his territory. He didn't consider himself a major do-gooder, yet he was no rebel either. Still, he kept on following Jessica around one corner and then the next. Along the way, he caught sight of several teachers still in their classrooms doing paperwork, but none of them noticed him passing by.

Further ahead, Kenta saw Jessica push through the large double doors into the gym. Before going in himself, he looked through the windows set into the doors and saw her walking with purpose across the gym floor to a far corner. There was no one else in there, and taking a steadying breath and a final glance around him, Kenta also pushed his way inside.

Their footfalls echoed slightly against the wooden floor as they cut a diagonal line across the gym's cavernous empty space. Jessica was heading for the corner where all the gymnastics equipment was kept in a small side area, and promptly disappeared behind one of the large wooden pommel horses and a tall stack of soft mats.

Kenta sped up, expecting some adult voice to call out his name at any moment, but none came and he reached the corner without incident.

He found Jessica already sitting down, back to the wall, in a narrow section behind the mats and pommel horse which was completely hidden from view.

"Glad you could make it," she said.

Sitting himself down as far from Jessica as the space would allow, Kenta looked around at his cramped situation and wondered just what the hell he'd got himself into. "How did you know about this?" he whispered, suddenly aware of how quiet it was.

"Just basic reconnaissance. It's always good to scout useful spaces in any building. I like to get away from people sometimes."

Jessica took a book out of her bag – *The Moonstone* by Wilkie Collins – and began to read as if this was all fairly regular.

"How long do we wait?"

Jessica shrugged. "At least till it gets dark. I don't expect a ghost will turn up in daylight."

"But that's more than two hours away!"

Jessica regarded him briefly over the top of her book. "You know where the door is if it's too much for you."

Kenta said nothing, only sighed resignedly and wondered again what he was doing. It was probably already too late to leave now without arousing suspicion. He had no choice but to go through with it.

Taking his phone out of his bag, Kenta began punching in a message to his mother. When he was done, Jessica said, "What did you tell her in the end? Your mum, that is."

Annoyed by the accuracy of her educated guess, he wanted to tell her to go to hell and mind her own business, but since they were now effectively trapped together, he opted for forced cooperation.

"I said I had another special football practice. We have a big game next week."

Jessica didn't look up from her book, only raised an eyebrow slightly in acknowledgement, though she didn't seem overly interested.

"What about your parents?" said Kenta. "What do they think you're doing?"

"I doubt they're thinking about it too much. They'll probably not even be home when I get back myself. They work a lot."

There was no apparent emotion in her voice or face as she said this, and Kenta found himself wanting to know more. But he held back. He didn't imagine she was one for discussing her personal life in any detail.

Seeing no other choice, he took out his maths textbook and began doing his homework.

After they'd been sitting in silence for a while, the oddness of where he was and what he was doing became even more apparent. While most of his friends would be at home with their families, or maybe out and about somewhere having fun, Kenta was still at school hiding in a corner with a strange girl he barely knew. Still, now that he'd relaxed a little, he couldn't deny there was a slowly creeping sense of excitement to it. He had, after all, dared to do something he'd never normally imagine doing, involving the flouting of school rules. And there was the possibility that he was doing something important, something that could help catch a vandal and perhaps offer some clues to Yudai's whereabouts. There was still, of course, the niggling issue of lying to his mother, but he did his best to ignore it for the time being.

Several times as he worked on his maths, Kenta glanced in Jessica's direction. She was deeply immersed in the book, seemingly oblivious to him and to the whole situation, as though she did these things all the time. He could see now what it was that made her a little different. There was an intensity about her, but not the sort that was visible on the surface. On the outside she was cool, detached, even a little emotionless. But it was her eyes that gave some hint of the energy fizzing away behind them.

Kenta realised he still didn't know what to make of her. His first instinct was to dislike her, plain and simple, and probably not trust her all that much either. And yet here he was doing as she'd requested, and without much of a fight.

He put this uncomfortable fact aside and took out his personal notebook now that he was done with his maths. It was in this notebook that he wrote ideas for his novel. He rarely took it out when anyone was around, but he had nothing else to do and figured Jessica wouldn't know or care what it was anyway.

He settled the notebook on top of his lap, with his legs raised a little and bunched together so that it was closer to his face and hidden from Jessica's view.

After a few minutes of scribbling away he soon found his stride. He was slowly working his way through a tricky plot point that had been bugging him for days, but then he found himself being pulled back out into the world by a voice.

He looked up and saw Jessica eyeing him. "Sorry?"

"I said, what are you writing?" she repeated.

Without thinking, Kenta's hands curled protectively over his scribbled lines as if to hide them from Jessica's X-ray stare.

Was she just nosy or had she sniffed out the fact he was doing something that was ordinarily a secret?

"Nothing really," he said, feigning nonchalance. "Just writing out a few notes for the English essay we need to do."

"Really?" She sounded totally unconvinced, and he guessed she'd sensed he was lying. She seemed to have that ability.

He thought for one moment that she might ask to see the notes since they were in the same English class, but she only continued reading.

"How's the book?" said Kenta, wanting to deflect her attention from himself.

"Quite brilliant." Jessica's face lit up for a moment as she glanced at the front cover. "I've read it a couple of times before. It's a classic."

"I know," said Kenta. "It's one of the first detective novels, isn't it? It was an influence for Arthur Conan Doyle when he started writing Sherlock Holmes. I haven't read it yet, but I've heard a lot about it."

Jessica feigned a look of astonishment. "Wow, so you're not a brain-dead jock after all."

"So that's what you think I am?" Kenta shot back, mildly irked at the sudden accusation. "Just because I play football?"

"It's more the company you keep. I mostly see you hanging around with the sporty types. Except for Yudai of course, but like you said, you guys weren't... sorry... *aren't* really friends any more."

"Is that what you go around doing all day, just judging people?"

Jessica let out a little yawn. "I just say what I see."

"Yeah? Well, what do you think people say when they see you?" There was an intended venom in Kenta's voice as he said this, and he watched Jessica's reaction closely.

"Oh, the usual... loser, weirdo, whatever other unimaginative words you can come up with for people who aren't the same as you."

Although she appeared unfazed, and Kenta himself had thought the same thing of her before, he felt a tiny sting of remorse for bringing it up.

"Do you like Kyoto?" he asked as if to make up for it.

"I haven't made my mind up yet."

"And you were in Beijing before?"

"Yes."

"What was it like?"

"Very Chinese."

Kenta could see her resisting. But he wasn't done yet. "So why did you come to Japan then?"

"I didn't have a choice. My parents decided to move here and that was that."

"You didn't want to leave?"

Realising she wouldn't be allowed to keep on reading just yet, Jessica placed the book face down on her lap, and a weary sigh escaped her lips.

"Would you want to leave a place just as you're starting to get used to it?"

Kenta considered this and shrugged. "I suppose not."

"There's your answer then. So, no offence, but I'm not exactly Kyoto's number-one fan just yet. Knowing my parents, we'll be off somewhere else before the year is out."

"What do they do?"

"Sell olive oil and jewellery."

"Olive oil?"

"Yes, you know? The stuff people pour over their salads."

Kenta gave a sarcastic snort. "Yes, I'm familiar with it. Which olive oil?"

"Morelli."

"Oh yeah, I've heard of it. Big Italian company."

"That's the one." Jessica was sounding bored again. "And you're half-Korean, right?"

Kenta couldn't hide his surprise. Once again, she appeared to be one step ahead of him. "Yes, my mom's from Seoul. How'd you know that?"

"I did my own research. I'm hardly going to trust a person to help me with this sort of thing without checking them out first."

"And your parents?"

"British and Italian. I was born in London."

Kenta nodded, secretly pleased to finally be learning something about her. "So do you believe in ghosts?" he said, surprising himself with his own question.

"Since I've never seen one and I'm yet to see any convincing evidence for their existence, I'd have to say no."

"So, what do you think is happening here?"

Returning to her book, Jessica's eyes began scanning the lines again. "We'll see, won't we?"

"And you're not a little freaked out or anything by the idea of a geisha wandering about?"

"Not especially. Are you?"

"No," he replied a little too quickly.

"If you don't mind," said Jessica, "I'd like to get a little reading done while we have some light."

This time Kenta didn't take much offence. He was getting used to her curtness, and guessed it was just her style rather than an attempt at being rude.

Up above, rays of ailing sunlight were streaming in through the gym's giant windows near the ceiling, the kind of golden sideways light that came with autumn and winter.

Watching the light fade, Kenta allowed his head to rest against a pile of soft mats behind him and closed his eyes just for a second.

***

"Hey, sleeping beauty! Wake up!"

It was a voice whispering in the dark. At first, Kenta wasn't sure where he was or who'd spoken, but then he felt the cold hardness of the wooden floor against his palms, and the stack of mats behind his head. He looked up and saw that the figure looming over him was not the ghost or a security guard, but Jessica Hunter.

"It's time to go," she said, more insistently this time.

"What time is it?" He struggled to his feet, blinking heavily.

"It's almost six."

"Six?" He looked to her with a start.

"You were asleep two hours!"

Gathering himself, Kenta swung his backpack straps over both shoulders and followed Jessica back out onto the gym floor.

It was almost completely dark, with only a hint of shadowy, silver-tinged light in the windows high above. Kenta noticed Jessica had a small torch on in her hand, though this didn't surprise him. She probably had a whole kit ready on standby for this kind of thing.

He took out his phone and switched on the torch, adding to the light from Jessica's.

As they crept across the floor, careful not to make their presence known, Kenta found his sleepiness falling away in an instant as the reality of what they were doing hit him with an almost physical force. They were creeping around at school in the dark where there were security guards patrolling and the phantom geisha lurking somewhere. That was all people at school had been talking about all day, that and the great defiling of the auditorium screen. Already the two things had merged, so that most of the pupils believed the geisha had also painted the mysterious giant circles using whatever dark magic she had at hand. How else had it been done without anyone being caught on camera? Earlier, Jessica's plan had seemed a brave thing to do, but now Kenta was confronted with the fact that he was genuinely scared.

Once they reached the double doors, Jessica turned to him. "Follow my lead. We'll start with the ground floor then work our way up. If you see any of the security guards then look for an open classroom door, most of them aren't locked, but be quiet about it."

Kenta found himself nodding, though his mind screamed no.

Jessica pulled open one of the gym doors an inch at a time, then put her head through the space. She looked left and right before turning back to Kenta. "Let's go."

The corridor was now plunged into an eerie darkness, more so than in the gym where the moonlight was still leaking in through the windows.

Jessica began walking to the right, filling the section of corridor ahead with her torchlight, which surprised Kenta with its strength. It was stronger than his phone, and offered some sense of safety and control, as if the light alone had the power to banish any lurking ghouls or ghosts.

Before turning the next corner, they paused and peered tentatively around. Kenta's heart flailed in anticipation of seeing something, anything, but there were only more stretches of darkened corridor, oddly lonely now that it was devoid of the usual sunlight and frenetic activity.

They kept on going, stepping softly yet at a decent enough pace. Jessica had her sights fixed firmly on the end of the corridor ahead while Kenta continued to look back over his shoulder. He kept close to Jessica's side, even convincing himself more than once that he was actually taking the lead. But in reality, he was impressed by her nerve and resolve. He couldn't think of anyone at school who would willingly do this, at least not without being babbling wrecks jumping at every little shadow and noise. And he was Kenta, a boy, and therefore bigger, stronger and supposedly braver, relying on the girl to lead him through the scary building.

At the next corridor, which turned left again, circling back towards the main central walkway to the foyer, they saw that one of the classrooms still had its lights on, flooding the centre of the corridor with a bright fluorescent glow. It was one of the Chinese rooms.

"It's probably just one of the teachers leaving them on and forgetting," whispered Jessica over his shoulder. "But they could be working late too."

Then as if this was no big deal at all, she crept forward until she was next to the small window in the classroom door. Kenta wanted to tell her to get back, that she was too close. He was sure this was the moment when it would all go wrong.

"There's no one there," said Jessica before walking on. "Let's go up to the second floor."

Allowing himself to calm down a little, Kenta caught up and joined her on the stairs. He was gradually adjusting to the dark and the need to be constantly watching, though he could still feel his heart beating its uncomfortably fast and frantic rhythm.

The second-floor corridor smelled more strongly of the sickly-sweet chemicals the cleaners used when mopping. The small green light of a fire exit glowed dimly near the end, and snatches of moonlight and the sports field's lamps outside bled through classroom windows so that they could see the outlines of lockers and fire extinguishers more clearly.

Although Kenta remained on high alert, he was now getting used to the drill, and becoming brazen enough that he was sure they wouldn't see anything of note – which would mean he'd done his bit, shown his mettle, and would soon be free to get on with his life instead of involving himself in Jessica's ludicrous schemes.

He was still checking behind him once in a while, but the novelty of having the school all to themselves had at least some appeal, and he was sure he'd remember this night for a long time.

Jessica remained doggedly vigilant as she swept each stretch of floor with her torch. Kenta was aiming his phone light into the classrooms, catching camera flash snippets of whiteboards, desks, chairs.

They were close to the next corner and a left turn when Kenta happened to casually look backwards and noticed a light. It was faint at first, a smear of illumination on the walls, but he could see at once that it was getting brighter. Someone was coming around the corner.

He reached out and tapped Jessica on the arm. She spun round, blinding him momentarily with the torch. He threw a hand up over his eyes.

"Someone's coming," he uttered in a harsh whisper.

Then Jessica saw the light too, as whoever was holding the torch was just about to turn into their stretch of corridor.

She moved quickly to the nearest classroom door and tried the handle, but it wouldn't budge. Kenta almost swore out loud as they dashed as quickly and quietly as their feet would allow to the next room along.

Jessica switched off her torch and Kenta followed suit, stuffing the phone into a pocket and nearly dropping it in the process.

Now he could hear footsteps. The light was coming around the corner. It was much brighter than their small torches. The person would catch them in their sights in a matter of seconds.

Jessica tried the door handle.

Hurry, hurry! Kenta was screaming internally, wanting to take over and shove her aside, but she turned the steel doorknob so that it wouldn't make a noise and was careful to push open the door softly in case it squeaked.

The light was on Kenta now. He was done for. But a hand seized his forearm and pulled him inside.

"Get under a table," Jessica commanded under her breath before closing the door as slowly as she'd opened it.

Kenta ducked beneath the teacher's desk, which was the largest, while Jessica crouched beneath the pupil's desk nearest the door.

There was a momentary hush in which Kenta could only hear his own stifled breaths, but then came the unmistakable sound of footsteps working their way methodically towards the classroom. There was a voice too. No, it was singing. A low murmured melody as though the person was singing along to a tune only they could hear.

They mustn't have seen anything, but then the footsteps were slowing down just outside. A bright shaft of torchlight split the classroom's darkness in half, hitting the surfaces of the desks closest to Kenta.

From his hiding place, Kenta peered up at the source of the light coming in through the row of classroom windows. There was the dark silhouette of a head and shoulders. The singing had stopped as the torch swept the room like a spotlight roving over the grounds of a prison at night.

Kenta held his breath and ducked down lower. He'd been wrong. The guard must have seen something after all and had bluffed ignorance with the singing. But then as quickly as the light had turned on them, it disappeared and the footsteps continued on, along with the soft out-of-tune melody.

They both waited until the footsteps had gone before daring to emerge from under the desks.

Jessica looked out into the corridor and turned the handle.

"Wait!" said Kenta, raising himself to his feet and brushing his knees. "This is stupid. It's not worth it. We should just go now while we still can."

Jessica switched the torch back on, and even in the dim light Kenta could see the defiant glare in her eyes.

"You go if you want," she shot back. "I'm carrying on."

And with that she crept back out into the corridor.

Shaking his head, and furious with himself, the world and Jessica, Kenta reluctantly followed her out.

The security guard's torch and footsteps had disappeared around the corner to their right.

"Let's at least be more careful," said Kenta. "The second we think someone is coming, we get the hell out of the way."

With a slight rolling of the eyes, Jessica mouthed "okay', and jerked a thumb back the way they'd come. "We should go up to the third floor. That way we'll probably avoid security."

"Fine, and then I'm done," said Kenta.

"Whatever you say."

They backtracked to the stairwell, this time pausing every few steps to listen for any sounds.

As they made their way up the stairs, Kenta felt a chill. He hadn't banked on being out after dark, and so had only come in his uniform with just his blazer for warmth.

They were reaching the top of the stairs where the art department was, and Kenta could see a selection of pupil's sketches on a giant display board.

Jessica held out a hand to stop him, freezing just as her foot was poised to take the last step. Kenta presumed she was waiting to ensure the corridor was clear, but she remained that way for a good few seconds, and from the side he could see the intense concentration on her face.

"Listen," she whispered eventually.

Kenta listened. He thought he was listening out for the rhythmical slap of the guard's footsteps, and simultaneously imagined there was one patrolling the third floor, and another behind them so that they'd be trapped.

But there were no footsteps. Jessica was still listening intently all the same.

"What is it?" said Kenta.

She waved her hand to signal more quiet.

Kenta didn't like just standing there. It was making him more and more nervous. At least with the walking there was also the opportunity to run and therefore escape, but to just wait like this – they were sitting ducks. Any guard, or any... thing could suddenly come upon them.

"Music," said Jessica. "I think it's behind us."

She turned back to the blank dark space further down the stairwell. Kenta strained for the sound of the guard's murmured singing, ready to make a dash in the opposite direction. But it wasn't singing. It was music all right, but there was no voice at all. It was an instrument.

Something lurched in the pit of Kenta's stomach, and his throat ran dry in an instant. "What is it?" he hissed croakily.

Casting about like a bloodhound, Jessica carefully picked her way back down the stairs to the second floor. As with everything else that evening, Kenta wanted to tell her no, to stop, but this time it wasn't down to a fear of getting caught. It was something else, something instinctive, which sent a shiver of dread through his bones.

Reaching the second floor, they looked both ways but there was no light or movement in either direction. Jessica stood motionless again, straining for sounds. Kenta could still hear it too. It was slightly clearer but remained faint.

"Down," she said suddenly, and before he could say anything, Jessica was moving downwards again to the first floor.

They'd barely left the last step before she jerked her head left. "There!"

She was moving quickly now, back in the direction of the gym, and Kenta almost had to jog to keep up. He couldn't say anything as she was too far in front, and he had no idea what they were chasing after. Jessica had lowered her torch as well, so that they were moving quickly into near-darkness.

When they reached the corner, she crouched down and craned her head round. "Look!"

Standing above Jessica, he looked around the corner. At first there were only more shades of dark and shadow infused with a little moonlight that had found its way inside. But then there it was, emerging into a weak shaft of moonlight as though it had materialised right there and then.

Kenta felt his heart fling itself against his ribcage. Something like pure horror gripped his innards and stole the air from his lungs.

It was there. It. Exactly what people had said. A geisha, or at least that was what it seemed to be. There was the long flowing white kimono adorned with a hint of darker patterning, and the tall mass of oil-black hair glistening around the head. And the way it moved, almost gliding along the smooth stone floor as if not even touching it.

An urgent inner voice was telling Kenta it couldn't be real. There was nothing in his understanding of life and the world that allowed for what was in front of him now.

He was already shrinking back as Jessica looked up at him. "We have to go," she said, and Kenta felt a profound relief until he realised she meant to go ahead, *towards* that thing.

He shook his head.

"We have to!" she hissed. "If we don't, we'll never figure it out."

This was madness. They'd seen it, that was enough. It was all true. She wanted to charge ahead but was most likely struggling with the same sense of shocked disbelief as he was. She didn't want to do it alone, but he also knew she would if she had to. He saw her readying herself and knew he should turn and run the other way, just as he should have done long before that point. Then without warning, Jessica stood and lunged forward, charging towards it as it was approaching the next turn at the far end.

At first, Kenta could only watch her go. He felt a strange paralysis keeping his limbs inert, yet the sight of Jessica running overrode the stifling panic in his chest, and the next moment he found he was also sailing along behind her.

The ghost must have heard them coming and turned to face them. The ghostly pale face was there as clear as the rest of it. Would it scream or vanish or do some other diabolical thing? Should they try and talk to it?

But instead of all these things, it let out a surprised gasp and began to run. The ghost was actually running.

Jessica seemed emboldened by the spectre's flight; a predator's instinct kicked in and she sped up.

The music was much clearer now. It was coming from the ghost itself, and as they turned the next corner, Kenta realised they'd almost caught up. He saw the kimono flailing about the figure as it ran and thought he could hear its desperate panting, but he hesitated at the crucial moment, and instead it was Jessica who reached out to seize its shoulder.

The girl yelped and spun round.

They were face to face, breathless and pumping with adrenaline.

Now it was the three of them – the geisha standing in the centre of the corridor, staring aghast at the two of them – and Kenta realised it wasn't a spectre at all but a solid form.

He thought it might try to run again but then Jessica moved to the nearest classroom door, and finding it open, beckoned the white apparition inside. "Hurry, before we're seen."

After a further hesitation, the geisha saw there was little choice and went in. Jessica followed, and a still utterly baffled Kenta went in last. He shut the door behind them while Jessica switched on the classroom lights.

"It's only for a minute," she said as the three of them blinked and squinted against the sudden burst of harsh fluorescent light.

Now it was undeniable. They were looking not at any supernatural being, but at a real person. In the full light, the girl's frightened expression revealed the heavy make-up which was not quite as thick or as accomplished as that maiko's had been at the school assembly. The hair was also clearly a wig, and with the effort of running had come slightly loose so that it leaned lopsidedly.

"Who are you?" said Jessica firmly.

The girl was standing against a desk in the front row while Kenta and Jessica stood near the whiteboard at the front, like two imposing teachers bearing down on an unruly pupil.

The girl's scared eyes flitted between the two of them. Her chest was still heaving a little from the effort. She moved her painted lips to speak, then instead pulled at the wig and tore it loose. It hung uselessly in her hand while her own natural hair shone in the light, pulled down tight around the scalp and kept in place with clips. Following this, she reached down the front of the kimono and pulled out a phone, pausing the koto soundtrack that was still coming from it.

The girl blinked and dropped her head guiltily. Perhaps it was the eyes or the way she moved, but something flicked a switch in Kenta's brain.

"Rina?" he said disbelievingly.

A further guilty glance in his direction confirmed it was true.

"Rina Mitsustuka?" said Jessica.

Rina gave a single, solemn nod.

"What the hell?" Kenta gestured at her dress, unable to hold back a sudden burst of anger. "You nearly gave me a heart attack!"

"I didn't mean to hurt anyone," muttered Rina, her eyes still cast to the floor.

Jessica took a step closer to her. "So this is why you were so keen to bring up all that crap about the curse in the assembly. You were priming us all for your little stunt."

Rina shook her head. "No, that bit's true... at least I think it is."

Jessica went on. "We need to know why you're doing this. It's important. We think it might have something to do with Yudai's disappearance."

A flash of confusion passed briefly across Rina's face at the mention of Yudai. She looked quite small now, huddled slightly as she perched on the desk. Her features were almost unrecognisable beneath the make-up, but Kenta knew her eyes and her small nose well enough. They'd been in many of the same classes for three years. She was normally pretty quiet, but very friendly and smart, and was generally well liked in the way quiet and harmless pupils often were. She'd always been the sort to keep her head down and never got into trouble. He couldn't think of anyone less likely to do such a crazy thing.

"I had no choice," she said, fidgeting nervously at some imaginary object in her hands.

"We know that," said Jessica, speaking calmly now. "But it's still very important that we find out. We're not going to tell anyone it's you, I give you my word."

Kenta looked to Jessica in surprise, but she ignored him.

"We just need to know."

"I can't," said Rina, shaking her head again more violently. "I really can't."

"Yes, you can," said Jessica, "you have no choice. It's us or the headmaster, and we all know how that would go."

As she continued to shake her head in small yet vigorous movements, tears began to bunch and glisten in Rina's eyes. "They made me do it. I couldn't say no." Her voice caught on a rising sob.

"Who made you?" said Jessica, more intensely this time.

"I don't know... they just... they knew something about me. They said if I didn't do this, they'd let everyone know."

"What exactly did they ask you to do?"

"To do this." She looked down exasperatedly at the dress she was wearing. "There was a kimono left in my locker and they sent me a music file to play. They said I had to do this every night for an hour until..."

"Until when?"

"Until the school festival performance. They told me I couldn't get caught." Rina swallowed down a further sob as the tears began to slide down her cheeks. "There's a place in the boiler room they told me to hide in if anyone saw me, but now I'm in trouble."

"How did they tell you if you don't know who they are?" said Jessica.

"They just started sending me messages one day. I don't know how they got my number. I don't even know if they're male or female."

"What about the name?"

Rina thought a moment. "No name, just two letters or two zeros... just like in the auditorium."

Kenta and Jessica looked at one another. The alarm bell that had already been ringing in Kenta's brain became even louder, and he could see the same alarm registered on Jessica's face.

"Do you have any idea why they wanted you to do this?" said Kenta.

Rina shook her head. "No, I thought maybe it was just for a joke or something, but then that thing with the guard happened in the auditorium. I didn't want to do it again, but they sent me another message this morning and said I had to carry on."

"Can I see the message?" said Jessica.

Rina went to hold out her phone, then in a moment of indecision drew it back again. "They didn't show their number."

"I just want to see."

"I can't." The tears were flowing freely now from Rina's red-rimmed eyes.

"Is it because of the thing you mentioned, the thing they know about you?" Jessica spoke quite softly, sounding almost like a teacher calming an upset pupil.

Rina nodded.

"Remember," Jessica continued, "this is just between us, no one else will know. Will they, Kenta?"

Double-taking at the sudden mention of his name, Kenta found both girls' eyes trained on him. "No, definitely not," he said, attempting to sound as honest and convincing as he could.

After further deliberation, Rina opened her phone and selected a message. Her hand was trembling as she offered it to Jessica who took it with a soft, "Thank you."

Kenta watched as Jessica stared at the screen.

"My parents..." Rina burst out, sobbing profusely. "If they find out, they'll kill me... they're not... they're very traditional."

Nodding, Jessica said, "I understand."

She handed the phone to Kenta, who first saw the photo. It was of Rina kissing a girl he didn't recognise on the lips. The photo had clearly been taken without the girls knowing. The message beneath read: "*You know what to do. You can't back out now.*"

"Your girlfriend?" said Jessica.

Rina managed a nod. "She's from another school. My parents don't know... I don't even know how this person found out... we've always been careful. They knew about my parents, knew how they'd react."

Handing Rina her phone back, Kenta said a sheepish, "Sorry."

She tucked the phone back into her dress and swiped the kimono's sleeve across her eyes and cheeks.

"Okay, Rina," said Jessica decisively. "This is what's going to happen. We're not going to tell a soul that it's you who did this, but you still have to stop doing it. If you don't, you'll get caught eventually, and whoever's behind this is planning something else, something nasty. You don't want to be associated with it, believe me."

"But—" Rina's mouth opened to protest.

"—It's not worth losing everything over this. Your parents are going to find out one day anyway. Best to do it sooner rather than later. You shouldn't have to hide who you are from the world."

Easy for you to say, thought Kenta, knowing that it was usually much easier for Westerners to come out about their sexuality. He could guess at some of the anguish Rina was experiencing. Some Japanese parents simply wouldn't accept it.

Rina's body shook now with heaving sobs, and she covered her face with her hands.

Jessica went to place a hand on Rina's shoulder to comfort her. It was obvious to Kenta that this didn't come naturally to her. She didn't seem the type who went for any sort of physical affection or contact.

"I'll help you. You should go to the police, or at least tell a teacher you trust. You won't get into trouble if you come forward. It's good you kept the messages. Now we have the evidence."

Still crying desperately into her hands, Rina said nothing as she allowed herself to be slowly guided by Jessica towards the door.

"We have to be quiet now," said Jessica. "There's a way out by the side gate, but we have to be careful, okay?"

Rina nodded again, and Jessica looked to Kenta.

He switched off the lights and went to open the door ahead of them. He turned the handle ever so slowly just as Jessica had, and was about to poke his head out to check the corridor when his eyes were filled instantly with a blinding light, and the way was suddenly blocked by a dark figure. But this was no apparition either.

Kenta saw the security badge and the torch, and heard the static emitting from the walkie-talkie on the man's belt. He didn't even try to run, only closed his eyes and sighed. They were finished.

CHAPTER 14

Neither one of them got further than the foyer the next morning. The deputy head, Miss Jennings, was waiting by the main doors for them. She picked each one of them out the second they crossed the threshold, and with a grave face and ominously businesslike tone, asked them to go straight to the headmaster's office.

They'd been expecting it of course. When the security guard had caught them in the classroom, they hadn't put up a fight or protested. They'd been seen and recognised and that was that. The guard had been as dumbfounded as anyone to find the infamous phantom and two pupils having a seemingly casual conversation in the classroom. It was the young security guard who normally watched over the koto.

When Jessica entered the headmaster's office, she found Kenta and Rina already there, seated at two of the three chairs lined up in front of the headmaster's desk. She'd expected to be interviewed one at a time, not all together, but this was better, she thought. He wouldn't be able to use the old divide and conquer approach and turn each pupil against the others by isolating them.

Mr Murphy was sitting at his desk typing something on his laptop. When Jessica entered, he continued typing, seemingly unaffected by the whole affair, although Jessica was sure she detected a hint of stiffening in his jaw and posture.

"Jessica, take a seat," he said flatly, aiming an upturned hand at the empty chair beside Kenta.

She glanced at the other two as she approached. She was pleased that Rina was there. Jessica hadn't been sure if she'd have the guts to show up, but in the end she'd obviously listened when, just before being marched out of the school by the security guard on Wednesday evening, Jessica had told her to be brave and turn up in the morning like she had nothing to hide.

Now Rina looked more than a little dejected, her shoulders slumped, head dropped forward. She was sniffling, staring down at the crumpled tissue she was clutching on her lap, but she was there, and so was her phone, which was good.

She looked up briefly as Jessica took her seat, and Jessica saw her face as she knew it, free of the thick make-up and haunting mask, albeit with a heavy puffiness around the eyes.

Kenta, on the other hand, ignored Jessica completely as she sat down beside him. She could sense his tension without even looking. He was angry with her, with the world. *Good*, she thought. She wanted him angry. She was angry too. She hadn't spent the night trembling with fear, terrified of Mr Murphy's wrath. On the contrary, she'd been rehearsing her words in her mind, and knew exactly what she was going to say.

A heavy quiet descended while Mr Murphy made a show of slowly closing his laptop and rearranging a pen, before folding his hands together on the desk and regarding the three of them with a dead-eyed look that almost made Jessica snigger.

"I don't need to say too much about how very serious this is," he began, sending a wave of minty-tinged breath across the space between them. "You're just lucky that the police weren't called. They still could be, of course, but that depends on what you tell me." He turned his attention to Rina who was still sitting with head bowed, sniffling into her lap. "I understand you're the person who was dressed up as a geisha, is that right?"

Just as she had during her interrogation by Jessica, Rina gave a couple of sorry little nods.

Watching Mr Murphy leaning forward over the desk, his formidable paunch bulging against the edge as he impressed his larger size and authority on the smaller, weaker pupils, Jessica knew what was coming. She could have written much of it out in advance, each point from the classic headmasters' rulebook. This wasn't her first rodeo, and she'd encountered far more intimidating figures than the one in front of her.

As Mr Murphy opened his mouth to continue and inevitably lay into Rina, Jessica chose her moment to butt in. "Sorry, Mr Murphy, can I just say something?"

The headmaster started. He jolted his head towards her in surprise. She could see his jowly neck quivering. Kenta and Rina were looking at her too. Kenta's face was saying 'No!' as usual, and as usual she ignored it.

"Excuse me!" Mr Murphy near-bellowed in response, but again Jessica cut him off as he went to add more.

"I'm sorry, sir, but you have to listen. This is extremely important and concerns the school's reputation, and potentially the safety of everyone in it."

The headmaster stared at her as though some bizarre alien being had suddenly appeared before him.

"Rina, your phone please," said Jessica with such conviction and natural authority, that after an uncertain, darting look in Mr Murphy's direction, Rina proceeded to reach down into her schoolbag and handed Jessica the phone.

For the next few minutes, Jessica told Mr Murphy everything, from Rina being blackmailed, to Yudai drawing O's on the koto's display box in addition to the worksheet they'd discovered in his locker. Jessica had also asked Kenta to produce it as evidence, and fortunately for her he still had it in his bag and had no choice but to hand it over.

"And so, as you can see, sir, there's something much bigger going on here. Someone is actively trying to damage the school's reputation, and we were simply trying to find out who."

After listening to Jessica's outpouring of facts and speculations with a look of dumbfounded amazement, Mr Murphy fell into a further confused silence while he considered the crumpled worksheet in one hand and Rina's phone in the other.

"So let me get this straight," he said eventually. "You're saying Yudai's disappearance has something to do with what happened in the auditorium and the person blackmailing Rina?"

Jessica replied with a firm, "Yes."

"Are you saying then that Yudai is behind this?"

"No," said Kenta before Jessica could reply. "Wherever Yudai is, he wouldn't do a thing like this."

Mr Murphy scratched his head and looked over the two pieces of evidence one last time before handing them back.

"Look," he said. "I'm very sorry Rina that this has happened to you. We will of course help you report this to the police." He shifted his gaze now to Jessica in particular. "And while I can appreciate that you were attempting to help things with your little escapade last night, the fact remains that we can't have pupils trespassing on school property with impunity. Thanks to your behaviour, a security guard is ill at home, and a senior pupil has been left totally traumatised."

"That wasn't us," said Kenta. "We didn't have anything to do with that."

Not appreciating being interrupted by a pupil yet again, Mr Murphy glowered at Kenta who faltered under the scrutiny.

"Frankly, I don't care who did what. You're all deeply involved in whatever this is, as far as I'm concerned. For all I know, you're also involved in that disgraceful act in the auditorium, and this is just another part of your ridiculous game. No, the school has had enough turmoil without pupils running rampage."

As Mr Murphy straightened up in his big leather swivel chair, his voice increasing in volume with each syllable, Jessica could see he was regaining his composure, doing what he did best, which was to give out the orders, not receive them. It was time to put him back in his place.

"Yes, I'm afraid I have no choice but to call in your parents and suspend the three of you while we investigate this further."

A small yelp of despair left Rina's lips on hearing this, and even Kenta stiffened suddenly, staring at Mr Murphy in pained disbelief. Jessica could see him wanting to remonstrate somehow, but the words wouldn't come.

Mr Murphy was about to dismiss them when Jessica piped up one last time. "Mr Murphy, I think you're missing the point."

"I beg your pardon?" said the headmaster, who'd clearly had enough of this cocky little newcomer, but Jessica wasn't going to stop now. She knew it was now or never.

"Those reporters outside," she said, referencing the one TV van that was still parked across the street from the school, probably after getting word of the vandalism incident. "I'm sure they would jump on any story about Yudai, especially if it could be connected with all the other crazy things going on."

Kenta's leg jerked sharply against Jessica's below the desk. She jerked hers back in return and went on. She had Mr Murphy's attention now. At the word *reporters* his lips had pursed up and his right eyebrow arched.

"I'm sure they would also be aghast to learn that one of our pupils was being targeted by a blackmailer on account of her sexuality, and that the school was suspending her on top of it. That wouldn't really go down well with the school's ethos of tolerance and global community, would it?"

Mr Murphy was glaring at her now, and she was glaring back. She had him, and he knew it.

"It wouldn't look good at all," Jessica continued, "if the pupils who were only trying to help the school rebuild its reputation were punished for it. It would be much better for the pupils and the school if this was all kept to ourselves so that we could all get on with things and find out what's going on. That way, Rina doesn't have to suffer any more than she already has, and no reporters need to hear anything about discrimination or anything negative about Yudai, who's still missing by the way. Lastly, you won't have any irate parents blaming the school for all of these unfortunate mishaps, especially when Kenta and Rina here have excellent academic records and no prior blemishes to their name. I think that scenario would be much better for all concerned, don't you?"

Jessica sat back and calmly waited for Mr Murphy to digest what had been said. She guessed at the rapid calculations he was making behind those steely eyes, while Kenta and Rina remained deadly silent beside her, no doubt expecting an oncoming fallout of nuclear proportions. But instead, with his jowly cheeks glowing an epic raspberry-red, he kept down whatever volcanic eruption was threatening to explode from within him, and with great effort said in a low voice, "Just get out of my office and make sure I never hear of you doing anything even remotely out of line again, do you understand?"

"Yes, sir, absolutely!" With a smile, Jessica stood up and slung her bag over her shoulder.

Kenta and Rina didn't seem to have fully understood what was happening and were still planted in their seats.

"Let's go," said Jessica, flicking her head towards the door, while Mr Murphy quietly eyeballed them all with a look of utter contempt.

As they were getting to their feet, the office door swung open, and the headmaster's secretary burst in. It was immediately obvious from her expression that something was wrong. She was about to say something, then seeing the three pupils present, quickly changed tack. "Mr Murphy, the deputy head says you're needed immediately."

"What is it?" he grumbled.

"It's... There's some sort of issue with the school's intranet system."

"All right, I'll be there in a moment."

Filing out past the flustered secretary, Kenta whispered to Jessica. "You just blackmailed the headmaster. You're insane."

"You're welcome," grinned Jessica. "Now let's find out what's going on with the school's intranet. I'd put money on it being something to do with our friend, OO."

CHAPTER 15

Of course, she was right. She almost always seemed to be right, which to Kenta was the most irritating thing about her on a long list of very irritating qualities.

As with the rumours of the ghost the other day, the school buildings were awash with excited chatter, and it didn't take long for Kenta to discover why.

On entering his form room, which was a hive of noise and activity like all the others he'd passed by, the first thing Kenta saw was the projector screen, or more accurately, the two giant letter O's emblazoned there. But this time they weren't painted on. It was a digital image coming from the projector itself.

Half the class was standing around Miss Bennett's desk while she sat hunched at her computer, shaking her head and hammering away at the keyboard.

"It just gets better!" called Milo to Kenta. Milo was sitting back in his corner chair enjoying the show. "It's the same in every classroom, just like in the auditorium. No one can get into the school's intranet. And the best thing is, they're saying it's been wiped or something, as in everything might be gone – records, marks, the lot! This is freaking awesome!"

With that, Milo laughed to himself and settled down even further into his seat.

A few days earlier and Kenta would have been gobsmacked, but nothing was surprising him any more. The school was under attack, there was no doubting it now.

His first instinct was to go straight to Jessica's form room, but he stopped himself. He was still reeling from the episode in Mr Murphy's office, during which he'd been certain it was all over. That was almost his entire reputation and school record down the drain in one fell swoop, and all because he'd allowed himself to be manipulated by that selfish lunatic who didn't seem to care what happened to him or anyone else as long as she was having her fun. But then she'd somehow done it. Kenta had never seen anything like it in his life, never seen a pupil not only answer back like that, and to the headmaster of all people, but completely and utterly outmanoeuvre him too. She'd effectively blackmailed her way out of major trouble, and done it without any shame or hesitation.

She was dangerous all right, thought Kenta. He had no doubt she'd lead him into some other perilous situation if he allowed her to, and he swore he would keep away from her from now on.

Still, there was a small part of him that couldn't help admiring her at least a little for the bravery she'd shown the night before, and the unbelievable audacity and cunning of her performance in the headmaster's office. She might have landed him in the shit, but she'd pulled him right back out of it too.

There was also the lingering sense of shame he felt at the fact he'd frozen up when Jessica had first chased the supposed ghost, then again when he'd had the chance to collar the fake phantom. He wasn't sure if Jessica had even noticed any of this, but it bothered him that when the moment had come, he'd faltered. It wasn't like a football match, where he never hesitated and always knew what to do.

Returning his attention to the class projector screen where the two O's continued to stare out at them all mockingly, Kenta knew he would need her again if he was going to figure this out, and for once he probably knew one vital fact that even she didn't.

He knew that whatever it was, it was a cyberattack that had brought down the school's server – that much would soon be apparent to everyone else. What all of them probably didn't know was that there was only one person Kenta knew of who was capable of pulling something like this off, and his name was Yudai Matsumoto.

Chapter 16

Things were happening. Already it was shifting into the next gear, and yet Jessica was no closer to knowing who OO was or what it meant.

On seeing the double O's emblazoned across the form room's projector screen, along with the screens in almost every other classroom along the corridor, a thrill and a shiver of anger had simultaneously coursed through Jessica's body. She was excited at the sense of a chase, yet she knew she was more than a few steps behind. She and Kenta might have foiled the geisha ghost plot, which was something at least, but as long as they knew nothing of these two cryptic letters or symbols that were turning up left, right and centre, or where Yudai was, then they were essentially nowhere.

After she left the headmaster's office with Kenta and Rina, Jessica had instructed Rina to come clean with her parents and contact the police as soon as she got home after school, though she didn't expect much to come from it. She hadn't seen or heard anything more from the police since the day after Yudai's disappearance, and she wasn't holding her breath. Police were rarely the most imaginative bunch in her experience; it didn't matter which country you were in.

Jessica only hoped that Rina's parents wouldn't kick up the storm she was expecting. Rina had thanked her profusely for at least getting her off the hook with the headmaster – Jessica did have to admit she'd excelled herself there – but the battle wasn't over yet for Rina, just as it wasn't for her. At least Rina had relieved herself of the terrible burden she'd been carrying. It even made Jessica feel some gratitude for her own parents who, like with anything else, would probably simply shrug or say, "That's great, Jessica," if she ever told them she had a girlfriend.

And that was another thing to be grateful for, she supposed – to not have all that relationship gunk to distract her further from what she needed to do. Something in what was happening all around them at the school was calling to her with ever greater urgency. She felt some new and compelling sense of purpose growing in her the more she delved into it.

The most pressing task, besides figuring out once and for all who or what was behind OO, was to start searching for the insider. Jessica knew there had to be someone in the school who was helping the perpetrator. There were just too many factors pointing towards a person with intimate knowledge of the school complex, as well as the access.

It was possible it was a pupil, or even more than one, but something in the audacity of the auditorium feat said that it was someone who knew more than any of her peers. This was someone with keys and knowledge of how things operated after hours when all the pupils were gone. Naturally, this pointed towards the staff members – teachers, caretakers, security. There definitely seemed to be something personal about the whole thing, as if maybe a disgruntled teacher was getting their own back on the school for some perceived slight. This, however, seemed a little too far-fetched for Jessica's liking. Any teacher with that big a grudge would surely have just upped and left or been fired first. On top of that, it was a fairly prestigious school, and it didn't seem plausible that any sane teacher would jeopardise their position with this insanely elaborate campaign of fear. But more than anything, Jessica didn't see how any of the teachers would have the time or energy to pull something like this off. They appeared even more harried than their overworked pupils, scurrying about between classrooms and offices with piles of exercise books in their hands, and dark bags under their eyes.

It was the same with the pupils. The amount of homework at the school was ridiculous, far more than any other she'd been to, and she'd thought Beijing was bad. She barely had any spare time herself with which to focus on her fledgling investigation.

That left the caretaker and the security team. Already Jessica had been watching them all more closely, even before the ghost hunt the previous evening.

The caretaker, Mr Takagi, and his assistant, seemed the most obvious people on paper. They had the keys to every room, and knew every nook and cranny of the school grounds. They could easily carry out a mass scheme of sabotage before anyone would know what was going on, but none of this seemed even remotely likely either. A couple of casual enquiries with members of the admin team – under the guise of *getting to know the school bette*r – had confirmed Mr Takagi had been at the school for over twenty-five years since it first opened, and his assistant, a man named Mr Saito, had been there over a decade. He was about ten years younger than Mr Takagi, possibly in his mid-forties. He was tall and slim, with sharp, bony features. Wherever he went, he always seemed to have a dopey yet friendly smile plastered across his face. He did most of the heavy lifting under Mr Takagi's supervision, and though he knew only one word of English, he liked to say an enthusiastic *hello* to any foreign person passing him by. Jessica just couldn't see these two amiable men bearing any kind of grudge, never mind one deep and dark enough to motivate the recent events.

Jessica had similarly ruled out the receptionists and admin staff, who never seemed to venture beyond the offices and the school foyer. Like the pupils, they would have no real reason to be roaming the corridors at night and would have stood out a mile if they'd tried.

Which left the security team.

The head of security, Mr Goto, was still on leave after his run-in with Rina's geisha, and the security team consisted mostly of middle-aged men who spent much of their time talking and laughing together when they weren't smoking during breaks.

There was, however, one outlier, namely the young security guard who'd busted her, Kenta and Rina, and who also happened to be the person watching over the koto most of the time, with the exception of when Yudai had scrawled on the display box, which she found to be suspiciously convenient.

Jessica had to admit to herself that he wasn't the most obvious of criminal sidekicks. If anything, he looked a little gormless. He didn't appear particularly suited to his current profession, since he was always dozing rather than observing a single thing going on around him. But then he was the closest thing to a suspect Jessica had. He'd been near to the action at the right time more than once, and despite the sleepy vibe he gave off, it was possible he was capable of taking a bribe and looking the other way. More than that, it was the security team's job to prevent what had happened in the auditorium, and therefore there was a large question mark over their reputation as far as she was concerned.

For this reason, Jessica had made a note to watch him more closely from now on. She would need Kenta's help of course, though how willing Kenta would be to offer it was no longer certain. He'd looked mightily pissed off during the meeting with the headmaster – even if she'd technically saved his neck too – and had stormed off to his form room before she could speak with him afterwards.

Jessica would be the first to admit she might have initially taken advantage of Kenta's friendship with Yudai. She knew the job of searching the school would be much easier with a Japanese pupil at her side, particularly one with a squeaky-clean record and who knew the school grounds well, and one with a personal motivation was even better. But then he'd only gone and surprised her.

He'd not only turned up after school as she'd expected, but he'd also shown some nerve during their hunt. She knew he'd wobbled initially, but she wouldn't hold it against him. When it was all said and done, he'd been there when it mattered, and he'd also shown integrity and loyalty to his friend, Yudai, which she supposed were fairly admirable and occasionally useful attributes. Furthermore, she knew he was a writer. It was so obvious in his furtive notebook scribblings, and with this came a sensitivity and acuteness of observation that could prove very useful. Yes, it was safe to say Jessica had seriously underestimated Kenta Higashi, and she was more than prepared to admit it, just not to his face.

***

As she'd expected, Kenta had made himself scarce during the morning, and Jessica couldn't find him anywhere during the first break. So instead of wasting further time, she went about finding out more on the morning's hacking incident.

The teachers were keeping quiet of course, saying it was just a glitch with the BSK intranet or something to that effect – which was plainly false to anyone with eyes and a brain, when all had seen the same symbols from the auditorium on every projector screen.

The most far-fetched rumours coming from her fellow pupils were that it was part of some terrorist campaign or a government-related conspiracy, though no one could offer any solid conclusions as to why they would target a school. The receptionists also weren't falling any longer for Jessica's attempts at language practice, which always seemed to be followed by a lot of questions about the school and its staff. When she asked them what had happened, they'd only repeated what the teachers had said. But whatever it was, it was still wreaking havoc. All the teachers had been forced to switch off their projectors and forgo the use of any computers during lessons until the issue was resolved. And it was obvious from the expressions on the admin team, which Jessica caught snatches of through the wall of windows behind the reception desk, that they were also stuck in the same technological quagmire.

The confirmation of a graver Issue came just as break was ending, when Jessica spotted a team of serious-looking technicians entering the foyer, all wearing the same dark blue overalls and badges bearing their company's name. They each had a large heavy-duty toolbox in their hands, and it only took a swift peek outside for Jessica to catch sight of their van parked at the side of A-block – *Kyoto Digital Solutions*.

A quick online search in the IT room shortly afterwards confirmed what she already knew – that KDS was no small-fry fixer of Wi-Fi issues. These were the guys you called in when you had a major network calamity on your hands. This in turn told her something else that was plain to see, namely that whoever was behind this hack was no small-timer. Something of this magnitude required serious ability and motivation, and she had some idea who might be involved.

***

She eventually bumped into Kenta during the final afternoon break before the last two periods.

He was leaving A-block, and caught sight of her waiting by the same decked area with benches where they'd previously discussed their ghost hunt adventure.

She threw Kenta a fixed enough look that he couldn't miss it. She saw him hesitate and look away, but he was also smart enough to know he couldn't ignore her for long, and once again he resigned himself to the inevitable by trudging over to where she was standing.

Once they were face to face, Kenta opened his mouth to speak.

"Let me guess," said Jessica, cutting him off before he could utter a sound. "You're done with all this, and you want me to stop pestering you, or something to that effect?"

Kenta went to protest then decided against it. "Yeah, something like that."

"Thought so. So, am I to understand that after all this, you're giving up now? Just when we're actually getting somewhere?"

"Getting somewhere? You mean getting my ass thrown out of school on your account?"

"Oh, don't be so dramatic!" Jessica snapped. "You were never getting yourself thrown out of school."

"Whatever you say, I'm not pulling any more stunts like the other night."

"Fine, fine. You don't need me to keep looking into Yudai's whereabouts anyway, you can do that yourself."

Kenta was eyeing her closely, no doubt trying to figure out her angle.

"And I know you think he's involved with this computer-hacking business," Jessica added, almost nonchalantly.

Kenta's mouth dropped open. "What?"

"It's not exactly a stretch. His face is plastered all over the walls in the IT room – top prize for a robotics competition, a special award for designing an app, and another for coding. Add to that the fact that he's some kind of genius, and it's not a big step to the next conclusion. Plus, we already know he's a part of this somehow, but you should at least be pleased that you're the only other person who made the connection."

After staring at her in quiet amazement, Kenta sighed heavily and shook his head. "So, what is it I'm supposed to do?"

Jessica shrugged. "That's up to you, you're not an idiot. If I were you, I'd maybe see if I could speak with someone else who knows him well. His parents perhaps."

"His parents?"

"You do know them, don't you?"

"Yeah, sort of. I met them a few times."

"There you go then. But like I said, it's up to you."

Jessica could still see Kenta was suspicious of her sudden willingness to let him off the proverbial leash.

"And what are you going to do exactly?" said Kenta.

"Find out the real missing piece, i.e. who or what the hell is OO."

"Good luck with that!"

"I do need one thing from you though," Jessica added.

Kenta raised an eyebrow.

"Just updates, that's all. If you find anything on Yudai outside school hours, I want to know. And I'll keep you posted on my end too."

With eyes slightly narrowed, Kenta continued to survey Jessica more closely as though checking for hidden motivations lurking on her person.

"All right then." He looked around for any watching teachers and removed his phone from the front pocket of his bag. "We can use Line. What's your username?"

"I don't have one."

"What?" Kenta balked. "You've been in Japan more than two months, and you don't have Line? It's what everyone uses. How do you chat with people?"

Jessica shrugged lightly. "What can I say? I'm not much of a chatter."

"What about in Beijing?"

"I got WeChat eventually, but then people started actually contacting me all the time, it was awful."

"Not even Instagram? Twitter?"

Jessica shook her head.

"Do you even use your phone?"

"Only when I have to. Usually, it's just for my parents to get hold of me once in a blue moon."

As he stared at her in amazement, it took a further moment for Kenta to digest this. "Do you have it with you?"

Jessica rummaged inside the small brown leather bag she had with her and pulled out a phone before handing it over.

"This is a new Xiaomi. What a waste!"

After half a minute of Kenta thumbing the phone screen, and Jessica waiting impatiently with folded arms, he handed it back.

"There, you are now officially in the twenty-first century. I've downloaded the Line app for you and added my contact."

"Thanks," said Jessica, at which point a loud wolf whistle pierced the air, and they both turned to see Milo passing close by. He waved and winked in Kenta's direction with a giant smirk added for measure.

Kenta rolled his eyes. "Great!"

"You don't seriously care what he thinks, do you?"

"I've got to go." Kenta zipped up his bag and traipsed off towards C-block, leaving Jessica to watch him go, equally as puzzled by this boy who was so eager to be seen a certain way while hiding the realest parts of himself. *It must be so exhausting*, she thought, before cutting her own path back to B-block.

**

The school day finished with extracurricular activities, or ECAs as they were known to pupils and teachers alike.

Jessica had been encouraged to do something she wouldn't normally choose, and so found herself in an arts and crafts class with an exceptionally smiley and sweet Japanese teacher named Miss Sagawa.

The class, while initially sounding tolerable, mostly turned out to involve cutting pretty shapes and patterns out of paper. It was made up almost entirely of girls, with just one boy, and all of them looked quite at home. It didn't appear as if they'd chosen something they wouldn't normally go for, and Jessica felt she'd been duped. Even badminton or football would have been better than this.

After the ECAs were over – and Jessica couldn't have left sooner – she knew there was still one more important task to complete.

Her head may have been swimming with the investigation she was privately building, but that didn't change the fact she had an ever-growing pile of homework to contend with. The English assignment was the most pressing of them all. She was due to deliver her PPT and essay in less than two week's time, and she'd been unable to find anything of worth on the history of the koto and its mysterious maiko owner. There was quite a bit of info online concerning the actual koto, as well as the nobleman who'd commissioned its creation, but there was virtually nothing on the geisha herself, and absolutely zero about a curse. Jessica didn't even have a name for her. It was as if she'd been wiped from the history books entirely.

Jessica was beginning to wonder if in her initial enthusiastic haste, she'd chosen a dud of a topic for the assignment, which would make up thirty per cent of her first-semester grade. And while she would have loved to do a quick job of it, it was perhaps a mixture of pride and an aversion to parent–teacher meetings that reminded her she needed to at least make it look as if a sufficient effort had been made.

She was starting to think a visit to the public library would be required, or perhaps the museum too. She remembered Miss Nakamura and her assistant, and knew they were the obvious people to ask.

But then she remembered the koto.

The museum's representative was still there in the foyer, standing or sitting nervously by it all day long with a small table piled with pamphlets. She'd had little to do during the first couple of days, but perhaps because of all the negative publicity concerning the school, there had been renewed interest from pupils, and the word was the headmaster would be opening the foyer up to the public as initially planned.

It was quite a clever move, Jessica thought. More than she would have given him credit for. After all, right now BSK needed something to deflect attention from all the other recent mishaps.

On her way out after the final bell, Jessica stopped by the display case where the koto was being kept and pretended to be taking an interest. She made a point of peering closely at the beautifully worn mahogany frame, adorned with its thirteen strings, and the elegant flowers painted along the bottom panel. On the wall behind the case, below the giant museum logo, was a blown-up vintage photo of a geisha playing a koto, although it was not the same one.

To her right, Jessica could sense the museum rep watching her closely. She allowed her eyes to meet the young woman's and faked pleasant surprise when the rep approached with a wide and enthusiastic grin.

"It's beautiful, isn't it?" she said in excellent, though heavily accented English, gazing admiringly at the koto.

"Yes, it's very impressive," agreed Jessica.

"Where are you from?"

"From the UK, London."

"Oh, wow, I really wanna go there one day."

Jessica, having had this particular conversation a thousand times before, decided to cut to the chase. "I was wondering if I could ask you a couple of questions?"

The rep's eyes widened briefly. "Yes, of course! I'm all ears."

"I'm doing some research on the koto's history, but I can't seem to find anything on the famous maiko it was made for."

"Ah…" The rep's lips, poised to spout the first relevant fact, withdrew slightly. "Yes, she was quite a tragic figure I believe, but there isn't much known about her, unfortunately. The koto itself is so famous that maybe her story was forgot a little. I could give you lots of information on the koto itself though, if you like?"

"No, it's okay," said Jessica, seeing the rep deflate further, her one chance at imparting some knowledge squandered. "Do you know how I could find out more about her?"

"Maybe at the National Library? They have an extensive history section."

"Okay, thanks." Jessica forged a weary smile.

She moved towards the main door then turned to the rep again. "Do you by any chance know what the maiko's name was?"

The rep's eyes went up to the ceiling. "Oh yes, I do know that one. Her name was Otake… Otake Okimi."

"Great, thank you!"

Jessica waved goodbye and went out into the brisk autumn air knowing she'd at least managed to gather one piece of important information for her assignment.

And then it hit her. How had she not realised immediately?

She repeated the name to herself. It had been there all along, right in front of her… Otake Okimi… OO.

CHAPTER 17

Kenta hadn't heard Yudai's name mentioned once all day. Already they were forgetting. It was just like any news in the end – one seemingly massive story forgot as soon as the next huge story arrived, and in the age of social media there was always some big news somewhere, or at least an endless array of smaller distractions to keep your mind off the real stuff, the stuff that was too difficult to think about for too long.

It made him sick to the stomach. They really didn't seem to care. There hadn't been any mention of the case in form time, no updates from the headmaster or further visits from the police. The headmaster, if anything, was actively trying to draw attention away from Yudai and all the events that had begun to plague the school ever since his disappearance.

There was very little on the local online news sites either, just snippets about the fact Yudai had yet to be found and the case was ongoing. It was as if he was already becoming some statistic rather than a real person missing from his home. Had he been a young child, it would probably still be big news, but a teenage boy – people seemed to presume he'd simply run away from home and would turn up eventually. Wasn't it just something teenagers did sometimes? It didn't help that Yudai had very few, if any, friends at the school. When he was winning competitions and designing cool apps, then he was at least useful. But of late he'd just been that strange and surly genius kid who thought he was better than everyone else and was now gone.

The Jidai Matsuri festival performance was going ahead next Friday, and already the auditorium was busy all day long with rehearsals involving pupils from every year group dressed in ancient Japanese costumes, acting out various famous scenes from the city's past. Even the foreign pupils, who often didn't seem to know or care about the stories, had to take part. The actual festival would take place that weekend when Kyoto's citizens, along with scores of visitors, would line the city's streets to watch the festival parade as it travelled from the Imperial Palace to the Heian Shrine. The festival itself was one of the most important of the year for Kyoto. It was a celebration of Kyoto's history and culture, and Kenta had been to the parade almost every year of his life. He usually enjoyed it too, but now it was the last thing on his mind.

The one thing that gave him some solace, however, was that Yudai's figurative fingerprints really did appear to be all over the hit on the school's system and the auditorium too, which meant he was at least okay and possibly nearby. The auditorium's screen had been covered up already with giant white sheets, but at the end of the day, the school's server was still down, and there were growing rumours about pupils' records and grades being completely wiped.

Kenta didn't want Yudai to get himself into any more trouble, but wherever he was and whatever he was doing, Kenta couldn't help but imagine him sitting somewhere with a very satisfied look on his face, pleased at the magnitude of what he'd done.

***

On his way out of school, Kenta cast one bitter look in the koto's direction as he passed through the foyer. Whatever was going on, it had seemed to start with that thing, and he wished it would conveniently disappear or crawl off back to where it belonged.

That morning after leaving the headmaster's office and narrowly escaping a suspension, he would have sworn to anyone who asked him about it that he would have nothing further to do with Jessica Hunter, and yet now he was carrying her contact on his phone.

But it wasn't just about her. Something had taken root in him since their escapade the night before. It was something he was barely acknowledging to himself, even as he could feel and sense those roots growing and flourishing inside him with each passing moment.

He felt he still had something to prove after he'd embarrassed himself by freezing. But despite the near-crippling fear he'd experienced that night, he'd also felt a thrill while they were chasing Rina, who at the time he was fully convinced was some supernatural apparition – yet he'd still done it. Most importantly, something good had actually come from it. Rina had been released from her trap, though he was still concerned about what else she would have to go through now. They'd also foiled part of the smear campaign against the school, which suggested they could do even more if they put their minds to it.

The feeling, Kenta realised, had been much like the thrill of scoring a goal in an important match, except the stakes had been far higher, and the sense of satisfaction that much greater. He felt he'd done something crazy but truly important, and the risk had been a part of it. More than anything, there was the feeling that he'd just let himself go. For a brief moment, he'd stopped worrying about being on time, or responsible, or sensible, and had allowed himself to run on pure instinct and wild adrenaline, which had felt surprisingly good.

But he was still wary of Jessica and her plans, of what she was capable of doing in order to get what she wanted, though she'd been right about one thing – he didn't want to stop. Not yet. There was more to do. They'd got closer to something, he was sure of that now.

And that was why he was going to do something else he wouldn't normally dream of, and this time he didn't need Jessica to hold his hand.

He was supposed to be in computer club on Thursdays after school but had fobbed it off with an excuse about needing to go to the dentist – another lie; he was getting the hang of it, as long as it was for a good reason. Instead, he found himself getting off the train at Karasuma Oike Station downtown. He came out into the early evening bustle of Karasuma Dori, the main road which cut through the city's heart from north to south. The Imperial Palace was a few blocks north, and Nijo Castle a few blocks west. Tall office buildings loomed overhead. An assortment of cafés, stores, restaurants and business headquarters littered the pavement in all directions. Like the subway, the streets were already busy, with traffic streaming by in ever greater numbers, and the pavement near-swarming with salarymen and -women, shoppers, and pupils returning home from school.

First Kenta went into a nearby Lawsons store and bought a small bag of oranges. Then he walked a block north, taking a left into a narrow residential street. He didn't have to think about where he was going or consult a map. He'd been here several times before, but still there was something close to hesitancy in his steps. He was starting to wonder whether this really was a good idea. Perhaps he was making a big mistake. He slowed slightly and almost stopped, but some deeper instinct carried his feet forward. He wanted to be a person of action. This was what he needed to do; he was at least clear on that.

After another fifty metres, Kenta came to a modest, traditional-looking single-storey house, nestled in between two double-storey modern houses with grey concrete façades. The smaller house had wood panelling along the front, and a sliding screen door. The roof was made up of traditional kawara clay tiles, and a tall magnolia tree was poking above the rooftop from where it stood in a central courtyard further back. Although it was much smaller than the buildings surrounding it, Kenta knew these homes weren't cheap.

Standing at the front door, he steeled himself then quickly pressed the doorbell before he could hesitate any further.

The door slid open a few moments later and a lady stood staring at Kenta. She'd pulled back the door with surprising speed and deftness, and for just a second had looked at Kenta with something close to bright-eyed hope. Her eyes went down to the school badge on his blazer, then back up to his face before narrowing in confusion.

It was then that Kenta realised Yudai's mother must have started at the sight of the school uniform. Perhaps she'd even mistakenly believed it was Yudai, if even for a split second. The realisation only made him feel worse.

"*Ojama shimasu*," said Kenta, apologising for disturbing her, as was custom. "Mrs Matsumoto," he added, bowing his head. "It's me, Kenta... Yudai's friend."

Mrs Matsumoto's clouded expression remained a short while longer as she studied his features, and then her lips broke into a thin smile as his words sank in. "Oh, Kenta! Yes, of course. How are you?"

"I'm very well, thank you. How are you?"

He felt immediately stupid on asking this and watched her smile waver before she readjusted it and resisted whatever inner forces were threatening to topple her composure.

"I'm doing okay, thank you for asking."

An awkward pause opened up, in which Kenta wasn't sure what to say next and Mrs Matsumoto remained slightly puzzled by his presence at her door.

"I just wanted to say sorry for everything that's happened."

Again, he watched as the struggle to maintain a smile quivered in the corners of her mouth.

"Thank you, Kenta. That's very kind," she said, her voice breaking ever so slightly.

She looked very tired, Kenta noted. There were dark black-grey smudges ringing her eyes, and she seemed much older than the last time he'd seen her, which couldn't have been more than seven or eight months ago.

Kenta faltered a second time. Behind him, a car horn blared loudly back along the street on Karasuma Dori. What was he doing there? Why was he bothering this poor woman?

"Would you like to come in for a moment?" said Mrs Matsumoto. "My husband isn't home I'm afraid, but you're welcome to have some tea."

"*Arigato*." Kenta bowed again, feeling relief tinged with a lingering guilt.

Mrs Matsumoto stood aside and gestured for him to come in. Kenta took off his shoes and placed them on a small rack by the doorway before placing his feet into one of the three pairs of slippers left there for guests. As Mrs Matsumoto closed the door behind them, he remembered the bag of oranges and removed them from his backpack before handing them over. This was another custom, and one he was so used to, he did it without thinking.

"You're most kind," said Mrs Matsumoto. "Please, come into the kitchen."

Kenta followed her along the hallway passage into the kitchen, which was just as it was the last time he'd visited. Despite the house's traditional exterior, it was mostly a typical modern home inside, except for one room with paper screens and tatami mats for receiving formal guests. Kenta hadn't been in there but had peered inside once when Yudai was showing him around the house on his first visit.

"Please sit." She pulled back a chair for him at the kitchen table and placed the bag of oranges on the counter. "Would you like some coffee or tea? Maybe a glass of water?"

"Water would be fine, thank you."

As Mrs Matsumoto poured him a water and prepared a small plate of snacks, Kenta studied his surroundings more closely.

The house was very quiet. Aside from the slight background thrumming of the nearby traffic, there was only the faint ticking of a clock that Kenta couldn't see. It was the sound of absence, he thought. Not just because Mr Matsumoto wasn't there and Yudai was missing. It was a felt sense of lack, of a missing piece in the house's puzzle.

In the hallway, just beyond the kitchen doorway, Kenta could see several family photos hanging on the wall. There was one of Yudai in his BSK uniform. It must have been taken when he was in Year 7 or 8, as he looked several years younger. There was a more recent one of him standing with his parents in front of a tree. They were all dressed casually. Yudai wasn't smiling in that one.

Mrs Matsumoto came to the kitchen table and placed a glass of water in front of Kenta, along with a small plate carrying a couple of KitKat bars and a handful of bite-sized rice crackers.

"Thank you." Kenta took a sip of water and munched on a rice cracker.

Mrs Matsumoto took the chair opposite. She had always been a slightly shy woman, and she glanced uncertainly at Kenta as he ate.

"How's school?"

"It's fine. Just the usual," Kenta replied, knowing this was very far from the truth.

"That's good," she said in a low voice.

As he sipped some more water, it was dawning on Kenta just how odd it was to be in the presence of a friend's parent without the friend being there too. Plus, he knew it was impossible to keep up any small talk without mentioning the only topic that mattered.

"Have you heard anything... about Yudai?" he asked.

Mrs Matsumoto's eyes went down to the table. "The police are still receiving tip-offs. They give us an update every day. They think he might have gone north, into the mountains. But they say they'll find him soon. That's the most important thing."

"Yes, that's good."

She nodded to herself. She looked so exhausted, Kenta thought she might keel over at any moment. Why was she alone? She should have been with friends or family.

"Thank you, Kenta," she said after a moment, looking directly at him. "I know you and Yudai might have drifted recently, but you were always a good friend to him."

Now Kenta was the one looking down at the table.

"Yudai was a little quiet of late," she continued. "Always working in his room. He wouldn't really talk about anything. I asked him about you, but he didn't want to discuss it."

"I'm not sure what happened either, to be honest."

Mrs Matsumoto let out a weary sigh. "I know things can be hard at your age, but I always wanted him to be happy. His father encouraged his talents but... there was no end. He didn't leave his room, wouldn't go outside. I tried to speak with him, but it just became more difficult."

Her voice grew louder as she spoke, almost as if she were trying to remonstrate with Yudai all over again. Catching herself, she clasped her hands in front of her on the table and drew a sharp breath. Kenta didn't know what he would do if she started crying. He tried to imagine what his own mother would be like if it were him that was missing. It was a grim thought.

"I'm sorry," said Kenta, not knowing what else to say and feeling rather useless.

"Thank you. You're a good boy, Kenta. My husband and I always said you were a good influence on him. I just wish..."

She didn't say what it was she wished, only stared listlessly at a point on the wall above Kenta's left shoulder. It was as if the last dregs of energy were slowly draining from her.

Swallowing another gulp of water, Kenta prepared himself for what he needed to do next. He went to speak then drank some more. He should just stand up, say thank you and leave. He'd done the right thing by paying a visit – that was enough. But then he knew what Jessica would do. She wouldn't hesitate. She wouldn't let feelings or petty doubts get in the way of finding out what she needed. Just as he had done with their ghost hunt, Kenta attempted to resist this line of thinking, but it was no good.

"Mrs Matsumoto?"

She jumped ever so slightly, her thoughts seemingly elsewhere, no doubt drifting towards her missing son. "Yes?"

Kenta swallowed heavily. "I hope you don't mind, but I just remembered that Yudai still has a book of mine that I lent him a while ago. I was wondering if I could take it back? It's just that I need it for an important assignment. I can return it when... when Yudai's home again."

He waited nervously while she took in his words. At first, he wasn't sure she understood. That cloudiness was washing over her eyes again, but she snapped out of it just as quickly and said, "Of course, I'm sure Yudai would be happy for you to have it again. I can show you to his room."

Kenta stood and followed Mrs Matsumoto back into the hallway. She took a left along an adjoining corridor, and Kenta caught a glimpse of the small yet beautifully tended courtyard garden at the house's centre.

When she came to Yudai's door, Kenta half expected her to knock and call Yudai's name as usual, but she only turned the handle and beckoned Kenta inside.

"Everything is still the same," she said, smiling more brightly now, as though for a moment, things were as they'd always been.

Kenta nodded hesitantly and made himself go in.

His first thought was that it was still as tidy as he remembered. Yudai was a clean and ordered person. There wasn't a heavy sweat smell or scattered books and clothes, which passed as normal for some of his friends. It felt suddenly wrong to be in there, and Kenta wondered if Mrs Matsumoto would stay in the doorway and watch his attempts to find the book, but she only said, "Please take your time," then flashed him a sad little smile walking away, leaving the door slightly ajar.

Turning to scan the room, Kenta questioned himself again, but the voice of action took control, and he began his search.

It was true that he'd lent a book to Yudai. It was a copy of *Dune*, one of Kenta's favourite sci-fi novels. He'd handed it to

Yudai over a year ago, thinking his friend might like it, but Yudai had never got around to reading it, and Kenta hadn't asked for it back before their friendship soured. At least that part was true. He wouldn't have been able to look Yudai's mother in the eye and say what he'd said if there hadn't been some grain of truth to it, though Kenta knew he didn't need the book in reality.

The room itself was quite small and unusually bare for a teenage boy's. Rather than being plastered from top to bottom with posters, the walls were mostly blank except for a patchwork of notes stuck to the wall above Yudai's desk. Kenta looked at them more closely. It was all code-related, probably something to do with the app Yudai had been working on, but it didn't mean anything to Kenta.

He took out his phone and checked the doorway before taking a couple of photos of the notes. Next, he quickly opened each of the desk's four drawers. The top two contained neat piles of school textbooks. One of the lower two was filled with an assortment of stationery – pens, pencils, eraser, various maths equipment. In the other were several small ring-bound notebooks, similar to the ones Kenta used for his writing.

He took two from the top. He checked over his shoulder again and listened for steps in the hallway before flicking through them.

Like the notes plastered to the wall, they contained Yudai's code-related scribblings. There was a bittersweet comfort in seeing his handwriting again, but Kenta reminded himself that time was tight, and turned the pages with increased urgency.

The fact the police hadn't taken them suggested there wasn't anything of importance in there, but he wanted to be sure.

He found no personal notes, nothing that resembled a journal or diary, only plans and calculations. Much of it appeared to be maths problems. Kenta knew Yudai liked working through complicated equations just for the hell of it. The other notebooks were the same.

He heard noises through the crack in the door. It was coming from the kitchen, which emboldened him to keep on looking despite the fact he was growing increasingly uncomfortable.

A quick rifle through Yudai's wardrobe and clothes drawers turned up nothing. The wardrobe was as ordered as the rest of the room, with several pairs of shoes lined neatly along the bottom, and the various sweaters, shirts and trousers hung with an almost freakish neatness. It was the same in the drawers, and Kenta recognised one or two of Yudai's T-shirts, even recalling the last time he'd seen him wearing them.

Kenta was running out of options as he turned to the bookshelf by the desk. There was an assortment of mostly maths and coding-related books, with the odd scientific text and a couple of biographies of people Kenta hadn't heard of, and sitting awkwardly in the middle of them all was Kenta's copy of *Dune*.

He pulled it out and looked over the familiar cover. He recognised particular creases in the corners and was glad Yudai had looked after it. He flicked through the pages, realising he'd missed having it around. At least he wouldn't leave completely empty-handed.

After seeing there was nothing in the wastepaper basket beneath the desk, Kenta eyed the narrow crack in the doorway one last time before turning to the only place left.

He got down on his knees and peered under Yudai's immaculately made bed. There were several larger textbooks in three piles, most likely overflow from the small bookcase.

With a small sigh of resignation, he went to raise himself back to his feet. But there was something else. A small object lurking in the corner beside one of the bedposts.

Pausing awkwardly on his elbows, half poised to stand, Kenta found himself calculating rapidly. Was it worth it? His instinct told him it was, and with the copy of *Dune* still clutched in his left hand, he dived under the bed and dragged himself forward on his elbows until he could make a grab for the little white ball.

When he fumbled his way back out from under the bed, Kenta, still crouched on the floor, opened up his hand to reveal a screwed-up piece of paper. It must have evaded Yudai's and his mother's rigorous cleaning.

Unfurling the scrunched ball, he saw immediately that it was a receipt. Along the heading ran the name of a place that sounded familiar – *Grand Central Café*. Kenta was sure it was a manga kissa, a twenty-four-hour internet café where people could work, read manga, watch anime, even sleep. There were quite a few of them in the city, and Kenta had been to a couple of them several times, mostly to read manga or a regular novel.

But he'd soon realised he preferred regular libraries where it was quieter and there was more space.

This particular café was on the eastern side of the city. Kenta hadn't been there, and he wasn't aware that Yudai went to manga cafés at all. He wasn't a gamer and was one of the only young Japanese people Kenta knew who didn't read manga books or watch any anime.

Kenta checked the date. It was from 29th September, only a few days before Yudai had stepped off the bus and vanished. The time said he'd been there for over four hours on a school evening. *What were you doing, Yudai?* He wasn't sure what this meant, but he knew it could be something.

"Did you find it?"

The voice came from the doorway, and Kenta couldn't help jumping slightly. He instinctively scrunched the receipt back up in his hand before turning awkwardly and getting himself up onto his feet.

"Yes, thank you. Found it," he said, covering his blushes with a forced grin. He raised the book up in front of him, hoping Mrs Matsumoto wouldn't notice anything amiss.

"Oh, I'm glad," she said, smiling benignly, and Kenta was relieved to see she didn't appear in any way suspicious.

He followed her back into the kitchen and stuffed the receipt into a back pocket, consciously slowing down his breaths and ignoring the blood pounding in his ears.

"Will you stay a little longer?" said Mrs Matsumoto, her tired red eyes widening at the sight of him preparing to leave.

Kenta looked at her, then at the half-drunk glass of water and the plate of KitKats and rice crackers on the kitchen table. It pained him to see the look of loneliness and borderline dread in her face, but with his heart still beating its panicked rhythm, and the shape of the mysterious receipt in his pocket, he wanted out of there.

"I'm very sorry, Mrs Matsumoto, but I should really be getting home. I have a lot of homework to do."

She visibly sank on hearing this, though nodded her understanding. "Of course, you're a busy boy. Please take the KitKats for the journey home."

Kenta thanked her and took the KitKats from the plate before dropping them in his rucksack, along with the book. He waited for Mrs Matsumoto to lead him to the front door.

Sliding it open and letting a gentle gust of cool evening air into the hallway, she looked up at Kenta who was several inches taller than her. "Thank you so much for coming, Kenta. It was lovely to see you."

Kenta bowed slightly. His cheeks were burning red, and he was glad to feel the cool air on his skin.

"I'm sure Yudai will be home soon," he said, unsure of what else to say.

"Thank you," she said in her little voice. "Please do come again."

Kenta nodded and waved, then the door stood shut, and he was standing alone in the narrow street. It wasn't even 6pm yet, but already the sky had turned a darker shade, and the air was much colder. Autumn was taking a firm hold.

A sudden movement to his left made Kenta's head jerk in the direction of a small alleyway running off the street, but when his eyes fell on its shadowy opening, there was nothing there.

Feeling utterly relieved, yet still burdened with guilt, Kenta made his way back towards the subway station. He wasn't sure whether what he'd just done was a good or bad thing, or some measure of both, but he had something at least, and surely that was what counted.

Just as he was reaching the main street, he reached into his bag and brought out his phone before opening up his Line app and searching for Jessica Hunter's contact.

Chapter 18

That evening, after learning Otake Okimi's name, Jessica's brain was fizzing with the excitement of her new discovery. She'd wanted to dash straight to the museum but realised to her great annoyance that she wouldn't have got there in time before it closed.

The solution was simple, she thought. She would bunk off school the next day and head straight there, but then recalled Mr Murphy's warning and knew she had to keep off his radar. If she so much as flaunted even the most minor of school rules, it would be enough for the headmaster and his radioactive red cheeks to put her on report or worse, and then she'd be no good to anyone.

Yuko would be at the house all of the following day, and Jessica knew her father would be home tonight, and so she resigned herself to visiting after school the next day when she would be able to leave earlier, and only hoped Miss Nakamura would be there.

Still, as she walked home from school, Jessica found the words *Otake Okimi* teetering on the tip of her tongue and announcing themselves on a loop in her mind.

She'd been so caught up in it, and so eager to get home to start researching, that she'd barely noticed anything around her. It was already close to dark as she approached the turn into her street. She was off the main road now and bathed in a suburban quietness. She was beginning to recognise some of the houses in the area, though many of them were near-identical, with similar neatly tended gardens poking over walls. Even the phone-line cables running overhead had a uniformity about them that fitted with the overall theme of careful, painful precision. It was all still so strange, and Jessica couldn't imagine seeing it as home for a long time yet, maybe never.

It was the scuffing of a shoe which made her turn and notice the figure walking behind her. They were around thirty metres away, dressed in a light-grey hoodie with black jeans. The hood was pulled low over the face, though the angle of the head suggested they were looking straight ahead in Jessica's direction. She couldn't tell if they were male or female, but the person's dress, size and gait suggested it was a young man.

There was no one else in the vicinity. The low-level thrum of busy traffic still hung in the air like a background frequency, but otherwise it was eerily quiet. Seeing her gate at the far end of the street, Jessica didn't think too much of it and only quickened her steps slightly, pulling her school jacket tighter around her as the cold breeze blew with greater intensity.

A light was twinkling in the distant hills ahead, above the multitude of rooftops. Jessica eyed it momentarily, allowing herself to let go of all things school-related – until some barely perceived sound, a hint of an encroaching presence, made her look back again over her shoulder.

The figure was still there, but they were moving much faster now, narrowing the gap down to twenty metres. It could have been a student returning home from a nearby college, or some young person on their way to or from work, rushing to get to their destination. But it was the dark mask of shadow beneath the hood which hid their face, and the hunched, aggressive posture that gave off an immediate sense of threat.

She could have turned to face them or moved out of the way to see if they passed, but simple instinct made Jessica pick up the pace even more. A look ahead and to the sides confirmed they were the only two people on the street.

The gate to her house was not far ahead. She looked back a third time. They were almost on her now, moving with an alarming burst of steps.

Immediately she responded, breaking into a jog, and unbelievably the hooded figure started running too. She didn't need to look. She could hear the ominous rhythm of their feet echoing in tandem with hers against the low walls of the houses they were passing.

Jessica had her house keys out before she reached the gate, her thumb poised over the green button for the electric lock. If necessary, she would spin round and jab her pursuer in the eye before they had a chance to lay a hand on her. Maybe then she would scream too, or shout – she wasn't one for screaming.

All these thoughts flashed through her brain as she came to the front of the house. She pressed the green button, heard the electric buzz of the lock, felt the gate mercifully give way as she pushed it and near-leaped inside, slamming it shut behind her.

The hoodie went by in a blur. She'd half expected them to charge at the gate, hands reaching, scrabbling for her like some crazed maniac, but they were nowhere to be seen.

With her breath catching at the sudden rush of adrenaline, Jessica stepped closer to the gate and peered through the space between the bars, looking as far to the right as she could. There was no one there, the street once again empty, returned to its early evening peacefulness.

She stood there a moment, dazed, puzzled. Had she really just imagined that? There was no mistaking the fact they'd sped up, but had she got it wrong? Was this her over-exercised imagination tricking her like she was some idiotic kid? But the way they'd moved, the hidden eyes she was sure had been fixed on her person alone – could her instincts really have been that off?

Shaking her head, and still rattled and baffled in equal measure, Jessica turned back to the house and opened the front door.

When she was in the hallway with the shiny polished wooden floors and bare walls – everything was still blank – she was surprised to see her father standing in the kitchen doorway.

"Hello, petal," he said with a grin. He was still wearing a suit. Jessica could see how tired he was from the grey smudges ringing his eyes, but as usual it didn't dull his good humour.

Jessica rolled her eyes. She hated it when he called her that and had done since she was twelve. "What are you doing back?"

"Clearly you're pleased to see me. I got away early. I know, it's a miracle."

Jessica removed her shoes and placed them neatly by the skirting board against the wall. She was getting used to this national custom, which Yuko had politely forced on the house, and which her parents also encouraged, but she ignored the set of house sandals waiting for her and walked into the kitchen in her socks.

"You okay?" asked her father. "You look a bit pale."

Fetching a glass from the cupboard, Jessica filled it with water from a filter jug. She wasn't quite okay, at least not yet. For a second, she considered telling her father what had just happened. But she still wasn't too sure herself and didn't want him to think she was being an overly dramatic teenager.

"I'm always pale," she replied dryly. "And anyway, it's getting cold."

"That's true."

Her father was still in the doorway watching her with interest as she drank the water. This was something he did more often these days, studying her as though she were some strange creature he couldn't quite understand.

"How's school?" he asked, which she had known was coming.

"Tolerable." She swigged the last of the water. She could feel her pulse settling to something approaching normality.

"Tolerable, eh? Well, that's not too bad." He nodded towards the oven. "Yuko left us some dinner. I told her she could go home early. I thought you and I could eat together and catch up."

Jessica let out an obvious sigh. She wanted to get straight to her research, but she was aware that resistance was futile. "Do I have a choice?"

Her father smiled. "Not really, but let's maintain the illusion that you do and you're choosing to indulge your old man."

They ate Yuko's version of fast food – chicken cutlets with a curry sauce and rice, which Jessica had already noted was quite popular in Japan. She did her best to humour her father by answering his questions about what she'd been up to and what she thought of the school. As he sat across from her, she saw him stifle several yawns, and his eyelids threatened to lower themselves against his will more than once, but his eagerness to chat won through.

"Met any interesting people?" he asked after they'd finished the meal.

Jessica raised her eyebrows ironically. "You mean, have I made any friends?"

Her father shrugged, pretending not to care one way or the other.

She had to think a moment before saying, "Not really, just the usual."

"Oh well." She could tell from his tone that he was slightly disappointed. "The most important thing is you're happy." When Jessica said nothing, he went on. "You are happy, aren't you?"

Jessica wiped her mouth with a napkin. "I'm ecstatic," she said in as flat a tone as she could muster.

"Just give it a chance, Jess... I really think you'll like it here. It's such a fascinating culture."

"That's what you said about China, and the name's Jessica by the way."

He raised his hands in mock surrender.

"Can I go now? This wonderful school loves to pile on the homework."

"Consider your daughterly obligations fulfilled." Her father winked playfully, and she tried not to smile.

After locking herself up in her room, Jessica raced through her homework so that she could research the name Otake Okimi, but again there was little to no information anywhere online. It was as if there was some conspiracy to erase her name and story altogether, which only made Jessica's need to visit Miss Nakamura at the museum all the more pressing.

She was attempting a second round of searching when she noticed the telltale light blinking on her phone, and saw that

Kenta had sent her a message. She read his update on his findings at Yudai's place, which came with a photo of the receipt he'd picked up.

Jessica nodded to herself. She was impressed. Kenta was continuing to surprise her and was turning out to be a far more useful ally than she could have imagined.

> Jessica: *Good work. Definitely worth following up. I found out what OO is – or at least what I think it is. It's Otake Okimi, the name of the geisha who played the koto originally, back in the 1800s.*

> Kenta: *Woah! WTF? How'd you find that out?*

> Jessica: *From the museum rep at school. Finally, she was actually useful.*

> Kenta: *But why? That OO's been dead I don't know how long.*

> Jessica: *I don't know, but I'm going to find out. There's zero information about her online. It's weird. I'm off to the museum as soon as I can to speak with Miss Nakamura. In the meantime, I'm keeping an eye on the security guard.*

Kenta: *Huh?*

Jessica: *So far he's the top candidate for the insider. If we can prove it, we can get to the person behind OO.*

There was a lengthy pause before the next message, and Jessica knew he was thinking it out, weighing up the risks, Captain Sensible to her Sergeant Reckless.

Kenta: *You sure? That's risky. He's probably already watching us too.*

Jessica: *It's okay, I'll be careful. I can keep an eye on him just as well as he can keep one on me.*

The radio silence that followed echoed Kenta's doubts and reluctance clearly enough. Jessica wasn't going to ask for his help on this one. She didn't want to spook him again. He could continue to follow the Yudai lead and see where it went.

Jessica: *Keep me up to date on the Yudai thing. It's probably best if we don't talk too much in school.*

Kenta: *Okay.*

Kenta: *Be careful.*

She turned off her phone and rubbed the tiredness from her eyes. She was still thinking about the person in the hoodie. She didn't like to admit she was spooked. It didn't fit her own self-image of resilience and detachment. She wasn't a person who was easily bothered by things. But when she got up from her desk and went to the window, Jessica found herself scanning the street outside for lurking figures.

It was empty, and all was stillness beneath the soft, yellow-tinged amber of the streetlights. She could see a hint of the hills and Mount Hiei in the distance, darker forms against a night sky bleached by the city's lights.

"Get a grip," she muttered to herself before returning to her laptop on the desk. She was going to email Miss Nakamura and ask for a quick interview for the purpose of a school project.

Searching the museum's website, all she could find was a "General Enquiries' contact email. There was nothing for Miss Nakamura or any other curators. Still, it was better than nothing.

Opening up her email, Jessica went to compose a new message with an "FAO: Miss Nakamura' in the subject line, but something else caught her eye.

It was the most recent email in her inbox. It was the odd address that she noticed first: oono@anonmail. The subject line simply said, "*Hi Jessica*'.

Normally she would have deleted it right away in the belief it was probably a spam email that had slipped through the net, but the sight of the two O's brought up her hackles in an instant.

Opening up the email, she saw it contained a single sentence typed in block capitals:

STAY OUT OF THE WAY LITTLE ENGLISH BITCH!

Jessica stared at the screen, blinking rapidly for a long while. It was from them, him, her... This was OO.

There was a tightening in her gut as she read it over a couple more times, a primal reaction much like the one she'd felt earlier when she thought she was being chased. But there was an excitement there too. She'd rattled OO's chains enough to get a reaction. They wanted Jessica to be scared, but they didn't know who they were dealing with.

She wasn't sure if she could respond to anonymous emails, but she typed in a reply anyway.

MAKE ME!

And then she pressed ''send'.

CHAPTER 19

As he entered the school's foyer the next morning, the first thing Kenta saw was Rina sitting in the waiting area close to the reception desk. On either side of her sat her mother and father, both looking every bit as worried and forlorn as their daughter.

Kenta briefly caught her eye and flashed her as reassuring a smile as he could, to which Rina attempted one in return, though it came across as more of a pained wince.

At that moment, the headmaster himself emerged from the admin office door to greet them with a ready smile. He happened to catch sight of Kenta moving towards the main building, and his professional grin slipped for an instant.

Avoiding his admonishing glare, Kenta went on to his form room where the talk was of nothing but ghosts and curses and whether their previous marks were gone forever. As the form tutor hadn't arrived yet, a number of pupils were passing around their phones. They were all showing the same thing – a short video of a serene-looking geisha smiling at the camera before the special effects kicked in and her face suddenly lunged at the screen, becoming some sort of grotesque phantom with bulging eyes and fangs, along with a howling scream that made each person watching jump in fright. Even with the shock factor gone, people continued to watch it in little groups, staring at the screen with greedy anticipation.

Kenta sat and watched it all with curious amusement as they worked themselves up into a mini frenzy. One boy claimed he'd seen the ghost himself after school the previous evening, except this time his description had a hint of the demonic about it, in keeping with the video that was doing the rounds. Another girl said she'd heard crying and wailing in the corridors in B-block, and her friend backed her up with a nod of confirmation. The third person began a debate over whether the geisha was getting revenge for the moving of the koto, while another said it was an evil spirit having fun.

This was exactly what OO wanted, thought Kenta. It didn't matter if the ghost was real or not; it was the rumours and the disruption that counted. Even Yudai's continued absence was coming second to the ghost. If anything, they were all enjoying it. It added some excitement to their otherwise typically dull school days.

And Kenta could only guess at his classmates' disappointment when during the special assembly shortly afterwards, Mr Murphy informed them all that the school intranet was back online without any lasting damage, and the person dressing up as a geisha had been caught and dealt with.

A loud collective hum filled the auditorium, and the headmaster had to raise his voice for a return to quiet. Behind him, the space normally occupied by the giant screen was a blank wall that was yet to be filled. Kenta didn't need to search out Jessica. He knew she'd be raising her eyebrows at this too. He was also half expecting Mr Murphy to turn his beady eyes on the two of them, followed by the rest of the school. Instead, he started waffling on about how BSK had been the victim of a nasty prank, but that they could look forward now to the upcoming Jidai Matsuri festival celebrations. And for once, Kenta agreed with what he knew Jessica would say to this... *Fat chance!*

Chapter 20

For the remainder of the day, the talk amongst the pupils had gone from ghosts to the identity of the person who'd reportedly dressed up as one. Jessica heard a couple of names mentioned here and there, but mostly because the pupils in question happened to be absent from school that day, and no one suspected Rina for even a second despite the fact she was also conspicuously missing in action. Perhaps her parents were pulling her out of the school? Jessica hoped not. That would be a crying shame. She hadn't really done anything wrong, whereas the supposed insider was still sloping about somewhere undetected.

Now Jessica's thoughts returned to her number-one insider suspect, namely the young security guard. He might not have looked anything special – he was pale and a little gawky, the kind of person who didn't appear fully at ease in their own body – but there was something about him, a hidden depth that said there was more to him than his appearance suggested. It had been there in his eyes when he'd found himself face to face with Jessica and Kenta beside Rina's geisha. After the initial shock, he hadn't behaved in the dim-witted manner Jessica had expected. In fact, his actions had been swift. He'd viewed the situation with a surprising sharpness, and rather than screaming at them, he'd simply asked the three of them to follow him to the reception where he would take down their names, which they did without protest. It was that cool and calm collectedness that might have given him away. He hadn't been as ruffled by the sight of Rina in her strange costume as Jessica would have imagined – almost as if he'd seen it before.

During each breaktime that day, she made a point of casually wandering the corridors and the field outside, aiming for a glimpse of the young security guard.

She caught sight of him mid-morning as he was doing his shift at the school gate, standing around the security kiosk. He stood apart from his older colleagues, reading on his phone while they huddled in a small group, laughing and chatting.

The school foyer was busier than ever, as was the museum rep who was speaking with a large group of adults, people no doubt drawn to the school and the koto by the recent controversy and rumours of ghosts which had leaked into the outside world. But Jessica didn't imagine Mr Murphy cared why they were there, so long as they were finally making his museum scheme look like a success.

Her next sighting came during the afternoon break.

Passing through the foyer again, doing her usual perusing act of pretending she was reading notices and posters, Jessica saw the guard was on duty near the koto, sitting in the same chair he should have been in that night she'd encountered Yudai and then Kenta. The rep was speaking with yet more visitors in front of the increasingly famous instrument, and there were plenty of staff and pupils buzzing about, and so the guard was doing his best job of appearing alert and watchful.

Glancing his way only occasionally as she loitered by a large bulletin board close to the reception desk, Jessica was reminded again of her first thoughts about the guard – namely that he really didn't look like any kind of criminal mastermind or even sidekick. He looked even more awkward than usual, wearing an expression of permanent boredom.

Jessica was reading the same poster about health and safety for the second time when the bell went to signal the end of break. Any pupil still in the area quickly scooted off to their next lessons while she hung back a while longer, positioning herself behind one of the four giant pillars which rose up from the foyer floor to the ceiling. Once the majority of pupils had left, Jessica peered around the pillar for another look at the guard.

The rep was already moving the group of people away from the koto and its display box, at which point the guard stood up, looked around, then approached the koto under the pretence of exercising his legs.

At first, he only seemed to be idly observing the koto's features, his head moving up and down as he scanned its length, but then he glanced around a second time before removing his phone from his pocket and taking several close-up photos of the koto from various angles.

There was definitely something odd about the furtive way in which he'd done it, but this in itself wasn't necessarily a crime. There was one detail, however, that caught Jessica's attention.

As the guard held his phone up for a photo looking directly down through the top of the display box at the koto, the sleeve on his right arm slipped down a few inches, revealing the unmistakable markings of a tattoo. Jessica couldn't see what it was exactly, but it looked like part of a much larger image that might have snaked up his arm to his shoulder.

"Jessica, what are you doing?"

Jessica spun round to find Miss Hart standing behind her. She must have come out of the admin office.

"Oh... I was just... checking the noticeboard. Sorry, Miss."

As she made her way back towards the main building, Jessica's eyes flitted in the direction of the guard, who was quickly stuffing his phone into a pocket and pulling down his sleeve. He glanced in her direction, and their eyes met.

Jessica wasn't sure if it was confusion, embarrassment or something else, but the guard's stare lingered before he sauntered back to his chair, and then again, he observed her closely as she went through the doors into the corridor, acting as if nothing of significance had happened. Perhaps he was baffled at seeing Jessica, when he would have expected her to be suspended for the after-school stunt, or possibly he sensed that she was on to him.

The tattoo, Jessica decided, was significant. She was no expert on Japanese culture as yet, but she'd watched enough movies and read enough books set in the land of the rising sun to know that tattoos were still considered a major no-no by much of traditional Japanese society. There might have been more and more young Japanese people getting them these days, but there was still a stigma surrounding it. She knew this had something to do with the Yakuza, the Japanese version of the Mafia, who were known for their ceremonial tattoos.

Surely it was odd then, she thought, for a person in a position of responsibility in a reputable school to have any discernible tattoos. It was possible he'd managed to hide it from his colleagues until now and had let down his guard for a moment when Jessica had been watching him.

Jessica had no idea what the man was up to, but she knew they had to find out.

CHAPTER 21

He only saw Jessica once that day during English in the last period.

When he entered the classroom, she was already in her solitary corner seat reading a copy of an Agatha Christie novel he'd never heard of before. They exchanged a glance but nothing more, as Kenta remembered her saying they shouldn't be seen together too much while the heat from the headmaster was still on them. This suited Kenta anyway. It wasn't exactly that he didn't want people to know he had some sort of strange partnership with Jessica, but a part of him was also quite happy to keep it under wraps. It was easier that way.

He took his seat beside Shun in the middle of the room, and they began chatting as Kenta removed his books from his bag. They were discussing that evening's game against a nearby Japanese school, who were one of their biggest rivals. Kenta could feel the first minor fluttering of nerves in his belly as they wondered who was playing.

Milo, who was busy throwing a paper snowball at someone, turned his attention to Kenta. "Hey, Kenta!" he called out, snagging the attention of half the room. "Why don't you go sit next to the new girl? Aren't you guys best buds now?"

It was obvious to everyone he was talking about Jessica, and with an inner groan, Kenta remembered Milo had seen the two of them locked in a heated debate the previous day.

Shaking his head to himself, Kenta only stared ahead at the whiteboard, hoping the teacher would walk in any second or that Milo would do what was good for him and keep his mouth shut. But Milo, who was grinning from ear to ear as usual, with a look of permanent self-satisfaction, had other ideas.

"No need to be shy, guys. We don't mind if you sit together!"

"Quit it, Milo," muttered Kenta casually enough, even as he felt his grip tighten on the pen in his hand.

"Hey, new girl!" Milo was calling across the room now to Jessica, with most of the class now watching the exchange. "I think Kenta will sit next to you if you ask him nicely."

A series of chuckles and guffaws filled the air, and Kenta hoped the heat rising in his cheeks wasn't too obvious. He didn't dare look Jessica's way, but he already knew what she would be doing anyway. She'd still be reading her book with a mildly bored expression, acting as if she hadn't heard and didn't care, which she probably didn't. But then to his and everyone else's surprise, he heard her voice coming from behind him. She was saying something, but it wasn't in English.

When Kenta swivelled round to see, he saw Jessica staring at Milo with a narrow dead-eyed look.

Kenta realised she was speaking Italian so that only Milo would understand, but even as the rest of the class watched on in bemusement, Jessica was delivering her message with such brilliant scorn that it was obvious they weren't having a casual exchange. And then as quickly as she'd begun, Jessica returned to reading her book, her face maintaining its default look of mild boredom as if nothing had happened.

Everyone was looking to Milo now for a response, but he wasn't grinning any more and was evidently too gobsmacked to open his mouth, at which point Miss Hart entered the room and demanded everyone's attention.

"What did she say?" Kenta heard someone whispering to Milo, but Milo was no longer in the mood for chatting.

A few wary and bemused glances were being aimed Jessica's way, and even Kenta raised an eyebrow in her direction, but she wasn't paying him or them any attention. Instead, as she read her book, he noticed the corners of her lips rising ever so slightly.

***

At the end of the match there was a cheer from the BSK crowd watching from the sidelines. They'd won 2–1, with Kenta scoring the first goal. He was named Man of the Match and handed a small token medal, his second of the season so far. He received a back slap or high five from each member of the team for good measure, but mostly he was just happy they'd won and that he'd played well.

In the changing rooms afterwards, with the air filled with cloying clouds of steam and the collective odours of multiple sweaty teenage boys, Kenta was feeling physically and mentally drained after a taxing week of high drama and a startling amount of homework. Still, the after-game buzz remained with him, and he felt mildly satisfied with himself as he put on his socks.

The boisterous chatter around him had gradually levelled off as the boys began to leave the room one by one, wishing Kenta a good weekend as they went.

Milo was the last one out and nodded Kenta's way with a mumbled, "See you," before he left. He'd been quiet since his run-in with Jessica, which people had been speculating on, though Milo still hadn't told anyone what she'd said.

As Milo's footsteps faded along the corridor through the open doorway, Kenta was suddenly alone, with only the sound of dripping water coming from the showers. He wasn't in too much of a hurry himself though, and often enjoyed these brief moments of solitude after a game.

Still, as his mind settled into the quietness, and he began to put on his shoes, his thoughts turned to Yudai and the receipt and the fact he would need to visit the manga café the next day, if only to see for himself if there was anything in it. He'd meant to catch Jessica before she left school just to get an update, but she'd left the English class in a hurry, and he hadn't seen her by the lockers.

Since it was after school hours and there was no one about, he took his phone out of his bag and switched it on. He put on the second shoe while he waited for it to load and stood to put on his school blazer. Then an SMS message appeared on the screen. He didn't recognise the number, and the message was a simple "*Hey Kenta*'.

He thumbed in a reply: *Who's this?*

He picked up his bag from the bench and swung it over a shoulder. The sound of light footsteps in the corridor made him turn around to face the doorway, but he couldn't see anyone there.

"Hello?"

When no one answered, he went to the doorway and peered out. The cool air hit him immediately like a breeze over his clammy skin. He hadn't realised how warm it was in the changing room.

Finding the corridor empty, Kenta guessed a security guard must have passed nearby. Since he was the last one out, he went to switch off the lights then realised he'd left his boots under the bench.

He went back in and dropped them into a plastic bag. The phone shivered in his hand. He looked at the screen and read the words emblazoned across it.

I have a message from OO: KEEP AWAY OR YOU AND YOUR LITTLE GAIJIN WILL BLEED!!!

The word *bleed* was the most troubling of all. It seemed to leap out and scream at him. Who the hell was this anyway? Maybe it was Milo, getting him back for what had happened in the English class, but Kenta was sure not even Milo would go this far.

A final message popped up on the screen.

p.s. Enjoy your gift!

With the first stirrings of alarm pricking at his skin, Kenta went to reply. His thumb hovered over the screen. He raised his head. He could hear something. It was coming from outside again. This time it wasn't footsteps, it was faint music.

He listened more closely and began to realise with a sinking feeling that he recognised the melody. It was the koto, and the very same recording he and Jessica had heard that night coming from Rina's phone as she'd fled from them in her ghost costume.

He wasn't hallucinating, so someone had to be messing with him. But who, and why? He didn't like it. Something felt wrong.

"Milo, that you?" he called out, but there was no reply or movement, only the music, which was increasing in volume and didn't sound far away now.

Not wanting to be there a second longer, Kenta headed again to the doorway. He switched off the light, closing the changing room door behind him.

Even with this sickening dread roiling in his guts, Kenta was angry enough that he was being toyed with like this and was ready to go after the source of the music – but no sooner had the door clicked shut than the music suddenly stopped.

He thought it had been coming from around the corner where the Year 12 lockers were, but there was no one there, not even a cleaner or teacher wandering about.

Kenta looked at his phone again, focusing in on the mention of a gift – what did it mean? Just the idea of it sent an unpleasant shiver up his spine.

Looking about him one more time and finding the nearby corridor empty, he went to his locker and crouched down to key his PIN into the number lock, wanting to be out of the school and into the free, fresh air as quickly as possible.

The locker door, which was sticking slightly these days, came open with a gentle tug.

It was the smell that told him something was wrong before his eyes could see what it was.

His hand had already reached for the pile of books inside out of habit, but his fingers found something wet and strange. He pulled back his hand. His fingertips shone crimson in the fluorescent corridor lights – and what was that iron-like smell?

To get a better look into the shadowy space, Kenta pulled the locker door back further. It was then that he saw the large OO painted on the inside of it in what looked suspiciously like blood.

Kenta felt the skin crawl on his scalp. He was disturbed enough to turn and flee, but he had to look into the locker, into the space at the very back.

And then he knew what his gift was.

CHAPTER 22

The Kyoto National Museum looked resplendent against the soft colours of the late afternoon sky. Jessica was taken aback by the grandiosity of it. She wasn't sure what she'd been expecting. To the left stood a brand-new ultramodern wing, but the original façade, with its long and elaborate approach leading from the ornate gates via a large circular fountain, was more than a little impressive.

There was a cold nip in the air as Jessica raced up the front steps. She'd left school the second the final bell had sounded, and had paid for a taxi to get to the museum as quickly as possible.

The time was just short of 5pm, which gave her roughly an hour before closing time. In the taxi on the way, she'd checked her emails on her phone, but hadn't received anything from the museum in response to her enquiry regarding an interview with

Miss Nakamura, nor had she had anything further from the anonymous sender. Nonetheless, she told herself she was going to keep on pestering the museum until she got what she needed.

She went in through the main doors into an appropriately grand space complete with pillars and tall vaulted ceilings, along with an air of age and importance like many of the old museums she'd visited. There were several free-standing banners dotted about the floor advertising various exhibitions – "*Masterpieces from Hatakeyama Memorial Museum*' and "*Coming soon: National Treasures of Kyoto, Japan's Ancient Capital*'. There were still a few people milling about, but the majority of visitors Jessica could see were heading for the exit.

There was a main reception desk to the right which Jessica made a beeline for. Behind the desk stood a pencil-thin young man and a stout middle-aged woman, both wearing the same white shirt and black jacket, complete with name badges pinned to their lapels. Together, they were a picture of competency.

Jessica opted for the woman. She approached the desk with her widest smile. The lady broke into a smile of her own and bowed in return. "*Yokoso*. Welcome to the Kyoto National Museum. How may I help you?"

The woman spoke with the practised ease of a person who'd said those very words countless times before, though her English accent suggested she wasn't too used to speaking the language at length.

"Hello," Jessica began. "My name is Jessica Hunter. I have an appointment with Miss Nakamura."

The woman's eyebrows went up half a centimetre. "Miss Nakamura?"

"Yes, I have an interview with her. It's for an important school project. I'm from BSK, the British School Kyoto." Jessica moved her coat to the side so that the school badge was clearly visible on the breast pocket of her blazer.

"Oh, I see." The woman grinned, betraying a hint of doubt as she glanced in the young man's direction. "What time is your appointment?"

"Five pm."

"I see, just a moment."

The woman picked up a walkie-talkie from the counter in front of her and spoke into it in Japanese. Jessica kept up her smile while she waited, aiming it the young man's way when she saw him watching. He dutifully bowed his head in return.

When she was finished communicating with the person on the other end of the line, the woman replaced the walkie-talkie and beamed her pearly white teeth once again. "I'm afraid Miss Nakamura is not available. She's busy helping with the new exhibit."

"Oh..." Without any need to think on her next move, Jessica's face automatically crumpled. "But... but she said she would meet me... I have a deadline."

Clearly uncomfortable with this new development, the woman looked to her colleague imploringly. "I am very sorry, miss."

"But... She promised me!" Jessica said, voice quivering. "I have to see her about the famous koto. If I fail this course, my parents will kill me."

With not a small amount of effort, Jessica made her lower lip tremble and widened her eyes in preparation for the tears.

"I'm so very sorry, miss," said the young man, also offering a final bow of consolation.

"What's the new exhibit?" said Jessica rather innocently, as though she'd already forgot what she was upset about.

"A new samurai exhibit," said the woman.

"Can I still walk around?"

"*Hai...* yes, of course. The museum closes in one hour. Please." The woman gestured into the museum, looking relieved to have avoided further difficulties.

"Thanks!" Jessica beamed a last smile and turned on her heels, leaving the two bemused and now slightly suspicious museum staff watching after her.

Crossing the large floor of the entrance area, Jessica approached the first assistant she came across at the entrance to a long room containing many statues – in this case an assortment of ancient-looking buddhas and other mystical figures.

"*Sumimasen*," said Jessica with a bow. She was getting used to this.

The assistant, a young woman with thick-rimmed glasses and a bob cut, who looked barely older than Jessica herself, greeted her with a shy bow.

"Sorry, where is the samurai exhibit?"

"Oh, samurai?" The girl looked surprised. "Sorry, English not good." She giggled nervously.

"It's okay. *Watashi no Nihongo mo heta desu*," added Jessica, telling the girl her Japanese was also bad. This was one of the first Japanese phrases she'd memorised, and it was proving extremely useful so far.

The assistant smiled and pointed through a window in the direction of the new museum wing. "Samurai over there. But not finish."

"Oh, okay. No problem." Jessica bowed. "*Arigato gozaimasu.*"

"*Doitashimashite.* You're welcome," said the assistant, waving Jessica off as she went on her way.

She passed through long galleries and corridors with parquet floors and tall, ornate ceilings. She went by collections of paintings and ceramics and mannequins draped in old clothing, making a note to come back soon and actually visit properly.

It didn't take long to find what she was looking for. In fact, she heard it before she saw it. It was coming from the other side of a darkly atmospheric gallery room where a large number of tall glass cases stood, dotted symmetrically around the centre, each one displaying a piece of jewellery of some sort.

Jessica could see the noise was coming from behind a set of double doors at the far end of the room, above which a sign read "*Gallery Closed*" in English, Japanese and Mandarin. Beside the doors was another free-standing banner with a "*Coming Soon*' advertisement for the samurai exhibit which wasn't due to open for another week.

Like in the other rooms, there was an assistant standing close to the doorway into the first space. This older man was looking at his phone and had barely acknowledged Jessica's entrance. The only other people present were two women in the opposite corner. They had their backs to her and were admiring one particular piece inside its glass case.

Seeing the opportunity, Jessica quickstepped it to the double doors into the closed gallery, and before the assistant could see what she was doing, she pulled at the handle and stepped quickly inside, finding herself in an entirely different space.

Unlike most of the other rooms, this one was a hive of activity. It was much wider and taller than the one she'd just been in, and there were far more lights blazing overhead, which gleamed dully in the polished black surfaces of the floor and walls.

Jessica counted at least ten people dressed in the same black T-shirt and black jeans, all milling about around several giant wooden crates. A couple of them were open, and the staff were carefully fishing objects out of the beds of straw which lay inside. The one object Jessica could see being lifted out by a man and woman in unison was instantly recognisable as a metal samurai helmet. Further back, a rudimentary mannequin had already been half covered in armour, with the helmet and slightly frightening mask covering the head.

For a moment, Jessica was taken aback enough that she forgot why she was there and instead gawked at everything that was going on.

A man carrying a small cardboard box was the first person to notice her. His eyes widened at the sight of the young foreign girl in school uniform standing in front of the doorway.

"Very sorry, this gallery closed."

"I'm here to see Miss Nakamura," said Jessica rather brazenly, making it clear she was meant to be there.

"Nakamura?" said the young man.

Jessica nodded. She saw him hesitate just as the staff at the reception had, but then he nodded and wandered further into the room.

She watched as he disappeared behind one of the giant boxes, and a few seconds later, a woman's head popped around the sides. Jessica recognised her at once. It was Miss Nakamura.

She peered in Jessica's direction with narrowed eyes and a baffled frown. Unsure if she was struggling to see her, or if she was simply confused, Jessica put on a wider smile.

After a few more seconds of deliberation, Miss Nakamura began to approach. She was followed by another woman whom Jessica recognised as Miss Yoshida, the young assistant who'd translated for Miss Nakamura during the special school assembly.

The two women cut a path between the assortment of boxes and crew members. Miss Nakamura was holding a clipboard in one hand and had the natural air of someone who was in charge. She was dressed the same way she'd been at the assembly, in a black suit jacket and pencil skirt with a white blouse and formal patent leather shoes. Like her boss and the staff, Miss Yoshida was also dressed mostly in black, with white polka-dot patterning across her shirt. She moved with the same dainty, birdlike manner Jessica remembered, whereas the shorter and sturdier Miss Nakamura moved boldly and with purpose.

As they came up to her, Jessica bowed and greeted them as politely and gracefully as she could, hoping the right words would come to her.

Miss Yoshida was the first to speak. "How may we help you?"

"I'm Jessica Hunter. I'm from BSK." She flashed her school badge once again. "I need to speak with Miss Nakamura about the koto at our school. It's for an important project."

Jessica waited while Miss Yoshida translated her words. Miss Nakamura nodded as she listened and then exclaimed, "Oh!" and grinned at Jessica before replying in Japanese.

A moment later, Miss Yoshida translated back to Jessica. "Miss Nakamura is very pleased that you have taken an interest in the koto. She would be very happy to assist you, but unfortunately she is currently engaged. Perhaps you could try writing an email?"

Miss Nakamura offered a supplicatory smile and was already backing away when Jessica said, "Please, I really need to speak with her, just for a few minutes."

"So very sorry. It isn't possible at this moment," said Miss Yoshida, all formality and apologetic smiles as she too began a slow retreat.

Jessica floundered momentarily. She'd tried and she'd failed. Maybe she should try emailing again and hope for the best. But she had to know, and she had to know now. "Please!" she called out. "I need to talk about Otake Okimi."

Miss Nakamura, who'd already turned away and was walking back to the other side of the room, stopped mid-stride on hearing the last two words and spun round to fix Jessica with a look of surprise.

"Gotcha!" muttered Jessica under her breath.

Chapter 23

Jessica was perched on a flimsy plastic chair at the furthest end of the gallery, with Miss Nakamura and Miss Yoshida sitting across from her on a viewing bench. Miss Nakamura had said she could spare ten minutes, at which point Jessica had thanked her profusely.

She took out a notebook and pen from her bag and switched on her phone voice recorder while the two women watched her closely. Jessica tried to arrange her thoughts. She almost hadn't expected to get this far and found herself wishing she'd done more preparation.

"I know that you gave a little bit of a backstory to the koto when you were at the school, but my project is about the famous musician who played it. I can't find anything about her online, and it's very important that I get something soon."

With one ear cocked slightly, Miss Nakamura took in Miss Yoshida's Japanese version with a look of grave seriousness. When the words were delivered, she thought for a moment and took a deep breath, as though preparing herself for some arduous task, then said, "Yes, it is true that Otake Okimi's name has been wiped from the history books. Unfortunately, this is not an accident. I don't normally speak about her, and there are few people who know her story well, but you have taken it to heart and taken the time to find me, so I will give you a little more."

She looked at Jessica more closely, as if to measure the young girl's seriousness, and Jessica met Miss Nakamura's gaze with a steady one of her own, signalling she was ready.

"Otake was born here in Kyoto in 1853 during the Edo period when Kyoto was still the capital. She came from a humble background, but in addition to her natural beauty, she was a very talented musician from a young age, particularly in playing the koto.

"She was encouraged to train to be a geisha, or perhaps chose it so that she could employ her musical talents. The training then was very rigorous, and still is. It takes many years of classical training and a period of apprenticeship as a maiko before becoming a fully fledged geisha.

"Otake was only twenty when she came to the attention of Minamoto Sojuke. He was what you would call a nobleman. He came from an old and powerful samurai family, and was an important and much respected man in Kyoto during this time.

Like most established men in those days, he would frequently visit ochaya, or teahouses, where geishas would entertain the guests. All geishas were very skilled in the arts, as well as in being consummate hostesses. Some were well known for their singing ability, others for the shamisen, another important traditional Japanese instrument, and others for their physical beauty. But Otake very quickly became famous for her exceptional koto-playing abilities.

"She soon completed her training and became a geisha, but she was not yet experienced enough to entertain the more important guests. One day, however, Minamoto Sojuke overheard Otake playing in another room and demanded that she play for him instead. It is said that he became enraptured by her playing. He was a lover of music and often heard the koto being played by skilled musicians, but he'd never heard anything like Otake's playing.

"From that day on, he asked that she play for him every time he visited the ochaya. Eventually he also requested that she play at other functions, at prominent people's homes and at official events. He paid her well for this, and despite rumours at the time, he was in love with Otake's playing, not with her. It is a common misconception in the West that maiko and geishas were more like courtesans, common prostitutes, but this is not the case.

"However, it was said that Minamoto became obsessed with hearing her play and would accept no other musicians, no matter how skilled. To show his appreciation for her talents, he commissioned the finest maker of kotos in Japan to craft the best and most beautiful koto anyone had ever seen. Minamoto paid a very large sum of money for this privilege, and the master craftsman certainly delivered on his promise. Now Otake's fame as a player became even greater with this prized koto, which was hers alone to play. She too was believed to be greatly attached to the instrument, and would practise playing with it long into the night after each working day.

"This arrangement, however, did not last very long. It isn't known for sure who instigated it. Some say it was Minamoto's wife, who had grown jealous of her husband's fascination with Otake's playing. Others claim it was an older geisha who had once been favoured by Minamoto and resented Otake's popularity. Whoever it was, she was accused of stealing money from another geisha's purse. She was almost certainly framed, but the other geisha was older and exerted more influence. This was considered a grave offence, and Otake was stripped of her geisha status and thrown out of the teahouse.

"The rumours also increased, and she was falsely accused of sleeping with some of the ochaya's patrons. Not even Minamoto would support her, and Otake's own family wanted nothing to do with her. She was effectively left out on the street, almost penniless and without any prospects for the future, but worst of all for her, more than losing her position and her name, was the loss of the koto.

"When she was thrown out of the ochaya, the koto was taken from her and returned to Minamoto. It was this loss that Otake couldn't bear. It drove her to madness. People say she roved the streets, dirty and crying out for her beloved instrument. With no protection, she soon became prey to scoundrels who forced her into the very act she'd been falsely accused of. She eventually became sick and was barely able to walk or feed herself, and this was all before she had reached the end of her twenty-first year. But the part of her story that is perhaps the most contentious and yet the most infamous concerns the curse."

At this point, Miss Nakamura stopped. Both Jessica and Miss Yoshida were watching her as she blew a weary sigh, shaking her head. Jessica could have sworn she looked visibly more tired, as though the telling of the story itself had sapped the energy from her.

"This is the part I don't always like talking about," said Miss Nakamura.

Don't stop now, thought Jessica, almost uttering the words out loud, her pen poised over the notebook. But she was relieved when Miss Nakamura's voice sounded once more.

"The story, or perhaps the myth, concerns Otake's hiring of a Shinto priest to curse the koto. She is said to have given her very last money and possessions to the priest so that he would perform a ritual ensuring misfortune would befall all future owners of the koto. It is likely she was not in her right mind when she did this, but whatever the circumstances, her young life was lost little more than a week later. Her body was found in a side street. She had died from a combination of malnutrition and exposure. It's a very sad story indeed."

She broke off again, her eyes looking off over Jessica's right shoulder. At the other side of the room, a clattering of metal parts erupted, snagging everyone's attention. One of the staff had accidentally dropped what looked like a pair of pleated shoulder-armour plates, and was busy collecting them up guiltily while Miss Nakamura looked on with an expression of scorn. She drew a sharp intake of breath and called out something Jessica presumed meant, "Be careful', or "You idiot!"

Fearing she would lose Miss Nakamura's attention altogether, Jessica fired off another question. "What about the curse? Haven't some strange things happened to people who owned or played the koto in the past?"

Still reeling from the clumsy crew member, Miss Nakamura was brought back to the conversation by Miss Yoshida's quiet translation. Perhaps it was her annoyance at what had just happened, or she didn't like the question, but she soon began shaking her head quite vigorously.

"Oh, this is the problem. People always want to focus on this part of it and forget about the magnificence of the koto itself."

"It's just so that I can have a full picture... for my assignment," said Jessica, cutting in with a broad smile.

It seemed to work, as a still slightly flustered Miss Nakamura relented and spoke again.

"While I don't believe any of it for a second, it is true that some strange things have happened to some of the koto's owners. Minamoto himself was thrown from his horse and broke his neck not more than six months after Otake's death. This was probably when the rumours began. The Minamoto family kept it for another generation until one of his sons also died, a drowning accident apparently. Then it was purchased by a wealthy merchant from Kobe."

Distracted again by something that was going on at the far end, Miss Nakamura pointed, issuing some instruction to a staff member who bowed and nodded.

Miss Yoshida looked apologetically in Jessica's direction while they waited.

"Where was I?" said Miss Nakamura.

"The merchant from Kobe... did he also have any bad luck?"

Miss Nakamura thought about it. "I'm not sure... actually, come to think of it, yes. He did lose his family home in a house fire. Fortunately, he'd already donated the koto to the museum by this point, but of course this is all coincidence. Tragedies occur at some point in most families, that's just the way it is."

Jessica nodded her understanding as she scribbled down a note, resisting a need to point out that tragedy hadn't just struck one or two of the koto's owners, but all of them.

"And at the museum?" said Jessica. "Has anything strange happened here around the koto?"

On hearing the translation, Miss Nakamura scoffed, waving a hand dismissively in front of her. "There are always rumours, staff members making things up about geisha phantoms and hearing the koto playing at night. It's all just silliness, stories to entertain visitors."

Jessica looked to Miss Yoshida for confirmation of this, but the younger woman looked away as though avoiding the question herself.

Miss Nakamura glanced at her watch and then at the growing bustle surrounding the wooden crates. "I'm sorry, I really must go now."

"Just one more thing!" Jessica said quickly. She reached for her phone on the bench beside her, and with it still recording, flicked through her photos until she found the one she was looking for. She held it out in front of the two women, who both peered closely at the screen. It was a photo of the auditorium immediately after the vandalism attack, with the two giant O's plain to see.

Miss Nakamura seemed to be struggling to understand what she was seeing, but she appeared troubled by it, nonetheless.

"This happened at our school a few days ago," said Jessica. "A pupil is missing, and another was blackmailed into dressing up as a geisha ghost at night. This all started when the koto arrived, and I believe someone is using Otake Okimi's name and memory to discredit the school. But what I want to know is why and how. How long ago was the partnership between the school and the museum announced?"

It took a moment for Miss Nakamura to take this in, the creases along her brow deepening further. "At least three, maybe four months ago." She looked to Miss Yoshida for confirmation and received a nod.

"So, anyone could have learned about it in advance?"

"Yes. We started advertising in the museum and online. It wasn't just the school. There are several institutions involved."

"Then what about the why? Why do you think they're doing it?"

Miss Nakamura thought a moment then shook her head. "I heard there were some problems at the school with a missing pupil, that's very sad. I never wanted the koto to leave the museum in the first place, but the museum's director said it would be good for us and insisted. As for why this is happening..." Miss Nakamura pondered this a moment then simply shrugged. "Who knows? The tourism industry is a very competitive one, you know? There are other museums, other organisations wanting their piece of the pie. I wouldn't put it past them to try and make the museum look bad. This initiative for the school was all about publicity, naturally."

Jessica raised an eyebrow.

"And from what I hear, the koto exhibit has been very popular at the school. If anything, these crazy idiots are only helping the cause. I should have thought of this myself!" She let out a strange little snort of a giggle the didn't fit her austere appearance. "But it won't be for long. Either way, the koto will be coming back after the school festival performance on Friday."

"On Friday?" said Jessica, sensing a light coming on somewhere in her brain.

"Yes, didn't you know? There will be one final performance with the koto at the school. Miss Yoshida and I will be there. It should be delightful. Hopefully we will see you there?"

This time Miss Nakamura consulted her watch with an air of finality and stood up from the viewing bench. Miss Yoshida followed suit, as did Jessica who still had more questions.

"I hope that was helpful," said Miss Nakamura. "Good luck with your assignment."

Jessica bowed and thanked her formally. Miss Nakamura turned her head back to the museum staff and her demeanour tensed up again as she switched back into boss mode and began barking orders.

"Let me show you out," said Miss Yoshida as Jessica packed away her phone and notebook.

The two of them walked together around the side of the giant crates where several more mannequins had been lined up, and the one already half dressed had been adorned with several more pieces of armour. From the tannoy overhead came a short burst of music followed by an announcement in Japanese and English that the museum would soon be closing.

Miss Yoshida pushed through the doors into the other gallery. She waited until they closed behind them before her nervous, darting little eyes met Jessica's.

"I didn't want to say this in front of Miss Nakamura, but it isn't made up, at least not the bit about the museum. There have been accidents. People working on the koto getting hurt." She looked past Jessica to make sure no one was nearby and lowered her voice further. "The staff here don't like the koto. It's bad luck. But we can never say it in front of Miss Nakamura. She gets angry. She is very passionate about the koto and its history."

The announcement blared from the tannoy a second time. "You'd better get going," she said to Jessica. "And please be careful. Like I said, there is something about this koto."

And with that, Miss Nakamura's voice sounded on the other side of the door, and the young assistant hurried away, leaving Jessica alone in the dark gallery.

CHAPTER 24

They watched as the girl came down the museum steps. So sure of herself she was, probably believing she was getting closer. They had to admit she'd got further than anyone else. Not even the police had looked much deeper into who OO was or what it meant. But soon they would find out. All of them.

They saw the school badge on the girl's jacket as she walked swiftly along the paved approach, towards the main gates. A flash of revulsion shivered through them at the sight of it, but it was quickly replaced by a sickening glee at what was coming.

But first they needed to take care of her and the boy. It had to be done.

They waited until the girl was beyond the fountain before emerging from behind the tree. And then they began to walk.

CHAPTER 25

Kenta's first reaction on seeing the dead rat was to gag. He felt a sickly acid sweetness attempting to rise up his throat and swallowed it down.

He jumped to his feet and moved back, then seeing the blood still on his fingers, wiped it on the back of his trousers, grimacing the whole time.

It couldn't have been there long. The last time he'd been inside the locker was before fifth period, meaning a little over two hours ago.

He dared to peer closer again. The rat was lying on top of his maths textbook. Its rope-like tail hung limply over the side, its yellow teeth bared in a sort of frozen sneer. On even closer inspection, it was clear its gut had been sliced open, and its pink and grey innards glistened slightly where they bulged from the incision.

Looking again at the locker door, Kenta could see the two circles had been smeared on the inside, possibly with a finger. The thought of it brought further convulsions to his stomach. What was he supposed to do now? He couldn't just lock the door and walk away. Some pupil's instinct, or was it habit, was willing him to tell the first figure of authority he could find and wash himself of the responsibility – but even if he did find a teacher, they were bound to get security involved, and Kenta wasn't sure if he could trust any of them. If Jessica's theory about the insider was right, then who was to say how many of the guards had been turned or influenced in some way? That was exactly what OO wanted, to freak him out and cause more of a stir at the school in the process.

The grimace etched across his features relaxed into something more determined. He was pissed off more than he was scared. He was under attack, same as the school was. And just like the football team when they were under pressure, he wasn't going to run. He had to hold the line and resist.

His first action was to take a photo of the inside of the locker with his phone before forcing himself to start cleaning it up. He removed his football boots from the plastic bag they were in and lay them on top of the locker. He checked for movement along the corridor and listened for anything in the adjoining one, then put his hand inside the plastic bag and took a couple of deeper breaths to steady his nerves before reaching into the locker.

He flinched slightly when his hand found the rat's body. He couldn't look at it, but he forced himself to take a hold of the fat little corpse and quickly reversed the plastic bag, clasping the top of it shut, stifling a retch in the process. He tied it off and dropped it on the floor beside him.

"Hey, Kenta!"

He almost cried out in shock and jumped violently enough that he bashed his elbow against the frame of the locker door. He looked up to see Mr Griffiths, the head of PE and the football coach, coming his way.

"It's Friday, Kenta. Get yourself home!"

Kenta recovered in time to close the door slightly without it being too obvious, and forced a nod. "Yes, sir."

"Have a good weekend," called Mr Griffiths over his shoulder as he kept on going past the lockers, half glancing at the plastic bag beside Kenta's feet before returning his gaze to the corridor ahead.

"You too!" Kenta called after him.

He waited until the teacher was out of sight, and with his heart still beating its semi-panicked rhythm, snatched up the bag and made a dash for the nearest boys' toilets just around the corner, feeling the rat's unpleasant weight as he went.

Once he'd disposed of it, he set to cleaning away the blood with a ball of tissue paper, and in a couple of minutes, all visible traces of the carnage had been erased.

He stood up, regarding the locker door with both relief and satisfaction, but the anger was still there, fizzing away inside him. He knew exactly where it was he needed to go as he marched with purpose towards the school gates.

***

The Grand Central Café was on the second floor of a nondescript building above a beauty salon. Most of the manga kissa Kenta knew of were in the downtown area, just across the river from Gion, whereas this one was all by itself in Northern Higashiyama, only a couple of streets from the Heian Shrine, an area usually swarming with tourists during peak season. Kenta had been there a few times as a kid with his parents, but not for a long while.

There was only one Grand Central Café in the city, so he knew it had to be the same one from the receipt he'd found in Yudai's bedroom. The idea of it made sense. If Yudai was still in Kyoto and needed computer access, he wouldn't want to go to one of the chain cafés in the busy areas where he could be easily spotted.

Before crossing the street, Kenta checked his phone. On the bus, he'd sent Jessica a photo of his locker, along with a snapshot of the text threat he'd received, but she still hadn't replied. He'd also tried to reply to the text itself, but they must have blocked his number, and he could find no trace of it online.

He put his phone away as a gust of cool autumnal wind swept along the pavement. It was already past 5.30pm and the sunset was almost complete.

He went in and climbed the stairwell which smelled faintly of bleach, reminding him of a hospital, but when he got to the

216

door of Grand Central Café, it was like a portal into an alternate universe.

It was much bigger than he'd expected. The café took up an entire floor of the building, with virtually every single piece of wall covered in shelving brimming with manga books and comics. On the other side of the huge space was a row of at least a dozen tall open bookcases running from one end to the other, all of them filled with every manga book and DVD a fan could want. Closer to the doorway was a large section of open computer terminals, half of which were occupied. Further away, Kenta could see an area of larger private booths, which looked more like wider toilet cubicles, and beside that was a small café counter with seating.

"*Irasshaimase!*"

Kenta turned to the reception counter to his left where the voice had come from. It had been spoken rather half-heartedly by a man with shaggy hair dyed an almost fluorescent green. He was about thirty, with a paunch pushing through his T-shirt. His eyes had a lazy, hooded appearance that fitted his general air of indifference.

Taking out his phone again, Kenta quickly selected a photo, and after greeting the man, held up the screen. "I'm looking for my friend. Have you seen him?"

Kenta showed him a photo of Yudai from the most recent school yearbook. He wasn't smiling in this one, which wasn't unusual. But at least he looked like the old Yudai that Kenta remembered well.

The man peered at it then shook his head. Kenta wanted to ask him if he was sure, but already knew what the answer would be and instead put his phone away.

"I'd like to use a computer," he said.

"Are you a member?" said the man with a lazy, unimpressed drawl.

"No."

"You have ID?"

"Travel pass?"

"Sure." The man pushed a form across the counter. "Fill this in."

Kenta filled in the form and showed his travel pass.

"Open seat or private booth?"

"Open seat," Kenta replied.

"That's two hundred yen for thirty minutes, then a hundred yen per fifteen minutes afterwards."

Kenta paid and went over to the open seat area where each computer sat between small wooden partitions, much like the computer study areas at school and in public libraries. He'd chosen a spot where he'd be able to scan the room easily, but even as he took his seat and began logging in, Kenta wondered if he was wasting his time. The chances of Yudai actually being here were slim. If he really was hanging about in the city, surely police would have picked him up by now. He might have been a computer genius, but he was no criminal mastermind. He wouldn't have been able to get into this café without ID, and his face was plastered all over the local news.

It occurred to Kenta that he'd allowed himself to get carried away. He was playing detective like Jessica, but that was her thing, not his. He just wanted to write and play football and hang out with friends like a normal person. Instead, he was skulking about in a café on a Friday evening playing the spy. Still, he'd paid for half an hour, and it was a decent café. He might as well see it through.

He checked his email and the local news for anything on Yudai's case, but wasn't surprised when there was nothing as usual. More and more people were coming through the entrance. Quite a few were students, mostly from local Japanese schools Kenta didn't recognise. From where he was sitting, he had a good view of all of them, but he couldn't see many of the other computer users close by, who were hidden behind their partitions. There was only a handful of people browsing the multitude of bookshelves, and he could only see one man in the café area.

Kenta's gaze fell on the block of private booths at the other end of the space. He'd never used one himself but had seen inside them a few times. They were much more spacious than the open seat booths, with a large reclining leather chair. Some had tables for food and drinks, clothes hangers and bedding too. He was aware that many people slept overnight in manga cafés, particularly young salarymen and -women who might have worked late and missed the last train home. It was a budget option for tourists as well, and Kenta had even heard of people living in cafés long-term. There were showers in the toilets, so it was quite possible to stay for more than one night if a person wanted to.

He checked his phone again, but there was nothing from Jessica as yet, which was starting to annoy him. He was used to friends replying quickly to any message, but then she wasn't exactly a friend, nor was she like normal teenagers, at least not any Kenta knew. He hadn't received any further anonymous texts either. He resisted an urge to read the message again and stood up on the premise of needing to stretch his legs and take a look around.

Leaving his schoolbag on the chair, Kenta walked from the open seat booths towards the rows of bookshelves, casually checking out the other open seat users as he went. At a glance he could see most of them had headsets on. A couple were gamers, boys around his age. A woman nearby was in the middle of a Skype call with someone.

After scanning the booths as closely as he could, Kenta was satisfied he didn't recognise any of the people there and moved on to the bookshelves. Pretending to be browsing the titles like anyone else, he walked by each row of bookcases, flicking a sideways glance in between them at whoever happened to be there.

He came across three schoolboys talking excitedly over a book one of them was holding. Elsewhere, he mostly encountered solitary browsers studying pages and looking over the covers.

Next, he made his way to where the private booths were. There were about twenty in total, with two rows of ten facing one another. Like the open seat partitions, they were comprised of simple varnished wood. They were about the height of Kenta's nose and around two by two metres in size. They were open at the top, so it was possible to peek inside if you were tall enough. But as he came alongside them, Kenta realised it wasn't exactly easy to wander by and casually take a look over the sides without seeming like a potential thief or pervert. And so, on his first pass by the booths, he felt too awkward to so much as glance in their direction, and instead pretended he was walking towards a shelf nearby.

He picked out the first comic he saw. It was one he knew, *Sailor Moon – Volume 8* by Naoko Takeuchi. It was a series an old middle school friend of his had loved, and Kenta remembered reading one or two of them himself.

After half a minute of fake reading, he passed his eyes over the surrounding area, half believing someone might have already identified him as a suspicious person. He realised he wasn't cut out for spying. He'd never be able to pretend he was someone else or hide his emotions. Still, he needed to take a look at those private booths. It was the only conceivable place where a person could keep a low profile for long stretches.

Kenta replaced the comic, and without much thought took out his phone and placed it to his ear. He approached the private booths a second time, and though his cheeks burned almost instantly at how stupid it felt, he began a fake conversation with no one at all, seeing this as the best option for checking the booths without it looking too obvious.

He fake-laughed at some non-joke his non-existent caller was making and started jabbering on about a football game that had never happened. He moved swiftly, keeping close enough to the front of each booth so that he could peer over the top as inconspicuously as possible.

It was clear the first two booths were empty, as the seats were vacant and the computer screens were off, and he could see no sign of bags or personal belongings on any of the surfaces. Another three on that side were empty too, and the others were occupied by a similar assortment to the open seats – gamers, young people studying and one foreigner, probably checking emails.

With the first pass done, Kenta relaxed just a little. He waited to make sure his antics hadn't been noticed by anyone, then continued his fake conversation at the end of the bookshelf before nonchalantly turning back and making his way past the opposite row.

Like the other side, half of the booths were empty, probably because it wasn't late enough yet for those who might want to sleep in them. In the booths that had occupants, Kenta could make out one older woman having a heated phone conversation as she lounged in her reclining seat, a couple in their late teens who were kissing and giggling on their chair while an anime movie played on the computer screen, a young guy wearing a red baseball cap, and a middle-aged man who appeared to be dozing. The only one Kenta hadn't seen properly, and who resembled Yudai in age and size, was the guy in the baseball cap.

When he reached the end of the booths, Kenta dared to walk back the other way almost immediately, speaking even more loudly on his phone and laughing half-heartedly as he went, homing in on the booth where the red baseball cap was.

As soon as the flash of red fabric came into view, he allowed himself to move even closer to the door, ready to look away quickly in the event the person turned around and saw him.

This time the guy wasn't sitting so close to the screen, and Kenta had a better look at his hair and profile. For a second, he felt his heart jolt as he saw Yudai's face partially hidden by the shadow cast by the cap's peak, but then perhaps he was speaking too loudly this time, because the person swung their head around and looked straight at him.

It wasn't Yudai. He wasn't wearing glasses and was probably a year or two older, with a larger nose and wider face. He looked at Kenta in mild surprise, followed by a flash of annoyance, before returning to the screen.

Kenta shoved the phone back into a pocket and walked dejectedly back to his open seat booth. He sat and stared at the screen. He still had ten minutes left, but what was the point? He could be home soon where a lovely home-cooked meal would be waiting, and he could talk with his mum. If he was lucky, his dad would get home early too, and maybe they'd watch a movie together, a Friday night tradition Kenta still enjoyed from time to time. Perhaps there'd even be a chance to write before bed. He hadn't had the time or energy to write much over the previous crazy week.

He found himself inspecting his hands again, checking both sides thinking there might be a spot of blood he'd missed. He tried not to think about the rat, its open lifeless eyes, the yellow teeth frozen in a strange little grimace.

Shaking off the image, Kenta logged out of his session, picked up his bag and made his way to the exit. What had he been expecting? At least he'd tried, as stupid as it all was.

The lazy-eyed man at the counter was too busy reading a manga book to notice him leaving. He pushed through the door, almost bumping into a young woman reaching the top of the stairs onto the third floor. He moved aside to let her pass. The unpleasantly clinical bleach odour filled his nostrils once again, which only added to the growing tiredness and disappointment that were beginning to weigh him down.

As his feet hit the first steps, Kenta saw another person below him reaching the middle landing between the second and third floors. It looked like a young male. He was dressed in black jeans and a light grey hoodie, a full and heavy-looking backpack strapped over both shoulders. The hood was up over his head, and Kenta couldn't see the face until the person reached the landing and turned to the right so that he was directly below him. He saw a fringe of peroxide-blonde hair peeking out from beneath the hood, which immediately told him it wasn't who he was looking for. But then at the sound of Kenta's descending footsteps, the person looked up and Kenta found himself staring into Yudai Matsumoto's eyes.

CHAPTER 26

Yudai froze mid-step, as did Kenta. There were perhaps ten steps between the two of them.

"Yudai!" He said the name, not for confirmation but out of sheer shock. It was like seeing a ghost.

Nothing more was said for the next two seconds, nor did either of them make another move. Kenta was still too shocked to formulate any other words, but seeing the fear and doubt in his old friend's eyes, he knew what he was going to do even before Yudai took a step back.

"Yudai, wait!" He said the words pre-emptively, but it was already too late.

Before he could utter another sound, Yudai was already hurtling back down the stairs.

Instinct kicked in and Kenta near-threw himself down the steps, nearly twisting his ankle as he leaped four at a time, landing heavily just short of the landing. He seized the handrail with his left hand and pulled himself around the turn onto the next flight of stairs. Yudai had a good head start on him and was already hitting the steps just below the second floor.

As Kenta hit the second floor himself, he heard a high-pitched yelp from below, and his head jerked around to see two girls standing on either side of the next stairwell, both still reeling from being shoved aside by the fleeing Yudai.

He muttered a breathless *"Sumimasen!"* as he also tore through the space between them, jumping the last five steps and hurtling past the half-open door already sprung by the fleeing Yudai.

He caught a flash of his target veering left on the pavement and followed, finding himself suddenly moving through the semi-darkness of the late evening, with the headlights of oncoming traffic filling his eyes, a far cry from the windowless cocoon of the café.

Yudai was ahead of him, careening down the pavement with surprising speed, not even attempting to dodge between oncoming pedestrians, some of whom had to jump out of the way to avoid a collision.

Relying on his own football skills, Kenta darted between people with ease. Now they were on a level playing field, and Kenta had the upper hand. He'd always been more athletic than Yudai, and though his friend was going like a bat out of hell, it was probably on sheer adrenaline. As long as Kenta had eyes on him, he knew he'd catch up soon enough.

His gaze was still firmly locked on Yudai, who was coming to a pedestrian crossing at an intersection. Kenta could see the red man blazing from the signs at each of the intersection's four corners, and a small group of people was already standing waiting to cross just ahead.

By this point, Kenta had narrowed the gap to about ten metres, and he prepared for Yudai to cut a quick left along the only stretch of pavement open to him. But to Kenta's amazement, he kept on going right into the road, streaming past the shocked group of waiting people. He barely even turned his head to check the oncoming traffic, only sped onward with insane momentum.

Kenta winced in anticipation of seeing Yudai tossed into the air by a car. He slowed to a halt as he came to the kerb. A car horn pierced the air, followed quickly by another, but there was no screeching of tyres as Yudai reached the opposite pavement.

The red man continued to blaze on all sides. Kenta cursed under his breath. He couldn't wait and found his right foot stepping out onto the tarmac.

He paused briefly to let a taxi pass, then moved forward, raising a hand in apology as he fought against every ounce of propriety and safety he'd had drilled into him his whole life.

Kenta got to the opposite kerb without incident and was just in time to see Yudai taking a left into a side street. He forced his legs to work harder, still riding the waves of adrenaline pouring through his system.

When he turned into the side street, he saw Yudai wasn't too far ahead of him. He was slowing down. It was the heavy backpack and Kenta's superior fitness. He'd catch up before Yudai reached the end of the street, he was certain of it. What he would do once he had a hold of him, Kenta still had no idea. There was no time for thinking; there was only the burning need to see his friend again and speak with him.

"Yudai, please stop!" he called out, his voice reverberating off the tall brick walls looming overhead on both sides, but Yudai ignored him.

The air here was saturated with food smells. On the left, Kenta passed a small bubble tea shop, then on the right, an open izakaya where four men in near-identical grey suits sat huddled around a small table. They were laughing at something. One of them looked up in surprise at Kenta as he raced past them.

He was closing fast. Yudai's sprinting had become more like a wild flailing. He was reaching his limit, but Kenta was only just getting started. The anticipation was growing, a frenzied relief tinged with uncertainty, but he knew the search was over.

When Kenta saw the man, it was already too late. He was a blur of limbs emerging from the darkness, stumbling forward with a carton of food in one hand and a beer can in the other, and Kenta could only open his mouth in a wordless gesture of disbelief as he crashed full on into the man's body.

After the impact of hitting the man's solid frame, he found himself flying through the air. He didn't know which way was up, only knew the searing shock of the blow as his right knee hit the ground first, followed by a rolling tangle of legs over head over torso.

By the time his senses had gathered again into something more coherent, Kenta understood that he'd collided with the man who was now laid out on his back several feet away, groaning. The carton of food he'd been holding lay scattered across the ground, and the beer can was still rolling away, spewing frothing beer as it went.

Kenta looked the other way. He saw Yudai slowing down and then coming to a stop. The hood had come loose from his head, and Kenta could see his full head of straw-coloured hair in the dim light.

"Wait, please!" said Kenta, groaning now himself.

He pulled himself to his feet and tried to take a step forward, but the moment he put his weight onto his right leg, it half buckled. His knee wasn't so much screaming with pain as vibrating a disturbing numbness. There was damage down there, but Kenta didn't care. He only wanted to keep on running, even as his legs rebelled against him, reducing him to a sorry hobble.

Yudai was still watching. He was close enough that Kenta could see his eyes, unshrouded by glasses, which he'd never seen Yudai without, and he could hear his laboured breathing.

"Don't run!" Kenta begged through his own ragged breaths.

After a further moment's hesitation, Yudai pulled the hood back over his head, turned and bolted away with new vigour – leaving Kenta to collapse into a broken heap, where he could only sit and watch Yudai disappear from his life for the second time.

Chapter 27

Jessica was just about to get on the subway home when she received Kenta's message. She'd wandered the streets around the museum for a while after her meeting with Miss Nakamura, her mind a frenzy of criss-crossing and looping thoughts. She'd been so caught up in figuring out what to do next that she hadn't checked her phone since entering the museum.

When she opened the first message with the snapshot of the threat Kenta had received, along with the photo of his locker, her first reaction was the expected disgust at what she was seeing. But then came a flicker of excitement. They'd targeted Kenta too, and it was ramping up. OO was really rattled now. Perhaps this was her and Kenta's chance to draw them out. They were bound to do something else, and now Jessica was certain the Jidai Matsuri performance was the key. That was where it all appeared to be leading, and the koto having its final performance there before its return to the museum only seemed to confirm this.

She stopped by the entrance to Kitayama Station and opened the next message.

> Kenta: *I saw Yudai. He got away but I saw him. We need to see Detective Yamada. Can you meet me now? I'll be at Kyoto Station, main entrance.*

Jessica blinked several times at the screen as she took this in, then with a shiver of anticipation running through her like electricity, she replied that she was on her way, and set off at once in the direction of the city centre.

CHAPTER 28

"What the hell happened to you?" said Jessica as she hurried up to the main entrance of the futuristic-looking Kyoto Station, where Kenta was standing off to one side. She was referring to the tear in his trousers at the right knee where the cut and dried blood were visible.

He was glad to see her, the one person he knew would believe him. "I'm okay. I'll tell you all about it. The police station's this way."

Kenta only had a slight limp now, and the sharp pain in his knee had been reduced to a dull, pulsating one. The cut wasn't as bad as he'd expected, and after limping away from where he'd fallen in the street, leaving the drunken man where he was, Kenta had quickly recovered from the shock and decided on his next move.

He was still bitterly disappointed that Yudai had got away, and yet he found his resolve tripled now. He'd been right the whole time about Yudai still being in the city, and now he knew his friend had dramatically altered his appearance. If he hadn't known Yudai so well, Kenta could have easily passed him by in the street without recognising him. Everything about him was different – his hairstyle, and that peroxide-blonde colouring, which was something Kenta wouldn't have expected from him in a million years. And then there were the clothes. Yudai wasn't one for fashion, he'd never cared about looking like everyone else his age, and Kenta had never seen him wearing a hoodie or decent trainers. Finally, there was the lack of glasses. Yudai probably had the worst eyesight of anyone Kenta knew. He never wore contact lenses, and he was useless without his specs, hence why he was never without them.

This only went to show that Yudai's disappearance hadn't been some hasty emotional response. His planning had been meticulous, from the way in which he'd executed his disappearance, to every detail of his disguise. And yet he hadn't really gone anywhere. He'd only made himself effectively invisible in plain sight, and if anyone had the brains to do this well, it was Yudai. But why? Again, the question was always why.

More than anything else, Kenta knew this couldn't go on any longer. The whole thing had gone further than he could have imagined, and now there were dead rats turning up in his locker, and missing friends turning up in disguise. It was time to get someone else involved.

Kenta had remembered that he still had the card in his wallet, the one the police officer had given him after the interview at school. It had the police station address on it, and Detective Yamada's number and email address.

He didn't want to call him. He doubted the detective would believe anything he had to say via a phone call, and it would be much better to have Jessica with him as backup. But he was aware he couldn't wait either. Yudai was out there, close by, and if they were going to find him, they would need the police's help.

After he'd finally got through to Jessica, Kenta had messaged his mother to say he was meeting up with some friends for dinner downtown, which was something he did occasionally. When she asked who he was meeting, he had no choice but to compound the lie and say it was Shun, since his parents had met Shun before and liked him.

As he walked now with Jessica to the police station, they quickly updated one another on all that had happened. Kenta went first with the locker and the dramatic chase after Yudai. Jessica plied him with multiple questions on all fronts, asking him about minute details he hadn't had the chance to think much about – *Do you think the main corridor cameras would have picked up the culprit? What was the music you heard? Was it coming from a phone? Did you ask the man at the café if Yudai had been before and what ID he'd used?* Kenta did his best to answer everything, although his own mind was still struggling to keep up with all that had happened.

When she was done with all the questions, Jessica told him first about the guard's odd behaviour in the foyer, along with the tattoo, which Kenta agreed was surprising and a point of interest. Then she told him everything she'd learned from Miss Nakamura, including her suspicions concerning the Jidai Matsuri performance at the school. Since he'd also divulged everything about the threat he'd received, she finally told him about the threatening email she'd got herself. Kenta wasn't happy that she hadn't told him immediately, although she explained she hadn't wanted to freak him out, and rather than protest this point, he went quiet.

"Oh, and something weird happened outside my home."

"Your home? What?"

She retold the strange incident with the guy in the hoodie on her way back from school.

"Wait!" said Kenta as they were turning into the street where the police station was. "The guy was wearing a hoodie?"

"Yes," said Jessica. "Why?"

"What colour was it?"

"Light grey."

"What about the shoes?"

Jessica thought for a moment. "They were white. Sports shoes. Maybe New Balance."

"Did you see his hair? Was it blonde?"

"Blonde? No, I didn't see. He had his hood up. Why are you asking?"

He told her more details about Yudai's new appearance, though he wasn't enjoying having to draw the conclusion that was creeping into his thoughts.

"Well, it definitely sounds like too big a coincidence to me," said Jessica. "He was around Yudai's height and size too."

"And you say he tried to hurt you?"

"Not exactly. He definitely scared me though."

Kenta shook his head several times. "It just doesn't make sense. None of this does."

They arrived at the steps leading up to the police station. It was the main one in the downtown area, and intimidatingly large as they stared up at the tall façade looming over them.

They exchanged glances. Jessica spoke first. "We tell them everything, okay? Emails, texts, photos, the lot. And if this Detective Yamada isn't here, we'll just have to tell the next most senior person."

Kenta nodded. "Okay. You ready?"

Jessica nodded in return, and they made their way up the steps, Kenta wincing slightly at the sharp ache in his knee each time it took his weight.

Once they were inside, they found themselves in a surprisingly corporate-looking reception area, more like the entrance to a bank headquarters than a police station. There were no criminals being dragged about with their hands cuffed, only a few people sitting quietly in a seating area off to the right.

As he had been since he was a child, Kenta was filled with the same dual sense of respect and guilt he experienced whenever he saw a police officer, as though he believed they might be able to suss out every bad thing he'd ever done just by looking at him. It was even stronger now as they approached the reception desk where a female police officer was on duty. She had a pretty face, and Kenta was momentarily embarrassed when he met her eye. She greeted them with a hard blank stare that gave her a mildly threatening demeanour.

"How can I help?" she said in a flat tone.

Kenta took out the card with Detective Yamada's number on it and pushed it across the counter so she could see. "We need to see Detective Yamada. We're from the British School. It's about Yudai Matsumoto, the missing boy. We have very important information."

The officer picked up the card and checked both sides, then considered Kenta and Jessica again, appraising them in more detail. Kenta went to smile but found it didn't feel natural, and instead opted for as non-guilty a look as he could muster.

"What are your names?"

"Kenta Higashi and Jessica Hunter. She's British."

Glancing at the card and the two of them one more time, the officer appeared to be thinking, which Kenta presumed was a good thing.

She pushed the card back across the counter. "One moment, please."

Kenta listened as the officer spoke to someone on the phone, relaying to them everything he'd just said.

When she put the phone down, she gestured towards the seating area. "Please take a seat. Someone will be here to speak with you shortly."

Kenta nodded and thanked her, then almost went to request that they speak with a senior officer if not the detective, but the woman's stern gaze made him think otherwise.

"What did she say?" asked Jessica as they made their way over to the several rows of plastic seats.

"She said someone's coming to speak with us. I don't know if it's him though."

They sat down beside one another. Neither of them spoke for a long moment, each lost in their own anticipatory imaginings of what was about to happen.

Kenta looked at his knee and hissed slightly when he prodded the flesh around it.

"That looks nasty," said Jessica. "Makes your story a bit more convincing though," she added without irony.

They didn't have to wait long. After a couple of minutes, they both perked up at the sight of Detective Yamada coming towards them from behind a locked glass door.

When he came into the reception area, Kenta found something tightening in his stomach. He imagined the detective scowling at them, telling them they were wasting precious police time, but in fact he greeted them with a warm smile.

"Kenta?" he said.

"Yes, sir."

He looked to Jessica, also greeting her with a smile and a nod. She smiled back.

"Would you both like to come with me? We can speak in my office."

He aimed an open palm towards the door he'd come through, and Jessica followed Kenta as he stood and walked behind the detective.

They moved along an official-looking corridor, where a couple of doors had windows through which Kenta caught glimpses of people working at desks much like in any office. It was only when they passed a police officer in uniform, this time a man in his thirties who nodded to the detective, that Kenta fully absorbed the fact they were being led into the inner sanctum of a police station. The strange guilt began to rear its head again, as though he were willingly heading towards his own cell.

After turning into another stretch of corridor, Detective Yamada opened a door and waited for them to go in.

Kenta had expected it to be more like the interview rooms he'd seen in films, with a single desk, bare walls and a two-way mirror. But it really was just the detective's simple office. It was quite small, with a single window looking out onto another building. There were several plants dotted about the place, with a peace lily on the windowsill, and a decent-sized bonsai tree sitting on top of a metal filing cabinet. On the walls there were framed certificates and a number of photographs, mostly of the detective in uniform alongside other police officers.

There was one seat facing the desk, and the detective pulled up another one from the corner before beckoning them to sit.

"Would you like some water?" he asked.

"Oh, yes please," said Kenta. He saw Jessica hadn't understood, but the detective pointed at the water dispenser on one side of the room, and she said yes.

He poured them a cup each and let them take a couple of sips as he sat in his own swivel chair on the opposite side. The desk itself was immaculately tidy. On one end there was a small free-standing photo frame angled towards the detective, but Kenta could see part of it – the detective a few years younger, standing beside a woman who must have been Mrs Yamada, and a teenage girl standing in front of them. There was another person in the picture, but he could only see their arm.

The detective continued to observe the two of them with a neutral gaze, his lips still drawn into a slight smile. He was slightly older than Kenta remembered from the assembly, perhaps in his mid-fifties. His neat hair was mostly a salt-and-pepper grey, and he was dressed in a simple brown suit, which made him look much like many of the older businessmen Kenta saw walking about the city. There was something about him that reminded Kenta of Mr Takagi, the school caretaker. Perhaps it was his shortness, and the grandfatherly presence he had about him. But unlike Mr Takagi, there was a shrewd sharpness in his eyes too, which gave the impression he was carefully assessing everything he was seeing and hearing.

"I must apologise," said the detective in Japanese. Then looking to Jessica, he spoke in English. "My English is not so good. *Sumimasen.*"

"*Daijoubu desu,*" replied Jessica, telling him it was all right, and surprising Kenta who'd never heard her speak Japanese before.

"I can translate," said Kenta.

"Very well," said the detective. "Now, I believe you have some important information concerning Yudai Matsumoto's disappearance?"

"Yes, sir."

"And you were both friends with him?"

"I was friends with him," said Kenta. "Jessica is new at the school."

"Ah, so you are both friends?"

Kenta looked to Jessica who clearly had no idea what he'd said. "Kind of... Jessica also saw Yudai the night before he disappeared. She's been helping me find him."

"A couple of detectives, eh?" he said with a chuckle.

Kenta smiled and looked down in embarrassment.

"How about you tell me everything that's been going on," he continued.

Taking a steadying breath, and ignoring his knee which was throbbing uncomfortably again, Kenta started from the beginning. He went over again the sighting of Yudai in the foyer that night, then the incidents at the school involving the geisha and how they'd foiled that particular plot, along with

Rina's blackmail. Next came the vandalism in the auditorium, and the hacking incident, followed by the threats they'd each received, and the rat in Kenta's locker. He finished with how he'd found the clue to Yudai's possible whereabouts and what had happened at the café. He raised his knee and torn trousers to support his account.

From time to time, Kenta turned to Jessica to translate a snippet of what he was detailing so that she would have some idea what he was saying. And even when he was speaking in Japanese, he could see her leaning forward and listening intently regardless of whether she understood or not.

Throughout Kenta's account, the detective only spoke a few times to clarify minor details. The rest of the time he simply listened, his eyelids narrowed ever so slightly, which Kenta took to mean he was listening carefully or was baffled by what he was hearing, or some combination of both.

"Don't forget all the OO stuff," said Jessica at one point. "Also, the worksheet and the photos."

Kenta had kept the folded worksheet in the front pocket of his backpack and slid it across the desk to Detective Yamada, who put on his reading glasses to take a look. Next, Kenta handed over his phone to show the vandalised auditorium and the locker, along with snapshots of the text he'd received. While he was doing all this, Jessica was relaying what she'd learned at the museum, along with her own run-in with the Yudai lookalike, and their theories concerning what OO meant.

At times, the detective looked more than a little bamboozled by the flurry of information being thrown his way, one moment glancing at an image, the next returning his narrow gaze to Kenta as a new piece of the puzzle was imparted.

When Kenta finally finished, he took a large gulp of water and waited for the detective to speak. Detective Yamada, in turn, looked at his notes, then again at the two pupils in front of him.

"Well, I certainly got more than I bargained for there. I was expecting to hear about Yudai's whereabouts, and instead you've given me more than enough lines of enquiry."

Kenta flashed a nervous smile. He could sense Jessica dying to know what had been said, but he didn't dare interrupt the detective.

"I have to say, Kenta. This is quite remarkable. You compiled all of this information yourselves?"

Kenta issued a single nod. "Yes, sir."

The detective raised his eyebrows, perhaps in disbelief or out of genuine admiration.

"And it seems you've both become a target of this prankster at the school. It certainly is an ugly business. I already knew about the acts of vandalism at the school, and also about your friend, the girl who was blackmailed. Some of my colleagues are following that up while I focus on Yudai's case. But you've given some pretty compelling evidence of a link between all of this."

Kenta felt a touch of relief settling his nerves, along with a smidgeon of pride at being a part of it all, even if he knew Jessica was the real driving force.

"If anything, you've made some of my team look quite bad. They've canvassed half the city, and they weren't able to come up with as much as you have."

Unsure whether to smile at this or not, Kenta remained quiet before the detective let out a chuckle and put him at ease.

Following this, Detective Yamada asked him more questions about Yudai, the address of the café, what time he'd seen him, where he'd been when he got away, what witnesses there were. He asked Jessica too about the time and details of her own possible meeting with Yudai.

Kenta told him everything, though stressed out of duty to his old friend that if it was Yudai, he didn't believe he would hurt anyone and had probably been tricked into doing all of the things he'd done. The detective scribbled further notes before asking Kenta and Jessica to send the images and the email threat to him, which they did right away on their phones.

With every detail and loose end documented, the detective clapped his hands as if to signal a full stop on the proceedings. "The last thing I have to say is a very big thank you to you both. You've done yourselves and the school a great service. You should be very proud, and your parents also."

Kenta, who was positively beaming inside on hearing this, though he tried to hide it, quietly translated what the detective had said to Jessica. She signalled that she understood and said thank you to the detective in Japanese, but Kenta couldn't help noticing that she didn't look as pleased as he'd expected.

"Thank you," said the detective in heavily accented English, then added in Japanese, "Do your parents know about all this?"

Kenta hesitated. "Erm... no, sir. Not yet. I didn't want to worry them."

"That's understandable, but I would advise you both to inform them right away. This is a serious matter after all. You may be asked to appear in court if it comes to that."

"Oh, right. Yes, of course."

"Ask him what's going to happen next," said Jessica rather brusquely.

Seeing the detective was about to get up from his seat, Kenta was hesitant to say anything further, but Jessica had fixed him with one of her determined stares.

"Detective... we were just wondering what'll happen next?"

The detective paused halfway through rising and settled back down into his chair. Kenta thought he might not have understood, but after a brief pause, he said, "Well, first I'll interview people at the café and check CCTV in the area. The same goes for the area near Jessica's home. Yudai is my top priority right now. As for the incident at the school, I will pass on your information to the officers working on that. I'll ask them to look into the threats you both received. I expect it might be some fellow pupils having some fun, but we should also take such things seriously."

"And mention our suspect," insisted Jessica. "The security guard."

Kenta went to speak again, but this time Detective Yamada got to his feet quickly and cut him off.

"Again, I really must thank you both, you've been a great help. Please do contact me if you find anything else, and I'll be in touch again if I have any further questions."

He was coming around the desk and moving to the door. Kenta and Jessica looked to one another. She was practically boring into him with her piercing blue eyes.

Kenta ignored her and got up. He bowed to the detective who was now opening the door for them, and thanked him for his help.

"I'll show you out," said the detective, beckoning them into the corridor.

He delivered them both back into the reception area. Kenta's knee had stiffened considerably while he'd been sitting down, and he did his best to stifle the groan lurking in his throat.

"You should get that seen to," said the detective, pointing to Kenta's knee as he paused in the secure doorway between the reception area and the private corridor.

"I will, thank you." Kenta bowed again, and Jessica did the same.

They were about to turn and go when the detective spoke one last time.

"And Kenta... keep your eyes open. The ones doing all this are not good people. Be careful and let us do the rest."

His friendly demeanour morphed briefly into something sterner that came across as a partly cautionary and partly friendly warning. And then he closed the door and was gone.

CHAPTER 29

"Let us do the rest?" said Jessica on the pavement outside the station. "He actually said that?"

"Yep," replied Kenta whom she noted was looking more than a little tired, and with his torn trousers and bloody knee came across as some semi-ragged street character more than a straight-laced pupil.

"So, basically he was telling us to piss off?"

Kenta shrugged. "I wouldn't say that."

"And he wouldn't listen to our theory about the security guard?"

"Look," said Kenta, betraying a flash of irritation as he turned to face Jessica. "We told him all the important stuff, and he said he's going to look into it. What more are we supposed to do? We're just pupils! They're the actual police."

"Pupils who figured out more than they ever did," Jessica muttered.

Kenta went to say something else, but perhaps the will to argue was leaving him, and he only stared mournfully at the passing traffic with the oncoming headlights glinting in his eyes.

A sharp and cool breeze came along the street. Jessica buried her hands in her coat pockets and realised then just how riotously hungry she was. Looking around, she had no idea where she was. She didn't want to go home yet, not with the fierce energy still burning in her.

"Do you know anywhere I can eat around here?"

Kenta, who'd perhaps been expecting more of a fight from her, seemed taken aback by the question. "Oh... yeah. A few. What do you like?"

Jessica shrugged. "I'm not fussed. I'd eat anything right now."

"You tried okonomiyaki yet?"

Jessica looked at him blankly. "Okonomi-what?"

"It's a pancake, a savoury one. The best places are in Osaka and Hiroshima, but there's a couple of good spots here."

"Sure, I'll try it. Point me in the right direction."

"I'll show you. There's a good place in Gion. It's just over the river."

"Okay, thanks." Jessica was more than a little surprised. She'd presumed Kenta would bolt at the first opportunity. She wanted to eat something quickly so she could get back to planning and researching, but the mention of Gion had piqued her interest. It would be a fitting end to the day, after all, to visit the very geisha district where the real Otake Okimi had once lived and worked.

"You sure the knee's okay?" said Jessica as they walked.

Kenta waved it off. "I'm fine. It's not so bad."

They were soon crossing the Shijo Bridge over the Kamo River, which took them onto Shijo Dori. It was more compact and even more bustling than the downtown area they'd just come from. They passed all manner of shops and restaurants. Food smells filled Jessica's nostrils – beef, cabbage, steamy noodle clouds, grilled chicken. She had a vague recollection of passing along this street on the whistle-stop tour she'd been forced to take on arriving in Kyoto, but as with most of the sights she'd seen that day, she'd been too annoyed with her parents and generally furious at the move to Japan to pay any of it any real attention. But when Kenta deviated from the main road and onto Hanamikoji Street, the famous pedestrianised route through Gion, she found herself quietly enthralled as suddenly they were amongst traditional wooden buildings, the kind she was familiar with from the handful of historical Japanese movies she'd seen. She noticed a difference in Kenta too. Gone was his frustrated listlessness from earlier. Now his eyes were wider as they cast about the street. He pointed out the machiya, the wooden merchant houses, and also the ochaya, the quaint little teahouses, some of which were still only for exclusive members, though many allowed tourists to experience a traditional tea ceremony.

Many of the narrow merchant houses were now restaurants, and Jessica caught glimpses of warm, dimly lit spaces through the open doorways. The street was busy too with the growing Friday night throng of tourists and locals – families, couples holding hands, young women dressed in kimonos and wearing geisha wigs. As Kenta explained, the real geishas wouldn't be seen out in the open like this, at least not normally. But maybe it was possible to catch a glimpse of one in the quieter side streets in the early mornings or late in the evening.

He took them left along a narrow alley which led onto another busy pedestrian street, though this one was narrower and lined with more conventional restaurants.

It wasn't long before he stopped in front of an unassuming doorway wedged between a locksmith and an izakaya, and partly covered by a pair of white curtains, like many of the places they'd already passed. Inside, they went up a steep set of stairs into a surprisingly small space with a wooden countertop running along three of the four walls where several people were already sitting and eating. There was an empty square in one wall which framed the kitchen's frenzied activity.

They took a seat and Kenta went over the menu with Jessica, who was becoming increasingly famished at the sounds and smells of frying and grilling in the background, along with the sight of the diners around them already tucking into their food.

"I'd recommend the Gion Yankee," said Kenta excitedly. "It's a Kyoto-style version. It's amazing."

Jessica nodded, knowing she would eat just about anything at this stage. She watched as the food was made on the large griddle in full view by a man wearing a red and white bandana. First he fried a large pouring of batter, before throwing on and mixing in all kinds of foods while slicing and dicing at it with something resembling a paint scraper.

When the dishes eventually arrived, along with two Cokes, Jessica decided it was a cross between a frittata and a pancake, with a large fried egg on top, and a lot of grilled goop everywhere else. It smelled delicious though, and she waited approximately half a second before tearing into it with her chopsticks.

"You can tell you've lived in Asia before," said Kenta, observing her dexterity with the chopsticks as she took the okonomiyaki to pieces with swift precision.

They didn't speak for a while as they shovelled in mouthfuls in between sips of their drinks. Close behind them, a man and woman in office clothes were chatting loudly and downing small cups of sake.

When she was down to the last bite of the surprisingly large portion, Jessica could feel the heavy weight of satisfaction settling into her stomach. "That was bloody delicious!" she said, stifling a burp.

"I knew you'd like it."

Looking around the warm cosy space, Jessica was experiencing something close to contentment for the first time in a long while. She wasn't Jessica the new girl or the strange outsider in the corner. She was simply Jessica, a person who now lived in Kyoto. Kenta wasn't just another dull and annoying BSK pupil either, but an increasingly reliable companion, or perhaps sidekick. She didn't want to think of him as a *friend*. That didn't seem correct – it was too much. Still, she was happy that he was there beside her at that moment in time.

When they were finished, they paid and made their way outside. The night sky had taken hold, and Gion's streets were even more alive with evening revellers.

"Have you even seen Gion properly yet?" said Kenta as they stood outside the restaurant entrance.

"Not really."

He looked at his watch. "Well, you haven't really seen Kyoto yet if you haven't seen Gion. I can show you a little more if you want?"

"Sure," said Jessica, suppressing any obvious signs of her relief. It was clear from Kenta's face that he was relieved too. Neither of them wanted to go home yet, to parents' questions and TV and sameness, not while the scent of adventure was still in the air.

With their bellies pleasantly full, they went through the red torii gates of the Yasaka Shrine at the eastern end of Shijo Dori. On either side of the pathway to the shrine stood a number of small stalls sending further grilled-food smells into the air.

By the shrine's main hall stood a pavilion-like stage adorned with multiple hanging rows of glowing paper lanterns running all the way around. Jessica recognised it instantly as one of those Kyoto landmarks she'd seen photographs of before, maybe in a guidebook somewhere. There were already a number of small groups surrounding it, snapping photos with their phones while Kenta gave her a little background info, explaining it was a Shinto shrine dedicated to Susanoo, a well-known kami, which was a form of Japanese deity. This was also where the famous Gion Matsuri festival was held each year in July.

They took a stroll in Maruyama Park where in spring thousands flocked to see the trees blossom. Afterwards they returned to the many side streets running between Shijo Dori and Hanamikoji Street, where Jessica was happy just to take it all in. Kenta chimed in from time to time to point out specific places, but otherwise they were simply comfortable walking side by side, looking like all the other pairs of young friends exploring Gion that night.

It was after 8.30pm by the time they'd explored much of the district, and Jessica sensed their evening was coming to a close.

"So what are we supposed to do now?" said Kenta, echoing Jessica's thoughts exactly. She knew he wasn't referring to their walk.

"I'm going to find out who OO is once and for all," she said in a low and intense voice, as much to herself as to Kenta. "I don't know how, I just know it has to be done."

"What about the school? We have to warn someone about the performance on Thursday."

Jessica thought for a moment. "We have to speak to Mr Murphy again. There's no other way around it."

"And our parents?"

"You can tell yours if you like. Mine probably won't be around even if I wanted to, which I don't. They definitely won't be going to the performance, that I can guarantee. I don't see what it has to do with them anyway – we've got this far by ourselves, haven't we?"

"Easy for you to say," said Kenta. "Japanese parents aren't always quite so cool about this kind of stuff."

"I don't know if *cool* is an adjective I would use for my parents."

They were passing along a narrow side street populated mostly by what looked like bars, though few of them had any sort of window to see in. Many had the traditional white curtains in the doorways which Kenta had told her were called noren. It was quiet too, with the hubbub of the main streets merely a faint hum on the air, and only one or two of the bars gave any indication of life inside with the occasional muffled laugh or voice escaping from within.

Jessica went to speak again, but there was something in Kenta's demeanour that made her hold fire. "What is it?" she said after a moment.

He looked back over his shoulder twice in quick succession. "That person's been walking behind us for a while now," he replied in hushed tones.

Jessica looked back herself. At first, she saw nothing but a length of darkness along the narrow street, punctuated by the lights from the bars. But it was in the soft glow of one illuminated sign that she saw it – a small figure moving along the alley in their wake. It was a woman. She was at least fifty paces behind them, and like many of the people they'd passed that evening, she was wearing a kimono. When Jessica looked a second time, she saw the shine of the hair artfully arranged on top of the woman's head, and as she came into the pool of light from the next bar along, her face beamed a bright white.

"Is it a real geisha?" said Jessica under her breath, still keeping pace with Kenta as they reached the end of the alley where it turned left.

"I don't know... I don't think so. They wouldn't walk around in the open for so long. She's been behind us about ten minutes now."

They emerged onto the quiet end of Yasaka Dori. It was pedestrianised and paved with flagstones like all the other surrounding streets and alleys, snaking gently downhill amongst traditional wooden homes. The way was lit by a number of lantern-shaped streetlights. Ahead of them, rising up into the midnight-blue sky, was the Yasaka Pagoda. Jessica had glimpsed it before from a distance, but now it was a majestic sight, an almost picture-perfect scene, the kind she'd always imagined of Kyoto and Japan before moving there. It was enough to make her forget everything for just a moment – school, geishas, Otake Okimi.

It was Kenta's obvious unease which brought her back to the street. Normally she might have joked and said he was being paranoid, but not tonight, not after the week they'd had.

They came to a fork in the road, and Kenta took Jessica's elbow, pulling her sharply along the right fork.

"Let's wait here... just to make sure," he whispered, backing up against the wood-panelled front of a small shop. They stood with their backs to the wall, where they were slightly hidden within a pocket of shadow on the fringes of the nearest lamplight.

They fixed their eyes on the point where the road diverged. Jessica wasn't sure what they would do if the person came their way – would they pretend to be talking or looking at their phones?

The road was eerily silent and empty of any movement. The only sound Jessica could hear was her own and Kenta's breathing. She strained her ears for sign of the footfalls coming around the corner, but there was nothing.

Another twenty seconds passed and still there was no sign of the woman.

"Maybe she turned left after the alley?" muttered Jessica, at which point Kenta's eyes widened and he pointed ahead.

"There."

Jessica looked and saw the woman's small frame finally emerging into the soft orange glow of the streetlamp. She was heading along the left fork where the road continued to curve downwards into further clusters of traditional housing. Jessica could see her more clearly now – the white silken flow of the kimono, patterned with the greens and pinks of a floral design. In the amber light, her ghostly make-up was less severe. She was moving swiftly and silently on slippered feet, which explained why they hadn't heard her coming. Seeing her moving amongst the traditional homes, and in the shadow of the pagoda, Jessica had a fleeting sense that they were intruding and she was the one who belonged there, almost as if they were being offered a minute snapshot of Kyoto as it had been when the real Otake Okimi was still walking the earth.

When the woman had passed out of sight, Jessica heard Kenta let out an audible sigh, and his frame visibly relaxed.

"Maybe she really was a real geisha," he said in his normal voice, perhaps even a little sheepishly. He nodded to where they'd just come from. "We'd better head back. You can get a bus home this way."

They stepped into the light and retraced their steps along the paved street towards the small alley. Kenta was hobbling slightly on the leg with the banged-up knee, though he did his best to hide it.

It might have been instinct, or a simple desire to see the pagoda and the moon one last time, but this time it was Jessica who looked back over her shoulder.

"Kenta!" She nudged his elbow sharply. He was a little slow to react this time, but when he saw that she was turning back to the road behind them, he did the same, and then they were both looking at her.

Now that they'd stopped, she too stood still around five metres from them. She must have come up on them quickly to cover this much ground in just a few seconds, and they hadn't

heard a thing. There was no longer any doubt that she was following them.

Nothing was said for the first few moments. There was only a tense pause in which each side took stock of the other. The woman had her head bowed slightly, and though her geisha's wig glistened in the light, her face remained partially hidden. All Jessica could see clearly was the white of the woman's jaw and bright red lips, which at that moment remained straight and expressionless.

"What do you want?" said Kenta in Japanese, though Jessica recognised enough to know what he was saying.

The woman said nothing, only remained absolutely still, hands motionless by her side. Looking quickly about her, Jessica could see there was no sign of other movement on the road either behind or in front. It was just them and her.

"I said what the hell do you want?" repeated Kenta, but still the woman gave no reply, nor did she move an inch.

It was then that it began to dawn on Jessica, and before Kenta could say another word, she found herself speaking instead.

"It's you, isn't it?" she said in English. "You're OO."

Kenta looked sideways at her in confusion, but Jessica didn't take her eyes from the woman's face. At first there was no visible reaction in the geisha's lips and mouth, and Jessica wondered if she hadn't understood after all.

"I know what the OO means," Jessica continued. "It's Otake Okimi. You're doing this because of her, aren't you?"

Again, Jessica watched the woman's blood-red lips intensely, and this time they twitched.

"Why don't you tell us what you want? Maybe we can help you."

Now Kenta was watching the woman too, waiting for something, anything. And then her lips did move, forming into a thin smile. But it wasn't one of amusement or recognition. It was something else.

The geisha took a step forward and raised her head, revealing more of her face. The features remained partially disguised by the heavy make-up, but Jessica could see that she was young, almost childlike. And then there were her eyes, glittering with a malignity so pure that it sent a shiver up Jessica's spine.

Her small hand went behind her back, then when it appeared again there was something held in its grip, something that glinted in the dim lamplight.

Now the woman's lips were parting, revealing the whites of her teeth as they curled into a snarl, and in one fluid, blood-chilling instant she was coming at them.

Kenta was the first to react, jumping forward and in front of Jessica. He must have seen before her what it was in the geisha's hand, as he dodged the sweep of her arm, keeping himself between Jessica and their attacker who cursed angrily as she missed her target.

Wanting a better look at what was happening, Jessica stepped out from behind Kenta's tall frame. She saw the woman facing Kenta, in a half-crouch, poised for another attack, her eyes flaring wildly, pouring their furious hatred out at the both of them. And the thing in her hand – it was a knife, about six inches in length, and wide, like the sort professional cooks used.

Jessica felt the skin crawl along her scalp as a cold bolt of fear struck her. But it wasn't a paralysing fear, or the kind to make her scream uncontrollably. There was a thrill in it too.

With a catlike screech, the geisha came at them again, and now Jessica was fully ready.

She didn't need Kenta to shield her this time. As the geisha homed in on her instead, she dodged right while Kenta went left, and the geisha stumbled forward as she again missed her mark, swiping wildly in the air with crazed malice.

Now Jessica and Kenta remained apart, their gut instincts telling them to make it harder for the predator, almost as if they were planning on herding and trapping her themselves. Jessica realised they both could have turned and run in opposite directions, but neither one of them retreated from where they stood. Kenta might not have been able to even if he tried, judging on the state of his knee, and though she was small, the geisha was quick too.

"Just tell us what you want?" said Jessica in between heavy adrenaline-fuelled breaths.

Kenta was panting too, and the geisha as well, her eyes roving wildly from one target to the next. Jessica was sure the woman had understood her, though she expected no answer. She was only distracting their attacker, keeping her attention divided for as long as possible. But to her surprise, the geisha opened her mouth and let out a disturbingly childlike snicker before uttering a couple of words in English. "Help me? Ha!" She spat on the ground in Jessica's direction, then with teeth bared went for Kenta once again, perhaps emboldened by the wound on his knee and his obvious limp.

Jessica could see his eyes shining wide in the gloom. He was scared all right, but there was an athlete's poise about him as he readied for the next attack.

Keeping herself low, the geisha moved cautiously towards him, and when she was a metre away, lunged for another violent, screeching blow. But Kenta had pulled his backpack from his shoulders and held it out in front of him, using it to deflect the blade as this time the geisha was more accurate. She landed a hit, which Kenta blocked. He sidestepped, but she came in again, now lower, aiming at his stomach. He brought the bag down low just in time, but the geisha was relentless, like some demented creature driven to madness, and she went in yet again, screeching like a banshee, this time driving the knife into Kenta's bag.

Jessica saw the panic register in Kenta's startled expression as he tussled with the bag that had absorbed the blade meant for him. She swallowed down her own red-hot ball of panic. This wasn't a game any more. This small geisha, who'd been the picture of grace and serenity only minutes ago on the street, was like a demon who would keep on coming no matter what they did.

As the geisha pulled the knife from Kenta's rucksack, Jessica wasn't sure if he'd be able to fend off the next strike, and she found her feet taking her forward, and a shout erupting from her throat.

"Hey!"

The startled geisha spun round, at which point Jessica's right hand, seemingly of its own volition, bunched into a fist and flew through the air.

It connected with the geisha's left cheekbone before she had a chance to raise the knife in defence.

The geisha stumbled sideways. The punch hadn't knocked her off her feet, but it had stunned her long enough for Kenta to move away.

Jessica, who was almost as shocked as the geisha at what she'd done, reeled from the shocking pain in her hand. She'd never punched anyone in the face before. It felt like punching a solid wall, and now she didn't know what else to do. She'd played her secret hand and it had only brought them a moment's reprieve.

The geisha shook her head. The wide eyes refocused as she readjusted her grip on the knife handle. Her teeth clenched in a furious grimace. Her murderous gaze was fixed firmly on Jessica's person, and all Jessica could do was stand her ground in the middle of the street and hope she could evade the knife again.

But as the geisha came for her killing blow, Kenta screamed "No!" and charged at her.

The geisha must have seen him coming before his shout, and she changed direction mid-charge, arcing her arm to the left instead where it struck the top of Kenta's right arm.

With a startled hiss, Kenta clutched at his arm where his coat sleeve had been sliced open. Jessica stood open-mouthed. She turned to the geisha, who appeared excited at having drawn blood for the first time, and she would have gone in for more if a chorus of laughter hadn't pierced the air.

The three of them swivelled round to where the noise was coming from. Four people were approaching them along the street. They were talking and laughing loudly. Jessica guessed it was two couples walking together.

There was a final cold exchange of glances between the geisha, Jessica and Kenta, each of them sussing out what the other would do as the cold night air between them filled with the clouds of their breaths.

Jessica discerned a flash of hesitation in the small white face as the approaching voices grew louder. She steeled herself for one more charge, but with a final hateful glare, the geisha took off along the street in the opposite direction, leaving her and Kenta to watch on stunned as her white form was swallowed by the darkness.

CHAPTER 30

This time there was a different officer at the desk in the police station, an older man with an even less agreeable expression than the woman who'd been there before him.

He stared at the two panting teenagers with a look that teetered somewhere between mild disgust and boredom. When Kenta tried to explain what had happened, the officer didn't even try to hide his disdain.

"A geisha, you say? With a knife? Where exactly was this?"

Kenta, who looked the worse of the two with his torn pants and now torn jacket sleeve, did his best to remain calm and provide the backstory so that it would all make more sense. But it only served to make the tale sound all the more improbable.

"And why was she attacking you exactly?" said the officer with a raised eyebrow, despite Kenta having already told him why. "Were there any witnesses?"

Kenta said no. They had been near the Yasaka Pagoda. It was quiet there. Four people had come along, but the geisha had run away by that point.

"Ah, right," said the officer, making a show of writing something down on a notepad, though Kenta doubted it was real. "Probably not too many cameras in that part of town either... very convenient."

"Look, just please get Detective Yamada. He already knows about this."

"Detective Yamada has already left," said the officer flatly. "And I doubt he has time for teenage pranks."

Kenta, who'd tried to keep his cool, but who was tired and in shock and hurting, slammed his palm down on the counter. "This isn't a joke! Someone just tried to kill us!"

The officer, who'd barely been humouring them as it was, did not take kindly to this tone. "Yes, a small geisha... with a knife... but you don't know who they are... in a place with no witnesses."

Jessica, who was standing by Kenta attempting to glean what was going on, gave up and started barking at the officer in English, even though he clearly couldn't understand.

The officer fixed them both with a look of firm displeasure. "Which school is it you go to? And what about your home addresses?" This time his pen was poised above the notepad with purpose.

Kenta shook his head and resisted the urge to scream the first obscenity that came to him. That was their cue to leave. They were still on their own for the time being.

"Well, it is slightly unbelievable," admitted Jessica outside the station on the pavement.

A frustrated Kenta was feeling absent-mindedly at his upper right arm where the slash in his coat sleeve hung open.

"You sure you're okay?" said Jessica.

"Yeah, I'm fine."

After the geisha had fled, and the two couples passed them by with only quizzical stares, Jessica and Kenta had caught their breaths and asked if the other was okay. Jessica said she was fine, but the main concern was Kenta's arm. On closer inspection, however, he saw to his relief that it had only pierced his jacket and not his school blazer or shirt. He'd got lucky. Instead, he was more worried about what his mother would say when she saw his clothes, and then there was his rucksack which now had a small gash in it. When he looked inside, he saw a dent on the cover of his maths textbook where it had absorbed the blade.

With the night's chill closing in, and the realisation of what had just happened dawning on them, they'd quickly made their way back to the police station, eyeing every shadow and woman in a kimono with paranoid suspicion.

Standing outside the station for the second time that night, Kenta had no idea what to do. He felt how he looked – tattered and exhausted. A part of him was still expecting a small geisha to come at them again from behind a nearby row of parked cars, like some terrible goblin. Already the attack seemed more like a nightmare than a real event, but the cut in his jacket told him otherwise.

When Jessica said they should go home, all Kenta could manage was a nod. When she said she was getting a bus, he insisted she get a taxi instead, since public transport wasn't safe. Was anywhere safe now?

"It'll be fine," said Jessica before getting into the first taxi they hailed. "We'll get in touch with Detective Yamada tomorrow. He'll be able to help us, and we'll speak to the headmaster on Monday."

"Sure, okay."

"And be careful," she said before closing the door.

"You too," Kenta mumbled. Even raising a hand to wave goodbye was an effort.

It would take almost all the money he normally received for a whole month to get a taxi home, but he hailed one anyway. He didn't have the energy to walk the short distance to the subway.

It was close to 10pm when he got in the door. His parents were sitting together in the living room watching an old Japanese movie. He wanted only to go to his room and lock the door but knew this wasn't an option.

Taking his bag from his shoulder, he dropped it by his bedroom door before entering the living room. To hide the cut to his jacket sleeve, he had taken it off and rolled it under his arm. There was no hiding the tear in his trousers though, but that would be easier to explain.

"Kenta! Your trousers!" were his mother's first words on seeing him appear in the doorway.

"Everything all right, son?" said his father, looking obviously concerned at the sight of Kenta paler than usual and a little dishevelled.

Standing there, looking at his parents' faces, he considered telling them everything – about all the OO controversy at school, and his part in it; about the dead rat and Yudai, and almost dying that same night at the hands of a demented geisha. It was all there in his chest, a painful pressure like something was pushing outwards from within. It was about to find its way to his tongue when he considered the flipside of the coin – that his parents would then find out what had happened at school the other night, and that he'd lied about his whereabouts more than a couple of times, and that now the police were involved. And worst of all was the thought of dragging them both into it, of infecting his home with all that chaos and darkness. In doing so, perhaps he would be endangering them too.

This made him think of the geisha, and the homicidal wrath in her, and the fact she was still out there somewhere. It was enough to send a shiver through him.

"I fell on the artificial grass at breaktime. I'll clean it up myself. Sorry about the trousers, though."

"It's okay," said his mother, more quietly now. "I can fix that."

"You sure you're all right?" said his father.

"Yeah, I'm okay. Just really tired."

"There's some dinner in the oven."

"It's all right, I'm not hungry. I ate with Shun. I'll have it in the morning."

"Okay," said his mother, who was unfamiliar with the concept of Kenta refusing food.

"I'm just going to read," he said, moving back towards his bedroom door. "Night."

"All right, goodnight, son."

He left his parents' worried expressions behind and near-collapsed onto his bed. But even with the exhaustion flooding him as he lay there, Kenta still couldn't sleep. And in the darkness, he could still feel her eyes on him, burning with hatred, waiting for the next chance.

CHAPTER 31

Yudai Matsumoto stared at the laptop screen in front of him, bleary-eyed and hungry. The room around him, a tiny bedsit barely wide enough for a small single bed, smelled of damp and something faintly chemical. The paint was peeling off the walls. In the corridor outside he could hear a radio playing somewhere.

He jumped slightly when the phone in his pocket vibrated. Reluctantly he took it out. He knew who it was, but his throat still tightened when he saw two letters on the screen. He read the message.

OO: *Are you in the new location?*

Yudai: *Yes. Here.*

OO: *Good. And make sure this is the last time. No more foolish mistakes. No more*

> *excuses. Not getting the girl's phone was one thing, but letting some schoolboy find you is unacceptable.*

For a moment he wished he could tell her where to shove it, but he knew that would be a bad idea. He didn't want to have to face her in person again any time soon.

> Yudai: *Yes. No one will find me here.*

He still didn't know how Kenta had found him. Maybe it was a pure fluke? Either way, it had been too close. Seeing that familiar face suddenly in front of him, hearing his name spoken aloud, had sent a shockwave through him. Yudai knew it was only down to luck that he'd got away. Nine times out of ten, Kenta would have caught him without breaking a sweat. Yudai didn't want to think about what would've happened if he had.

The phone buzzed again.

> OO: *Anyway, I don't think your friend will be eager to do much searching now, not after last night.*

Last night? Yudai's throat tightened. Had she found him after the chase? There was something in him that still resented his old friend for his ability to befriend anyone he wanted, for his ease in navigating the world, his willingness to do what everyone else did. But Yudai didn't want him to get hurt. He'd seen Kenta the other evening outside his family home. He'd seen his mother in the doorway talking with him. It had enraged and confused Yudai all at the same time, and more so because in that moment he'd longed to simply run across the space and back into the safety of his home.

> Yudai: *Last night?*

He knew it was a risk to ask, but he couldn't help it. The answer came after a lengthy pause.

> OO: *Not your concern. Let's just say he and his girlfriend got a big fright when they saw me. You just focus on what you need to do. Is everything in place for Friday evening?*

Yudai couldn't help registering a slight relief on reading this. At least it meant Kenta wasn't badly hurt or worse.

> Yudai: *Yes, everything is fine.*

> OO: Good. *No more mess-ups, not like with the school's server. Just do what you said you'd do.*

He smarted slightly at this. It still infuriated him that he hadn't damaged the school's server beyond repair. He'd worked on that for weeks. She hadn't been happy about it. In fact, she'd put a knife to his throat. But he had to remember what they were fighting for. It was all part of something much bigger – bigger than him or Kenta or the school. *Unity is power.* That was their motto, and he said it to himself now as he swallowed down any rebellion and thumbed in a final reply.

Yudai: *Yes.*

OO: *Don't message again. I'll contact you before the event.*

Yudai put the phone away, happy to be free of her for the time being.

He cast another look over the sorry little room with the single cracked window looking out onto an old warehouse. He shivered against the damp air and returned his focus to the laptop screen, feeling it there in his fingertips and just behind the eyes – the rage and resentment that was never too far away, that would drive him on no matter what he faced.

And he took a deep breath and got back to work.

CHAPTER 32

Kenta: *You okay?*

Jessica: *Yeah, fine. You?*

Kenta: *Okay I suppose. Haven't left home all weekend. My parents think I'm sick or something.*

Jessica: *Did you get hold of Detective Yamada yet?*

Kenta: *Nope. I only have the email and phone number for his assistant. She just says he's too busy at the moment but she'll pass on the message.*

Jessica: *God, that is annoying. That's basically a great big "piss off"! How difficult can it be to report a crime? You still haven't told your parents?*

Kenta: *No. Not yet. I think they'd kill me themselves if they found out about even half of it. Look, what if she comes for us again?*

Jessica: *If we find out who she is first, then she won't be able to.*

Kenta: *How the hell are we supposed to do that? We're getting nowhere. And Yudai's still out there. Maybe he's in danger too?*

Jessica: *I've got a new idea. But it'll have to wait until we're at school. I reckon she'll think we're too chicken now to do anything else, which is to our advantage. In the meantime, we keep our heads low and stay in busy places. She won't try anything in a crowd. As for Yudai, he'll turn up. I'm sure of it.*

Kenta: *So we just go to school tomorrow and pretend everything's normal?*

Jessica: *Yes, that's exactly what we do. But we have to warn the headmaster first. He has to know that they're planning something for Thursday.*

Kenta: *I can't stop thinking about it though. She was insane. It still freaks me out.*

Jessica: *And soon she'll be insane behind bars. We're getting closer, I'm telling you. It'll be okay.*

Kenta: *Sure. The famous last words.*

Jessica: *I'll see you tomorrow. Keep your eyes peeled.*

Kenta: *My eyes what?*

Jessica: *Come on! It's an expression –
keep your eyes open, as in look out for
anything unusual. And watch out for that
security guard because he'll be watching
out for us too, that's for sure.*

CHAPTER 33

If Jessica had been a tad wary the morning after the close scrape with the hooded figure, whom she now firmly believed had been Yudai, she was now reaching new heights of paranoia on her walk to school.

Every female the size and height of the geisha was a potential threat amidst the crowds of pupils and professionals heading to school and work. Although she hadn't told Kenta, she too had spent the weekend cocooned in her bedroom, peering outside the window every so often for sight of a kimono. But at least being holed up at home wasn't an unusual activity for her. It had given her the opportunity to write up her notes from the interview with Miss Nakamura and do a little work on her English project.

But as for the one thing that continued to plague her every thought, Jessica found it almost unbearable that she could go no further with her investigation while stuck at home. She knew they were approaching the core of what this was all about, but there was an undeniable fear there too that she would never willingly own up to, namely the possibility that she wouldn't get to it in time.

As she approached the school gates, however, she managed to shake it off for now. She'd got there without incident, although she had to assume she was being watched at least some of the time. What was important now, though, was that she had a plan and intended to execute it as soon as possible.

She eyed the two security guards at the gate, though they paid her no attention in return, and there was no sign of their younger colleague.

When she was inside the foyer, Jessica didn't need to look for long to catch sight of Kenta, who was sitting on one of the shiny white benches in the waiting area. He came over as soon as he saw her. She noted a hint of a limp and a more pronounced darkness under his eyes, but otherwise he appeared his usual self.

"How's the leg?" said Jessica.

"Still attached."

"Should we do this?"

"Yes."

Without need of another word, they both headed straight for the headmaster's secretary.

"We need to see Mr Murphy," said Jessica to the headmaster's assistant, who was seated at her desk by his door. "It's very important."

The assistant looked up at them from her computer screen, her expression and posture hardening. "The headmaster's very busy this morning."

"She's right. It's very serious," added Kenta.

She replied in a disinterested monotone. "He's busy all morning."

Not waiting for another put-down, Jessica went to the headmaster's door and rapped it with her knuckles.

"Excuse me!" The assistant got up from her desk. "I said he's busy."

"Well, this can't wait," Jessica barked coldly over her shoulder. She knocked again, but there was no reply from inside. Next, she peered over the frosted glass for a better look, and seeing his desk was empty, cursed under her breath.

"We'll try him again later," she said to the assistant, already on the way back out. "Please tell him Jessica Hunter wants to see him."

She left Kenta standing there, and he nodded awkwardly at the flabbergasted assistant before following Jessica out.

"It's just like the sodding detective," spat Jessica as she marched across the foyer to the main corridor. "These morons aren't taking us seriously! Well, they'll bloody well have to soon."

Kenta hurried to catch up. "Why don't we send him an email or leave a note?"

"He'll just ignore them. It's pointless. We have to tell him to his face, make sure he gets it."

As they joined the pupil rush to lockers and form rooms, they both overheard pupils discussing yet more geisha sightings at the school. And when they got to their own lockers, there were several figures huddled around one particular door.

Jessica nudged one or two of them aside and found two large O's scratched into the door of Milo's locker. His wasn't the only one either. Two more doors bore the same marks, and Jessica wouldn't have been surprised to hear that lockers all around the building had them too.

"This is crazy," muttered Kenta, shaking his head.

"This is her, or her little helper," said Jessica quietly so only he would hear. "This is what she wants. It's part of the build-up, but these idiots all just think it's some bloody warm-up to Halloween."

Milo, who was rubbing at the scratches on his door, looked up and saw Kenta then Jessica beside him. This time there were no wisecracks or knowing winks, and he returned to inspecting the locker as if he hadn't seen them at all. Further along, the two A-block cleaners were busy trying to wipe away the O's written on two lockers in black marker pen. The shy young cleaner had her head down and didn't look at the nearby crowd while her older colleague was cursing under her breath as she struggled with the task.

"I'll see you in English," said Jessica. "We can try the headmaster again at breaktime."

And they did try again, but found his office empty once more and his assistant even more dismissive. In the foyer there were actual queues now of people wanting to see the koto, and the museum assistant had another museum employee helping her out. On top of that, there were pupils wandering about all over the school in Japanese costumes for the festival performance dress rehearsals – samurai, emperors, noblemen and -women scurrying to and from the auditorium.

"This is all messed up," said Kenta as they went back into the main building. "Everyone is still acting like there's nothing wrong. It's all just a joke."

"It's the calm before the storm," said Jessica, taking in the same scene of frenetic school activity around them.

Up ahead they caught a glimpse of a familiar figure moving towards the auditorium. Jessica was the first to react. "There he is! Now's our chance."

They caught up with Mr Murphy as he was approaching the auditorium doors, head bent to his phone as he walked.

"Mr Murphy!"

The headmaster spun round, his raspberry face barely hiding his irritation as he saw who it was. "I'm very busy right now, Jessica. Can we do this another time?"

His steps slowed only momentarily before carrying him forward at an increasing speed.

"But, sir! This is important. It's about Friday. Something's going to happen."

Mr Murphy's hulking frame disappeared into the auditorium. Jessica almost went to follow then thought otherwise. Instead, she stood glaring at the closing double doors.

"Bastard!"

"We'll try again later," Kenta offered gently.

"It's useless. Sod him! Sod all of them. We should just leave OO to do whatever it is she's planning, then they'll be bloody sorry!"

Two Year 12 boys dressed as Heian-era warriors brushed past them, laughing as they went into the auditorium. Jessica turned her murderous glare on them, then seeing Kenta's tired eyes and *what now?* expression, she suddenly charged off back towards the school reception area.

Kenta started. "Where are you going?"

"To follow our only lead."

"What lead?"

"The insider, of course! I'm going to wait for the security guard and then I'm going to follow him. He's our best shot right now. We're wasting too much time."

Kenta followed hesitantly as Jessica began heading for the main doors. "Wait! You can't, it's not safe!"

"We don't have a choice. He's the rat. We can't just let them carry on like nothing's wrong."

Now they were outside in the cool autumn air, moving towards the gates with all the other students.

Kenta hurried to keep up with her as she sped up. "But she could still be out there," he said imploringly.

The word "she' seemed to hang in the air, and for a second Jessica registered a hesitance attempting to take hold of her. But she pushed it away like everything else. She couldn't stop, wouldn't stop now.

"You stay here if you want. I'm going to follow him, and I'm going to get some answers while I'm at it."

"I can't help this time," said Kenta as they passed through the gates and onto the pavement outside. "I need to go home. I can't stay out late today. Let's wait till tomorrow. You shouldn't be out here alone."

Jessica stopped and turned to face him. She saw a genuine fear for her well-being written in his face and found an unexpected comfort in it. But it wasn't enough.

"Sorry, I'm going. I'll keep you posted."

She turned and headed across the street.

"This is crazy!" called Kenta behind her, but she only walked faster. When she reached the opposite pavement, Kenta was still watching her. They exchanged a brief stand-off look before he shook his head and walked off.

"Typical," she muttered to herself, experiencing a confusing mixture of both relief and something like a sinking dread at the sight of his tall figure disappearing amongst the school crowd. Still, there was work to do, and she focused on the bus stop further down the street, where she'd be able to keep an eye on the school gate without being too conspicuous.

She was still there an hour and a half later. She'd already seen the majority of remaining pupils leave. The sky had turned a midnight blue, only a few shades short of true nightfall. It was also then that Jessica acknowledged to herself that she was keeping an eye out for more than just the security guard. Her paranoia from the morning had increased tenfold now that the sun had abandoned her, leaving her stranded in a world of shadows where anyone or anything could be lurking. More than once she jumped at some perceived movement on the pavement around her and found herself ready to run. As it grew colder too, Jessica felt horribly exposed. She was making a mistake. Stupid Kenta was right, she couldn't be out there alone.

"Shut up! Shut up!" She found the harsh whisper in her mind coming to her lips. She did her best to silence all internal rebellion. Instead, she let all the rage return, at OO and the world in general, even at Kenta. She let it fuel her burning need to finish the job.

She checked her watch. It was almost six when she finally saw him leaving the front gates. He was still in his uniform, although with a light-green jacket over his black security guard's sweater. He waved to the guard in the kiosk and then moved along the pavement in the direction of the subway.

Jessica pretended to look at her phone so as to avoid being seen, then put it away and began walking.

Staying on the opposite side of the road, she made sure to remain at least thirty paces behind him. He was looking down at his phone as he walked, but she didn't want to take any chances. She'd never followed anyone before, though she'd read about it and seen it in more than enough books and films to have a rough idea of the correct protocol. She didn't know what she expected to find either, or what she would do if he got on a bus or hailed a taxi, but at least she was doing something.

After another ten minutes, the guard was still on foot. He'd been on his phone almost the whole way, glancing only occasionally at the pavement ahead of him.

He turned into Kitayama Dori where the evening rush-hour traffic was now in full flow, meaning Jessica found a growing barrier of cars and headlights between her and her target. And so, at the next pedestrian crossing, she swapped over to the other side so that she was now directly behind the guard.

He glanced periodically at the many cafés and shops they were passing and at one point went into a 7-Eleven convenience store so that Jessica had to hold back and linger behind a lamp post. She wasn't too far from her home now, where it would be warm, and Yuko would have food ready for her. She wouldn't stop until she at least saw where the guard was going. If she was lucky, perhaps she'd catch him mid-rendezvous with some shady character, or even with OO herself.

The guard came out of the 7-Eleven with a small Coke in hand and took a swig from the bottle. When he continued onwards, Jessica resumed her steps, maintaining the appropriate distance as she began to wonder how long she'd have to keep this up. She was getting colder, and the creeping sense that she too was being followed became such a distraction that she found herself checking over her shoulder almost as much as she looked ahead to the guard, trying desperately to stave off nightmarish visions of knives flying at her from all directions.

The guard turned right into a smaller street, and Jessica looked behind her one more time before also doing the same, which was when she nearly walked straight into a dark figure standing in her path.

She didn't scream or shout, only recoiled instinctively. There were about two metres between them, and then she saw that it was him, the guard, and he was staring straight at her.

Simultaneous urges to scream, run and fight jostled amongst Jessica's nerves, but after the run-in with OO she found herself surprisingly ready for whatever was coming.

She went to ask what he wanted, but he spoke first.

"Why are you following me?"

His voice was surprisingly clear, and though he had a heavy local accent, he'd spoken in perfect English.

Jessica found herself floundering. What she was seeing and hearing didn't seem to compute. "I..."

"Don't deny it!" he added before she could reply. "And your friend too."

"My friend?" Jessica frowned. "It's just me."

"Really?" In the dim light from the nearest streetlamp, Jessica saw the guard raise a knowing eyebrow, and he gestured with a nod over her shoulder.

She turned in confusion, and right on cue, Kenta came around the corner.

CHAPTER 34

Kenta was moving at a jog and starting to limp again when he came around the corner. He was worried he'd let her get too far ahead of him, but then there she was, looking back at him, and the guard too, staring at both of them.

"Kenta?" Jessica's confused voice cut through the strange silence hanging in the air.

Kenta didn't reply. His focus remained on the guard. Was he going to have to fight again? He didn't think he had the strength to beat up a grown man, even if he was a little taller. His knee was aching badly now, and if the guard had a knife... Kenta didn't want to think about it. But still, he found his hands forming into fists and his muscles tensing in readiness.

"I'll ask again. Why are you both following me?"

Jessica turned back to the guard. "You know why."

In the tense pause that followed, Kenta took a few more steps forward so that he was standing by Jessica's side, and together they stared down the guard.

"You think I have something to do with all the things happening at the school? I've seen you both watching me."

Eyeing him closely, Kenta could see the guard's nerviness, but there wasn't anything obviously threatening about his stance. If anything, the man appeared baffled.

"Well? Can you blame us?" said Jessica.

The guard thought a moment then shook his head. "It's the tattoos, right? People always think I'm a bad guy."

"That and the fact you happened to be there when we caught Rina in the geisha costume, not to mention you taking secret photos of the koto, and oh, there's also your access to the whole school."

A cat screeched in a nearby yard, but none of them looked away. Kenta was expecting the guard to rise in some way to Jessica's challenge, but instead he appeared to visibly deflate, and with a sorry shake of his head and a laboured sigh, he reached into his pocket and removed his wallet.

Jessica and Kenta watched his movements with strange interest as his fingers rummaged around inside before appearing again holding a small square of paper – or was it a photo?

He held it out. "Here."

Neither of them moved at first but then Kenta stepped forward warily, bridging the gap between them and the guard. He looked him in the eye as he reached for the square, seeing in them a defiance, but something else too: a vulnerability or pain perhaps that was at odds with what Kenta had expected.

It was a photo, slightly larger than standard passport size. It was too dark for Kenta to see properly, and he held it up where it caught the light from the streetlamp. His eyes narrowed while he looked at it more closely, aware the whole time of the guard scrutinising him.

The photo was of three people standing together – an older man and woman standing on either side of a younger man. They were in a park somewhere, the three of them smiling. Kenta saw almost right away that the young man in the photo was the guard. He had his arms around the two people, whom Kenta assumed were his parents, but it wasn't until he looked more closely at them that he understood.

He looked at the guard in amazement, then back at the photo before taking it over to Jessica, who repeated the same process of struggling to understand what she was looking at, followed by the shock of recognition.

Still holding up the photo, Jessica looked to the guard, incredulous. "You're Mr Takagi's son?"

"*Hai*," said the guard. "Tomo Takagi. You can call me Tomo if you like."

"But why didn't you just say?" said Jessica, her gaze still flitting confusedly between him and the photo.

"Why should I have to? Anyway, no one knows besides the other guards. I don't want everyone to know I'm the caretaker's son." The young guard looked at his watch. "Look, I've been working all day and I have to study for a class. There's a café just up here." He aimed a thumb over his shoulder up the side street. "I'm grabbing a quick coffee if you want to tag along."

Kenta and Jessica exchanged glances, but there was no need to voice their thoughts.

Jessica nodded. "Okay."

***

Three minutes later they were sitting across from Tomo Takagi in a small café close to Kitayama Station. It was an old-fashioned establishment, with tired maroon leather seats arranged into booths that made it look like a cross between an old American diner and a canteen. It reminded Kenta of how some cafés in Kyoto used to look when he was a child. There was a smoking room off to the side, separated by glass panels and a glass door. Kenta could see two old men in there, reading newspapers, and imagined his grandfather on his father's side would have drunk his coffee in a place like this.

Tomo had a cup of filter coffee on the table in front of him. He hadn't added any sugar or milk, and Kenta could smell the strong odour wafting across the space between them. Kenta himself had a hot chocolate, and Jessica had opted for a glass of water which she'd poured for herself from a communal jug beside the sugar stand. Once or twice, he caught the man behind the counter looking their way. He was in his forties with long hair tied into a ponytail. He had an impassive expression that

296

bordered on unfriendly. This was no Starbucks, thought Kenta, although a part of him liked it.

There was an awkward pause while the three of them took their first sips, each one adjusting to the oddness of their meeting.

Tomo was the first to speak. "So, I bet I can guess your first question."

Kenta looked to Jessica, but she seemed equally clueless.

A hint of a playful smile crossed Tomo's lips. "I bet you're wondering how a dumb security guard like me can speak English fluently."

"The thought had crossed my mind," said Jessica with typical forthrightness, whereas Kenta blushed slightly and looked down at his drink.

"Fair enough, I would've asked the same thing." Tomo blew on his coffee and lifted the cup for another sip. "I went to a good school, and I was a good student. It's pretty simple really. So now you're wondering why I'm a security guard?" Tomo didn't wait for a reply before continuing. "It's a fairly typical story. I got in with the wrong people. Guys I respected, the kind I wanted to copy, you know? I was getting into street art, graffiti, that sort of thing. They weren't all bad guys, some were really..." His brow furrowed while he sought the word. He looked to Kenta and said it in Japanese.

"Talented," said Kenta quietly.

"Talented! Yes, that's the one." He tapped the table lightly and smiled again. "See, I'm rusty. They were very talented, some

297

of them. But, you know, I was young. I followed along. Next, I was stealing from shops. It was just dares at first, nothing serious. A packet of chips from Lawsons, that kind of thing. My parents knew I was hanging out with these guys by then. My father and I, we had a lot of fights then, real bad ones. That's when I got my tattoos. He didn't speak to me for two months, said I'd thrown my life away, and then, well..."

Tomo twirled the cup slowly on the table, his attention snagged briefly by the dark pool of coffee.

"That's when things went wrong. I got caught stealing spray-paint cans from an art store. I was sixteen, so they sent me to one of those training centres."

Tomo raised both hands to indicate inverted commas as he said these last words.

"Like a juvenile detention centre?" said Jessica.

"Yes! That's exactly what it was. Prison for kids. A place just outside Tokyo. They had Zen gardens and all that to make it nice, but basically we were prisoners. Six months I was there. Only my mum came to see me the first three months. My father didn't want to look at me. I got thrown out of the school obviously, and I knew no good university would take me after that."

"What did you want to do?" said Jessica. "I mean, for a job?"

Tomo considered this for a moment then shrugged. "I wanted to be an artist, have my own gallery. I don't think I was ever good enough though. I thought about advertising too, maybe I could've used my art skills that way."

"What happened after the detention centre?"

"I bummed around in different jobs for a while... porter in a hotel, cook's assistant in a ramen restaurant. It wasn't easy getting work once people found out about my past. I was living in a bedsit then. My father and I still weren't speaking much, but eventually we both came round. Then he got me the job at the school last year. He had to call in a favour for that, made me promise I wouldn't let him down again. The money is all right though, better than anything I had before, and I'm going to art school at night. I figured it's better late than never."

"So that's why you were taking photos of the koto?" said Kenta.

"Yeah, it was for a project. I wanted to sketch it, it's beautiful. Look, like I said, my father got me this job, and that's why I wouldn't do anything to spoil it. I don't have anything to do with what's going on at the school."

"Don't worry, I already know that," said Jessica a little dejectedly. "It was also you who wiped away the two circles from the display cabinet, wasn't it?"

Tomo whistled softly. "Woah, you're good. Yep, guilty as charged. That shit happened on my watch. I didn't wanna get the blame, so I wiped that crap off before anyone else saw. But it freaked me out when I saw the same stuff in the auditorium after. I know something's not right. I'm not the superstitious type, but it did all begin when that koto turned up."

"You can say that again," muttered Jessica. "And if you're not the insider, that means we're back to square one."

Tomo raised an eyebrow. "Insider?"

Kenta said the equivalent word in Japanese and Tomo nodded.

"I thought you guys were in on it too after I saw you with the geisha girl. I didn't get why the school didn't throw you out or something."

Between the two of them, Kenta and Jessica filled him in on what had happened with the headmaster, as well as everything else they'd discovered since. Tomo sipped his coffee as he listened intently.

When they were done, Tomo shook his head in disbelief. "First thing, you basically blackmailed the headmaster, which is seriously cool."

On hearing this, Jessica considered Kenta with a look of mild satisfaction.

"And everything else – the dead rat, the psycho geisha, that's crazy. And the police won't help?"

"They don't believe us," said Kenta.

"Not even about your friend, the missing boy?"

Kenta shrugged. "I told the detective everything that happened. He said thanks, but he isn't answering any of my emails or calls."

Tomo shook his head again. He was almost finished with his coffee. Behind them, a taxi driver was entering the café for a takeaway, but otherwise it was quiet.

"So, who's doing all the crazy stuff at the school then?" said Tomo. "Must be kids."

Jessica pushed away her water, which she'd barely touched. "No, I don't think so. It's still someone with special access to the school. What about the other security guards?"

Tomo coughed loudly. "No way, not those guys! They wouldn't know how to do anything like that even if they tried. They're all bored old dudes waiting for retirement, trust me."

"Not even for money?"

"Nah, those guys are okay. Plus, they're all idiots, apart from Mr Goto, the old-timer. And he's still off sick after that girl nearly scared him half to death in her outfit."

"The office staff?" said Kenta.

Tomo considered this a moment and screwed his face. "I don't think so, man. I don't buy it. They don't ever leave the office except to get food at the canteen. They wouldn't be able to walk around at night without being seen. The only people who are in the school after hours, apart from security, are students and teachers. If you ask me, one of them is in on it."

With that he swallowed the last of his coffee and checked his watch. "Look, I'm gonna help you guys as much as I can, but I'm not getting myself into any shit either. I like my job. If there's someone at the school pulling all this crap, then we'll find them."

"Before Friday night?" said Jessica with a hint of a challenge in her voice. "If we don't find them by then, it won't matter."

"Like I said, I'll do my best to help. I'll let you know if I see anything. Mr Goto's back tomorrow. He won't let any more funny business go on, believe me."

As he stood up from the table, the sleeve on Tomo's right arm hitched up slightly, revealing the edge of one tattoo. He instinctively pulled it back down again.

"I've got to study. I have homework for my class, just like you guys."

"Thanks," said Kenta. "Sorry we, you know... suspected you."

Tomo waved it off nonchalantly. "No worries, man. At least someone is trying to solve this shit. But if I were you guys, I'd stay well out of all this. There's some crazy dark shit going down. Tell your parents or try the police again or something. You guys are smart. I don't wanna see you get yourselves into some messed-up stuff like I did."

"Thanks," said Kenta, and Tomo waved them farewell before strolling out onto the street.

Kenta considered his hot chocolate, which he'd barely touched. When he looked at Jessica, he could see she was deep in thought, her brow knitted, eyes boring into the table with a furious intensity.

"Don't you think he's right? About telling our parents and all that?" said Kenta, but Jessica wasn't listening.

"There has to be something," she said suddenly, more to herself than Kenta. "Something we're not seeing, some angle or other."

"Like what?"

"Well, that's the bloody point, isn't it? I don't have a clue."

Kenta glanced at his phone and found his heart sinking as he realised he was going to have to make up yet more excuses for his parents. "Look, I have to go."

Jessica didn't respond at first. She was too locked in her internal machinations. "Yeah, sure," she uttered distractedly, only getting up from the table herself when Kenta was halfway to the door.

He nodded to the man behind the counter who responded with a curt, "Thank you," and a blank expression.

Once outside, Kenta checked the street before stepping forward onto the pavement. The drone of the busy traffic on nearby Kitayama Dori hung in the air, but the side street the café was on remained quiet.

When Jessica came outside, hands stuffed into her coat pockets, her eyes were still observing the workings of her own mind rather than what was in front of her.

"I'll walk you to your house. It's nearby, isn't it?"

"Yeah, thanks," Jessica mumbled, not looking at him.

During the ten-minute walk to Jessica's house, Kenta remained highly vigilant, checking constantly for movement ahead and behind them while Jessica continued the discussion about what to do next. The conversation was mostly with herself, and Kenta only murmured a word of agreement every so often, noticing how worked up she sounded, which only made him more nervous.

He looked at the neighbourhood houses as they passed by, at their pleasant gardens and high walls. He imagined what it would be like to live in one of them, but only for a moment.

Jessica was so lost in thought that she almost walked past her front gate and looked a little startled to see she was home. "Oh... this is me."

Kenta looked up at the house and thought how odd it was that this English girl was living in this Japanese-style house in the cultural capital.

"Okay, see you tomorrow," said Kenta, noticing in the light from the streetlamps just how pale and tired Jessica looked. That was how he felt too, bone-tired.

He waited until she was through the gate, then began making his way back towards Kitayama Dori, wishing he could be transported straight to his bed and to a time when he'd neither seen nor heard of the famous koto or OO, when he didn't have to live in fear of being attacked every five minutes. In the far distance, above the mountains, Kenta saw a milky-white flash of lightning. He glanced up at the sky overhead, which remained cloudless, then kept on walking. He didn't want to think about whatever hare-brained scheme Jessica was dreaming up. He wasn't sure he had the mental power even if he wanted to, and nor did he have any idea of the storm that was brewing much closer to home.

CHAPTER 35

Jessica had barely slept, yet she was buzzing with energy when she got up to dress for school on Tuesday morning. She'd spent most of the night thinking over the next step in their investigation and had achieved a major breakthrough around 4am, after which she'd remained even more wide awake, chastising herself for not having thought of it before.

It wasn't until the morning break at school, however, that she was able to get the ball rolling. Picking her way through the breaktime rush of bodies streaming along the corridors, she made a beeline for the reception desk in the foyer. Himari, the receptionist, who was now used to Jessica's frequent visits and requests, greeted her with a friendly enough smile.

"Yearbooks!" exclaimed Jessica, forgoing the usual niceties. "I need to see the older ones, from before it became digital. Do you have any?" When Himari raised an eyebrow, she added, "It's for a school project."

Perhaps it was the intensity in Jessica's stare, but Himari didn't attempt to fob her off as she had the last couple of times.

"Well, let me see. We should have some somewhere. Please wait a moment."

Jessica watched her go into the admin office, and through the half-open blinds she could see Himari talking with one of the staff in there. After a brief exchange, she disappeared behind a door at the far end of the office before emerging shortly afterwards carrying a small cardboard box.

Jessica's eyes lit up as Himari plopped it down on the reception desk in front of her.

"Here you go. We do keep some of them after all. We went digital in 2015, and these go back to almost 2000. Is that far back enough?"

"Perfect!"

Snatching the box away, she only half heard Himari saying something about bringing them back.

She headed for the library and settled herself at a table in the furthest corner of the room, where she was hidden behind several bookshelves. Although she was sure it was too early, she started from the very beginning of 2001. She had to be thorough, had to be certain. She also had only a vague idea what she was looking for, but she knew in her bones that she would recognise it when she saw it.

Flicking through the pages, she began scanning face after face. The pupil population had been noticeably smaller back then, with less diversity in nationalities – namely, far more Brits. But at least she knew she was looking for a Japanese face, which narrowed it down considerably. Still, it would have been better to have Kenta there helping her out just in case. The bell signalling the start of the third period sounded overhead, but she paid it no attention. It was PE next anyway, which Jessica couldn't stand. But it didn't matter what subject she had next; her brain was on fire.

She got through the first three years fairly quickly. It was strange to think that all of those bright young faces would now belong to adults in their thirties. Like the pupils, the yearbooks themselves had changed in design and style over the years, becoming thicker as they went on.

By the time she got to 2013, the bell signalling the end of third period was already bursting from a speaker overhead. It was English next, but still Jessica wouldn't leave her seat. There were only two more books to go and still she hadn't found anything definitive. She started writing down a list of possibilities in a notebook, but they were all long shots, with not one of them fully meeting the strict criteria she'd had in mind.

By the time she was halfway through the 2015 book, a thin film of sweat was forming across Jessica's brow. She realised she'd put everything on this last-gasp idea. If she didn't find OO this way, she probably never would, and then what would they do? Simply fail? The idea of it was unthinkable. Not only had she assured Kenta, whom she knew was putting his faith in her even if he didn't always show it, but this thing had become personal too, and not merely because her life had been threatened. It was simpler than that. She had locked eyes with her foe. She knew beyond a doubt that the geisha was OO herself. They had been face to face and measured one another. Like every other adult seemed to be doing, OO had also probably written Jessica off as just a girl, not a real adversary. But she would have to show them. There was no other way.

When she'd flicked through the last page of the last book, Jessica pushed down the mounting rebellion in her gut, and on a hunch went back to 2007 to start again. She knew the answer wasn't to be found in the recent digital yearbooks from 2015 onwards, which she'd already picked over several times. OO was no university pupil fresh out of high school. This felt like the work of a mature mind, albeit a mad one, which meant the truth had to be locked away in these physical pages stacked up in front of her.

With a feverish intensity, Jessica doubled down on the search, scanning each face and name with even greater scrutiny, her eyes roving for what she'd missed the first time around.

It wasn't until she was halfway through 2010 and buzzing with an almost electric nervousness that Jessica saw something she'd only given a cursory glance the first time around – from 2009 onwards the yearbooks had a section at the back dedicated to special achievements. This ranged from pupils who were national fencing champions, to local ballet competition winners. So far, Jessica had been too focused on the individual pupil photos and profiles with their lists of hobbies and ambitions, but now she went back to the 2009 book and trained her mental spotlight on the bonus section.

She looked over each achievement carefully, reading the details in the accompanying articles. In that year there had been a girl who was a promising horse rider and a boy who won a provincial science competition, but there was nothing else Jessica was interested in.

It was the same in 2010 and the following two years. There was absolutely nothing that was jumping out at her, and again the sickness grew, the sourness of vomit reaching its way up into her throat. But then halfway through the 2013 section, she saw what she'd been searching for. It was there as plain as day. She couldn't believe she'd missed it, but there wasn't time to chastise herself.

Snapping the book shut and dropping it into her bag, Jessica scooped up the box of remaining yearbooks and hurried out in the direction of the music department.

CHAPTER 36

Kenta was just leaving the sixth-form common room at the start of the lunchtime break when Jessica, red-faced and out of breath, charged up to him with a small cardboard box in her hands.

"Where were you?" was the first thing he said, since she'd been inexplicably absent from classes despite the fact everyone knew she'd come to school that morning.

"It doesn't matter!" she said breathlessly, drawing confused stares from their fellow Year 12s as they passed by. "I think I found her!"

"What?"

"I'll explain on the way."

"On the way where?"

"To the music department. Let's go!"

A thoroughly bemused Kenta watched her speed off, box in hand. His stomach rumbled at the sight of the others heading to the canteen for lunch.

"Kenta, come on!" came Jessica's voice from further down the corridor, and Kenta was only embarrassed for a second or two before his curiosity got the better of him and he went after her.

He caught up to her as she was going up the stairs to the second floor. "What's in the box?"

"Yearbooks. From before they were digital. I had a hunch we'd find her in there."

"OO? How?"

"I knew there had to be a music connection, why else would they plan everything around that bloody koto? And it has to be someone closely connected to the school, or else why would they hate it so much? And who hates school more than a student?"

They reached the second floor and Jessica veered right, forcing Kenta to speed up to try to keep pace with her, even with the extra weight in her arms.

"And she spoke English too," Jessica went on as they came to the music department. "She spoke well, and almost with a British accent."

Not even pausing for a breath, and with the box balanced in the crook of one arm, she knocked heavily on the door to the main music room. They heard a faint reply come a moment later.

When they went in, Miss Shimada, the music teacher, was in the far corner packing away a set of mandolins. She was one of the older teachers at the school. Kenta put her in her early fifties at least. Dressed in her long grey skirt and black cardigan, she fit the stereotypical image of a teacher. Her shoulder-length hair was now a fifty-fifty mix of black and grey, and though she was what Kenta considered a fairly old woman, he often thought when looking at her long, narrow face that she must have been quite beautiful when she was younger.

She turned to see who it was and recognised him immediately. "Kenta!"

Though he no longer took music as a subject, she'd taught him when he was in the lower grades. She greeted Jessica, however, with a quizzical frown. "And who's this?"

"Hello, Miss. I'm Jessica Hunter. I'm a new pupil in Kenta's year."

Placing the last of the mandolins in a large plastic container, Miss Shimada walked towards them. "Yes, I've seen your face. Nice to meet you. What can I do for you both?"

With a relieved sigh, Jessica dropped the box of yearbooks on the nearest table. She was still a little agitated and out of breath, and Kenta watched her with a mixture of fascination and hesitancy as he wondered what she was going to say and do next.

"We need help with something. It's a... it's for an important project."

Miss Shimada glanced up at the clock above her teacher's desk. "Aren't you hungry?"

Kenta felt another stab of hunger at the mention of lunch, but Jessica didn't even acknowledge the question. Instead, she pulled one of the yearbooks from the box and flicked rapidly through the pages. When she'd found what she was looking for, she turned the open book towards Miss Shimada.

"Do you know this girl?"

Miss Shimada took a step closer, eyes narrowed as she peered at whoever it was. Kenta also moved closer for a look but couldn't see the photo. What he did see though was the flare of recognition in Miss Shimada's eyes.

"Hikaru," she said quietly, as if to herself. "Hikaru Kai... yes, I taught her when she was at the school. That was, what... almost ten years ago now."

"Yes, ten years exactly," said Jessica.

Miss Shimada remained caught in some brief private reverie before blinking and looking up from the photo. "I'm sorry? You say this is for a project? What does Hikaru have to do with it?"

Jessica and Kenta exchanged a look.

"It's connected with the koto in the foyer. I'm doing an English project on its history, and I also wanted to include something on a local koto player."

Kenta watched, more than a little impressed, as Jessica maintained an absolutely straight face while saying this. He wondered if she'd just made it up on the spot. Miss Shimada scrutinised her more closely, then her critical gaze fell on Kenta who found himself wanting to look away in embarrassment.

"That's an interesting topic," she said. "And you need Kenta to help you with this?"

Jessica opened her mouth to speak, but Kenta found himself butting in first. "I agreed to help her translate a few documents, and I'm also quite interested in the koto's history... Jessica's helping me with my assignment too."

Now it was Jessica's turn to look impressed. Clearly her knack for spouting spontaneous bullshit was rubbing off on him.

"Really, Kenta?" Both Miss Shimada's thick eyebrows went up on hearing this. "I don't remember you taking that much of an interest in anything music-related when I taught you..."

This time his cheeks burned, and Kenta avoided his old teacher's searching eyes.

"But anyway, of course I would like to help you, although it's been a long time since all that happened." Miss Shimada glanced at the clock a second time. "I do have to eat, but I can spare ten minutes."

She gestured for the two of them to sit at the closest pupil table while she took a chair facing them.

Now Kenta was finally able to see the yearbook when Jessica placed it on the table in front of her. He pretended to look casually but was taking in the photo with great interest. It was a girl, around fourteen years of age, standing on a stage in front of a koto with a trophy in her hands. Above her ran a banner for a Kansai music competition. The caption beneath

315

the photo confirmed it was Hikaru Kai. Kenta hadn't heard the name before, nor did he recognise her face. She looked much like any other teenager her age – dark shoulder-length hair in a ponytail, a small, rounded face registering a shy expression. She was noticeably short, but bore no distinctive birthmarks or features, and the fact she was wearing a school uniform only made her stand out that much less. How she could be OO or anyone associated with her was beyond Kenta. She certainly bore no resemblance to the demon geisha they'd encountered the other night, who still made Kenta shiver inwardly whenever he thought of her.

Miss Shimada pulled the book towards her for another look. She shook her head very slowly as she scanned the photo and article. "I hadn't thought about Hikaru in such a long time. It was a very unfortunate case."

As when she first saw the photo, the music teacher seemed to retreat into her own private memories for a moment before she pushed the book back across to Jessica.

"She was an incredibly talented musician," Miss Shimada went on. "Certainly the best I've encountered as a teacher. She was as good a koto player as you're ever likely to see. She'd been playing since she was five or so. Her father was the pushy sort, had a clear plan for his daughter, but there's no doubting she was a real natural. She won competition after competition. I think she won the Kansai regional championship twice in a row. She would've won the national one too, I'm quite sure about that…"

316

Miss Shimada trailed off, letting out a heavy sigh.

"Would have won?" said Jessica.

"Yes..." She joined her hands on the table and looked down at them fixedly. "Her parents wanted her to go to the Wells Cathedral School in the UK. It's one of the oldest and best music schools in the world. She was offered a place for the high school. In fact, she was offered a scholarship if I remember correctly. I was so proud of her as her teacher. You always hope for a pupil of her quality during your career. She had so much ahead of her, but..."

The classroom door burst open and all three of them turned to see a breathless little Year 7 boy standing in the doorway.

"Sorry, Miss!"

"What did you forget?" Miss Shimada called out, switching immediately into classroom teacher mode.

The boy stared at her in puzzlement.

"You forgot to knock."

"Oh yeah... sorry, Miss." The boy then proceeded to knock on the open door, which would have amused Kenta and Jessica if they weren't both so annoyed by the boy's terrible timing.

"I presume you've come for the clarinet that was left this morning?"

The boy nodded.

"It's on my desk. Hurry up and be more careful next time."

"Thanks, Miss." The boy scurried to the desk and picked up the long black clarinet case from Miss Shimada's desk. He threw

Kenta and Jessica a curious little look before scurrying back to the door. "Thanks, Miss."

Kenta feared Miss Shimada's annoyance would derail her story. He could virtually feel Jessica's burning anticipation at his side, but after a couple more seconds the teacher collected herself and continued on as if nothing had happened.

"Yes, it all went very badly wrong at a national competition in Tokyo. There was no question she would've won, at least in my opinion, but for reasons I'll never fully understand, she did something incredibly stupid."

As if she were seeing it all happening before her yet again, Miss Shimada shook her head, and a flash of annoyance crossed with disbelief momentarily contorted her features.

Kenta noticed Jessica leaning closer over the table. "What did she do?"

"She cheated," said Miss Shimada, forcing out the words.

"Cheated?" blurted Jessica, rather too excitedly in Kenta's opinion.

"Yes, it was such a reckless act. There was no need for it, none whatsoever. Perhaps it was the pressure, or some other psychological issue we weren't aware of. Either way, she was disqualified from the competition, and then when Wells Cathedral found out about it all, they withdrew their offer."

"What did she do exactly?" asked Jessica.

"She tampered with a competitor's instrument. They caught her red-handed. I wasn't there at the time, but there was no denying her guilt. She didn't even attempt to deny it. After that, none of the top music schools would go near her. Then to make things worse, the school expelled her too. Some silly rule about zero tolerance when it came to cheating in exams. I tried to convince Mr Murphy not to do it, but he wouldn't listen, said she'd tarnished the school's reputation."

"Mr Murphy?" Jessica perked up further. "He was still the headmaster back then?"

"Yes, it was his first year at BSK I think. He's been here a while now."

Instinctively, Kenta and Jessica glanced sideways at one another, their meaningful looks uttering a hundred things without a word being spoken.

"What happened to her after that?" said Kenta.

"As far as I can remember, her parents moved her back to Nagasaki, their hometown. Her father was a doctor if I remember correctly. I don't know what happened after that. They didn't keep in touch, and I didn't hear about her playing again... such a terrible waste."

"Nagasaki?" said Jessica. "And she'd be around twenty-five now? Do you know where she is now or what she's doing?"

Miss Shimada shook her head. "No idea. I don't think her parents wanted anything to do with me or the school after that. Maybe it was the shame... I did wonder about her for a long time afterwards though... such a talent."

"What about brothers? Sisters?" Jessica pressed.

"I think she had an older sister, but I can't be sure."

As Miss Shimada fell back into yet more sombre daydreams, staring off at the wall above Kenta's head, Jessica was already getting up.

"Well, thank you so much, Miss. That was extremely helpful."

Slightly startled, Miss Shimada came to. "I'd prefer it if you didn't mention what I've said about Hikaru's exclusion," she said, the doubt creeping back into her tone as though she was realising she had said too much.

"Of course, it's all off the record. It's just useful to know, that's all," said Jessica with absolute confidence, already picking up the box with the yearbooks.

Miss Shimada still looked quite unconvinced as the two of them began their retreat to the door. "Well, all right then..."

"Thanks again," called Jessica over a shoulder, and with that she pushed her way back out into the corridor with Kenta at her heels, leaving Miss Shimada still sitting at the table.

"It's her all right," said Jessica as she marched back towards the stairwell.

"You sure?" said Kenta. "That Hikaru doesn't look anything like the geisha... and you heard what Miss Shimada said, they went back to Nagasaki. That's miles away."

"Don't be ridiculous! That was ten years ago. She could be anywhere now."

For a second, Kenta found himself stung by Jessica's tone. Wasn't he the one helping her out and missing his lunch? But as usual he resisted the pang of annoyance and carried on walking.

He could see she was in the zone again. It wasn't personal, and she wouldn't have cared anyway even if he'd said something.

"We need to find out all we can about Hikaru Kai – where she is now, what she's doing. I'd put a lot of money on her not being in Nagasaki right now."

Jessica was racing down the stairs now in a hurry.

"Shouldn't we pass this on to Detective Yamada?" said Kenta, knowing the reaction he'd get before he even spoke.

"Ha!" Jessica snorted. "You've got to be joking! They'd look at that photo of a little schoolgirl from ten years ago and laugh at us all over again. Besides, there isn't even any solid evidence yet, but I just know it's her."

A further note of doubt rang amongst Kenta's thoughts, but he said nothing. Jessica was a person possessed, her voice rapid and frenetic like her movements. There wasn't a force in the world that would change her mind now.

When they reached the first floor, Jessica stopped quite suddenly and turned to Kenta. Looking him directly in the eye with an almost wild stare, she said, "It's just you and me, okay? Just like it has been from the start. The police, the headmaster, none of them are going to do a thing. This is about the school and Mr Murphy, just like I said. Something is going to happen on Thursday if we don't stop it."

Like a rabbit in headlights, Kenta could only blink and stare in response.

"I'm going to need your help finding info online. Meet me in the library last break. And bring your laptop."

And with that, she tore on along the corridor, disappearing around a corner with the box in her hands while a befuddled and very hungry Kenta watched her go, knowing full well his life was continuing along an ever-stranger path, with no way to turn back.

CHAPTER 37

When she got to the library she found Kenta waiting in a quiet corner, away from prying eyes.

"I can't be late for next period," he complained. "Mr Simmons will kill me."

"Whatever, let's get to it then. First thing is to see if there's any mention of her online."

The first online searches only turned up one or two old articles about Hikaru's victories in regional competitions. One had a photo which was nearly identical to the one from the yearbook – a young, smiling schoolgirl standing beside a koto with a trophy in her hands. Jessica almost felt pity for her. If only that girl knew what would become of her and her talents. There was a reference to her being disqualified from the national competition for cheating. There was no photo there and only a few basic details. After that, there was nothing else they could find on her.

"Didn't Miss Shimada say she had a sister?"

"I already asked at reception," said Jessica. "All they would tell me is no sibling of Hikaru Kai's ever went to BSK. They couldn't even find an address for the family. The only thing for it is to find her father, the doctor. Can't be many Dr Kais in Nagasaki."

"Japanese people don't give their personal information out easily," said Kenta. "People are more private here."

A minute later and he was regretting those words when a name showed up.

"There!" Jessica pointed at an English entry on the screen. "Dr Benjiro Kai. The Nagasaki University Hospital."

They clicked through to the hospital's website, and quickly found the doctor's details. He was a senior surgeon. The photo accompanying his profile presented an unsmiling man in his sixties with rounded spectacles on a round face.

"Call the hospital now!" said Jessica excitedly.

"Now? We're still in school."

"So? No one can see us here."

"What am I supposed to say anyway?"

"Just say '*Hello, can I speak to Dr Kai, please.*' It's easy!"

"You serious?" said Kenta incredulously. "No way. I'm not doing it now. I'll email them if there's an address."

Jessica rolled her eyes. "Do you want to solve this or not?"

"Yes, of course I do. But I'll do it my way. You can't just call someone up like that, it's not right. Anyways, I'm the Japanese speaker, not you."

"Fine, fine," Jessica groaned. "But do it now, time is of the essence!"

Despite wanting to tell her where to go, as usual he saw it was futile trying to resist the onslaught of her laser-like focus, and he opened his email instead so that he could be done with it.

Jessica dictated a message, filled with the usual made-up crap, this time concerning a research paper into the school's talented alumni which wouldn't be complete without a profile on the famous koto champion, Hikaru Kai. Kenta, who was not at all happy at putting his name to so brazen a lie, translated it into Japanese and pressed send before his conscience could get in the way.

"There, it's done!" he said, closing the laptop. "Now what?"

A burst of laughter erupted from a table of girls at the other side of the library, followed swiftly by a warning to be quiet from the librarian.

"So, what do we do now?" said Kenta.

The girls broke into yet another round of muted sniggering, and it seemed to Jessica that like OO and Detective Yamada, and pretty much everyone else, they were really laughing at her, the schoolgirl who thought she could solve real crimes. But they wouldn't be laughing for long.

"We just wait," said Jessica, getting to her feet. "I know this is it, I can feel it. We'll have OO in our sights in no time."

There was nothing obviously amiss as they went downstairs to retrieve the necessary books for the last two periods. Jessica's mind was still fizzing with all manner of possibilities and outcomes even as she approached the small crowd gathered by the Year 12 lockers. *What is it this time*, she thought, *some idiot pupil's graffiti again or something more serious?*

Pushing her way through the semicircle of people observing whatever the spectacle was, Jessica found that the centre of everyone's attention was her own locker. Kneeling in front of it, removing items, was Mr Takagi, while the headmaster stood over him, watching the proceedings as though supervising an act of grave importance.

She saw too that Kenta's locker was open and that several things had been taken out of it and left on the floor. Jessica wanted to ask just what the hell they were doing but already eyes were pivoting in her direction, and to her left there was a commotion as another figure was pushing through the wall of onlookers. And then Kenta was there, surveying the scene with an expression of befuddlement followed by a growing horror.

They could only swap the briefest of startled glances as their persons became the source of even greater scrutiny, with even Mr Murphy casting an accusing look over the two of them.

There were other familiar faces regarding them with a mixture of suspicion, disgust and disbelief. Milo was there, eyeing Jessica with complete contempt. A bewildered Rina looked the two of them over with her big sad eyes. Tomo was present too, just arriving at the back of the opposite group of spectators, watching on helplessly. And then Jessica already knew what it was. She didn't need to be read her rights. She'd been outmanoeuvred plain and simple. It was all too late. So very late.

CHAPTER 38

From Jessica's locker they'd removed three near-empty cans of black spray paint matching the paint used to deface the auditorium, a geisha costume and several posters bearing the letters OO. In Kenta's they'd discovered a single USB which purportedly contained the malicious software used to hack the school's server.

When Jessica demanded to know how they'd come across this information, sitting across from the headmaster in his office, he said only that an anonymous tip-off from a concerned person had led them to her and Kenta's lockers.

Jessica let out a single guffaw. "Ha! How very convenient. If you believe this, then you'll believe anything."

This time it was her alone in the office. She'd been kept apart from Kenta, who was sitting outside waiting for his turn on the stand.

Mr Murphy glowered at her. "I knew there was something wrong about that whole thing with the geisha. I should have trusted my instincts. I knew it was you really, playing your twisted little games, thinking you could undermine me and my school. Well, I'm afraid your time at BSK will be rather short-lived. Needless to say, you are suspended with immediate effect while we investigate, pending a likely expulsion. Your father's been called and is on his way. This is probably going to be a police matter too."

Sending back every ounce of disdain she was receiving from the headmaster, Jessica held her tongue with great effort while he spoke, then said, "It wouldn't be the first time, would it?"

"I beg your pardon?"

"It wouldn't be the first time you've expelled a pupil. That's exactly what you did to Hikaru Kai, isn't it?" She watched as the headmaster's eyebrows rose ever so slightly at the mention of the name.

"What are you talking about?"

"I'm talking about the pupil you expelled back in 2013 when you were the new headmaster. She was a star koto player, and you expelled her for cheating in a competition."

There was a glimmer of remembrance in the headmaster's dark hazel eyes. "What the hell has that got to do with anything?" he barked, his fledgling jowls shivering.

"It has everything to do with everything," replied Jessica with calculated calm. "Your past is coming back to haunt you,

Mr Murphy, and you'll find out on Thursday evening, if not before."

The headmaster stared at Jessica as he had during their last meeting in his office, as though she were some strange anomalous object that both perplexed and infuriated him. But then he found his feet again, and the jowls shivered further as he worked his way up to one of his apoplectic rages.

"Is that a threat?" he growled.

"No, it's a simple fact. Framing Kenta and me is part of their plan, and if you just did the most basic of investigations, you would see that. You're doing exactly what she wants."

"Enough!" The headmaster near-shouted, waving his hand dismissively. "Get out of my office! I'll speak to your father when he arrives."

"It's your funeral." With a surly flash of a grin and a bow, Jessica got up and left the room, positively brimming with virtuous indignation, but the sight of Kenta's face as she walked past where he was sitting slowed her steps. He looked utterly broken, and when she went to say something, he turned away from her and went straight into the headmaster's office without a word.

CHAPTER 39

Kenta's parents arrived together an hour later, having been forced to leave work after receiving an emergency phone call from the school. They'd presumed Kenta was hurt, and didn't quite believe it when they were told he was in trouble – at least not until they were sitting beside him in the headmaster's office listening to the list of charges levelled against him, with the headmaster's secretary translating for Mr Higashi's benefit.

His father remained stony-faced throughout, perhaps in disbelief, while his mother couldn't hide her distress, sitting open-mouthed as she listened, glancing occasionally at Kenta beside her, though he only stared down at the floor in front of him.

"But there has to be some mistake!" said his mother once Mr Murphy had finished. "Kenta was at computer club that night."

Mr Murphy looked at Kenta. "I'm afraid your son hasn't been honest with you at all about his recent activities. I have to admit this is very surprising, Kenta. You've always been an exemplary pupil, and the current football team captain."

"Kenta?" His mother was staring at him now imploringly.

A drawn-out silence followed as all eyes fell on Kenta, waiting for him to speak, after which he had no choice but to admit to being there that night with Jessica, although he denied any wrongdoing other than hiding in the school after hours. But then the questions kept coming about all the other nights he'd come home late from school recently, including the Friday when he'd been attacked at knifepoint and had visited the police station twice. Unable to lie about any of it, Kenta admitted to the slight deception on these occasions.

"Why, Kenta?" said his mother, while his father only shook his head, but when he tried to explain why, he could see he'd already exhausted any trust his parents had placed in him. His protestations about only trying to stop OO seemed to fall on deaf ears, and when Kenta attempted to pull up his trouser leg to show his knee injury as proof of the close scrape with OO herself, his mother snapped at him to "Please, stop!"

"But ask Jessica, she'll confirm all of this!" Kenta protested further, banging down a balled fist on his good leg.

"I think that's the problem," said Mr Murphy in a condescendingly knowing tone. "Everything was going well for you until your association with Jessica Hunter began. It's possible you've been deceived. I think that's something you need to reflect on."

Rather than nodding or agreeing immediately as he would have done once, he felt instead a surge of hot bile rising up in him, enough so that it almost made him scream in the headmaster's face, and at his parents too for not believing him, and then at himself for letting it all go so far. But instead he kept it in, so that it pulsed painfully, and he went inside himself, barely hearing anything any more.

It was the same in the meeting room where he had to speak with the policewoman who'd interviewed him the previous week. This time she wasn't quite so friendly. Her questions were focused around the USB and the school cyberattack, as well as his claims about seeing Yudai.

He denied having anything to do with the USB or the intranet hack, and stuck by his account of tracking down Yudai, and his belief that his old friend was behind the whole hacking incident. It was also at this point that his parents were informed of Kenta's previous secret visits to the police, and his claims of being attacked – it was a serious offence to waste police time, didn't Kenta know that?

It was clear from the police officer's questions that no one believed him any longer. Not even his mother, the person who'd always believed in him his whole life.

"Please, Kenta. Just tell them the truth!" she told him at one point, her voice breaking, after which he had to lock down the rising anger once again and resorted to "Yes" and "No" answers,

while simply wishing this new and hostile world would all just
fade away.

CHAPTER 40

Jessica, back in the headmaster's office beside her father, was resorting to a similar display of single-word responses.

Mr Hunter, who had initially been furious at being called away from a meeting in Nara, grew increasingly quiet during the headmaster's breakdown of her misdemeanours. Jessica was sure he was relishing it now and could only shake her head and snort contemptuously every few seconds.

When he'd heard everything, her father could only turn to her in wide-eyed wonder and say, "Jessica?", almost as if he were asking for her reassurance that this was in fact all nonsense.

"I'll say it for the last time, I deny absolutely any wrongdoing," she announced defiantly, crossing her arms in front of her chest. She wasn't going to back down now or cower as the headmaster hoped. The more they pushed, the harder she'd push back. It was the only way she'd ever known. "I was simply trying to save the school from impending doom, part of which is Mr Murphy's fault."

"Excuse me?" The headmaster gawped at her, open-mouthed.

"Jessica!" exclaimed her father.

She went on, ignoring both of them. "So, if attempting to stop a criminal is a crime in itself, then yes, I'm guilty as charged. Lock me up!"

While her father remained speechless, Mr Murphy could barely hold back the sneer of contempt from his face. He repeated his spiel about Jessica being suspended with a view to permanently expelling her, noting that her poor attitude and contempt for the teachers and her school had already been noted before any of the koto business had taken place. He finished by recommending she receive a psychological evaluation, at which point Jessica laughed out loud.

"Good luck this week!" she muttered on her way out the door, meeting the headmaster's eye one last time while her father was doing his best to apologise profusely for everything.

It was as she crossed the foyer on her way to the meeting room and more questions from the police, that she saw Kenta coming out with his parents.

It wasn't necessary to ask him how he was. If before he'd appeared broken, now he looked like an empty shell of himself.

His parents came up behind him, looking every bit as weary as Kenta. His father was much shorter than him, with neat greying hair, and dressed in an oversized grey suit. His mother was a graceful-looking woman with shoulder-length hair and a white cardigan over a floral dress. She looked a few years younger than her husband, and Jessica could see the Korean features that figured so strongly in Kenta's own. Her eyes were red and puffy from crying, and she walked as if she were sleeping or not quite fully conscious.

Kenta also looked out of it as Jessica made a beeline for him, ignoring a warning to keep away from him from Miss Eguchi, who'd been tasked with shepherding Jessica to the police interview.

"Don't ever admit to anything," she said to him, after which he seemed to come to. "You haven't done anything wrong, don't forget that!"

It was at this point Kenta's parents must have cottoned on to who this pale, gangly foreign girl was – and immediately they spirited Kenta away to the main doors as though saving him from the clutches of some murderous creature.

"And don't forget the doctor too! He's our only hope now!" she called out one last time as Kenta went through the open doors with his parents on either side of him.

Chapter 41

The remainder of that Tuesday passed like a blur for Kenta. He could do nothing but lie on his bed and stare disconsolately at the ceiling. He didn't want to eat, didn't want to speak with either of his parents, who remained more than a little shell-shocked themselves. His mother had cried during the car journey all the way back home, while his father remained silent and grave, flashes of the strain showing occasionally in his hard stare through the windscreen.

The crying continued at home. Kenta could hear his mother weeping in the kitchen, and his father consoling her. It was the worst thing he'd ever heard in his life. It made him want to collapse off the bed and be swallowed up by a dark endless void so he'd never have to see anyone or anything ever again.

Later there were knocks on his door from his father, but Kenta said he didn't want to talk. If he had his way, he'd never utter another word to a living soul for the remainder of his days. The anguish roiled in his guts. The fury, the helplessness, the despair. But at the same time that he believed he'd let his parents down terribly, he also felt utterly betrayed by them and the world at large for not believing him, as unbelievable as some of his story probably sounded.

More than anything, it was the dreamlike unreality of it all that was most disturbing. He'd wake from fitful naps and for a second would forget that he'd effectively been permanently expelled from school and still faced a possible investigation by the police. But then it would all come flooding back and he'd groan all over again, imagining the burned-out shell that was his future life, a future without university or job prospects or any kind of happiness.

His parents had taken his phone from him, probably so that the demon Jessica wouldn't be able to get in touch. He still had his SIM card, which he'd removed beforehand just in case, and a battered old spare phone in his desk drawer. But he didn't dare look at his messages, at least not yet. He knew Jessica would try to contact him even if she wasn't supposed to, but she was the last person he wanted to talk to. It was as if the mere act of reading a message from her would incriminate him beyond redemption. He imagined the police were monitoring every last thing he did. He'd already had to give up his laptop at school to the police.

But it wasn't just that either. Some part of him wanted to blame her for what had happened, even as he knew he'd gone along willingly with every one of her schemes. The police, the headmaster and even his parents had encouraged him to effectively denounce Jessica, laying the blame on her as though she were some evil mastermind who'd used him as an unwitting pawn in her diabolical plans. He'd refused of course, telling them she was as innocent as he was. He also had to explain more than once with great exasperation that she wasn't his girlfriend, or even really a friend, only a school colleague with a mutual interest. But still, that didn't stop Kenta from having dreams that night in which Jessica, complete with a maniacal grin, led hordes of faceless beings in taunting and laughing at him while he remained unable to respond or get away. He even woke up on Wednesday morning with freshly paranoid thoughts which had him questioning absolutely everything, including Jessica herself.

It wasn't impossible that she could have actually somehow been behind it all, that it was all simply a game for her, a way to play everyone against each other simply for her own enjoyment. She certainly had the brains and the scheming nature to pull it off, and he'd seen first-hand her willingness to flout the rules. Maybe he'd been wrong all along. Perhaps he really was some bumbling fool who'd allowed himself to be manipulated by an evil sociopathic genius.

When his clarity returned, Kenta angrily dismissed such thoughts. It wasn't possible. He shouldn't entertain them for a second. But it had shaken him nonetheless, so much so that he wasn't sure who he was supposed to believe or trust in any more.

That Wednesday morning, both his parents went to work. His mother knocked on his door softly and left food for him on a tray outside, but he wouldn't collect it until she was gone, by which time the omelette was cold.

It was hard to get the food down, as he still didn't have much of an appetite, but Kenta managed a few bites and a glass of orange juice. He might have wanted to be alone, but now that he was truly by himself in the apartment, he only felt even more hopeless.

In a fit of loneliness, he put the SIM card into the old phone from his drawer and held his breath while he waited to see who'd contacted him.

As he'd feared and expected, there were six messages from Jessica and another six missed calls. He gulped and made himself read a few of them.

Tuesday, 2.05pm

Jessica: *Are you seriously going to take this lying down? We can't let them get away with this!*

Tuesday, 3.30pm

Jessica: *Come on, Kenta! I don't care if you're feeling depressed or whatever, we can't give up, not now!*

Tuesday, 5.20pm

Jessica: *Really? Is this what you're reducing me to? A serial texter? Do you want me to beg or something? Okay, I can't do this without you! It sickens me to say it, but we work pretty well as a team. Now message me for god's sake!*

Tuesday, 8.08pm

Jessica: *Right, that's how it is then? Or maybe you're in a fit of despair, maybe you don't even have your phone... I'll email then. Either way, I'm not giving up, Kenta Higashi!*

Tuesday, 11.48pm

Jessica: *This is getting very boring. At least send me something so I know you're still a functioning human being. And what about Dr Kai? Have you heard from him yet?*

Wednesday, 8.45am

Jessica: *I give up. If you want to bury your head in the sand, be my guest. I, on the other hand, will be at the school Friday night even if it kills me. We've come too far. I'm not letting that lunatic beat me. This is my last message.*

Kenta re-read Jessica's last message several more times. "*I'll be at the school Friday night even if it kills me.*" The phrase had a terribly ominous ring to it. The school had made it very clear that neither of them were to set foot on school property until they were allowed back, which would probably never happen now anyway. He didn't doubt her for a second. If she wanted to be there, then she'd find a way. That was Jessica in a nutshell – fearless and totally reckless. Well, it was her life, not his.

Disregarding her messages for the time being, Kenta pored over the others he'd received. Shun and Milo had been the first friends to contact him, followed by a few other members of the football team.

Tuesday, 6.40pm

Shun: *Kenta, dude. What the hell, man? What's going on? They say you've been expelled? :-o No way! I told everyone it's bullshit. What's going on?*

Tuesday 5.16pm

Milo: *You really been expelled, bro? And crazy bitch Hunter, too? People are saying all kinds of mad shit... like you both did all that OO stuff.*

The other messages contained similar exclamations of disbelief, some of them firmly on Kenta's side while others, like Milo, couldn't help voicing at least a little doubt. A painful flinch struck Kenta somewhere in the chest when he realised some of his friends even believed he was guilty. Like his parents and the headmaster, they probably blamed Jessica too, which instead of giving Kenta any solace, only made him angrier. It was as if no one believed he possessed his own agency, his own sense of right or wrong.

The same fury he'd experienced at times the day before began to bubble its way back up to the surface. It reminded him that he'd been framed, that someone had intentionally planted that USB in his locker and informed the headmaster, knowing it would ruin his life. He wanted to hurl the phone against the wall above his bed, then failing that, fought an urge to punch the wall over and over, if only to feel something.

Instead, he punched his pillow once, twice, and kept on going, punching and punching until he found himself almost screaming. When he stopped, there were tears in his eyes.

Exhausted, Kenta fell back on his bed and resumed his vigil of staring at the ceiling. Beneath his leg he felt a slight shiver and realised it was his phone. He considered ignoring it and found himself staring at the screen anyway. Unusually, he'd received an SMS rather than a Line message. He didn't recognise the number either, and when he opened it up, he saw it contained only a single word:

Sorry.

The sight of this lone word made Kenta sit up, at first confused, then curious. *Who is this?* he typed in response, but the message remained undelivered. Next, Kenta tried to call but found the sender had already blocked his number.

He stared at the message a while longer, baffled even as he knew deep down who it was and why they'd sent it, which only confirmed what Kenta had feared all along – that if the USB in the locker really did hold the virus used against the school, then the only person he knew who could have made it was none other than his old friend, Yudai Matsumoto.

CHAPTER 42

Like Kenta, Jessica pretty much found herself under house arrest for the remainder of that Tuesday. While she was sitting at her desk, furiously scribbling in the notebook every last detail and scrap of evidence she could think of concerning the case, she could also clearly hear her parents arguing downstairs. Her mother had come home early from whatever conference she'd been at, while her father had cleared the rest of his working day.

"For god's sake, Peter. I think you're overreacting," her mother was saying with her usual Italian lilt.

"Overreacting? Are you serious? Our daughter is about to get expelled from her new school for some pretty disturbing behaviour, and you think I'm overreacting!"

"She's just bored. She's a highly intelligent girl. She needs the proper stimulation."

"She's not bored," replied her father, doing his best not to sound irate but mostly failing. "This is a cry for help if ever I saw one. We've been neglecting her. I told you something like this would happen if we didn't spend more time with her."

"A cry for help? Oh, come on! This is just a hissy fit. She's stomping her feet because she didn't want to move again. It was the same when we left Mumbai. She'll get over it soon enough."

"A hissy fit? This is pathological. She's been terrorising the place, for Christ's sake!"

Her mother let out a short high-pitched laugh. "Pathological? Now you really are overdoing it."

"My god, Eleonora! Listen to yourself... our daughter needs help. She's too much like your father, as in she has absolutely no morals whatsoever."

"Oh really, Peter? You don't seem to complain when you take a pay cheque from him every month."

"God, please don't start that again."

And on it went as Jessica's manic scribbling and sketching produced page after page. She too refused food and wouldn't answer any knocks or soft voices on the other side of her bedroom door. She tore out pages and stuck them to the wall until it resembled the noticeboard of a detective's office, or at least the ones she'd seen in movies.

When she'd exhausted this exercise with no result, she began messaging and calling Kenta, though she wasn't the least bit surprised when he didn't respond. Perhaps she'd never hear from him again. They'd both be turfed out and sent on to whichever school would accept them.

Seeing no other choice, Jessica attempted to contact Dr Kai herself, but no one was replying to her d emails, and no one could speak English when she called the hospital's main contact number. Since she had zero Japanese friends to speak of and knew Yuko wouldn't be able or allowed to assist her, Jessica could only stare at another big fat dead end.

Like the previous night, she'd barely slept. Her mind raced and calculated, seeking desperately to find some scrap of hope and reason amongst the chaos, but Wednesday morning brought nothing except exhaustion and a sinking feeling of dread that wasn't like anything she'd experienced before. It was as close to admitting defeat as Jessica had ever come. She hadn't realised just how important unmasking and therefore beating OO was to her until it had been snatched away.

She'd even been starting to imagine something of a future in Kyoto. It wasn't so bad after all. She was warming to the strange combination of ancient history and wacky contemporary culture, and in all this investigating she had found, for the first time in her teenage life, something that really inspired and fired her up. She wanted to know, wanted to solve the peculiar and chaotic mysteries life sometimes presented. But now they might have to leave again, and this time it would be because of her.

Her father had taken the day off work to be in the house with her, which was pretty much unprecedented, though she was aware it was as much to guard over her while she languished in her prison as it was to attempt to reason with her through the door. The headmaster had made it quite clear – if she and Kenta at least apologised for what they'd done, then it would go some way to mitigating the damage. "Just own up to your part in it, there's no harm in that," her father had said gently more than once, which made her want to kill him and cry all at once. It wasn't easy being falsely accused, she'd come to realise. But at least she knew the truth, and Kenta too. There was a righteous indignation in this knowledge which kept her going.

But of course, there was at least one other person who knew as well.

Several times over the course of Wednesday and Thursday, Jessica found herself staring out of a bedroom window towards the distant hills and mountains, imagining her, the enemy, laughing wholeheartedly at her victory. Just the thought of this knotted Jessica's insides with a fury so white-hot she thought she might scream, which was when she knew there was still a spark in her. It was at least enough to get her to the school on Friday evening no matter what it took, if only to have the chance to see her nemesis face to face – because she was certain OO would be there. She wouldn't miss the icing on the cake of her master plan.

And so, Jessica continued to stare over the rooftops, her eyes fixed on some unknowable point, her eyes tired and sore but her heart still aflame.

CHAPTER 43

On Friday morning the school was already a hive of activity before the first bell had even sounded. In the foyer there was a lot of fuss around the koto, which was being removed from the glass case by a team of museum staff dressed in black trousers and T-shirts, much like the ones Jessica had encountered at the museum itself.

Mrs Nakamura was there too with her assistant, supervising and issuing commands every so often. The museum crew was slowly lowering the koto onto a large trolley before transporting it to the auditorium in preparation for the evening's event.

The school's security team was more active than usual, and the museum had brought in one of their own security guards as well, perhaps just as a precaution, but also possibly in light of all the recent goings-on at the school.

Elsewhere, pupils in kimonos and warrior garb and other official historical dress wandered the corridors to and from rehearsals while the headmaster zipped past them, checking constantly between the foyer and auditorium, carrying a general air of heightened tension which he covered up with copious practised grins. But overall, there was a buzz in the air, an excitement tinged with nervousness. The pupils and teachers alike were eager to put all the controversy and drama behind them now, and the festival performance tonight, along with the Jidai Matsuri festival itself that weekend, would naturally signal a new chapter.

But there was one amongst them, already walking the corridors even as they rehearsed, who knew differently. Tonight would be the night only for endings. It wouldn't be long now. They'd waited all this time for this day and there were only a few more hours until it was done.

CHAPTER 44

A sombre atmosphere continued to hang over the Higashi household. The two parents were now barely speaking to one another, partly because they were both similarly terrified for their son's future, and also because they were beginning to resent one another for not having seen that there was something the matter with Kenta.

Kenta, on the other hand, was keeping up his vow of silence, emerging from his room only to use the toilet and collect the food that continued to appear at his door. He ignored passionate and tearful entreaties from his mother to see sense and write a letter of apology to the headmaster before it was too late. Her tears didn't move him quite so much any more, and his father's attempts at resorting to angry voices and threats had also had little effect. Even his sister had been calling the house from her university dorm in Tokyo wanting to speak with Kenta and no doubt chastise him too, but he'd given her the cold shoulder. He'd gone overnight from being that most unusual of teenage boys – one who rarely argued with his parents – to one who wouldn't even acknowledge them.

This is my life now, Kenta thought, lying on his bed on Friday morning. To be locked up in his room, away from school, friends, normal life, a stranger to his parents. This was just how it was. Kenta Higashi, school football captain, Grade A pupil, was no more, a figment of his imagination. Now it was Kenta, ex-captain, ex-pupil, fledgling dropout and loser. He might as well get used to it.

He was alone in the apartment now that his parents had each gone to work, but still he couldn't rouse himself for a shower. He'd only been at home a couple of days but looking at himself in the mirror was already starting to become an unpleasant event, what with his unkempt hair, bloodshot eyes and sallow skin.

Since homework had been rendered pointless, he at least had the opportunity to write some of his novel, but even that was beyond him. He'd tried a couple of times, but it had been so long since he'd had the time or energy to write, that he couldn't even remember where the story had been going and only stared blankly at the pages of his notebook.

In the end, the only activity he could manage was to watch anime movies on his laptop, which demanded the least amount of brainpower and was an effective distraction from all the disturbing thoughts vying for his attention.

At one point, around 11am, he opened his email, partly out of morbid curiosity and partly from a desperate need for connection with anyone at all. The mystery sender of the "sorry' text hadn't been in touch again, and some part of him perhaps hoped to find an email from them instead, or a message from the school forgiving him for everything and welcoming him back with open arms.

Of course, there were no such emails in his inbox when he opened it up. He disregarded the one he'd received from Jessica, which would just repeat what she'd already said in her phone messages. He couldn't help wondering if she was still planning something for that afternoon, and if so, what it would involve. But that kind of thinking was what had landed him in this mess in the first place.

Elsewhere in his inbox, he scanned a few sci-fi fan club emails and one or two special offers that had evaded his spam. But there was one subject header that caught his attention. He didn't recognise the sender's name at first, but on closer inspection saw the name "Kai' in the email address.

Kenta sat up with a start. He swallowed hard and clicked on the email.

The first words he saw in scanning the message were *Nagasaki University Hospital* in the signature at the bottom, along with the sender's name, Dr Benjiro Kai.

There was no greeting or sign-off, not even a "yours sincerely', and the automatic signature at the bottom was the only indicator of the sender. The email itself was a single sentence.

Please consult Dr Kutsuna Higuchi of the Katsukune Clinic in Kyoto for all matters relating to Hikaru.

That was it. It was as curt and matter of fact as it could be, but at least it provided a lead.

Without thinking, Kenta found himself searching for Dr Benjiro Kai's name again online, and found a picture of him on the Nagasaki University Hospital's website. He was a relatively regular-looking older Japanese man, probably in his early sixties with short grey hair and a stern look across his bespectacled face.

Next, he searched for Dr Kutsuna Higuchi. He got a hit right away on the Katsukune Clinic website. It was quickly apparent that it was a clinic for plastic surgery and eye laser treatment. There was a photo of her along with the other team of surgeons. She was quite young, in her early to mid-thirties. He figured she must be their prime suspect's sister, but there was nothing in her appearance to suggest it. In her photo she was smiling, giving her a far more welcoming air than Dr Benjiro Kai.

Slowly it began to sink in. This might actually be it, the missing link. If Jessica was right, and the culprit was Hikaru Kai, then this person could be the one to lead them to her.

There was no email address for the doctor, only a general one for the clinic, along with a phone number. Kenta's first instinct was to message Jessica, and he found himself picking up his phone automatically, but his finger only hovered over her name on the screen. She'd know what to do. Even if she was locked away somewhere, Jessica would find a way out, but then Kenta imagined the secret police descending on him the moment they were together, waiting for the infamous criminal duo to continue their scheming. No doubt Jessica would receive the brunt of the blame again, while Kenta would be seen as the gullible sidekick, duped into her latest plan. No, he could do this one himself.

Returning to the clinic's website page, Kenta considered first emailing then calling, but what the hell was he supposed to say? *"Hello, may I please speak with Dr Higuchi about her psychopathic little sister?"* Besides, it would take too long. The clock was ticking. The performance was only a few hours away.

Kenta peered out of his window over the river, eyeing the outside world from which he'd been temporarily banished. Next, he looked to his bedroom door, then by habit at his trainers where they sat against the wall, untouched since Tuesday. It would be so much easier to let it go, to leave OO to her twisted plans, to let his parents and friends keep on believing he was some reprobate in the hope it would one day blow over. But then he thought too of his friends sitting in the auditorium, and then came the image of the geisha's knife, the blood on his hands from the dead rat. He didn't want to think about what was in store for the real targets of OO's malice.

Kenta didn't even leave a message for his parents. His trainers were on his feet and jacket pulled over his shoulders before he even knew what was happening. And then he was charging down the stairs, feeling himself being drawn towards something big and frightening, though he didn't yet know what it was.

CHAPTER 45

Katsukune Clinic was only a five-minute walk from Katsura Station in West Kyoto. The imperial villa was nearby too. Kenta remembered visiting the famous gardens there once when he was a kid, but he hadn't been to this part of Kyoto in a long time. There was never any need to unless you were playing tourist, and this kind of district, with its fancy residences and wealthy inhabitants, wasn't his kind of place. This was where the rich kids of BSK belonged.

The entrance to the clinic was in a brand-new corporate block set within a residential area of small yet expensive-looking houses, a mixture of modern and traditional homes with carefully manicured gardens, much like in Kitayama where Jessica lived. Kenta looked up at its reflective windows and fresh cream-coloured walls and felt rather shabby. He still hadn't showered in a while and he was wearing old jogging pants and the same T-shirt he'd slept in beneath his jacket.

For a brief moment, as he stared at the clinic's glass front doors, Kenta found himself wavering. His mouth went dry at the same time his paranoia was returning in floods. He looked about him. The street was relatively quiet, yet still he imagined hidden pairs of eyes watching him, just as he'd done on the train journey over. But then he pictured Jessica at his side, heard what she'd say if he was hesitating – *"Suit yourself, I'm going in anyway."*

Shaking off the last of his resistance, Kenta bunched his fists, took a large steeling breath, and pushed on through the doors.

He found himself in a profoundly white and pristine reception area. The floor was comprised of polished white tiles, which gleamed in the light. The walls were the same, along with the ceiling. Even the reception desk was a long snowy white island, and the soothing lighting, along with the many tall indoor plants littered about the place, was obviously designed to offer a highly calming environment. To Kenta, it all looked so utterly fake and sterile.

There was no one sitting in the waiting area. The only other person was the receptionist, a young woman with a practiced gleaming white smile that went so well with the decor. Emblazoned across the wall behind her was the Katsukune Clinic name and logo. Overcoming yet more urges to retreat, he made himself walk to the counter.

The receptionist bowed her head ever so slightly. "Hello, how may I help you?"

Kenta swallowed hard and cleared his parched throat. "I'd like to see Dr Higuchi, please."

"Do you have an appointment?"

"Erm... no, but it's important."

Her professional smile gave way to a light frown. "I am afraid she's due to have a consultation shortly and is booked into surgery for the rest of the day. Perhaps you'd like to make an appointment for another time?"

Kenta noticed her looking him up and down, probably in judgement of his scruffiness – or was she trying to ascertain what was wrong with him, why he might be there in the first place?

"Please tell her it's about her sister, Hikaru. It's very important."

The receptionist tilted her head ever so slightly at the mention of the doctor's sister. Kenta saw her lips part to say something, then she thought otherwise.

"Please, this is no joke," he added imploringly.

After further deliberation, the receptionist picked up the phone, and with one more doubtful glance in Kenta's direction, quietly repeated what he'd said into the receiver.

She'd barely replaced the phone when Kenta heard a door opening along a narrow passageway at the back of the reception area. A figure approached them, and Kenta recognised Dr Higuchi instantly. She was slightly older now than in the website photo, but still possessed the same impressive businesslike grace. She was dressed in a black suit with a pale blue blouse.

She looked first to the receptionist and then to Kenta, giving him the same bemused up-and-down assessment. "Can I help you?"

Kenta floundered momentarily under her sharp scrutiny, then remembered to breathe. "I need to speak with you about Hikaru."

"Is she in trouble?" the doctor replied, letting her more professional voice drop for a second.

"She might be. That's why I'm here."

He watched as she digested this information, and after a brief moment the look of alarm that had crossed her features quickly retreated.

"You'd better come with me," she said to Kenta, glancing towards the receptionist to let her know it was okay.

Kenta followed the doctor back along the passageway. She opened the door and beckoned for him to enter. There was a sternness in her face and posture that made Kenta instantly nervous, and the trauma of the other day, when he'd been led into the school meeting room with his parents to face the police officer's questions, came flooding back.

The doctor closed the door behind him, then gestured for him to sit in one of the two chairs facing her own. "Please, take a seat."

Kenta did as he was told, giving the room a quick visual sweep while he waited for the doctor to take her place in the leather swivel chair behind a large mahogany desk.

The office itself was slightly smaller than Kenta had expected. Like the reception area, it had a polished clinical look about it, with more gleaming tiled flooring and fresh white walls decorated with framed photographs of beautiful Japanese nature scenes. Above the doctor's head, there were several framed professional certificates and awards, and a large family portrait of her with her husband and two little girls in formal dresses. It was a perfect image of a happy, attractive family.

Once she'd taken her seat, something in the doctor seemed to change. The semi-smile she'd been holding collapsed into something more neutral, and her general demeanour appeared to cool several degrees in an instant.

"Look, I'm not sure who you are or how you know about my sister, but I'd like you to get straight to the point. I have a client arriving very soon."

Kenta couldn't be sure if it was the sudden iciness in her tone or her hard stare, but for an agonisingly long few seconds he had no idea what to say. It was suddenly all too real. He'd actually followed through and done it, and now here he was, possibly only one more step from the truth.

As he'd done in front of the doors outside, Kenta imagined Jessica beside him. He knew she wouldn't be fazed by this adult doctor. She'd just get straight to the point as requested.

"I'm a pupil at BSK," he said, at which point the doctor seemed to perk up a little. Now he really had her attention. "I'm not sure if you're aware of what's been happening, but there have been some problems at the school."

"Yes, I saw something in the local paper. Some sort of vandalism," the doctor conceded. "But what has any of this got to do with Hikaru? She left that place a long time ago."

In his mind, Kenta heard Jessica spouting off her customary bullshit about researching Hikaru for a school article, but he knew that wasn't going to fly this time, and so he just went for it, starting from the beginning with the arrival of the koto and all the mysterious misdemeanours that had occurred since, including Yudai's disappearance and Kenta himself being framed. He finished off with Jessica's discovery of Hikaru's story and how the vengeful nature of OO's campaign of disruption appeared to revolve around the school and the koto. The only bit he missed out was the part where he was almost killed by OO herself. He didn't want to accuse the doctor's sister of being an all-out maniac, at least not yet. The doctor listened carefully throughout, giving little away other than the odd narrowing of the eyes as ever more salacious details were revealed.

When he was done, Kenta waited for her to speak. At first, she only continued to watch him closely, as though trying to figure something out from his face. It was her job, after all, to study and alter people's features. Maybe she could see things in a person's complexion that others couldn't.

Eventually the doctor did a slight double take as if only just understanding what she'd been told. "So, you're telling me that you think my sister is involved in all this? And this is based on a schoolgirl's hunch?"

Hearing it put like this, Kenta had to admit it sounded faintly ridiculous on paper, but then he wanted to tell her that she didn't know Jessica – this schoolgirl's hunches had been right all along, and he hadn't lost faith in her yet. But he didn't say any of this. Instead, he found himself channelling Jessica yet again.

"Yes, that's what I'm saying," he replied, adding some of his own coolness. "And you haven't said that any of this is ridiculous or crazy, at least not yet. Is it because you know something?"

The doctor's eyebrows went up in surprise, and Kenta wondered if he'd gone too far, but instead of ordering him out of the office, she changed tack. "How exactly did you know that Hikaru is my sister?"

"We knew she was from Nagasaki and that your father was a doctor. I found his details online and emailed the hospital. It was my friend Jessica's idea to pretend we were researching her for a school project. Dr Kai gave me your name, said you were the one to ask."

Now the doctor's eyebrows went even higher. "You're lucky that my father replied at all. He and Hikaru haven't spoken to one another in many years. I'm the only one who's had any contact with her, and I rarely speak with her myself. My sister is... well, she's a complicated person. She took it very hard after her expulsion from BSK, which damaged her relationship with my parents. But I really don't see how she could have anything to do with this. These are quite serious allegations after all, and anyway, Hikaru has been living in Kobe for over three years now."

"Kobe?" Now it was Kenta's turn to raise his eyebrows.

"Yes, she's working at a public library there part-time – at least she was last time we spoke."

"When was that?"

"Around a year ago... Hikaru isn't the most social person. She keeps herself to herself. I'm not even sure where she's living right now, she moves around a lot. We used to be close, but..."

A wave of something crossed the doctor's face, a sadness perhaps.

"Did she continue playing the koto?" said Kenta, wanting to stay on the topic while he still could.

"I believe so, although she never composed again, and she kept that side to herself. It was such a shame. She was so talented."

"What happened after she left BSK?"

A tired little sigh left the doctor's lips. "She moved back to Nagasaki with my parents not long after. It was a source of great shame for them. I was studying here at Kyoto University, so I stayed. I don't know why they had to go to such lengths." She paused to shake her head ever so slightly, then continued. "They still had dreams of getting her into a fancy college somewhere, maybe in America, but Hikaru stopped practising for a long time afterwards. It was difficult just to get her to eat during those days.

"We had to hire private tutors to come to our home for her entire two years of high school. She wouldn't study music at all in any formal sense, and only took up the koto again after a year or so, although she would only play alone behind a locked door. Then all hell broke loose when she said she didn't want to go to university. She didn't want to study any more. It was like she'd given up or simply wanted to spite my parents somehow.

"Things got bad enough that she came to stay with me here for a while. I was coming to the end of a very stressful medical degree, so looking after my depressed little sister wasn't the easiest thing. I did my best, but we started arguing too when I pushed her to find her own place and get a job if she didn't want to do a degree. That's when she started accusing me of being on my parents' side. She was always so bitter and paranoid. She had so many grudges. That's when she really went off the rails. She started drinking a lot and hanging out with some losers she met on the internet. She got a job at a music shop and found her own place in Kyoto eventually, but she could never hold down either for long.

"There were spells when she really struggled. I found her a therapist for a while, which helped a little. My parents kept sending her money as well, even though she didn't want to see them, and that's generally how it's gone the last few years – I'll hear from Hikaru once in a while, maybe when she's a little better. Sometimes it's to ask for money, other times it's just to get in touch or answer my own calls. She's only met her nieces, my daughters, a couple of times... and then she'll drop off the radar or move places without telling me. She doesn't even have a phone half the time. I didn't know she'd moved to Kobe until she'd already been there three months."

The doctor said these last few words with such exasperation that she caught herself and readjusted her chair in an attempt to regain her full composure.

Kenta had been listening avidly throughout. At times he was sure she wasn't even speaking to him but to herself, or some invisible audience. He was also slightly amazed that she was telling him, a mere school pupil, so much. Jessica had been right again. If you asked the right questions in the right way at the right time, then most people would tell you what you needed to hear.

"When you said Hikaru held grudges, what exactly did you mean? Who did she hold them against?"

"Oh, everyone at times: my parents, me, her old school friends, the headmaster at BSK."

With this last admission, the doctor seemed to realise she'd said too much. The sad, almost dazed glint in her eye was quickly replaced by the slight standoffishness of earlier.

Kenta, who tried not to show his surprise at what he'd heard, fired off another question. "Was Hikaru ever interested in Otake Okimi's story?"

The doctor frowned. "I don't know. She had quite a few obsessions back in those days. Sometimes European musicians and composers, other times Chinese or Japanese artists. Look, I've told you all I know. If the police aren't even able to find this OO person, then I don't see how this would help."

Normally Kenta would have shrunk slightly from the admonishing tone of an adult, particularly someone like a doctor, but this time he held firm.

"Has she been to Kyoto recently?"

"Not that I'm aware of."

"Which library does she work at in Kobe?"

"The main municipal library, I believe. I really don't have any more time for this."

"Do you have any recent photos of Hikaru?" said Kenta, still pressing.

"Excuse me?"

"Any recent photos of her... we've only seen photos of her as a teenager."

The doctor shifted again in her seat. "No, I don't," she said flatly. "And anyway, she doesn't look the same any more."

"What do you mean?"

"That's none of your business. I really must get ready for my client. This is becoming ridiculous."

A flash of irritation darkened the doctor's expression even further.

Don't back down! A voice in Kenta's mind sounded, almost as if Jessica herself were there, whispering in his ear.

Seeing the doctor was about to stand up, Kenta piped up with added urgency. "Dr Higuchi, please! My friend is still missing, I've been suspended from school, people have been hurt. You've answered all my questions and you haven't once told me to get out. I think that's because you know more than you're saying. Your sister is a complicated person, right? Maybe very angry? Even if there's just a tiny chance Hikaru is somehow involved, this could help her, and the school."

The doctor's hand remained perched on the armrest of her chair, but she kept on sitting, regarding Kenta with a mixture of suspicion and perhaps even fear. Kenta himself was trying to hide his rapid breaths. He couldn't believe he'd just said what he'd said.

She closed her eyes and let herself sit back in the chair.

"It was the last time I saw her. That was why she came here a year ago. She'd been begging me for a long time to help out."

"Help out with what?" Kenta was really finding his flow now. Unbelievably, he felt in control of the conversation.

"With my skill set." The doctor gestured vaguely with a hand at the examination bed on the other side of the room. "I didn't exactly choose this profession, you know? I was supposed to be a paediatrician, but then... well, other opportunities came my way, and this pays the bills better than public hospitals." She looked deflated now as she spoke, so much so that Kenta felt sorry for having brought it up.

"Hikaru wanted me to help her with her nose and some other things. She was never happy with the way she looked, how many young women are? Anyway, she'd never have the money for such a procedure, and I didn't want to mix business with family, but I just thought... I thought it might solve some of her problems, help with her self-esteem. It was all done off the books. I didn't even take pre- or post-op photos as usual. I didn't want any record of it. I could've got into hot water for a family freebie like that."

"And Hikaru looks quite different now?"

The doctor nodded reluctantly. "The work was quite extensive in the end. I haven't seen Hikaru since. I doubt my parents would recognise her either. She's not the sort for family photos or selfies. The only recent photos I have of her were taken when she was eighteen. She's twenty-five now."

In the solemn silence that followed, Kenta realised to his great surprise that he'd asked everything he'd planned to, and there was little else the doctor could give him now. "Well, thank you, Dr Higuchi," he said gently. "I'm very grateful for your help."

She tried to raise a hint of a smile but failed. "Kenta..."

The sound of his first name coming from the doctor took him aback.

"I may not have much of a relationship with my sister, but I don't want to see her get into any trouble... that is, if she is in any kind of trouble... perhaps if you manage to find her, you could contact me?"

The doctor met his eyes briefly, as though tacitly communicating something, though he wasn't quite sure what.

"Of course, yes. I understand," he said.

Kenta got to his feet and gave the doctor a grateful bow. He was already halfway to the door when she spoke again.

"And please could you not mention to anyone what I've told you regarding Hikaru's operation?"

Kenta turned to face her. "I won't, please don't worry."

The doctor nodded, her relief plain to see. "Also... she did mention that name... Otake Okimi... Hikaru often talked about her, especially back in the time after her expulsion. It became one of her little obsessions."

The doctor wouldn't look him in the eye as she said this. She only stared guiltily at her hands on her lap.

"Thank you," said Kenta. "I hope everything will be okay."

Then he closed the door and left.

Chapter 46

It was 2pm and Jessica was finally free. She stood at her bedroom window watching her father leave the house and get into the company car that came to pick him up whenever he had a meeting. He'd been at home the previous two days and that morning, keeping up his prison warden duties as Jessica saw it, but he had a meeting he couldn't miss in Osaka, and so Yuko had arrived to take over, with strict instructions not to let Jessica out of the house.

As she'd been doing ever since her suspension had begun, Jessica refused to respond when her father shouted, "See you later' up the stairs, but even he was probably getting used to the routine of locked doors and zero communication by now.

Yuko had already come upstairs and asked sheepishly on the other side of the door if Jessica was hungry. As much as she didn't feel like engaging with anyone yet, Jessica couldn't bring herself to ignore Yuko too and replied with a simple, "No thank you," after which Yuko had eventually shuffled away back downstairs.

The performance would be starting in less than two hours and there were still things she needed to do. She knew she had to get into the school building no matter what. Getting there and inside was the easy part. What she had do once she was in, however, was another matter altogether. She'd have to figure it out on the way.

Grabbing her purse, phone and a light rucksack, Jessica put on a baseball cap before leaving. It was a Chelsea FC cap her dad had given her the previous year, but she'd never worn it until now.

She put on her trainers, then crept out of the room, closing the door slowly behind her. Standing at the top of the stairs, she listened out for Yuko's movements down below. She could hear her humming faintly to herself in the kitchen. She was probably preparing vegetables.

Jessica unlocked her phone and selected "Home' from her small list of contacts. It was the number for the landline her father had insisted on having for both business and family emergency purposes. Jessica hadn't needed to call it yet, but today she was very thankful for its existence.

She dialled the number, and as the phone sounded downstairs, she waited for Yuko to scurry across to the other side of the living room to answer it.

"*Moshi moshi?*"

On hearing Yuko's Japanese greeting, Jessica crept quickly yet light-footedly down the stairs and darted into the kitchen. She opened the cabinet above the counter by the fridge and fished out the spare set of keys her parents kept there, half hidden beneath a pile of utility bills.

Yuko continued to speak into the phone, now in her broken English. "Hello? Mr Hunter-san?"

Jessica was about to creep out into the hallway when she heard Yuko putting the phone down around the corner.

Jumping back into the kitchen, she quickly dialled the number again. She heard Yuko muttering to herself as the phone blared once more, and waited a couple of anxious seconds to see if she would turn back.

A second later the phone stopped ringing and Yuko spoke again, this time with a hint of confusion in her tone.

Seeing her chance, Jessica dashed along the hallway and delicately unlocked the door before opening it and closing it behind her with extra care. Then before there was any chance of being detected, she pressed the release button on the front gate and ran out onto the street, making straight for Kitayama Dori.

CHAPTER 47

Kenta stopped on the street corner just a short distance from Katsura Station. He checked the time on his phone. It was already 2.20pm. He needed to act fast.

With the adrenaline of his successful interview with the doctor still energising him, Kenta searched on his phone for the Kobe Municipal Library website and dialled the first contact number he could find, still not quite believing what was happening and that he was actually doing it.

A moment later a woman's voice sounded. "*Moshi, moshi.* Municipal Library front desk. How may I help?"

For a couple of seconds, Kenta had no idea how to respond, then instinctively he replied in a deeper voice. "Excuse me, is this the Kobe Municipal Chuo Library?"

"Yes, it is."

"Yes, hello, I'd like to speak with Hikaru Kai, please."

"Oh... please wait a moment."

Kenta heard muffled voices, and a second or two later another woman spoke. She sounded much older and tougher than the first and reminded Kenta of several teachers he'd had over the years.

"Hello, this is Miss Kikuchi, senior librarian. Miss Kai is no longer working here," the woman said. "Who am I speaking to?"

Another second's hesitation, then Kenta said in a lower voice, "This is Detective Yamada of the Kyoto police force. I was hoping to speak with Miss Kai in connection with an investigation."

His heart began racing. The words had come without any thought at all.

"Kyoto?" said Miss Kikuchi, surprised.

Holding the phone away from his mouth, Kenta took a deep breath and braced himself. "Yes. Miss Kai once lived here and has a family connection in Kyoto. Do you know how I could contact her?"

"Miss Kai left quite suddenly. The phone number we had on record is no longer working. We did try to contact her."

"Do you have an address?"

"No, I don't think so."

"And why did Miss Kai leave?"

The head librarian went quiet for a moment. "As I said, she left quite suddenly. There were some difficulties..."

"Difficulties? What kind of difficulties?"

"Miss Kai was... she was not the easiest employee. She only worked part-time and was here little more than half a year, but she was frequently absent and wasn't the most cooperative of people."

"And when exactly did she leave the library?"

"Oh... about four months ago."

This was great, thought Kenta. People were so responsive if you were a police officer. He would try it more often if it weren't technically a crime.

He pushed even further. "Would you happen to have a picture of Miss Kai?"

"Oh... I'm not sure." The senior librarian said nothing further for what felt like an age, during which Kenta was silently willing her to speak. "Did you say you were a detective? I'm not sure if we're supposed to divulge that kind of information."

Kenta swallowed hard and hoped she hadn't heard. He nearly said thank you, and wanted to end the call, but he'd heard the wavering in Miss Kikuchi's voice. She didn't sound so threatening now. He was almost there.

"Yes, as I said, this is Detective Yamada. You may contact the central station in Kyoto if you wish to speak with my superior, but this is of the utmost importance. A photo of Miss Kai would be enormously helpful and may be very significant for the case. Your cooperation would be greatly appreciated."

Kenta wished Jessica could have heard him now. It was the performance of a lifetime, surely Oscar-worthy.

After a further momentary silence on the other end of the line, the librarian finally spoke. "Yes, of course I would like to help. We no longer have any official photos of Miss Kai, but I believe there is one from a staff event a few months ago. Would that do?"

Kenta punched the air then quickly composed himself. "Yes, that would be most helpful."

He was about to suggest she email the photo, then realised she'd see his email address which bore his own name. It was the same for his Line profile.

"Could you please send it to this number via SMS."

"SMS?"

"Yes, please. As soon as possible."

"Oh... yes, of course. Thank you, Detective."

"Thank you, Miss Kikuchi."

He ended the call, feeling ripples of excitement quickening his breaths. He started walking in the direction of the station, staring at his phone screen the whole way, barely aware of anyone or anything around him.

Two minutes later and still Kenta hadn't received anything. He checked he had enough of a signal. He did.

A minute later he was at the entrance to Katsura Station. Still there was nothing. He checked the time: 2.32pm. He imagined the school at that moment, the auditorium, the buzz of activity and expectation.

When after a full five minutes the librarian still hadn't sent anything, Kenta's elation began to rapidly fade. Perhaps she really was calling the Kyoto central police station to verify the detective's credentials. He'd used his own number. It was only a matter of time before they traced it to him. On top of the school stuff, this was jail time for sure. He felt sick.

Kenta took a step inside the station but paused again when his phone vibrated in his hand. He looked at it. It was an SMS message from an unknown number. There was an image file attached.

Kenta's heart sang and thumped with the quiet drama of it all while he waited for the photo to open.

People continued to stream in and out of the station while he stood off to the side, eyes wide and fixed on the screen. And then there it was – a colour photo appeared suddenly.

Kenta flipped the screen to landscape mode. The first thing he saw was faces. Lots of them. At least thirty people lined up into rows for a formal group photo. They were in what looked like a park somewhere, standing on a wide expanse of grass in front of a statue and a grouping of trees.

His eyes searched the many features, an alarm bell ringing somewhere in his mind when none of them jumped out at him.

In the middle there was a rather stout and stern-looking woman whom Kenta guessed was probably the senior librarian he'd just spoken to, but like most of the people in the photo, the majority of whom were female, she was smiling.

And it was the total absence of any smile on one face that drew his attention.

Just then a second SMS arrived bearing a short line of text. It said: "*Miss Kai is third from the left in the front row*". But Kenta didn't need it. He'd already spotted her. And then he knew.

CHAPTER 48

Jessica was hurrying along Kitayama Dori when her phone began to buzz in her pocket.

It was an unusual enough event that it made her slow down as she took the phone out. She presumed it was her father who would have already received a frantic call from Yuko, and was ready to switch it off, regretting her decision to bring it at all. But it was Kenta's name on the screen.

Jessica stopped in her tracks and pressed the green button.

"You were right all along, it's her!" blurted Kenta's voice on the other end of the line.

She could hear him all right and see the letters of his name signalling the caller, yet after two days of being stonewalled and speaking to no one else, it took her a few seconds to realise it really was him.

"Jessica…? Are you there?" Kenta was speaking excitedly. She could hear that he was walking quickly and a tad breathless. A station tannoy, or something like it, sounded in the background.

"Yes, I'm here."

"You were right, it's Hikaru Kai. I know for sure. I have the proof."

"Really? How?"

"I'll explain everything. I'm just getting the train now. I'm in Katsura Station. Are you at home?"

"No, I'm outside. Not far. Can you meet at Kitayama Station, exit one?"

"Yeah, I'll be about twenty minutes though."

Another loud station announcement cut him off for a second. Jessica could hear the rattle and hum of a train approaching.

"I'm sending you something," he added. "See you soon."

When the call ended, Jessica remained slightly stunned. She didn't realise she was standing in the way of a small lady, who threw her a disgruntled look when she eventually stood aside.

What had just happened? Had Kenta, whom she hadn't expected to ever see again, just gone and found the last piece of crucial evidence they needed? And without her, too?

A Line notification flashed up on her screen. She opened the message and saw the photo. It only took her a moment to find the right face. She blinked heavily then looked up in astonishment at the traffic passing by in the street, each one of the drivers utterly oblivious to the magnitude of what she was looking at. She could have almost laughed if she weren't so shocked. OO had been there all along, right under their noses, and they'd never given her so much as a glance.

Checking over the photo a second time just to be sure, Jessica realised it was beyond doubt. She was looking at an image of the small and diminutive cleaner from the school, the same one she'd passed by countless times and even said hello to, the one who worked A-block with an older cleaner and never looked anyone in the eye. She looked nothing like the schoolgirl Hikaru from the article Jessica had seen. It was like another person entirely.

She looked different too in the image on her screen, which Jessica guessed was a fairly recent staff photo. There was an almost malicious frown on her face, as though she were glaring with single-pointed hatred at the camera person, whereas as the cleaner she'd always looked so frightened that no one even noticed her. It was brilliant, masterful even. Jessica had to respect the audacity of it, the sheer skill, but yet the hot anger was glowing again inside her. They'd been made fools of the whole time. Hikaru was both OO and the insider. As the invisible cleaner she had the most perfect of disguises. But not for long.

***

Almost exactly twenty minutes later, Kenta came half running out of the exit at Kitayama Station. He saw Jessica immediately.

Kenta himself was looking uncharacteristically dishevelled. She nearly didn't recognise him in his jogging pants and with his hair unstyled, but she couldn't deny feeling something like relief at the sight of him. More than that, she was happy, and could guess from the look on his face that he felt the same. They were each the only ally the other had left in the world. This was probably one of those times when people felt the need to hug one another. Her father was a hugger, though he only tried it very occasionally now that Jessica was older. She was more like her mother, who avoided any kind of embrace at all costs.

There was a brief awkward pause while they sought the appropriate words for the moment.

Jessica spoke first. "The cleaner."

Kenta nodded. "Yeah."

"Your parents know you're out?"

He shook his head. "Yours?"

"No. Would yours call the school or the police?"

"I don't think so. Not the police anyway."

"Right." Jessica checked her phone. It was 3.06pm. "We don't have much time. We need to get costumes."

Kenta threw her a confused look. "Costumes?"

"I'll explain on the way, and you can fill me in on your end. Looks like you've been busy."

Walking further along Kitayama Dori, Jessica listened as Kenta explained everything about the email from Dr Kai, the interview with Hikaru's older sister, the plastic surgeon – the surgery revelation made Jessica shout out "Of course!" – and then he casually relayed his successful Detective Yamada impersonation over the phone with the librarian, which he was clearly quite proud of.

"Sorry, am I speaking to the same Kenta Higashi who didn't want to break a single school rule a few days ago?"

Kenta lowered his head and Jessica made a mental note to give him a break. It must have been tough for him just to leave his apartment against his parents' wishes, never mind the other stuff. And the fact he'd got the doctor to tell him so much was incredible, and yet he'd done it, and Jessica saw that in many ways she'd found her equal, someone prepared to do whatever it took to get to the truth.

She said none of this to him of course, only that he'd done "Good work', which she knew very well was an understatement.

Jessica managed to find the costume shop without consulting a map. She'd clocked it previously on one of her neighbourhood explorations, tucked away just off the main street beside a small florist.

She gave Kenta his instructions and helped him choose something appropriate before grabbing something for herself.

Ten minutes later, they both emerged from their separate changing areas to find one another transformed almost beyond recognition.

Dressed in a traditional yukata, a more casual kimono-like bathrobe worn by both men and women, and with a long ponytailed wig clipped to his scalp, Kenta looked a million miles from the scruffy teenager who'd entered the shop. The yukata itself was a long, dark blue robe wrapped around him and tied at the waist with a thick black sash. It reached down to just above his ankles, and on his feet he wore black leather sandals.

Jessica had thrown on a basic white kimono, tied up her hair, and added an ornate hairpin for measure. As for footwear, she had on some black slipper-like shoes. It was obvious from Kenta's wide-eyed look of surprise that he was equally taken aback at seeing her dressed in traditional Japanese clothes.

"We need something more," said Jessica, scrutinising him closely. She turned to the shop assistant. "Excuse me? Can you put some make-up on us? I'll pay you double, but we need to be quick."

A full fifteen minutes later and their transformations were complete.

Kenta had a full face of foundation, along with face-paint to add more definition to his eyebrows. Jessica had a light white powder added, and heavy mascara.

When she checked herself in the mirror, even she was surprised. "You're a genius!" she said to the shop assistant, who beamed at the compliment.

They paid their deposits and stuffed the old clothes and shoes into their rucksacks before going back outside.

The sky above them was already blending with the oncoming colours of an early autumn sunset, a precursor to the approaching darkness they both knew was coming. And then they looked to one another and began to walk in the direction of BSK.

CHAPTER 49

In Kyoto there was nothing unusual about two people being dressed up in traditional Japanese clothing, especially the week of the Jidai Matsuri festival, and so Jessica and Kenta made their way to BSK virtually unnoticed.

They were about five minutes away from the school when Kenta felt his pulse begin to quicken with the anticipation. "Shouldn't we at least call Detective Yamada?" he said in a hushed, nervous tone.

"What? I already told you, we'd just be laughed at again. It'd probably land us in even more crap anyway, so it's just us, like it has been from the start."

Kenta nodded uncertainly. He knew she was probably right, and yet the thought of facing a deranged criminal single-handedly made his mouth go suddenly dry.

As they approached the last corner before the school gates, Jessica checked her phone. "Three forty-six. At least we'll have a chance to poke around before it starts."

"What do we do once we're in?"

"I guess we should split up. We don't really have a choice."

"What if we get Tomo to help us?" said Kenta, doing his best to swallow away the bone-dryness.

"Good idea! Keep an eye out for him too and avoid Mr Murphy at all costs!"

They could see a large group of people congregating in front of the gates along the pavement. The closer they got, the more obvious it was that they were mostly parents, along with a few grandparents and pupils' little siblings.

The sight of so much parental might in one place only increased Kenta's nerves. He half expected to see his own mother and father there, eagerly scanning the crowd for their delinquent son. He kept his head down and prayed he wouldn't bump into any parents who might recognise him.

"I'll go first," whispered Jessica as they came to the line.

He watched as she walked straight to the front, bypassing the queue completely, her costume and make-up convincing enough that no one appeared to realise who she was. Even Kenta had to remind himself it was Jessica, the strange, tall, pale girl who wouldn't normally dream of touching make-up. But it wasn't just the cosmetics; it was the whole costume and the way her hair was tied and clipped up on top of her head that made her look so... well... like a regular girl, except surprisingly striking.

When she tried to walk straight through the gates, the guard nearest to her put out an arm and asked for her ticket.

"*Watashi wa gakusei desu.* I'm a pupil," said Jessica, surprising Kenta and also the two Japanese people at the front of the queue who'd only just realised she was a foreigner.

"ID," said the guard rather flatly, but it was quickly apparent that Jessica didn't have her school ID on her.

She began to remonstrate in English, which Kenta could see was causing a scene, and the guard, who wasn't budging, didn't seem to understand anyway.

Before they attracted any further attention, Kenta pulled his own ID from his wallet and hoped his name wasn't on some blacklist the guard had with him. He moved alongside Jessica and flashed the card in the guard's face. "We had to go out to get our costumes. The teachers will kill us if we're late!"

The guard surveyed them both with barely disguised contempt, then beckoned them in with a flick of the head.

"Thanks," said Jessica as they hurried towards the school's front entrance. But their relief at getting in was cut short by the sight of Mr Murphy and the deputy head standing in the foyer, greeting everyone who was coming in. Beside them, two Year 13 pupils dressed in kimonos were bowing to each guest.

"Shit!" Kenta muttered under his breath. "What the hell do we do?"

They slowed down. It would have been better to dart quickly to the right and down the side of A-block, but their approach had already been spotted.

"Just keep your head down," Jessica whispered out of the corner of her mouth. "Follow me."

Kenta, who was imagining being arrested in front of the whole school, watched as Jessica stood off to the side, pretending to be receiving a call on her phone.

"Oh, yeah, hi Dad... yeah, okay. That's great."

Standing awkwardly beside her, Kenta kept his back to the doorway and the headmaster, who was little more than ten metres away. He had no idea what Jessica was up to; he was just praying she knew what she was doing.

She stayed on her fake call until two separate sets of parents were coming by with one small boy. When they were passing Kenta and Jessica, she quickly darted behind them, beckoning him with a subtle flick of a hand.

He quick-marched it until he was at Jessica's left elbow. She was still speaking into the phone. "Yeah, just got here. I'll see you after the show."

She positioned them at the rear of the group, directly behind the tallest person, a blonde man whom Kenta thought looked German or possibly Dutch. They hadn't even noticed the two costumed pupils trailing them.

With his head slightly bent, Kenta had to remind himself to breathe as they approached the doorway. He could already hear the headmaster's deep voice as he greeted the first couple in both Japanese and English.

Jessica had ended her fake call, and with a sharp tug of Kenta's sleeve, pulled him along with her just as the tall German man was face to face with Mr Murphy.

Eyes down, heads lowered, they zipped past the group into the open space of the foyer. Kenta could see the headmaster's tall, bulky figure in the corner of his eye, could almost sense his eyes on him, and was waiting for the sound of Mr Murphy's voice over his shoulder, calling out Kenta's name for all to hear, his formidable voice booming and echoing up to the lobby ceiling. But it never came, and then suddenly they were in.

CHAPTER 50

Niko Haruki stared at herself in the mirror. She'd already applied the heavy white powder to her face and was adding the finishing touches to the blush around her eyes. Her hair was neatly in place, and the formal kimono was already on.

They'd put her in some small storage room and added a shabby little table and mirror to make it look like a dressing room. There were piles of boxes stacked around her, a mop and bucket in the corner. Beyond the door, she could hear the frenetic milling of the school staff and pupils running around backstage in their own costumes.

She sighed heavily. This was how it was these days. She'd always imagined her skill as a koto player would land her in far more glamorous locations, and though she'd performed at high-end hotels a few times, mostly for corporate events, it had mainly been weddings and schools and other less impressive functions. The agency she worked for even tried to pass her off as a real geisha some of the time. When she'd played at BSK a couple of weeks ago, Niko had seen the reaction from the young pupils, a wide-eyed fascination. But then like most people, they didn't truly appreciate the art of playing the koto, nor had they willingly signed up for it. It was often this way. Perhaps if she really were a geisha and not a pretender, then she'd get the respect she deserved.

But then that koto, the antique from the museum she'd played on the school stage and was due to play again that very evening, now that was special. She'd never played as fine an instrument as that before. She'd heard vague stories about it, of some tragic gifted geisha who'd once owned it, but it was the thought of playing it again in less than an hour which made it all worthwhile. She would happily play to all those pushy parents and clueless pupils if it meant she could lay her hands on that delicate instrument one last time, and then she'd really give them a performance they'd never forget.

There was a knock at the door.

"Yes?"

She presumed it was a pupil or teacher letting her know how much time she had left, but instead there was a short woman in a cleaner's uniform peeping through the gap in the doorway.

"Sorry, miss. May I empty the bin?" she said in a squeaky little voice.

Niko looked her over in the mirror. She thought it was an odd time and place to be cleaning but waved her in and went back to finishing off her make-up.

The cleaner gave a nervous little nod and scuttled into a corner, where she proceeded to take the rubbish bag out of the small metal bin. Niko, slightly irritated by the intrusion now, hoped she would hurry up so she could be alone again and continue with her mental preparations in peace.

As she reapplied some eyeliner, she could hear the cleaner rustling away over her shoulder, but when she glanced her way in the mirror, all of a sudden the little figure was no longer there.

Niko turned fully around in surprise. How had she left so soundlessly?

Shrugging to herself, she turned back to the mirror and let out a little gasp. The eyeliner fell from her hand and clattered against the floor before rolling under the table. The cleaner was there at her side, staring at her in the mirror.

Niko went to say something once she'd got over the shock, but it was the look in the cleaner's eyes that stopped her tongue from moving.

Gone was the coy, frightened little look Niko had witnessed a few seconds earlier. Now the woman was staring at her with a glare so profound, it could only be described as hateful, murderous even. She couldn't stop herself from staring into the other woman's eyes, transfixed.

And then the cleaner's hand went up in the air before sweeping downwards in a flash, bringing with it a sharp pain at the back of Niko's skull, followed by darkness.

CHAPTER 51

After leaving the foyer, they made the decision to split up, with Kenta going in search of Tomo while Jessica would hunt Hikaru down. They agreed to communicate via message if necessary.

Moving swiftly while she still possessed the advantage of anonymity, Jessica made a beeline for the small room in A-block which she knew acted as a breakroom for the block's cleaners. Along the way, she passed a couple of pupils from the lower years, but no one who might recognise her.

The room itself was tucked away in a back corridor beside the first-floor geography classrooms. When she got to it, Jessica knocked on the door. If someone answered, she would use the excuse of informing them of a spillage in the canteen, but no one came. She tried the handle, but it was locked. She checked her phone. 3.55pm They would be starting in five minutes.

Hurrying back the way she'd come, Jessica found the auditorium doors were still closed. People were beginning to form a line outside, but the two Year 13 pupils at the doors hadn't yet been given the nod to let them in. The majority of people were still in the canteen, which was acting as a sort of waiting room. She'd have to try her luck in there first.

She turned around and had only taken a couple of steps when she heard a voice over her shoulder.

"Jessica?"

The sound of her own name made her freeze. She spun round to find Rina staring at her. She was wearing her uniform. Presumably she was one of the volunteers.

Jessica watched as first a palpable shock and then bafflement competed for dominance over Rina's expression.

"What are you doing here?" she said eventually.

Casting about, Jessica rapidly assessed whether anyone else had seen or heard this exchange. When she was sure no one had, she took Rina by the elbow and gently led her away from the growing line.

"I thought you were suspended?" whispered Rina.

"I was," Jessica replied matter-of-factly. "I still am."

"But why—"

"Wait!" Jessica shushed her, glancing back to check no one was following. She waited until they could turn into a quieter corridor further from the crowd. When she was certain they were alone, Jessica looked to Rina who was still gazing at her in amazement. "Rina, do you believe what everyone's been saying?"

Rina shook her head. "I've been saying it couldn't be you and Kenta, but nobody believes me. I couldn't tell them how I knew, though." She looked down at the floor, crestfallen.

"It's okay, I understand. But I'm going to need your help. I want you to listen carefully, there's not much time."

Perking up again, Rina listened as Jessica filled her in on the most important details.

"Kenta's here too, but we need more eyes. That's where you come in. We need to find one of the cleaners."

Rina, who'd been struggling to comprehend all that she was being told, lit up at this. "I know where the cleaners are!"

Jessica raised an eyebrow. "You do?"

"Yes, they're up on the second floor. They had their own little party. I saw them earlier when I passed by."

"Are they still there?"

"I think so. I was only there about twenty minutes ago."

"Great! Let's go."

Rina led the way to the nearest staircase. Jessica took out her phone with the intention of messaging Kenta. She was punching in the words with half an eye on the steps as Rina raced ahead, bringing to mind the time she'd been fleeing from Jessica and Kenta in the dark.

Stopping just short of room A14, one of the economics classrooms, Rina put a finger to her lips and pointed at the door with her other hand. "They're in there," she whispered.

Jessica was almost finished with her message. She was typing in the room number as Rina pulled open the door. Was she just going to burst in and have it out with Hikaru there and then? Perhaps she should wait for Kenta. But then there wasn't time. He could have been caught already for all she knew. She'd have to rely on Rina for translation instead.

When she came to the open doorway, Jessica was already sensing that something wasn't right, but she'd been so caught up in the sudden dash to find Hikaru that her reactions were a fraction slower than usual.

She had only a moment to register that the classroom was in fact empty before the phone was snatched from her hand and she felt a violent shove in the small of her back. Stumbling forward into the classroom, Jessica managed to stay on her feet, but by the time she could turn herself around, the door was slamming shut.

In a moment of confusion, she looked around for Rina. Then came the sound of a key turning in the lock, and it was only when a face appeared in the door window that she fully understood.

Their eyes met. Rina threw her a fearful look. "I'm sorry," she said through the glass, her voice trembling. "I don't have a choice."

Jessica tried the door handle then cursed when it wouldn't budge. "I have to give it to you, Rina," she replied bitterly. "You had us fooled good and proper."

Rina shook her head. "No, I wasn't trying to fool you. She said she'd hurt her if I didn't help."

"What are you talking about?"

"It was never about my parents finding out. I always knew that would happen one day. She said she would hurt Miki."

"Miki?"

"My girlfriend. She said she'd kill her. And she would too, you don't know what she's like."

Unusually, Jessica was at a loss for words. She could see in the twisted anguish in Rina's face that she was telling the truth, as much as she didn't want to believe her.

"Look, Rina, no matter what she's told you, you don't have to do this. They'll charge you with aiding a criminal."

The tears were streaming from Rina's eyes now. She shook her head again before her face disappeared from the window. Jessica called out her name, but she was gone. She hammered her fists on the door and called out for help, but as the corridor lights went out, all she could hear in return was her hammering blows echoing down the empty space.

Chapter 52

He spotted Tomo patrolling with one of the other guards close to the doors into the foyer. At first, Kenta wanted to just walk up to him, but thought that would draw too much attention. He was already feeling painfully self-conscious in his costume, with parents, teachers and pupils alike scrutinising him and perhaps wondering why he wasn't in the auditorium with everyone else. At least no one had seen it was him yet.

Instead, Kenta overtook the two patrolling guards before swiftly turning around and coming back the other way. He made sure to catch Tomo's eye and motioned with a jerk of his head for Tomo to follow him.

He saw Tomo's initial confusion then surprise as he narrowed his eyes at the strange boy in the costume.

Kenta continued walking, turning to see Tomo saying something to the other guard before heading his way.

Stepping through double doors out into the playing fields, Kenta felt the late October chill had strengthened its grip further. He shivered, wearing only the yukata's synthetic material over a T-shirt.

He sidled over to a row of bushes beside the volleyball court where there was a darker patch of ground away from the field's lights. Tomo made his way over, checking behind him every few steps.

When he got to where Kenta was waiting in the shadows, he said, "Kenta? What the hell, man? I thought you were suspended?"

"I am," he said quietly, continuing to scan the area for potential eavesdroppers.

Tomo shook his head. "Boy, you've got some balls! But it was messed up what happened to you guys. I know you didn't do any of that stuff. I felt bad, but there wasn't anything I could do."

"It's okay, but will you still help us?"

"Us?"

"Jessica's here too, somewhere."

Tomo grinned, still shaking his head. "You two are something else! Damn right I'll help, so long as it won't end with me behind bars by the end of the night."

Kenta quickly told him what they knew about Hikaru and the cleaner.

"The little one?" said Tomo, almost shouting it then forcing himself to be quiet. "No way!"

"I know, but it's true. I don't have time to prove it now, you'll just have to believe me."

He waited an anxious couple of seconds while Tomo thought it out, then relaxed when the corners of Tomo's lips rose up into a smile. "Of course I believe you! You guys were on it right from the start. What do you need me to do?"

"We need an extra pair of eyes. The show's about to start, and we know she has something planned. We just don't know where she is."

"Absolutely, man!"

"What about any of the other guards? Will they help too?"

Tomo frowned. "Not sure... those guys are sticklers. Maybe my dad, though. I could just pretend we need to find her for something else."

"Okay, good idea. And if you see her, be careful. She's a lot more dangerous than she looks, trust me."

"I should go with you, it's not safe," said Tomo.

"Don't worry. There's not enough time. Just message me if you catch sight of her."

Kenta held out his phone and the two of them quickly exchanged Line contacts.

"The show's starting any minute," said Tomo, checking his watch.

"I'm going to try the canteen," said Kenta.

In that moment, Tomo's walkie-talkie burst into life. Kenta could hear a voice asking him where he was.

Tomo lifted the walkie-talkie to his mouth, but first he raised a thumb to Kenta. "Good luck, man. Be careful."

Kenta gave him a thumbs up in return, then made his way back inside. A part of him wanted to stay out there in the cold where no one could see him, or even better, head to the exit while he still could. But he wouldn't. The same deep inner force that had driven him to go and see the doctor was driving him still. He wasn't sure if it was bravery or just stupidity. It didn't feel like either. It just felt like doing what needed to be done.

The canteen was still brimming with guests waiting to be called into the auditorium. The sheer sight of them all caused him to falter as he crossed the threshold, making him think his face-paint had melted away and that at any moment hundreds of eyes would turn their gazes on him. But as they'd done all day long, his legs took him forward anyway.

On one side of the canteen, long tables had been set up, complete with offerings of snacks. Teams of private catering staff were milling about between guests, offering more drinks and collecting empty glasses. Several people glanced Kenta's way, looking him up and down. One or two smiled, and a couple pointed him out and chuckled. It seemed they thought he was part of the pre-show entertainment, which worked in his favour. Not even the several teachers he could see had clocked him.

Walking swiftly between groups of people, he heard conversations in English, Japanese, Spanish, even French. The foreign parents were mostly together in their own groups while the Japanese and other Asian parents did the same. Not so different from the pupils themselves, he thought.

With every second that passed, Kenta was praying to catch sight of Hikaru even as he feared it too. He only hoped she would be fooled by the costume like everyone else.

After a couple of tours around the canteen, during which he was beginning to sweat under the strain, Kenta still had no positive sighting. He snatched a quick look at his phone, but there was nothing yet from either Jessica or Tomo.

Cursing under his breath, he put the phone away and saw immediately that he'd been recognised.

Someone was staring at him. It was Milo. He was standing around twenty metres away with a group of four adults who were all similarly tanned and dark-haired. Kenta recognised Milo's mother, the diplomat, and his businessman father, and he guessed the other two people were also Italian.

Kenta stopped moving. For a moment, neither one of them showed any visible reaction. Milo's parents hadn't noticed their son gawping at the costumed figure in the centre of the room.

"Kenta?" Milo mouthed the word silently.

Kenta resisted an urge to simply walk away and instead placed a finger to his lips. To his relief, Milo nodded his understanding.

"Ladies and gentlemen!" A voice rang out. Kenta jumped slightly and turned to see the deputy head in the doorway. "Please could you make your way to the auditorium. The performance will begin shortly."

The hum of collective conversation stopped dead for a few seconds, then rose up once again with even greater fervour as people began making their way towards the auditorium.

Unsure of where to go next, Kenta moved instinctively against the flow of bodies, heading instead to the doorway on the other side of the canteen.

He felt a buzzing in his pocket. His heart lurched violently at the sensation. He took out his phone.

Jessica: *Meet me outside A14.*

Again, he felt all the moisture in his mouth and throat evaporating in an instant. Was this it?

As if fearing others could sense his alarm, Kenta quickly put the phone away. But looking back at the room one more time, he saw something that made him freeze.

It was Milo again on the other side of the canteen. But he wasn't leaving with the flow of people going out the doors. Instead, he was saying something into Miss Eguchi's ear and pointing in Kenta's direction.

A disbelieving Kenta watched Miss Eguchi listening intently, saw her eyes follow Milo's finger and alight on his own person, saw her shock and Milo's apparent indifference – or was there a smirk there, a look of satisfaction?

There was no time to utter even a WTF. Kenta knew he had to get out of there fast.

Room A14 was only around the corner, and he hurried out of the canteen, peering over his shoulder to see if he was being followed. He was still struggling to process what he'd just

414

witnessed. Was Milo a part of this too, or was it just some sick payback for the fact that Kenta was friends with the girl who'd humiliated him in front of the English class? Kenta snapped out of it. He'd deal with Milo later.

Seeing the corridor ahead empty, Kenta began to run, and as he sped around the corner to where A14 was, he was still expecting to see Jessica there even as he encountered someone else entirely.

There was no Jessica there at all by the classroom door, and as he slid to a halt, Kenta found himself face to face with the headmaster, who himself was flanked on both sides by Rina Mitsustuka and a security guard.

A disbelieving Kenta stared into Mr Murphy's dark brown eyes.

"Hello, Kenta," he said wryly. "How very nice of you to make it."

CHAPTER 53

After two minutes of pounding her fists on the door and shouting for help, Jessica's hands and throat were worn out. There was still no light in the corridor, and no sound of approaching footsteps. She was in a corner of A-block where no one would need to go after normal school hours, and as it was a corner classroom, there were no windows looking into the corridor either unlike all the other classrooms beside it. Rina had thought of everything, or perhaps she was simply following orders.

The thought of her own gullibility only inflamed Jessica further. She punched and kicked the door one more time for good measure. Normally her rage remained very much internalised, cool and sardonic, but now she could have almost torn the room apart.

How could she have been so blind? She normally took so much pride in sussing people out. Maybe Rina was that good. She'd learned from the best after all, namely Hikaru, aka OO, the great deceiver at the heart of it all. They were probably laughing at how easy it had been.

This brought Kenta to mind, and she wondered whether he'd be able to do this without her. God knew how many other secret little helpers Hikaru had enlisted, how many had been helping her the whole time. The sheer magnitude of it sent a chill through Jessica.

Turning to the empty room, she drew a sharp, deep breath in order to focus her senses. *Think, Jessica, think!*

The window in the door was far too small for her to fit through and smashing it would do no good since there wasn't anyone near enough to hear it. Next, she searched for a fire alarm switch, but it became quickly apparent that the nearest one was on the other side of the door in the corridor, taunting her in full view.

That left the row of windows that looked out over the glass roof of the covered badminton courts.

Walking over to them, Jessica stared down at the giant transparent roof only a metre below. To the right, she could see the adjoining second- and third-floor corridors in another wing of A-block, both as dark and empty as the one she was currently in. To the distant left there was the canteen and A-block's busier wing, but it was too far for anyone to hear her, and even if she did scream out her lungs and someone raised the alarm, it would only result in her being carted off to some other location until the police or whoever came.

She looked directly ahead to where a row of plane trees fringed the edges of the covered area, and beyond that where the playing fields lay. The distance from the classroom to the trees was a good thirty metres – too far, she thought. The corridors across the way were also beyond reach, and there was no guarantee the roof was strong enough to carry her the whole way.

No, it would be better to shimmy along to the classroom next door in the hope there was at least one open window she could climb into, followed by an unlocked classroom door once she was inside. It was a long shot, but it was all she had.

Flipping the latch, Jessica slid the centre window across. The cold evening air washed over her, making her shiver slightly, but it was refreshing too. She leaned out and looked down, surveying the glass roof where it joined with the side of the building. It was certainly within reach.

She eyed the glass more closely. It looked thick enough, and there were several lines of reinforcing steel running off in a grid pattern, offering a sturdier path if necessary.

Placing a hand on either side of the open window frame, Jessica raised one foot onto the windowsill and lifted herself up. Standing with her feet hanging over the edge, and the chill air biting at her face, Jessica, who'd never imagined she was afraid of heights, found an unexpected reluctance taking hold of her. She looked back at the classroom door and nearly lost her balance in the process.

Come on, you idiot, she chided herself. *Think of Kenta. He's on his own now. He needs you!*

And with that she lowered herself, delicately placing one foot down on the glass.

CHAPTER 54

The shock went through Kenta as he met Rina's eye. He had to do a double take just to make sure it was definitely her. She looked away, seemingly in shame. He was so utterly gobsmacked that he almost didn't hear when Mr Murphy said, "You'd better come with us."

The headmaster took him by one arm while the guard seized the other. He didn't try to stop them as they began leading him away. He couldn't even speak at first. He could only look back in time to see Rina standing in the corridor watching him go. By her side stood Milo, a sick grin plastered across his face as he watched on.

The force of the realisation felt like a physical blow. Milo wasn't simply on a revenge mission. He was deep in this whole evil mess, and with the girl they thought they'd been saving. Kenta realised it must have been one of them who'd messaged him from Jessica's phone, which meant... what did it mean? That Jessica was also locked up somewhere, or worse? Whatever it meant, it was all falling apart.

He almost went to ask the headmaster if he'd locked up Jessica too, but some unexpected instinct halted his tongue. It was possible they didn't know Jessica was there yet.

The corridors were mercifully empty as Kenta was taken on his march of shame, with most people being in the auditorium already. One or two teachers and volunteer pupils walked by, gawping at the costumed figure being led away by the headmaster himself.

"The police have been called," said Mr Murphy rather nonchalantly. "And your parents have also been informed. They'll be here shortly."

Perhaps it was the combination of hearing the words "police' and "parents' in the same sentence that kick-started Kenta's survival instincts.

"But sir, you don't understand!" he suddenly bellowed. "It's the cleaner, the small one from A-block. She's really Hikaru Kai, the pupil you expelled years ago. She's OO. I can prove it!"

The headmaster only shook his head. "I do have to say again, Kenta, how terribly disappointed I am in you. You had a very promising pupil career ahead of you before that Hunter girl came and filled your head with all this nonsense."

Kenta tried remonstrating further, but it was no use. The headmaster wasn't listening any more.

As they came to Meeting Room B, close to the foyer, Kenta imagined breaking free and running away, but instead he found himself being led inside the room.

"Mr Watanabe here is going to watch you until your parents get here. I'll take your phone until then."

Mr Murphy fixed him with a firm stare and held out his hand.

Kenta opened his mouth to speak. He even glanced at the open doorway behind the headmaster, half expecting Jessica to burst in any moment. But she didn't. And all that happened was he watched himself handing over the phone resignedly, not quite believing that it was over for good this time. He could hardly hear that other voice inside him, the one that was telling him to dive past the headmaster and find Jessica, the same voice that had driven him there in the first place. And he was still standing there, blinking in a daze, as the headmaster closed the door on him.

CHAPTER 55

The auditorium was alive with excited chatter as the headmaster and deputy head entered the room and took their seats in the front row. Not even during whole-school assemblies was the place this full. There wasn't an empty seat in the house and a few extra stools had been set up in the aisles to accommodate the overspill.

The stage itself was adorned with an impressive backdrop consisting of a brand-new giant screen showing a painting of old Kyoto with its many pagodas. At each side of the stage, large painted wooden cut-outs of trees and a wall added further authenticity while hiding what was going on just behind the curtains. Long gone were the giant painted O's, and the scenery was impressive enough in that moment to make everyone forget that unfortunate incident had ever happened.

At the foot of the stage, on floor level, a professional photographer was busy snapping photos of parents eager for a sighting of their own progeny, while at the back a second cameraman was readying a large video camera for the show's live recording. Nearby, in the control room in the rear left-hand corner of the auditorium, a technician, assisted by a Year 13 pupil, was testing the stage lights one last time.

The backstage area, meanwhile, was a hive of furious activity, with nervous performers obsessively checking and adjusting their make-up and costumes, or going over their lines while Miss Lewis, the drama teacher, was busy barking orders at the stage crew.

Slightly apart from the chaos, two museum staff members were guarding the famous koto from marauding teenagers, ensuring it was ready for its big performance. Standing nearby was the museum's own security guard, ready to step in if needed. And only a few metres away, in her private dressing room, the geisha was putting the finishing touches to her make-up, regarding her own image in the mirror with a look that spoke of deep satisfaction. She was almost there.

CHAPTER 56

Jessica closed her eyes and braced herself as she dropped her full weight down onto the glass roof.

Seconds went by. She opened them and looked down. There were no hairline cracks forming, branching outwards from her shoes like splintering ice, nor were there any ominous sounds of something breaking.

Looking past her feet, she could see all the way down to the illuminated badminton courts. She felt a tight knot forming in her throat, which she quickly gulped away, and with it the mild panic attempting to ensnare her. *Come on, Jessica! Move!*

She began sidestepping her way to the next classroom along, keeping her back close to the side of the building and placing her feet on the metal girders in between the glass squares. Her white kimono billowed lightly around her as a cool wind blew across the space. She was glad of the cold. It kept her focused.

When she reached the first of the windows in the next room, Jessica attempted to slide it along. When it wouldn't budge, she shuffled along to the next one and did the same, and then the next one and the next. When it was clear they were all locked, she cursed quietly to herself and continued onto the next room, knowing there were only three more classrooms left in the row before she ran out of glass roof and options.

She checked over her shoulder several times to see if there was anyone in the nearby corridors overlooking the covered area. Once or twice, she made herself look down too, but the badminton courts remained empty of movement.

She continued on and was almost at the next classroom along when she instinctively looked upwards to the right and saw the figure of a security guard ambling along the opposite wing's third-floor corridor. The corridor's lights were on, meaning she could see him clearly. It wasn't Tomo, that was for sure.

She froze and looked down, hoping that to take her eyes off him would somehow render her even less visible, but she was standing at the point where the lights over the badminton courts beneath broke through the roof and shone over her top half. Still, the guard was halfway along the corridor now, and there was no reason why he should look at this point.

So then perhaps it was some bitter twist of fate, or simply that the sight of a girl standing on the roof was too glaring a thing to miss, that made the guard glance quite innocently out of the window and across the space before homing in on Jessica.

The guard stopped dead, and the two of them locked eyes. No one made a move at first until suddenly the guard was lifting the walkie-talkie to his mouth and starting to run.

Jessica's eyes scanned the glass roof while her brain calculated at lightning speed. She didn't need to be a maths genius to know the odds of the next few windows being open were less than favourable, and even then, they didn't guarantee escape. The only option was straight ahead of her at the furthest edge of the roof where the row of tall trees poked over the top.

She had only another second or two to dither before she forced her legs into action and propelled herself forward.

At first, she half expected to plummet to a painful death, but her feet continued to find solidity rather than nothing, and Jessica was surprised to discover herself moving quickly across the roof.

She maintained a steady line along the single stretch of steel girder beneath the glass, imagining herself as a tightrope walker, but her steps faltered when a loud shout sounded behind her.

Whirling round, Jessica saw the guard was now leaning out of a window in the second-floor classroom she'd just tried to get into. He was shouting angrily in Japanese and motioning for her to come back, but she took off again, losing her balance slightly and landing a foot heavily on the glass. There was a loud thud and the glass square shuddered under the impact, but she could see now they were more than solid enough, and carried on at even greater speed.

The edge of the roof and the trees were only ten metres from her now, and already a niggling voice in her mind was asking what the hell she was supposed to do when she got there – but there was no choice, she had to keep going.

The guard's shouts continued to ring out behind her, reverberating off the surrounding walls so that he sounded much closer than he was. She knew she shouldn't, but Jessica paused again to look back and saw the guard was stepping out onto the roof.

Again, she lost her footing, slamming a foot down on the glass, and this time there was a sharp crack.

Her eye caught a snapshot of splintered glass glistening in the light, a web-like pattern swirling out from where her foot had been, but it hadn't collapsed. She was okay and still moving.

When she finally reached the edge of the roof, Jessica resisted an urge to leap without stopping. The gap between the edge and the trees' foliage was slightly wider than she'd anticipated, at least a metre. But then she couldn't see the branches for the leaves and had no idea if she could even grab onto something when she jumped.

She looked back again towards A-block. The guard was heading her way, though moving more tentatively, looking down through the glass before taking each step. Behind him, two more guards were now in the second-floor window watching his progress.

Turning back to the tree, Jessica stupidly looked down at the row of bushes below. It made her stomach lurch, and the clattering of the guard's approaching steps, coupled with the shouts from his colleagues, only intensified the feeling. She envisioned the guard carting her back to the window, saw herself being taken away in a police car, but the threat of further disgrace meant nothing. It was only the reality of OO finally winning that was truly terrifying.

In the end it was this which made her turn back to the tree in front of her, and before she could stop herself, she leaped out into the night air.

CHAPTER 57

Already the performance was in full swing. Mr Murphy had kick-started things with a few words in both English and poorly pronounced Japanese, and now the head boy and head girl were hosting with their brighter smiles and impressive traditional costumes.

One Year 10 boy had already done his part as Emperor Kanmu, who had relocated the ancient capital from Nara to Kyoto in the eighth century. Next up was a mini re-enactment of the Onin War in the Middle Ages, with pupils from various youth groups dressed as samurai and pretend-riding on wooden sticks glued to cardboard horse heads, while parents applauded gleefully in between near constant photos on their phones.

And waiting now in the shadows, within sight of the koto, she was counting down the minutes.

Chapter 58

Kenta couldn't sit. He could only pace backwards and forwards, his restless eyes flitting from the floor in front of his feet to the closed door on the opposite side of the room.

Watching him from the opposite end of the large mahogany meeting table was Mr Watanabe. Kenta supposed he was Mr Goto's second-in-command, as he was older than the other guards and the two of them were often seen together. A couple of times Kenta tried reasoning with him, offering deference as he did to all Japanese elders, explaining that the whole thing was a misunderstanding and that the school was in danger. The first time around, Mr Watanabe simply ignored him, choosing to inspect his fingernails instead. The second time, he glared at Kenta and said, "Save it for the police," before proceeding to ignore him all over again.

Kenta wanted to scream at the old man, wanted to pick up a chair and hurl it against the wall and shout obscenities in his mother tongue that he wouldn't normally dare utter in front of an older person in a million years. He wanted to scream at himself for being tricked so easily, for being so trusting, for being caught and giving up without a fight. He only hoped Jessica was okay, that whatever trouble she'd run into she would be able to get out of it as only she could, and show the headmaster and the school how wrong they'd been.

He checked the clock on the wall above Mr Watanabe. The time was 4.35. They would be well into the performance by now. He half listened for screams or running feet outside in the corridors, or some horrible bang from a bomb or whatever dark plan Hikaru had in mind. The sight of the clock's second-hand moving was like a form of torture, and with it came images of his parents standing beside Mr Watanabe, staring at him with looks of pure sorrow and disappointment. The police were there too in his mind's eye, and Detective Yamada, all appraising him with utter disdain. But the anguish from all that came second to his fears of what was happening around the corner, right under his nose.

Kenta looked again at Mr Watanabe who was now hunched forward on his chair, scrolling through something on his phone. He eyed the baton on Mr Watanabe's belt and wondered if he'd ever had to use it. Occasionally the guards toyed with them harmlessly while on duty, but that was about it.

A recent memory came to him, of a conversation with his father at dinner about history and how it was acceptable to do something that seemed wrong at the time if it was for the right reasons. Kenta couldn't recall what historical event they had been talking about, but his father's words took on new significance as he rehearsed the possible scenarios – if he rushed at the door, how quickly would the old guard get up? And if he did, would he have time to grab the baton and strike? He didn't like the idea of tussling with an older man, or worse, injuring him, but he saw now that the alternative was far worse.

With his eye half on the clock, Kenta stopped his pacing for a moment and made himself pull out a chair and sit down. Mr Watanabe glanced at him suspiciously for a moment then returned his attention to his phone.

Keeping his head down, but with one eye on his exit route, Kenta slowly positioned his feet so that he could explode forwards without any obstructions. Again, he looked at the clock, then to Mr Watanabe and back to the clock. There was no more time to wait. It had to be now.

He laid one hand down on the edge of the table for extra support and was tensing his every leg muscle in readiness for his escape when the door burst open.

A blur of possibilities raced across Kenta's mind – it was Jessica, or his parents, or the police. But the person who came in was none of these.

Tomo near-fell into the room, he was in that much of a hurry. He half glanced Kenta's way but didn't acknowledge him, choosing instead to nod at Mr Watanabe.

"Sorry, sir. You're needed at the badminton courts. There's a problem."

Mr Watanabe stood up. "At the courts?"

"Yes, there's someone on the roof there. They told me to get you."

Mr Watanabe frowned. "Why didn't they radio?"

"It just happened. I was told to get you."

The older man puzzled over this then shook his head and jabbed a thumb in Kenta's direction. "Keep an eye on him. His parents are on the way."

Tomo bowed his head. "Yes, sir."

Throwing Kenta a final surly glance, Mr Watanabe hurried out, closing the door behind him.

Immediately, Tomo let out a long, relieved sigh. "I thought he wasn't going to buy it!"

"You mean there isn't really a problem at the badminton courts?"

"No, there is, but I heard them say something about a boy in costume being held in here, and I knew it was you."

Kenta got up from his chair. "Look, it's not just Hikaru, the cleaner. She's got help from pupils. Rina, the girl who was dressed as the geisha, and Milo, an Italian in Year 12."

"What?" Tomo screwed up his face. "This is some messed-up shit, man."

438

"You need to get to the auditorium right away. It could happen any minute!"

Tomo smiled and opened the door. "Why don't you lead the way?"

Kenta gawped at him. "You're letting me go?"

"Of course, man. Why d'you think I'm here? Let's go!"

"But what about Mr Watanabe?"

Tomo shrugged. "I'll tell him you ran out before I could stop you. I mean, it's not every day we get stuff like this happening."

"You sure?"

"Yeah, I'm sure. Don't worry, man. If you're right, then the shit's going down soon. We'd better move."

"Thanks, Tomo. I owe you one!"

And with a last exchange of nods, Kenta popped his head out of the door then together they ran along the corridor.

CHAPTER 59

For one sickening moment she was falling. And then there was the sudden rush and scratch and stabbing of leaves and branches in her face, and then she was scrambling, clawing for a grip on anything at all.

Seizing hold of a thicker branch, she managed to keep a grip, and though it bent heavily under her weight, it didn't snap. Next, Jessica placed her foot on a weightier branch below and suddenly she wasn't falling any more, though her position was still precarious. She'd been swallowed up by the foliage, which was already starting to shed like all the other trees, but there was still enough cover to keep her hidden.

Carefully, she edged her way along the branch, which strained and lolled under her feet, as she grabbed at any other sturdy holds her hands could find. As she moved closer to the trunk, there were more thick branches to step down onto until she was as low as she could get.

Looking down, she could see there was still some way to go from the lowest branches to the ground, and no clear foothold on the trunk. Jessica hung on while she thought. Her face was stinging, and she knew she'd been scratched somewhere, but it was the continued shouts and clambering footsteps nearby on the roof that shook her out of her hesitation and made her crouch low before swinging down from the branch and letting go.

She landed heavily between two of the bushes separating the badminton courts from the running track, letting out a harsh grunt as her right thigh smashed into the soil.

She tried to get up immediately, thinking they'd already be swarming across the badminton courts to grab her, but her right leg was half dead as she struggled to her feet, and she was winded too.

Across the courts, she saw another guard hurrying along a ground-floor corridor towards the stairs, but not across the courts. Overhead, the guard on the roof had frozen halfway across. Maybe he wasn't sure if she'd made it down or not.

Keeping low while she caught her breath, Jessica shook her leg. "Come on!" she hissed under her breath. She knew if they found her now, she wouldn't have a chance of getting away.

The guard on the roof was heading slowly back to the window. They were bound to start looking for her any second now.

Scanning the court area, Jessica saw no other guards arriving yet, but before getting to her feet, she scooped up a handful of cold soil from the ground around the bushes then made a dash for it, limping diagonally across one of the courts and back into A-block.

CHAPTER 60

Kenta and Tomo went out through the school's front entrance and around the side of the building. Kenta figured the chances of simply walking into the auditorium's main entrance unnoticed were exactly zilch. The only option now was to creep in through the back and hope no one was there.

But just as Kenta was turning the corner, a voice rang out behind them. It was one of the guards by the school gates. He was saying something to Tomo as he approached. Kenta froze. He was sure the guard hadn't seen him, and as he peered around to where the two men were talking, he saw Tomo gesturing with one hand behind his back for Kenta to keep moving.

Reluctantly, Kenta continued along the narrow alley between the side of the school building and a high perimeter wall, passing a collection of industrial-sized bins where the canteen staff dumped leftover food, as well as giant air-con units lying dormant in the cold autumn air. The only light came from a couple of lamps atop the wall, as well as the few windows in A-block where the rooms remained illuminated.

When he came to the steps leading up to the fire escape door at the back of the auditorium, Kenta was relieved to find it unguarded and the door slightly ajar. Finally, something was going his way.

Through the narrow gap he could hear the performance. The hosts were talking, which meant it was still going on. Maybe Jessica had stopped her already, or most likely, Hikaru was still waiting in the shadows somewhere, and Kenta was the only person currently in a position to do anything about it.

The full weight of this conclusion, which he'd already reached before leaving the foyer, hit him now with full force. He paused at the bottom of the steps. How was he going to do this? And on his own too?

"She said you might keep on trying."

The voice startled him. He swivelled round, but there was no one there. A light footstep turned his head back around.

The figure was emerging from the darkness behind the staircase. It didn't take long for Kenta to figure out who it was.

"Milo?"

"*Ciao*, Kenta."

"What the hell's going on? Don't tell me you're mixed up in all this crap too?"

Milo took a few steps closer, stopping nearly within arm's reach of Kenta. The light from a nearby window cast a soft yellow glow across half his face. He was smiling.

Milo shrugged. "What can I say?"

"How long?"

"Long enough."

"But why?"

"It makes sense, Kenta," Milo replied excitedly, the same way he did whenever he was discussing football. "Everything they say is true. All this—" He gestured with a look and a flick of the hand at the school building. "It's all bullshit. The way they make us work like slaves, like we're just parts in a machine. They don't give a shit about us, none of them do. Parents, teachers, politicians – they're all the same."

He delivered this last part with added bitterness, and Kenta could see his eyes widen in the dim light. He looked high or wired somehow.

Not quite believing what was reaching his ears, Kenta said, "Milo, this is all totally crazy. Hikaru, she's insane. She tried to kill me!"

Milo looked genuinely puzzled. "Who?"

"OO... Hikaru's her real name."

"Oh, her." Milo's confusion lifted, and a sly grin worked its way across his mouth. "You think this is all her?" He chuckled mockingly. "You've no idea."

Kenta wasn't certain he was hearing right. He wasn't certain of anything any more.

"It's way bigger than OO," Milo continued. "That's just the beginning. They're just getting started."

"They?" Kenta said, baffled. "What are you saying? Who's they? You mean Hikaru?"

Milo didn't answer. He only continued to grin in a way Kenta found unnerving. Then he said, "How'd you like the rat?"

"That was you?"

"Just following orders," said Milo.

A burst of music sounded overhead through the open fire escape, just as Kenta found his patience disappearing.

"Look, Milo!" he snapped. "This isn't some joke. Something seriously bad is about to happen if we don't stop it. You don't want to be a part of this."

Milo's grin fell away. "Tut-tut, Kenta. You always were the good guy, but in the end you're just as dumb as the rest of them. That's why you all need waking up."

"I'm going up there, and you're not stopping me."

Kenta placed one foot on the bottom step, at which point Milo came at him with surprising swiftness.

With his teeth gritted, eyes flashing wildly in the half-light, his fists flew at Kenta's head before Kenta had time to block them.

The first blow struck his right ear, which exploded instantly with a hot, searing pain. The second caught him full on the right cheekbone, rattling Kenta's skull.

Falling sideways onto the concrete stairs, Kenta found himself dazed. For a second, he wasn't sure if he was still up or down, or where Milo was.

Another blow caught him full in the chest, snatching the air from his lungs – was it a kick? Milo was standing over him at the bottom of the steps, his tall figure blocking out the light.

"The Syndicate won't let you interfere," he said in a low voice.

It could have been panic or sheer reflex, but rather than waiting for the next punch, Kenta found his right foot shooting out.

The heel caught Milo full in the stomach, sending him stumbling backwards with a groan.

Kenta made himself stand while he still could. His ear continued to buzz loudly with pain, and his left cheek burned, but he had a grip again. Milo was still half bent over, clutching at his stomach.

"Keep the hell away, Milo. I'm telling you!"

Grunting like an injured animal, Milo looked up at his teammate. He swore in Italian and lunged at Kenta again, but this time Kenta was ready.

He knew Milo was fitter and stronger than his skinny frame suggested. He'd seen him fight at school more than once, and he knew how to use his fists, whereas Kenta had never been one to get into scraps. But today was different. Milo couldn't have reckoned on the sudden, unexpected surge of rage that sent Kenta's right fist into his face with shocking force, followed by the left, until he was pummelling the person he'd called a friend the past three years, and Milo was down on the floor cowering from the blows.

"Is Yudai a part of this?" Kenta shouted down at the huddled figure. "Do you know where he is?" Breathing sharp and ragged breaths, Kenta waited for Milo's reply. "Say something!"

He saw Milo turn his face upwards towards him, his bloodied teeth clenched. "Fuck you!" he spat.

With his fists still bunched, Kenta felt the fury rising again until a voice made him spin around.

"Kenta!"

There were three figures standing there in the alley.

"Kenta, it's okay, man. We'll take it from here."

It was Tomo, and beside him were his father Mr Takagi and Mr Saito.

Confused and still a little startled, Kenta stepped away from where Milo lay. He looked down at his battered Italian classmate and then at his bloodied knuckles, shocked to find he was the one who'd done all that damage.

Tomo rested a hand on Kenta's shoulder. "It's okay, let's go. My old man will take care of him."

Shaking off the pain in his ear and cheek, Kenta nodded and said thank you to Mr Takagi and Mr Saito who were already helping Milo to his feet, keeping one of his arms twisted up behind his back.

Wrenching uselessly against the restraint, a bloody-nosed Milo looked at Kenta one last time. "You won't stop it!"

But Kenta wasn't listening. He was already turning back to the steps and making his way up to the door above.

CHAPTER 61

Kenta had to stop himself bursting in through the fire door. Instead, with Tomo right behind him, and the adrenaline of his fight with Milo still charging his blood, he slowly pulled the door back and quietly stepped inside. His head remained a swirl of confusion from what Milo had told him. There were so many questions and doubts, but now he had to block them out.

There was no one near the door and nobody noticed their entrance as they gently closed it behind them.

"I'll go down near the front," said Tomo in his ear. "I'll signal if I see anything."

Kenta gave a nod and watched Tomo going down the steps until he was near the stage, where he stopped and stood with arms folded, glancing at the audience in between snatches of the performance.

Casting his own anxious eye over the room, Kenta saw only a sea of heads all aimed in the same direction, their attentions caught entirely by the action on the stage where the koto was already set up and the geisha had begun playing. Her perfectly painted face blazed a magnificent white beneath the stage lights. He wasn't even sure if it was the same performer from the assembly – if it was, she looked quite different. Kenta couldn't quite put his finger on it. Perhaps she was even more striking this time. Or was it her poise, which came across as even more delicate, yet with an impressive and confident grace?

If the room had been quiet during the assembly a couple of weeks earlier, now it was consumed by a profound silence, save for the sound of the koto itself, which was one of the most beautiful things Kenta had ever heard. The first time around, he hadn't paid it the attention it deserved. But this was different, something else entirely. The geisha was playing with such sad intensity, plucking notes that seemed to float then soar magnificently through the air.

When she had played the last note, the stunned silence continued briefly before it was broken by a rapturous round of applause and cheers, with many people rising to their feet for a standing ovation.

Performing another scan, Kenta hoped to at least search out a familiar face, but with the main lights down and the difficult angle, he didn't recognise anyone besides the back of the headmaster's large head down in the front row. He considered going down to join Tomo, but the fear of being recognised himself, especially by Mr Murphy, held him back.

Looking to his left, Kenta peered through the partly open door into the small sound room where a technician and pupil assistant were busy tweaking levels, their eyes flitting constantly between the large control board and the stage.

Amidst the explosion of sound and movement, Kenta found his senses heightening. The geisha remained where she was, head dipped a fraction, and he wondered if she was going to play again. But then a voice bloomed through the speakers, breaking the spell with a jolt.

The audience members who were standing took their seats again, and the applause died down as people listened to this new sound.

"Many years ago," the voice began. It was a woman's voice. She sounded older than any pupil, and the accent suggested she was Japanese, but Kenta didn't recognise it. *"In this very city, there lived a young woman whose supreme talent would go unnoticed. A young woman used and abused."*

With the last couple of words, the giant auditorium screen, which had been showing the same painted Kyoto backdrop throughout the performance, went suddenly black.

The voice continued.

"Otake Okimi is one of Japan's great forgot talents. She was a pupil who worked hard to perfect her talents, but she was let down by those who should have protected her."

Kenta's ears sharpened further at the mention of Otake Okimi's name. Tomo threw him a concerned look from further down the aisle, but the rest of the auditorium appeared blissfully unaware of anything untoward.

In the control room to his left, Kenta noticed a commotion. He popped his head inside to find the technician scrambling over the control panel, flicking switches and pressing various buttons with an air of panic. "What's wrong?" he said.

"Nothing's working," barked the technician. "None of this is on the programme!"

The Year 13 assistant, who up until that point had only been watching on helplessly, began pointing frantically at the stage.

Both Kenta and the technician looked up at the same time to see the two giant white O's that had appeared on the screen.

The technician's eyes widened further. "What the hell? This isn't me. We're not doing any of this."

Stepping back out into the aisle, Kenta could see and hear the audience reacting now to the sight of the two ominous O's on the screen. Almost as unnerving was the geisha herself, motionless in front of the koto while all this was going on. But stranger still was the figure emerging now onto the stage behind her.

They were dressed entirely in a black cloak from head to foot. Even the hair was covered, but where the person's face should have been, there was instead a Noh mask, the kind used in traditional Japanese theatre. This was a male mask with an eerily blank expression.

The masked figure stopped in the centre of the stage a few steps behind the geisha and the koto. They didn't move or speak, only stood there like some menacing statue, after which the audience's unease became more palpable and the voice continued through the speakers.

"OO will stand always for the forgot ones, the ones banished and cast aside, the ones taken advantage of, used and abused for their abilities, for all victims of injustice, for all those forced by parents and teachers to live lives that are not their own," said the voice, which was getting louder.

Tomo was looking to Kenta again. They both knew something was wrong, but neither knew where the threat was coming from.

"She was banished through no fault of her own, her life in tatters, her dreams shattered..."

Kenta signalled to Tomo to push the fire alarm button by the main doors, but Tomo was either unsure of his meaning or was reluctant to do it.

"But her story does not end here," the voice boomed, getting angrier with each syllable. *"Her story will no longer remain in the shadows."*

Now Miss Lewis, the drama teacher, was marching across the stage to the masked figure who still hadn't moved, but before she could reach them, a hand emerged from under the black cloak. It went up to the white mask, lifting it from the figure's face.

The audience gasped in unison as they all found themselves staring into the eyes of Yudai Matsumoto.

Yudai's face was pale beneath the stage lights. His hair had been dyed black so that it resembled its usual colour again. Looking out over the rows of stunned faces before him, he appeared a little stunned himself, almost as if he'd been pushed onto the stage against his will. But when the geisha stood up from the koto, he seemed to snap out of it.

"*Today OO is free!*" The voice roared from the speaker. "*All of you can be free. Say no to oppression. Say no to control!*"

The geisha was standing by Yudai's side as together they each raised a bunched fist in the air, staring defiantly at the room.

That was all Kenta needed to see as he began making his way down the steps. All around him the audience was alive with confused chatter, pointed fingers, gawping faces. He could see Miss Nakamura now getting up from her seat at the front along with Mr Murphy.

The geisha was brandishing something in one hand – a bottle?

Kenta paused when he came to where Tomo was standing at the foot of the steps. "It's her!" he said. "The geisha. She's Hikaru!"

Tomo looked to the small figure on the stage. "Shit!"

"Get everyone out."

Tomo nodded, but before either of them could move, they watched as the geisha began squirting water – or was it something else? – all over the koto.

Miss Nakamura was shouting now, gesturing wildly with her arms, and two museum staff in black T-shirts came running onto the stage, but they weren't fast enough.

With a glimmer of dark glee flashing in her black eyes, the geisha's hand came out from somewhere in her dress. Now she was holding another object, something smaller. But it wasn't until Kenta saw the tiny flame flicker that he knew it was a lighter.

In those few milliseconds, he was sure that time stopped completely, that a vacuum poured into the space so that all was silence as the lighter left her hand and flew through the air.

The explosion of flames was more sudden and shocking than Kenta could have imagined; the koto was entirely engulfed in an instant.

Miss Nakamura was the first to react. Her scream of "Yamero!" – "Stop!" in Japanese – pierced the air, sending a shockwave back through the auditorium, which had the stunned audience bursting into their own screams and shouts.

Tomo and Kenta looked at one another in speechless awe as chaos erupted all around them. Tomo jumped towards the fire alarm box on the wall and smashed it with his fist, but nothing happened. No alarm. No sprinklers.

"What the hell?" He punched the button a second and third time, but still nothing. "Something's wrong."

On the stage, behind the leaping flames, the museum staff and security guard were encircling the geisha, who was keeping them back with a knife, slashing wildly at the air. And if Kenta had been in any doubt that it was Hikaru, he knew it now as he saw her snarling and screeching like a cornered animal at the encroaching figures, all the grace of her performance completely gone.

Already people were barging past Kenta and Tomo in the panic to get away from the flames, which rather than dying down, were growing and spreading along the stage's wooden floorboards.

On the stage, Hikaru was swiping and slashing at the air as the museum staff surrounded her and Yudai, who remained by her side, seemingly frozen in place. Mr Murphy was there on the other side of the stage, attempting to talk her and Yudai down, while close by on the floor level, Miss Nakamura continued to watch on in dismay as the koto burned, shaking her head over and over while her assistant attempted to console her.

By the time Kenta was able to leap his way down over the last few rows of seats and evade the escaping crowds, the smoke was thickening around the stage. It caught in his throat and stung his eyes, and a blast of heat made him flinch as the fire began to devour one of the stage curtains.

Miss Nakamura was now backing away from the flaming wreckage of her beloved koto, and up on the stage one of the museum staff was fleeing from the spreading fire, leaving only his colleagues and the headmaster to face Hikaru.

Making his way to the steps on the right-hand side of the stage, which was furthest from the fire, Kenta climbed to the top, one arm clamped over his mouth against the fumes. He could hear Mr Murphy remonstrating still, asking them to see reason as the fire began to encircle them further.

"Yudai!" shouted Kenta, and the two of them locked eyes.

At first, Kenta wasn't sure if his old friend recognised him in his make-up and costume, and he took his arm away from his mouth, eyes blinking painfully against the smoke. "It's me, Kenta! Come with me!"

With a hand, he beckoned Yudai towards him and even saw amidst the chaos the desperation written across Yudai's face.

Mr Murphy turned to where the new voice had come from, as did the raging Hikaru, who sent Kenta a hateful glare on seeing him. But then her attention shifted to the headmaster's looming figure, and Kenta knew what she was going to do before she even moved.

The museum security guard and remaining staff member were finally beating a retreat as the smoke and heat became too much, and there was no one to stop her now as Hikaru lunged forward, teeth bared, blade poised to strike.

The headmaster was too late in turning back to face the threat, as was Kenta in shouting a warning. But not one of them saw the white figure emerging from the smoke, storming from the back of the stage as if they'd come from the flames themselves.

They ploughed into Hikaru before the blade planted itself in the headmaster's chest. Hikaru and the white figure went flying, two blurs of white flowing fabric twisting in the air.

They both landed heavily on the floorboards close to the burning heat of what was once the koto. Hikaru went over the edge of the stage and tumbled to the floor below while the headmaster's mystery saviour lay on the stage's edge.

Kenta rushed forward to help the person up. It wasn't until they turned over that Kenta saw the one face he'd been hoping to lay eyes on.

CHAPTER 62

For the second time in the space of ten minutes, Jessica found herself falling to the ground.

After clambering onto the stage from the back and seeing Hikaru there, instinct had carried her forward, making her forget her sore ankle as she found herself charging straight for her. She'd driven her right shoulder into Hikaru's side, rugby-tackle style, and the two of them flew briefly through the smoky air before slamming against the stage's wooden surface.

Jessica landed heavily on her side and saw Hikaru rolling off the edge of the stage.

Her first thought was not of the pain in her hip, which only added to the various other parts of her body that were hurting, but of the smoke. There was a lot more of it than she'd realised, and the fire had taken out half the curtain on the stage's left. Breathing was becoming difficult, and she was a little

461

disorientated as she attempted to pick herself up, but then a hand took a hold of her left arm and helped her to her feet.

"Jessica?"

The voice was muffled and far off, mixing with the crackling of the flames. Then all of a sudden it was close and familiar, and she knew it was Kenta. Behind him, looking similarly astonished, was Mr Murphy himself.

"Hikaru!" she yelled as she came to her senses, shaking off Kenta's hand and limping over to the edge of the stage – but when they both peered over, there was no sign of the little geisha.

At the back of the auditorium, panicked audience members were still filing out of the emergency doorway, but there was no telltale flash of her white kimono in sight.

"Damn it!" Jessica banged a fist on the floor.

Kenta looked behind him. "Where's Yudai?"

Mr Murphy, who was coughing heavily now, pointed a bulbous finger in the direction of the backstage. "He ran off."

A team of school security guards came charging in carrying fire extinguishers, only to rear back from the blaze.

"Go!" Mr Murphy screamed. "Get out!"

"Come on," said Kenta in her ear, and together they made their way down the stage steps and out into the bright fluorescent light of the corridor outside.

CHAPTER 63

They could see the telltale flashing red lights of police cars out front way before they reached the foyer, and police officers were already running into the building followed closely by a team of firefighters.

Kenta's first thought was that they were coming for him, but that wasn't his main concern. He was looking for where Yudai and Hikaru could have gone, and it didn't take them long to find the first clue.

Slumped against the wall of the main A-block corridor they found Mr Goto, the head of security. Crouched beside him was one of the other guards, tending to the deep cut on his shoulder. Mr Goto had his hand clamped over it, though blood was still seeping out over his fingers and down his arm. He winced and hissed sharply when the guard tried to take a look.

Not that long ago, Kenta would have been truly shocked at the sight of his injury, but tonight nothing surprised him. "Where did they go?" he said, breathlessly. "The geisha and the boy."

Mr Goto looked up at the two costumed pupils peering down at him, both still coughing slightly from the smoke. Kenta was sure he would call the police over to arrest them, but he only pointed with his good arm towards the nearest stairwell.

"They went up," he said through gritted teeth. "A-block is surrounded. They won't get out."

Without a second's hesitation, they both headed for the stairs.

He noticed Jessica was limping slightly as they ran. "You okay?"

"It's nothing. Keep going!"

Racing up to the second floor, they looked both ways, listening for any sounds. Kenta strained to hear. "They could be hiding anywhere."

"No, she wouldn't just hide. She wants a fight."

He could see it again in Jessica's eyes, that fixed, determined look that said her mental gears were turning rapidly.

Then they heard it: an echoing set of running footfalls somewhere above them, followed by a loud clanging and a metallic crash.

"That's the roof!" said Kenta. "This way."

He continued up onto the fourth floor, channelling all his attention on the space in front of him, then slowing his steps once they came to the stairs leading up to the roof.

He put out a hand to halt Jessica and together they listened into the darkness around the corner. Echoing somewhere below they heard distant shouts, but above them only silence, punctuated by the thumping of Kenta's own heartbeat in his ears. He was half anticipating that little demon of a geisha to be standing there, waiting for him with her blade, ready to complete the task she had been unable to finish near the Yasaka Pagoda. But as he came around to face the stairs, there was only more empty space above, and he allowed himself to breathe again before stepping upwards and onwards towards the night sky.

CHAPTER 64

They found the roof door slightly ajar at the top of the narrow stairway. A chilly night air poured in through the gap, washing over their faces.

Jessica had never been up there before. She knew there were some sports activities that took place on the roof, but none of them involved her, and her curiosity about the school hadn't extended that far upwards.

Kenta was two steps ahead of her. He stopped just short of the door to listen, and as she listened too, Jessica felt the hot itch of an oncoming cough working its way up her parched throat. She staunched it with a sleeve to her mouth, but the muffled sound still filled the stairway. Kenta looked back in alarm, then returned his attention to the doorway. He cocked his head, listening further, then when there was nothing, he took two more cautious steps up to the door.

It creaked slightly when he pushed it open a few more inches. There was a weak light somewhere nearby, but Jessica could mostly see varying degrees of dark in the gap. She knew Kenta was hesitant to go out there. She was too. It could be a trap. She thought of their night-time hunt for the ghost geisha. It seemed a long while ago now. Back then it had been her leading the way around corners with a reluctant Kenta at the rear, but here he was on the front line, and she was grateful for it. She wouldn't have been able to do it alone, she could fully admit that much to herself now.

It took a further few seconds for Kenta to find the resolve to go forward. Jessica wasn't sure whether he'd peer out first, but then instead he turned to her, signalled ''3-2-1' with his fingers, and then to her surprise kicked the door open sharply before leaping through the open doorway.

Jessica was slow to react. Her left ankle was still throbbing viciously, but she hauled herself upwards and outwards as quickly as she could, ready for the onslaught of screams, screeches, the glint of the blade cutting the air. But it was only them, side by side at the heart of the roof's wide-open space.

She hadn't expected it to be quite so large. It was like a sports field in itself, spreading out over the entire expanse of A-block. Beyond the parapet, the downtown area twinkled brightly. It seemed much closer than she'd anticipated, and was beautiful enough that Jessica found herself momentarily diverted from the reality of the peril they were in. There was no longer any time for hesitation or a loss of concentration. She knew Hikaru was up there somewhere, waiting.

When it was clear they wouldn't be ambushed just yet, Kenta went cautiously around the side of the utility block which housed the stairway door. Jessica heard the flicking of light switches, a whole panel of them, and in seconds the roof was ablaze with light from a series of tall powerful lamps dotted about the space.

Their eyes sought out any scurrying movements, but again they saw no sign of their adversaries.

In the light, Jessica could see the layout more clearly. Almost the entire roof was covered in artificial grass, much like the fields below. To the left, there was a row of practice cages where she presumed people practised baseball or golf. On the right, there was a gym area with benches, weights and hanging bars. In the distance they could hear the wailing of more police sirens and fire engines.

Standing dead centre, they both seemed unsure of which direction to take. Jessica herself was leaning towards the right, and exactly on cue they both heard a distant clanging sound coming from the far-right corner, like metal glancing off metal.

They looked to each other. There was no need to speak. They knew what they had to do. But first Kenta hurried over to the practice cages. Jessica had no clue what he was doing until after a few seconds of fishing around, he came back holding a short golf club someone must have left behind after practice. He gave

Jessica a nod, and slowly they made their way to the far corner where the sound had come from.

Most of the roof was well lit, except for some odd shadowy patches in and around the grouping of small maintenance outbuildings in the corner.

They passed the gym area, their joint gazes directed at the large concrete blocks ahead of them. Jessica dared a sideways glance at Kenta who was brandishing the club in front of him like a sword, his knuckles white where the hands gripped the handle. In his expression she saw the twin workings of fear and total concentration.

Leaning against the parapet to the right was a wooden sweeping brush, which Jessica quickly retrieved. It was long and awkward in her hands, but she held it like a staff and felt better for it.

The further they went, the louder the whirring sound Jessica had noted earlier became, like a giant fan was spinning somewhere. And it was only when they were five metres or so short of the first outbuilding that she realised they were all vents for the building's air-con and heating system, and that there probably was a giant fan or a series of them inside. The vents themselves were large concrete blocks with grids on three sides and a maintenance door on one. They were around three metres wide and a couple of metres high. The doors bore warning signs and were almost certainly locked.

There were three of these vents grouped together in the right-hand corner of the roof, and another two close beside one another in the left-hand corner. The mechanical hum was much louder here, so much so that Jessica was straining to hear what other sounds lay behind it.

Again, her and Kenta's eyes met, and each saw mirrored in the other an acute awareness of the danger they were in and a reluctance to go any further. With a sickening dread, it occurred to Jessica that they were doing exactly what Hikaru wanted, that rather than hunting her down, they themselves were being lured to somewhere she could finish her job. She'd never intended to escape. This was her last stand, a final chance to take out the two people who'd plagued her campaign of revenge.

But rather than paralysing Jessica as she expected it might, this dread only angered her. It was what Hikaru wanted her to feel, and Jessica wasn't granting her enemy a single thing.

To her left, she sensed Kenta wanting to step forward, which was when she spoke aloud.

"You think you're so misunderstood, don't you?" Jessica's voice rang out, startling Kenta slightly. "But I understand you."

In the moment that followed, the humming of the giant vents seemed to heighten. Kenta readjusted his grip on the golf club. Jessica peered into the shadows between the vents, searching out any minute sound or movement.

They both jumped when they heard it, their makeshift weapons shaking in their hands. It was a laugh, a sneering cackle that had come from the vent nearest the corner at the back.

"What do you understand, little rich gaijin?" Hikaru's voice rang clear. It had come from behind the right side of the

471

rear vent. "Don't talk to me about understanding. You know nothing!"

These last words came with a vitriolic hiss, as if the sound itself was intended to cut flesh.

Jessica took a step closer. "It's not rocket science, Hikaru. The slighted genius takes revenge on the school that threw her out and ruined her life. It's pretty textbook, really."

She sounded calm, indifferent even. Kenta threw her a questioning sideways look, but Jessica was focused on where she thought Hikaru was.

There was no reply, then a scuttling in the murky light between the two vents towards the back, a shadow flitting through yet more shadow.

Stepping sideways for a better view, but keeping a safe distance, Jessica focused now on the rear vent to the left where she'd seen the movement.

"What I want to know," Jessica continued, "is why burn the koto? Why destroy Otake Okimi's treasured possession?"

Another tense silence followed, permeated by the whirring vents, whose maddening drone seemed to take on its own malice as though infected by Hikaru's presence.

"It was made for her alone," came Hikaru's voice, shouted now from behind the left rear vent. "If she can't have it, no one should have it. And I wanted to see that bastard Murphy's face when his precious performance went up in smoke."

"What about Miss Shimada? All she could talk about was your talent, how exceptional you were. Why did you waste it? You could've carried on. You still can. You could play for yourself, no one else."

"What are you doing?" whispered Kenta.

They didn't have to wait long for Hikaru's response. "Waste!" she almost screamed with a frightening viciousness. "The only waste was my childhood at the hands of greedy parents and back-stabbing teachers. Miss Shimada never did a thing to stop them throwing me out. It's like what they did to Otake. They just use people."

"But Otake was innocent of the charges against her, wasn't she? You, however... you really did cheat, didn't you, Hikaru? Maybe the school shouldn't have been so harsh, maybe your parents pushed you too far, but no one made you cheat. You did that all yourself. There's no one else to blame."

"Jessica, what the hell?" muttered Kenta sharply, but she only listened further into the dark.

And then another shadowy movement, and all of a sudden Hikaru's furious, scathing voice was right there, just behind the nearest vent only a few metres away.

"Shut up! Shut up! Stupid gaijin bitch. You messed it all up, ruined everything. But oh, we're going to make you pay. We'll make you all pay!"

Kenta and Jessica both took a step back from the nearness of the threat, then held their nerves and stepped forward again.

"Who's this *we* you're talking about?" said Jessica. "Rina and Milo are finished. It's just you and Yudai now."

473

"You stupid English bitch! What do you know? They're more powerful than anything you could dream of." This time the furious volley of words came from the opposite side of the vent.

Jessica looked to Kenta. Now was the time. With a flick of the head, she signalled for him to go around to the left side of the vent while she indicated she'd go around to the right. Kenta visibly gathered himself then nodded.

They began moving away from one another, creeping slowly enough that their footsteps wouldn't be heard.

"Why don't you give it up now, Hikaru? You can't fight for a cause from prison. This is no way to prove a point."

One step. Then another. Jessica listened for a response, but none came. Now she had tunnel vision, her sight aimed solely on the rear corner of the nearest air vent, from where she expected Hikaru to burst out any second.

Kenta was out of sight behind the vent's opposite side. Jessica felt her pulse beating wildly in her neck and attempted to swallow it away. Sweat was spreading across her palms, and she re-gripped the wooden brush handle, feeling utterly exposed now as she realised she'd brought a brush to a literal knife fight. *Too late to back out now. Hold steady, Jessica*, she murmured silently to herself. *Hold steady*.

When she was one more step from the back of the vent, Jessica paused. She took a large breath, ignoring the wild protests of her speeding heart. And with the brush ready to strike or parry any lunging attacks, she leaped around the corner.

Jessica couldn't help the yell that burst from her mouth, a primal, guttural "Aaaahhhh!!!" that she hoped would both startle Hikaru and make herself sound bigger and more threatening than she was.

The commotion had set Kenta off too, and he jumped around the opposite corner half a second later, letting out his own fearsome battle cry.

And then they were facing one another across empty space, Kenta with the golf club raised up above his head, Jessica with the brush held diagonally across her chest. There was no Hikaru, only shadow and confusion and the ominous all-consuming drone of the air vents.

They stared wide-eyed at one another. She'd duped them, and now they were sitting ducks.

Jessica spun round, anticipating an attack from the rear. Kenta did the same. But there was only more emptiness between the vents, which to Jessica were becoming almost deafening. Something was wrong. She'd made a mistake. They shouldn't be there.

The movement could only have registered for a fraction of a second, a hint of a disturbance in the space in the corner of her eye, and perhaps it was luck too, or sheer instinct, or some other factor beyond her perceptions or understanding, but Jessica found herself turning rapidly again, swinging the broom as she went. And the girl who'd never been one for any sport, especially those involving bats or clubs, swung the brush with all her strength as though intending to launch it into space.

It connected with Hikaru's head just as she was exploding out from behind the next vent, knife in hand, her mouth open in readiness for a scream of her own, the scream of a would-be murderer.

But she never got the chance to utter any sound except a startled moan at the sheer force of the blow.

The brush head broke off on impact, spinning into the air. Hikaru stumbled sideways and fell heavily onto the artificial grass. The knife left her hand, dropping to the floor a few inches away.

Dazed by the blow, Hikaru was trying to get up. Jessica, who was still in shock at having hit her, saw the knife too, and Hikaru's fingertips reaching out for it. She leaped into action once again, bringing down the broom shaft on Hikaru's arm before the hand could re-grip the knife handle.

Hikaru's scream filled the night air. Her arm retreated like an injured creature, and she lay crumpled up on the ground, whimpering.

Jessica kicked the knife away and stood over Hikaru's shrunken figure. Kenta was by her side now, peering down at their fallen foe in pure shock and amazement.

"Who are *they*?" said Jessica in a low but firm voice.

Hikaru continued to whimper.

"I said, who were you talking about when you said *they*? How many are there? Or is it just some crap you fed Yudai and the others?"

"Go to hell!" Hikaru hissed, looking up at them with malevolent eyes that were drowning in tears. It was difficult for Jessica to imagine this was the same deadly geisha they'd been fighting all this time.

At first, she didn't know what to do or say next. There was something so pathetic and defeated about the person lying at their feet, but she couldn't let it go. She needed to know.

Tossing away the broom shaft, Jessica knelt by Hikaru's head. "Tell me!" she said sharply, close to her ear.

"No!" shouted Hikaru, turning her face away.

"Is it the syndicate?" said Kenta, surprising them both.

Jessica saw the flicker of recognition in Hikaru's face at the mention of the word. She turned to Kenta, wondering what he was saying.

He spoke again. "Milo said something... about a syndicate."

Jessica could feel something welling up inside her, something cold and fierce. She seized Hikaru's arm, the one that had been struck. Hikaru yelped, but Jessica no longer cared.

"Tell me who they are." Jessica was nearly shrieking now. "Who's behind all this?"

Hikaru grimaced, flashing her bloodied teeth. Two of them were broken and her lip was bleeding heavily on one side. With a look of utter hatred, she spat a wad of thick blood in Jessica's face. It hit her on the left cheek, but Jessica didn't even flinch or wipe it away. Instead, she slapped Hikaru hard across the face.

The strike was hard enough to sting Jessica's hand. "Tell me who they are, I won't ask again!"

Smarting from the hit, Hikaru winced and grimaced again. "No! Fuck you!"

In a flash, Jessica was upon her, pinning down Hikaru's arms with her knees. "Tell me!" she screamed, hitting Hikaru again, across the other cheek, this time even harder.

"Jessica!" said Kenta behind her. "What are you doing?"

Now Hikaru was too dazed to respond. Beneath Jessica's weight, she looked so small and young, much like the pupil she'd once been, but Jessica was in the midst of a frenzy of her own. She didn't even hear Kenta and would have hit Hikaru a third time if at that moment the police hadn't come charging up to them across the roof.

"Jessica, stop!"

This time Kenta's shout got through to her. She looked up to find Detective Yamada and three other police officers staring at her. Just behind them was Tomo.

"Jessica, it's okay," said Kenta, more softly this time. "It's done. You can let her go."

Staring down into Hikaru's frightened, resentful eyes, Jessica saw that it was true. It was over. At least this chapter.

With some effort, Jessica got herself to her feet and stepped back while the detective signalled for two of the police officers to get Hikaru up.

She stood beside Kenta, and the two of them watched the officers pick up a squirming, squealing Hikaru, who kicked out at them and screeched when they touched her left arm.

Detective Yamada looked to Jessica and Kenta and nodded. He pointed to the knife lying a couple of feet away and instructed the third officer to retrieve it.

As she was being led away with an officer on either side of her, Hikaru looked back, sending one last sinister glare Jessica's way. "You're dead, gaijin! They'll find you. Just wait!"

Jessica didn't react. She only watched Hikaru being led away with a mixture of frustration and relief. Frustration at not having got the name she wanted, and relief that she wouldn't have to fend off any more frenzied knife attacks.

Hikaru was still struggling as she went, cursing and screaming. The detective and Tomo were also watching her go. They probably thought it was over too, but when Hikaru was more than halfway to the door, she managed to pull one arm away, then reeling back from one of the officers, she stamped on the other's foot, yanking her injured arm free in the process.

She yelped at the pain, but it didn't stop her, and she was away before they could seize hold of her again.

Detective Yamada yelled for them to grab her at once, and even Tomo was giving chase, but the small figure in the flowing kimono was too quick for all of them.

She made a beeline for the parapet on the western side of the building, and before the nearest officer could get to her, she'd already climbed up onto it.

The chasing officer stopped dead just short of the ledge, fearing they'd scare her into jumping.

Jessica and Kenta, who'd both been too stunned at first to react, were moving quickly to where Hikaru stood on the parapet. She was facing them.

"Miss, no! Please! Get down," said one of the police officers, but Hikaru only laughed, looking down on him with a crazed amusement.

Now they were all grouped together, staring in unison at the spectacle of a wild-eyed woman standing on a roof ledge dressed as a geisha.

For a few seconds no one moved or said anything, until Detective Yamada took a few measured steps towards the parapet, both his hands raised to signal he was no threat. But Hikaru wasn't looking at him. Her gaze went over the detective's right shoulder and found Jessica.

"Hikaru, don't!" The words raced up Jessica's throat, but they didn't come in time. With a final demented smile, Hikaru stretched her arms out wide and simply fell backwards into the open darkness.

Chapter 65

Everything seemed to go quiet. Even as the police officers were rushing to the parapet and leaning over, Kenta couldn't hear very much. Jessica too stood motionless at his side, mouth open, but there were no words for what they'd just witnessed. They didn't hear any impact down below, and it was as if Hikaru had simply fallen into the open air and vanished.

The shock wasn't to last too long. There was already excitement elsewhere on the roof. One of the officers pointed and spoke, and then Kenta saw him.

It was Yudai breaking his cover from behind one of the air vents on the other side. Kenta saw his billowing black cloak first, like a patch of darkness breaking away from the night.

He was running. Not for the door as Kenta might have expected, and with a sickening lurch in his heart, he knew where Yudai was going.

Kenta found himself running too, as fast as his legs could take him. He quickly overtook the detective and Tomo and reached the other two officers just as Yudai was climbing onto the parapet.

Kenta stopped a couple of metres short of the roof's edge. "Please, let me speak to him," he said to the two officers. "He's my friend."

They looked back uncertainly to Detective Yamada who nodded for them to let Kenta go ahead. The two men stepped back slightly, perhaps relieved at not having to contend with yet another suicidal maniac. Behind them, Tomo and the third officer had already run down the stairs, followed by Jessica, probably to find where Hikaru had fallen.

Kenta looked at his friend. He saw written in his stricken face just how frightened and broken he was, nothing at all like the impassive school genius he'd once known. Tears glistened on Yudai's cheeks, and the dark smudges beneath his eyes suggested he hadn't slept in a week. His gaze flitted nervously between Kenta and the others, then down at the ground four floors below. His hesitancy was clear, and Kenta hoped it would last a little longer.

"Don't bother trying," said Yudai, his voice quivering. "I'm not coming. Not with you, not with anyone. They said we couldn't get caught."

Resisting a strong urge to ask who *they* were as Jessica had done with Hikaru, he said, "Yudai, it's me, Kenta. I'm not the police. I'm not a teacher. I'm not taking you anywhere. I just want you to be okay."

Kenta spoke softly, edging closer with hands raised slightly to show they were empty, while Yudai watched his every move.

"Don't!" Yudai roared. "Please!"

Pausing a moment, Kenta unpinned the fake ponytailed wig from his scalp and threw it to the floor.

"Yudai, I don't understand. Why are you doing this? All the hacking, the running away? Why?"

"I couldn't take it any longer," said Yudai, choking back tears. "Every day they wanted more, everyone wanted more. More results! More wins! Higher scores! More, more... I don't want it, to play the goddam genius. I don't want it!"

"Your mum misses you, Yudai. She just wants you home. You should've seen her."

"Shut up! Shut up! Stop! My mother doesn't understand either. She didn't stop any of it. Her and Dad like it. They like having their little genius on show. But the syndicate, they really understand. They made me see how things really are, that we don't have to do anything for anyone else any more. The syndicate can—" He stopped himself mid-sentence, his red-raw eyes still fixed on Kenta.

"Who are they? What's the syndicate? Do you mean Hikaru or someone else?"

Yudai went to say something then stopped himself. "You'll never find them. It's already started. They won't ever stop. They'll give us all a voice again."

More siren bursts split the night air on the street down below. Yudai flinched slightly at the sound.

Resisting further urges to dive at Yudai and pull him back, Kenta said, "Whoever it is, they've used you, Yudai. Look where you are, what they've made you do."

"Shut up! Shut up," spat Yudai. "You're wrong. They helped me be myself. They helped all of us."

"Who's all of us? You mean Rina and Milo? They've already been caught. The fire department are putting out the fire now. Hikaru's gone too. It's over."

Kenta was sure he saw a flicker of doubt cross Yudai's face. He thought he might even be ready to step down from the parapet, but then whatever paranoid delusions he'd been brainwashed with took Yudai over again. He smiled mockingly. "Over? Ha! You've no idea. It's more than Hikaru and her little geisha. She was just a foot soldier. She lost sight of what really mattered. For her it was just about her stupid revenge on the school, but the syndicate... they're about so much more."

In the open doorway behind them, distant voices echoed somewhere down below. Maybe it was more police heading their way.

"Yudai, please. I don't want you to be anything else, just my friend, like you used to be. It's not too late if you stop now."

Kenta dared to take a couple more steps in Yudai's direction. He was now so close that he could almost reach out and touch him. Again, Yudai's gaze darted nervously from Kenta to the police and then behind him at the sheer drop. He stepped back half an inch so that the ends of his heels were hanging over the edge, but Kenta's instincts were still telling him to keep back for just a while longer.

"I know you don't want to do this, Yudai. I know you."

More fire engines were arriving outside the front of the school, their sirens blaring along the street. Smoke continued to billow from the far end of the block. It filled Kenta's nostrils, a pungent scent that smelled unnatural, of plastics and fibres and man-made things, but it was calming down now.

The tears were flowing again down Yudai's cheeks. There was no more defiance left in him, only despair – as though he saw his options narrowing ever further to one singular point.

It was then that several more police officers came pouring through the doorway onto the roof, slamming the door back against the wall as they barged in.

The detective and the other officers all turned instinctively to see what was happening, but something told Kenta not to, some wordless whisper in his ear. And just as he feared, the loud intrusion set off Yudai's already frayed nerves.

He wasn't sure if the fright made Yudai lose his footing, or if this had been the final straw. All he saw was his friend falling backwards just as Hikaru had, except there was no smile on Yudai's face as he went, only a look of confusion and terror.

But Kenta didn't freeze as many would have. He had an athlete's reflexes and agility, and he used them now with every fibre of his being, diving forward and reaching into the empty night air in the wild hope of grabbing something, anything.

And in the darkness he found it, a flaring of fabric as Yudai's feet left the parapet altogether. Kenta's hand seized hold of it and immediately he was almost dragged over the parapet himself. The jolt of catching Yudai's full weight near tore his shoulder from its socket, and Kenta let out a pained groan as he took the strain. But somehow he held on, and the fabric didn't tear, and Yudai remained wrapped in the black cloak which flapped and rippled in the breeze.

Before his strength gave in, Kenta reached down with a second hand. He saw Yudai dangling upside down, saw him look up at his saviour in abject terror, too terrified even to scream.

Kenta himself was trying to call for help, and it came just as his strained arms felt as though they couldn't take any more, with every muscle and sinew holding on for dear life.

It was first one officer on his left, then a second on his right, both reaching down themselves, taking hold of the dangling figure below.

Together they hauled him up, and once it was done, Kenta near-collapsed from the strain of it all. The police officers were shaken too. They were both young, in their early twenties.

Lying at their feet was Yudai. At the sight of him there, still intact and breathing, a profound wave of relief washed over Kenta. Yudai was sobbing heavily now, his face buried in the crook of his arm, his whole body shaking.

The two officers helped him up. He didn't resist.

"Take him downstairs," said Detective Yamada behind them, his voice soft and quiet. "Get him checked by a paramedic first."

The two officers nodded and began leading Yudai away by the elbow.

"Wait!" said Kenta, holding up a hand to stop them.

The officers paused, watching as Kenta stood before Yudai. His old friend's gaze remained lowered to the ground. He appeared utterly defeated, but he raised his chin in surprise when Kenta suddenly stepped forward and embraced him.

There was nothing to say, nothing either of them could say even if they wanted to. Or perhaps a simple hug said more than any number of words.

Yudai didn't move. He simply stood, arms dangling loosely by his side, still wrapped in his black cloak. The officers let go of him for a moment while the two boys said their wordless goodbye.

Kenta felt Yudai shivering against him. He felt the dampness of his cheeks brush against his own skin, and when he finally let him go, Kenta found there were tears in his own eyes.

Just for a moment, Yudai looked up at him. "It wasn't me... the USB. She tricked me, took it without me knowing."

And then gently, and with a solemn air, the officers took Yudai by the elbows once again and led him slowly towards the doorway.

As he watched Yudai go, Detective Yamada came up beside Kenta and placed a hand on his shoulder. "Well done," he said. "I'll see you downstairs."

Then he followed the officers out, leaving Kenta alone on the roof, with all of Kyoto's lights blinking around him in a world that would never be the same for him again.

CHAPTER 66

They found Hikaru's broken body lying on the ground in the middle of the alley running along the side of A-block.

Jessica was standing over it, alongside Tomo and the third police officer from the roof. Unreasonable as she knew it was, she'd half expected to find Hikaru gone completely, or struggling to her feet before attempting an escape, but no. She was lying a few feet away from a set of three giant bins. There were no mangled limbs or unsightly contortions. She simply lay on her back, arms and legs slightly outstretched like someone attempting to make an angel in the snow. Her eyes were wide open, staring blankly at the night sky above. Across her lips there remained a faint smile, and even in the dim light, the growing pool of blood beneath the smashed skull was plain to see, a puddle of near-black liquid spreading over the dark tarmac.

The officer knelt close to the body to check for a pulse, a simple formality, while Tomo and Jessica watched on.

"Oh man," muttered Tomo to himself.

Jessica had never seen a dead body before. She'd imagined she would be shocked, and although she was, there was an undeniable fascination there too, along with an unexpected feeling of sympathy. She felt no satisfaction at seeing Hikaru dead, even if she had tried to kill her and Kenta more than once. Looking down at the lifeless painted face, Jessica could see Hikaru as she once was, an innocent schoolgirl with an incredible talent and a world of possibility ahead of her. And now she'd destroyed herself, and for what?

They were soon joined by several other police officers, and Jessica and Tomo were led away by a female officer who directed them inside.

In the foyer, Jessica found Kenta sitting on a chair in the waiting area, hands clasped between his knees, eyes staring blankly ahead. When she sat next to him, he didn't appear to even notice her presence until she said his name, and then he returned to the waking world as if being plucked from a daydream.

When Kenta heard Hikaru was dead, he simply nodded, and Jessica said she was glad Yudai was alive.

All around them, people were rushing backwards and forwards: police, firefighters, teachers, security guards. At one point, a paramedic came and knelt in front of them both. She asked if they were okay, and they both said they were even though Kenta clearly had an injured shoulder and Jessica a swollen ankle.

The paramedic checked their eyes and gave them a once-over before handing them each a blanket and telling them their parents would be there soon to collect them. It was like a scene from a film, thought Jessica, one where after a disaster the survivors lie or sit around with blankets around their shoulders, their faces lit up by the flashing lights of police cars and fire trucks.

On the far side of the foyer, she saw a shell-shocked Mr Murphy talking with police. For once his face was something approaching a normal colour. He even glanced in Jessica's direction at one point, then quickly looked away. She would have grinned at this if she weren't feeling so wired and suddenly exhausted all at once.

Their parents had been held outside until it was considered safe, and all of them came in together.

Jessica was surprised to see her mother and father together, along with Yuko. Her mother even appeared concerned, and her phone wasn't in sight. As they approached, she noted the bafflement in their faces at the sight of her in costume and make-up in the school she'd been suspended from, surrounded by police and firefighters. But these were all questions that would have to wait.

Her father reached her first. "Come here," he said, arms outstretched.

She struggled to her feet and let him hug her.

"Oh, my poor darling," said her mother, stroking her hair. "What on earth have you been up to?"

To their right, Kenta's mother was crying as she wrapped her arms around her son. Kenta held her too, looming several inches above both parents. His father watched on stoically, perhaps bemused by it all.

"Oh, Jess-ca, Jess-ca," said Yuko repeatedly, fussing over Jessica once her father let her go, checking her head and face and stroking her cheeks as though searching for cracks, and Jessica herself was too tired to resist any of it.

"Are you okay?" said her father.

"I'm fine, I just have a sore ankle."

"The detective explained everything." He looked in the direction of Detective Yamada, who was speaking with Mr Takagi a few metres away. "He told Yuko what you both did. I think it was extremely foolish, dangerous and incredibly brave. You don't have to worry about anything, we're proud of you."

"Okay," said Jessica rather flatly. It was about all she could manage.

She took a step forward and grimaced at the pain in her ankle. When she looked down, she saw the swollen flesh there and wondered how she'd managed to do so much running on it.

"Here, let me help." Her father pulled her arm over his shoulder and took half her weight as he guided her towards the exit. "This is going to be a chapter in your memoir, that's for sure."

On her other side, Yuko continued to fuss over her, stroking her arm and tutting and sighing. Her mother, still dressed in her smart work clothes, looked more like some visiting official sent to supervise proceedings as she walked with them, appearing unsure of what to do with herself.

Jessica looked over to where Kenta was also being guided away with his mother and father on either side of him. She saw him groan at a pain in his shoulder, but he shrugged it off and walked on.

Before they all reached the door, Detective Yamada caught up with them. He bowed dutifully to both sets of parents, who returned the gesture, then looked to the two pupils and did the same.

"I humbly apologise to you both," he said in slow yet clear English, surprising Jessica. "We were wrong to ignore your information. You have done a great service to your school."

"*Arigato gozaimasu,*" said Jessica, as did Kenta, after which the detective explained they would still need to give statements, but that it could wait a day or two.

Bowing a final time, the detective excused himself, leaving the parents to stare at one another a little confusedly.

For a second, Jessica wondered if Kenta's parents still saw her as that evil English girl who'd corrupted their son, but his mother looked her in the eye, and with a weary smile said, "Thank you," in English.

That would have been a fitting way to put an end to this whirlwind of a day, but a sudden commotion at the far end of the foyer made them all turn to look.

It was Tomo and a police officer escorting Rina across the floor, each of them holding her by the arm, but halfway to the doors she suddenly snapped and tried to wrestle herself free, though with no success.

Jessica, Kenta and their groups moved aside to let them through, and it was as she was led outside that Rina sent a final look of shame in the direction of her two schoolmates before being ushered into the back of a police car.

Jessica and Kenta watched the car pull away. Despite the continued flurries of movement around them, a kind of peace and quiet seemed to descend on the scene. The two of them looked at one another. Jessica could see he was as weary as she was and imagined that behind his eyes there no doubt swam all the images of what they'd seen that night.

"Yudai said it too... about a syndicate," said Kenta in a low, tired voice. "Do you think it's real?"

Jessica thought about it for a moment, then shrugged. "I guess we'll find out."

Kenta only nodded sleepily. Whatever else was to be found out, it would have to wait a little while. He raised his good arm and waved goodbye. Jessica smiled and did the same before each group walked off in separate directions to their cars.

CHAPTER 67

The following Sunday morning, the official Jidai Matsuri festival took place without incident. Many thousands of people, both locals and tourists, turned up to watch as usual, but keener observers may have noticed the heightened security on the streets that day, and the event was no doubt overshadowed slightly by the news reports of the scandalous drama at BSK.

Fortunately, the fire in the auditorium had been put out before it spread beyond the stage, and no one in the audience was hurt. But this all came second to the confirmation of the famous koto's destruction, along with growing reports of a conspiracy led by Hikaru Kai, a derailed former pupil who'd jumped from the school roof before she could be arrested.

Then there was the dramatic reappearance of Yudai Matsumoto, the BSK pupil who'd been missing for more than two weeks and who was now a lead suspect in the conspiracy and believed to be behind recent cyberattacks on the school, as well as Hikaru Kai's main accomplice. According to police, he'd been taken to a nearby psychiatric facility for further assessments and observation.

All in all, the storm that had descended on the school was of such magnitude that no one seemed to know which part of the whole thing was the worst. But there were some positives. Kenta Higashi, a local boy, and Jessica Hunter, an English national and fellow pupil at BSK, were both acknowledged as having helped uncover and foil the conspiracy after they themselves were wrongly accused of involvement. One article even referred to them as a *duo* and *young detectives*, which had made both Jessica and Kenta chuckle to themselves when reading it.

The school itself was closed until the auditorium could be cleared up a little and declared officially safe, which could take a few days. It was also an opportunity for pupils who'd been there to recuperate, and for the many irate parents to calm down a little. Mr Murphy was placed on immediate indefinite leave. The official story was that he also needed time to recover, but the rumours behind the scenes were that he'd been shunned by the school's owners for his failure to heed warnings about what was going on. There was also his involvement in Hikaru's expulsion ten years previous, which was under review. More than anything, he was the one who'd been in charge when things had gone wrong, and like any good captain, he had to go down with his ship. A new face was therefore needed as a means to put the whole mess behind them. For the time being, Miss

Jennings, the deputy head, had been appointed as the school's new leader, while Mr Tanaka, the IT teacher, had been made the new second-in-command.

In an effort to improve their bad PR, the school had also reviewed their homework policies in an attempt to reduce pupils' stress, and two extra counsellors were being hired to ensure there was more of a support network for those who needed it. This in turn had a knock-on effect throughout the city, with other international schools and even several local ones changing their homework policies in order to avoid their own potential pupil revolts.

This was at least one positive thing that had come out of all this, thought Kenta when he read about it on the following Monday. He was resting at home on his parents' orders, though he had no real intention of going outside just yet. He was on a break from the outside world for a few days, at least until he could try and get some of his head around everything. The shoulder still hurt, but it was only a mild tear in the muscle and would heal soon with rest. His parents were being particularly attentive and contrite, most likely on account of their guilt at having doubted Kenta in the first place, but he never blamed them for one second; he was only glad that it was over. There were also the regular calls from members of the press wanting to speak with the young local hero who had saved the school, but Kenta had no wish to talk to anyone about it, especially not some prying reporters.

He'd already had to revisit the whole thing the day before when he went with his parents to the police station in the city centre to give an official statement. Detective Yamada had been present in the interview room while a younger detective asked the questions. They wanted to know everything, from when he and Jessica had discovered Rina dressed as the geisha, to the moment he pulled Yudai Matsumoto off the edge of the school roof. The questioning was gentle and respectful, yet rigorous. More than once, Kenta's mother asked that they stop and let him rest, but Kenta said it was okay, providing as many details as he could.

He also learned something of Hikaru's accomplices. He knew that Yudai was in a psychiatric ward and was not currently allowed visitors except for his family members. The thought of Yudai being there pained Kenta, but then it was at least some comfort to know he was safe and being cared for. And although he was still facing serious charges, Detective Yamada hinted he would escape any real punishment on account of his mental health.

As for Rina, she was expelled from the school for her part in events. She'd apparently denied any knowledge of Hikaru's plans to burn the place down but admitted her part in framing both Kenta and Jessica, as well as in the vandalism of school property. Kenta and Jessica had both told the police what Rina had said about being blackmailed, which they hoped would be enough to save her from any serious charges.

According to the detective, Milo and his family had already left Japan and returned to Italy. Milo's involvement in the whole thing was deemed bad publicity for his mother, the diplomat, who was quickly relieved of her post, but not before using what influence she had to keep her son from being arrested. Kenta wondered what Milo would do now. No doubt he'd land on his feet no matter what.

Although it was technically confidential, Detective Yamada also divulged some of what they knew about Yudai's movements during his disappearance. He was apparently never more than a few kilometres from the school the whole time. First, he'd moved between a number of manga cafés, including the Grand Central where Kenta had found him. He'd effectively bribed the café staff with cash to avoid being detected.

After Kenta had blown his cover, he moved to a bedsit in an old industrial area in one of Kyoto's southern districts, not far from Kenta's home. Hikaru's fingerprints were over all of it. The money he received had come directly from her, and numerous phone calls and messages between them told a story of regular communications which mostly involved her issuing orders. Furthermore, Yudai had admitted being behind the cyberattacks on the school, including the one that had interfered with the auditorium lights and sprinkler system on the night of the fire. He'd done it all under orders from Hikaru herself who'd apparently recruited him, Rina and Milo at least three months earlier at a student competition.

It still wasn't known why Hikaru had targeted them in particular, and so far there was nothing linking anyone else to the whole thing. This was despite Kenta's insistence that Milo and Yudai had let slip about some sort of syndicate. Detective Yamada had taken this into account, but since there was no evidence of anyone else's hand besides Hikaru's, and since Hikaru herself was not around to confirm it one way or the other, this theory of another person or persons being behind her schemes was quietly brushed aside.

"We thank you again for your bravery and assistance with the case," the detective had said, gently ushering Kenta and his parents out. "It looks as though you could have a future as a detective yourself."

***

Jessica, who had also visited the station with her father later that day, told the detective the same thing and found her own testimony being politely fobbed off.

"We will certainly keep an eye on the situation," the detective told her via a translator, his apparent English skills now conveniently absent yet again.

The official story, apparently, was that Hikaru had acted alone and had effectively brainwashed the three BSK pupils. It was never explained where Hikaru had got the money to finance the secret plot, especially as she'd been a part-time librarian and hadn't even worked in some time. The money hadn't come from her family either, and it was presumed she'd been saving money for a long while before beginning her hate campaign against the school. Rather than going quietly, Jessica had rolled her eyes at this and informed both the detectives in the interview room that if they weren't going to investigate further, then she would have to do it herself, just as she'd done before.

Like Kenta, she'd also been resting at home while ignoring requests from reporters. Even a couple of journalists from the UK had been in touch and similarly shunned.

Her ankle had been sprained during the jump down from the roof, and she hobbled around the house for a few days. Her mother stayed home that entire weekend after the fire, which was almost unheard of, though she was back on the road on the Monday morning after Jessica rejected offers of counselling from both the school and the police, insisting for the hundredth time that she was okay.

Yuko remained at the house much of the time, attending endlessly to Jessica, much to her annoyance. Her father also took some time off work to be at home more that week. Like Kenta's parents, his attention seemed more than a little fuelled by guilt, which Jessica had no shame in milking, using it to barter promises that they would at least stay in Kyoto until her high school studies were over. Her father agreed happily, but not without some confusion.

During that week, Jessica kept herself busy, searching online for hours a day in the hope of finding something, anything that would shed more light on the mysterious syndicate. Once or twice she half doubted herself. Maybe Detective Yamada was right on this one. Maybe the whole thing was a cover by Hikaru to get herself off the hook, or some elaborate distraction designed to throw people off the scent. She was, after all, someone who'd manipulated teenagers into helping her terrorise the school. She'd been unhinged. Jessica had looked into her eyes and seen a broken human being, one beyond despair and reason.

But there also lay the problem.

Jessica had looked into those same eyes when she'd spoken of this *they*, and there had been a fervour there, a sort of twisted fandom that felt very real, and in Rina's it had been a genuine fear bordering on terror. More than anything, Jessica's gut told her she was right to keep looking. After all, no one else was going to do it.

And so, the search continued, but so did those visions of Hikaru's eyes, the lifeless ones staring blankly at the sky where she'd lain, dead and shattered like a little geisha doll. And behind Jessica's closed eyes at night, they continued to stare endlessly.

***

On the first day back at school after its reopening more than a week after the fire, there was a special assembly in the canteen on account of the auditorium still being under construction for a further couple of weeks. Miss Jennings, as the new headmistress, addressed the whole school, offering the expected speech about hard times and moving on to a brighter future, et cetera. She thanked all the teachers and pupils involved in the performance for their bravery, but special mention was reserved for Jessica and Kenta, who were applauded for their quick thinking and loyalty to the school in the face of great danger and adversity.

Both of them kept their heads down as all eyes turned towards them. Jessica noted there was no official apology for the initial suspension, but she wouldn't hold it against them. She didn't care so much about any accolades, and though part of her missed the thrill of the chase that the OO episode had offered, she was also at least a little happy at the prospect of being simply a normal pupil at BSK for a while.

They eventually bumped into each other by their lockers after the morning break. Jessica was walking normally on her ankle, though it still ached a little, and Kenta's shoulder was much better. He'd had a haircut and looked as if he'd lost a little weight too. There was an added sharpness to his cheekbones, and his uniform appeared a tad looser around his frame.

For the first few seconds there was an awkward shyness. It was as if they weren't quite sure how to communicate now that there wasn't a sinister conspiracy to work on together. Or was it the fact that there was little they could say after the mayhem of the previous weeks?

Kenta spoke first. "Hi, how are you?"

"Good. You?"

"Yeah, good. Thanks."

Jessica noticed the curious looks they were getting from other pupils passing by, eager to see the dynamic duo together, back as heroes after their disgrace. She shrugged it off herself, but she saw Kenta's discomfort under the scrutiny.

"It's a bit weird being back," Kenta added.

"I guess so. It's great not being suspected of being a criminal though."

Kenta smiled. "Yeah, I guess it is."

"You still got journalists contacting you?"

"Some, not so much now though. Old news I suppose. You?"

"Nah, lost interest."

Kenta nodded. He looked down at the floor, scuffing his shoe absent-mindedly.

"It was her funeral yesterday, in Nagasaki," he said, referring to Hikaru's small private service in her hometown, attended only by her sister and parents.

"Yeah, I saw something about it in the news. It's Rina I feel bad for, though. I don't think she was brainwashed like the others. Still... who knows? I was wrong about her the first time. Maybe we'll never know."

Now it was Jessica's turn to look down at the floor. There didn't seem to be much else they could add to this, although there was so much more she wanted to say. She could feel the words bubbling somewhere behind her thoughts, and she sensed it was the same for Kenta too.

"Did you tell Detective Yamada about... you know, about *they* and the syndicate?"

Jessica gave a single nod. "I did. Fat lot of good though, as expected. They just said they'd *look into it*."

"Same here... but you aren't going to just leave it, are you?" Kenta looked her directly in the eye.

Jessica couldn't help an eyebrow from lifting ever so slightly at this, along with the corners of her mouth. "Why? You interested in helping out?"

He chuckled and shook his head. "I need a break from playing the detective... got a ton of stuff to catch up on."

"Fair enough," replied Jessica, unsurprised yet unable to hide a mild disappointment.

The bell sounded for the approaching second period.

"Okay, I'll see you then," said Kenta, awkward once again.

"See you."

Turning, they both went off in opposite directions, but Jessica paused when she heard Kenta call out her name.

She turned back around. "Yeah?"

"It was full on, wasn't it? The whole thing, I mean. Not just the fire and all that. Some crazy things happened."

She noted the anguish swimming in his eyes. "You're right, it was. I still see Hikaru's face sometimes, the way it was before she... you know..."

Kenta didn't reply, but she knew he understood.

"You going to be okay?" Jessica added.

"Yeah, I'll be all right. You?"

505

"I'll manage."

A final meaningful look passed between the two of them, one only they could possibly understand.

"Oh, and by the way," added Jessica, "let me know when you've finished your novel. I'd love to read it."

With that she gave him a knowing smile and left a thoroughly puzzled Kenta standing there, wondering just how the hell she knew.

CHAPTER 68

There was a definite early winter nip in the air as Jessica walked home from school two weeks later, dipping her hands into the pockets of a new coat as she went.

It was already mid-November and dark by the time she was done with her after-school studies in the library. That same day, she'd finally delivered her English presentation on the real Otake Okimi after being given an extension and had received a round of applause and an ''A' for her efforts. It had certainly felt like a full stop on the OO affair, a natural closing of the book on a figure whose history had almost brought about the school's destruction. It was also a tribute, Jessica supposed, to the real person behind the name, the one who hadn't tried to kill anyone but had only defended what was hers after being snubbed by the world.

It was a Friday evening, and Jessica was tired and looking forward to relaxing a little in her nice warm house which she'd grown accustomed to. She was even looking forward to seeing Yuko, who'd essentially become another family member, a kindly aunt who only spoke a little English, but who was always on hand with a smile or a gentle admonishment.

Once she was in the door, Jessica had her usual exchange with Yuko in Japanese. She was in the lower Japanese second-language class at school, which basically meant she was a rock-bottom beginner, but she was learning fast and enjoying it more than she'd expected, even if it was more than a little difficult.

Jessica ate a snack from the kitchen while Yuko was busy preparing dinner, which both Jessica's mother and father were expected to be home in time for.

Mr Hunter had insisted they watch a film together afterwards, which was something they'd done often when Jessica was younger. He'd told her it was her turn to choose a film, but there were other things on her mind, and she made her way upstairs instead.

Once she was in her room, Jessica closed the door behind her. She breathed a lengthy sigh, happy to finally be alone. She didn't bother changing out of her uniform. Rather, she first went to the window and stared out over the twinkling lights of Kitayama. Already it was becoming a familiar, almost cosy sight.

Next, Jessica went to her desk and sat down. She pulled open the bottom-right drawer, and from beneath a pile of old textbooks, retrieved a light-blue cardboard folder. Opening it up, she pulled out several pieces of paper – some of them A4 documents, others newspaper clippings. She spread them out on the desk and re-read all the details she'd already been through several times before. It was a selection of news reports on the fire at BSK and the other events surrounding it, including Yudai's disappearance and his and Rina's arrest. Some were in English, others in Japanese with a printed English translation attached. There was even a report about the museum suing the school for negligence and breach of contract following the destruction of the koto.

Jessica could well picture Miss Nakamura still fuming over the loss of her beloved instrument, but then perhaps that meant the school would be the last victim of the koto's curse, if one believed in such things. Perhaps though, quite ironically, it was actually Hikaru who was ultimately to be the koto's last victim, as well as its destroyer. Maybe that was a good thing, an end to a sad and unfortunate history. As for the legal action, Jessica had heard it would be thrown out of court, since the museum's own security had been present at the time and had failed in their duty to protect the museum's property. Whatever happened, she didn't imagine they'd be loaning out any exhibits again any time soon, but perhaps it would mean an end to all the strange goings-on that Miss Nakamura's assistant had alluded to.

Once she'd read them over again, Jessica opened up her laptop with the intention of continuing the hunt for clues regarding the mystery syndicate that she still wasn't even sure existed, but first she checked her email in case one of the teachers had sent any homework instructions.

And then she saw it. The third email down from the top. The sight of it caused Jessica's hand to stop dead where it hovered over the tracking pad. Her lips parted an inch or so while her eyes widened.

The message had come via the same anonymous email service as the threat she'd received several weeks earlier, presumably from Hikaru.

She felt her pulse quicken in dark anticipation as she opened it.

Hunter and Higashi... has quite the ring to it. You must be pleased with yourselves. Enjoy it while you can. We'll be seeing you.

Jessica's eyes took in every word, then instantly scoured them a second, third, fourth time before she collapsed back in her chair in a state of utter amazement.

Downstairs, she could hear the front door opening, followed by both her mother's and father's voices, but she was too flabbergasted to go and greet them, even when she heard her father calling out her name from the foot of the stairs.

She sat up and read the email one more time, her gaze resting on that final line: *We'll be seeing you.*

"Finally," she said, smiling to herself. "It's on."

***

Hunter and Higashi will return in *The Osaka Syndicate,* Book 2 of THE HUNTER & HIGASHI MYSTERY SERIES. Keep reading to find out what happens when Jessica and Kenta come face to face with the real perpetrators behind the attack on BSK.

YOUR EXCLUSIVE FREE BOOK IS WAITING...
Download your free exclusive copy of *Death on the Bullet Train*, a standalone mystery-thriller by S.J. Cullen. You can get your free copy by going to www.SJCullen.com

She's a tourist in Japan.
It's her first time on the bullet train.
What could possibly go wrong?

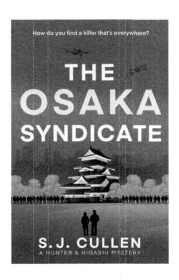

How do you stop a killer that's everywhere?

This is the dilemma facing young detectives, Jessica Hunter and Kenta Higashi, when they discover a nefarious group known as The Syndicate is behind a brutal murder in Osaka.

Fresh from saving the British School of Kyoto from a vicious attack, the two school friends are lauded as heroes, but they alone know the real perpetrators are still at large. When a talented young hacker is found dead in Osaka, Jessica is the first to link it to The Syndicate whose powerful network runs far wider and deeper than even she could have imagined.

Why are they building a secret army? And what is The Syndicate's connection to a major organisation in Osaka?

Outgunned on every level and surrounded on all sides by an invisible foe that will stop at nothing, Hunter and Higashi must live on their wits if they want to survive.

The Osaka Syndicate will be available in August, 2024. For more information, go to www.SJCullen.com where you can also sign up for the S.J. Cullen Readers' Club and receive a free, exclusive mystery-thriller novella. You'll also get release information before anyone else, exclusive stories, special deals and more.

Last but not least, please consider leaving a review on Amazon if you enjoyed this book. Reviews are very important for independent authors as they help other readers discover the story. Just a line or two would be greatly appreciated.

g

Printed in Great Britain
by Amazon

43542710R00293